BLAZE OF GLORY

MAJOR **JEFF STRUECKER** AND **ALTON GANSKY**

NASHVILLE, TENNESSEE

978-0-8054-4854-2

Published by B&H Publishing Group,
Nashville, Tennessee

Dewey Decimal Classification: F
Subject Heading: ADVENTURE FICTION \
TERRORISM—FICTION \ POST-TRAUMATIC STRESS
DISORDER—FICTION

Jeff Struecker is represented by Wheelhouse Literary Group,
1007 Loxley Drive, Nashville, TN 37211.
www.WheelhouseLiteraryGroup.com

1 2 3 4 5 6 7 8 9 10 • 14 13 12 11

To Jacob,
I hope you will live your life in a blaze for His glory.

THE TEAM

Sergeant Major Eric "Boss" Moyer, team leader.
Master Sergeant Rich "Shaq" Harbison, assistant team leader.
Staff Sergeant Pete "Junior" Rasor, communications.
Sergeant First Class J. J. "Colt" Bartley, weapons and explosives.
Sergeant First Class Jose "Doc" Medina, team medic.
Sergeant First Class Jerry "Data" Zinsser, surveillance and
    communications.

PROLOGUE

Spring, present day, near Fort Jackson, South Carolina

IT FELT HOT IN his hand. *Not possible.* Bronze should not feel warm, not after it had been sitting on a bathroom sink for the last two weeks, untouched, away from sunlight.

Still . . .

Jerry Zinsser closed his hand on the metal and ribbon. He knew everything about the object he held: bronze, cross-shaped, two inches high, one-and-thirteen-sixteenths inches wide.

His hand shook. He tightened his grip. The points of the cross and tips of the eagle's wings bored into his sweaty palm. A forty-watt bulb in the bathroom's ceiling fixture struggled to push back the predawn darkness.

Distant sounds entered his ears. *Pop . . . pop . . . tat . . . tat . . . tat.* A thousand tiny explosions pounded his eardrums. Familiar sounds. Terrifying noises. Sounds of 5.56 mm rounds blazing from the barrel of an M4A1 weapon.

"No . . ."

He raised his hands to his ears.

The gunfire disappeared.

He lowered his arms and opened his hand. The pointed bronze medal left four bleeding punctures in his palm. Gently he returned it to the cold tile of the sink and smoothed the red, white, and blue ribbon.

Something exploded behind him. Zinsser spun with raised hands to deflect any shrapnel coming his way. No shrapnel came. He saw no smoke, no damage to his wall. He saw only the empty, dry shower.

The sound of gunfire returned: staccato blasts pierced the air. AK47s have their own haunting sound.

Zinsser pressed his eyes closed and tried to protect his ears from the noise: an impossible task. The sounds were coming from inside his head.

"No . . . no more."

He knew what was coming. Knew it was more frightening than the sound of automatic gunfire.

"Data, it's Echo. I'm down. Repeat . . . I'm hit."

Zinsser pressed a finger in each ear, deeper and deeper, hoping the pain would drive the voices away.

"We need support. Data, where is our support?" A scream of pain. *"Oh dear, God. Don't let me die in this dump."*

Zinsser dropped to his knees, the hard tile offering only a cold, unforgiving surface.

"Chief is gone! Data, get us that support!"

Something hammered his sternum from the inside, like a prisoner using a mallet to break down the wall that kept him confined.

"Data, do you read me?"

"I read you, Boss . . . I'm . . ." Zinsser rolled onto his naked back and began to weep.

Winter, four months earlier, Kismayo, Somalia

JERRY "DATA" ZINSSER SPRINTED from behind the stucco building and hunkered behind an old car. Three Somali militia moved to the entrance of a rug factory. The hand-applied plaster bore pockmarks of bullets fired over the years. Zinsser hid behind a car in one of the world's most dangerous cities: Kismayo. Slowly he peered over the vehicle's hood. The three militia men split up, moving to the windows that framed the door.

A glance up and down the street revealed a dozen or more men moving in on the position. They shouted in Somali and Arabic. He turned his attention to the three men again: two stood by one window; one by the other. He knew what they were about to do—and what they'd leave behind when they finished.

Inside the old building were fifteen crewmen of the *Burltown*, a South African cargo ship that floated less than a mile off the coast. The Navy was responsible to take the *Burltown* and rescue what crew remained. His team was to secure the safe extraction of the crew sequestered here by Somali pirates.

He had done all he could. He remained hidden to keep radio contact with Ops while his team went in. Clockwork. It had all gone like clockwork. Boss, Chief, and Echo made entry and dispatched the guards in short order. Then . . . the clock broke.

The best Zinsser could tell, the pirates had hidden guards among the crew. After the initial assault, more gunfire erupted. Ten seconds later it stopped.

"Data, it's Echo. I'm down. Repeat . . . I'm hit. Chief is gone. Boss is dead."

Zinsser did his job and reported the situation. The approaching horde of men from the north and the south would arrive in two minutes or less. There was nothing Zinsser could do. His training told him to retreat and wait for air cover, to hide and report until he could be extracted. Echo would have to wait for reinforcements.

Zinsser started to move back when he saw one of the men at the window raise his AK47 and aim. He could only be aiming at Echo. Zinsser hesitated. He had his orders—

Zinsser rose, shouldered his M4, and then ticked the trigger and sent two copper-clad rounds into a spot just behind the man's right ear. He fingered the weapon to automatic and pressed the trigger to the stops. A long burst of bullets cut the other two men down.

"I'm coming in, Echo. I'd appreciate it if you didn't shoot me."

Echo didn't reply.

Zinsser rounded the car, jogged across the road, kicked open the door, and waited to be gunned down. Nothing struck his body armor. With weapon raised, he entered the large room.

Echo lay against the south wall. Boss, the team leader, stared around the hole between his eyes at a ceiling of peeling plaster. Chief, second in command, lay face down in a growing pool of thick blood.

A sound to his right made Zinsser spin, his weapon leading his eyes. Three men with AK47s by their side lay dead on the concrete floor. Six other men knelt or stood next to the north wall, their legs shackled to metal cleats in the floor.

"We . . . we got them all," Echo said. "I think."

Zinsser studied the men, waiting for one to draw a weapon. The six raised their hands. "Sailors," one said. "Don't shoot us."

Without a word, Zinsser picked up the AK47s and moved them out of reach of the prisoners. He wasn't taking chances and didn't have time to think of a new plan. He moved to Echo.

"How bad is it, Brian?"

"Took one in the hip, just below my armor. Wouldn't you know it—ahhh!" He took two deep breaths. "Took another in the shoulder. I'm bleeding out."

"No you're not."

"I'm the medic. I should know."

"Well, I say you're not dying. If you do, then I die alone, and I'm far too admired to go that way. Can you hold a weapon?"

"Maybe a nine."

Jerry pulled his 9mm pistol from its holster and set it on Echo's lap. He then pulled Echo's from its place and set it on the ground by his working arm.

"We got company, pal. It's about to get noisy. You see that window there?" Zinsser pointed at the southernmost window. "Shoot anything with a face. Got it?"

"Yeah, got it." Echo paused. "Is help coming?"

"As we speak."

Echo nodded. "You know we're going down, don't you?"

"Maybe, but if we do, we're going down in a blaze of glory."

The shouts grew louder. Zinsser stepped to the room with the captives. "Get down. On the floor. Now!" A moment later he stood in the middle of the room, his M4 aimed at the door.

BOOK I

CHAPTER 1

Present day, Fort Jackson

"MARRIED? WHO?" RICH HARBISON rose from his seat in the Special Ops briefing room in the Concrete Palace of Fort Jackson. The master sergeant ran a hand over his black, bald head. "I don't think I heard you right."

"Come on, Shaq, you heard me." J. J. "Colt" Bartley expected to be razzed by his team, but it didn't mean he had to like it. Or tolerate it.

Rich turned to the others in the small group. He was a tall man with the build of a Dodge pickup truck, hence his mission nickname, Shaq. "Did anyone else hear this, or am I the only one hallucinating?"

"I heard it," Eric Moyer, team leader, said. "But I don't believe it. Our baby seems so grown up."

The others who rounded out the five-man team laughed.

"I'm twenty-seven, Boss. I'm nobody's baby."

"So if I'm hearing you right, Colt, you're going to tie the knot."
Shaq furrowed his brow.

"That's right."

"Usually marriage means a man weds a woman."

"That's what's happening here."

"You see," Rich said, "that's where I'm having trouble following you. You're telling me that there is a woman out there who will marry *you*?"

"Of course there is."

"Tell me the truth. Have you ever been on a real date? You know, where you pick up the girl, do a movie and dinner, kiss on the doorstep, and all that."

"Of course."

Moyer grinned. "Of course he has, Shaq. The question is: Has he ever had a second date?"

"Come on, Boss. I expected a *little* support from you." Despite his protestations, J. J. had to laugh. Moyer, a stout man of thirty-eight years and the most courageous man J. J. had ever met, could be the poster boy for Army leadership.

"You're right," Moyer said. "I feel horrible."

"Thanks."

"For the girl."

J. J. did his best to look angry. "Great. Just great. I've traveled to half a dozen countries with you guys; been shot at; held prisoner; and done my best to lend a little class to this group, and what do I get? Snide remarks that pass for jokes."

"Marriage is a big step, son," Moyer said. "Think you can handle it?"

"After all the danger we've faced together, you have to ask?"

Shaq put his big hand on J. J.'s shoulder. "Listen to me. Do you remember that firefight in Afghanistan where the Taliban had us pinned down, outnumbered ten-to-one, and it looked like we were all dead? Do you remember that we had to call for close cover air support to drop bombs all around us?"

"Yeah, what about it?"

"Marriage is worse."

The men guffawed.

"So if I repeated that to your wife—"

"I would hunt you down and gut you like a fish."

J. J. smiled. "Still afraid of the wife, eh?"

Shaq's faced hardened. "Maybe."

The door to the briefing room swung open, and Colonel MacGregor swept in, followed by a tall man with Master Sergeant stripes on his uniform. "As you were," he said before anyone had time to come to attention. "Take your places."

J. J. and Rich took two of the ten seats available to them. The room was familiar territory. Every mission began here with a briefing from the brass and research conducted on the several computers that lined the back wall. Just to get in the room, J. J. had entered a code on a keypad by the only entrance door in the large, plain, ugly concrete building. Once in the lobby, a sergeant with the military police electronically scanned his fingerprints, relieved him of his cell phone, and checked for any other electronics he might have on his person.

Once the MP was satisfied, J. J. approached a second door, entered another code that granted him entrance to the office corridor, a long hallway bordered by closed doors. In this building, doors always remained closed.

Just like every other time he had entered this building, he made his way to the last room off the corridor. The mission briefing room had no windows and had been designed to keep every word spoken confined to that space.

Colonel "Mac" MacGregor's expression seldom changed. He looked today as he had since J. J. first met him: constipated.

"Before we begin, Colonel," Shaq said, "we think you should know our dear J. J. proposed to his girl last night."

"Don't tell me she said yes."

"Roger that, Colonel. We're thinking of throwing him a bridal shower."

"Isn't that usually done for the bride?"

"No one will know the difference."

The men laughed. Even Mac risked a smile.

"You know," J. J. said, "someday you're going to need me to back you up. Don't be surprised if I hesitate."

"All right, ladies, can it. We got business to do." Mac turned to the tall man who entered with him. "Since you guys drove off the last two men I gave you to replace Caraway, I'm going to try one more time, and you *are going to like it*. Is that clear?"

The answer came in a chorus of "Hooah."

"Good. This is Sergeant First Class Jerry Zinsser. He's your new surveillance man. He's also skilled in communications and will help Pete out should he decide to sleep in late."

"Zinsser?" Moyer's forehead creased. "Jerry Zinsser. That name rings a bell—" Moyer straightened. "Kismayo? The *Burltown* mission?"

Mac nodded. "I see you've heard of him."

"Who hasn't."

"Um, I haven't," J. J. said.

"We have a hero on deck," Moyer explained.

Mac raised a hand. "If you don't mind, I'd like to run my own meeting."

"Yes, sir. Sorry, sir."

Zinsser gazed at the beige vinyl floor, clearly uncomfortable with talk of heroism.

"As you know"—Mac cast a hard look at J. J., and he felt it pierce his heart—"or, as you should know, Sergeant Zinsser was awarded the Distinguished Service Cross for heroic actions against superior forces and for saving a wounded team member despite receiving several wounds. He's fully rehabilitated and your new team member."

J. J. joined the others in a short round of applause. The Distinguished Service Cross was the second highest medal awarded for bravery; second only to the Medal of Honor. J. J. was impressed.

Mac continued. "Moyer, introduce your men. You can leave out their favorite things, like walking in the park and picking flowers."

Moyer rose. "Yes, sir." He faced Zinsser. "I'm Eric Moyer, team leader. Like most team leaders, they call me Boss." He pointed to Rich, who stood. "Rich Harbison, assistant team leader. Goes by Shaq. I'll let you guess why."

Zinsser's eyes widened at Shaq's size. "I think I can figure that out."

"Don't let his size fool you. He hates sports and loves Broadway musicals."

"What can I say," Rich retorted. "I'm a Renaissance man."

Moyer ignored him. "This is Pete Rasor—Junior. As the colonel said, he's the team's communication specialists. Next to him is Jose Medina, team medic. He goes by Doc."

"Not very creative," Pete said, "but it beats other nicks I've heard."

"On your feet, Colt," Moyer snapped.

J. J. bolted to his feet.

"Meet J. J. Bartley. Weapons and explosives. Those who like him call him Colt."

"And if they don't like him?"

"Everybody likes me," J. J. said before Moyer could answer. "What do we call you?"

"My previous team . . ." Zinsser cleared his throat. "When on mission they called me Data."

"Oooh. A Star Trek reference," J. J. said. "The name fits a surveillance and comm guy."

"Now that we're all buddies," Mac said, "we can get down to business. I hope your social calendars are clear because you're going on a little trip."

THE WOMAN LOOKED TEN months pregnant, even beneath her long, black abaya. Dr. Hamid al-Jaburri watched her enter the hospital lobby waddling with each step, steps that seemed to cause her pain. Standing next to her was a young girl. Dr. al-Jaburri guessed her age to be ten, certainly no more than eleven.

"I don't know how you women do it."

The nurse standing next to him looked up and saw the object of his attention. "Allah gives us peace."

"Peace. There hasn't been much of that in Baghdad over the last few years." He motioned to the woman. "She looks confused. I wonder how much prenatal care she has received. Get a wheelchair and take her to OB/GYN. From the looks of her, she could deliver any moment."

"Yes, Doctor."

Dr. al-Jaburri watched as the young nurse moved toward the pregnant woman. Even twenty feet away he could see the woman's eyes dart from side to side. They were red and he assumed she had been crying. "So much pain in the world—"

A piercing ring stabbed Dr. al-Jaburri's ears. It took several moments for him to realize he was no longer standing. Plaster from the ceiling fell around his supine body. Dust and acrid, burning smoke filled the air and flooded his lungs. He tried to close his eyes but only one worked. He touched the left side of his face and felt bone where skin should be. There was no pain; he experienced no emotions.

Someone, half buried by debris, screamed. Ululations joined the moans, groans, and weeping. Moments later, the choking air carried the pitiful sounds of damaged and dying humans.

A dozen people cried for Allah's mercy. Dr. al-Jaburri felt he should do the same, but he couldn't force a syllable from his throat.

He tried to rise. He was a doctor. People needed him. He managed to sit up, but his legs would not move. Somehow he knew he would never stand again.

The sound in his ears quieted, as if someone had filled his ears with cotton. He glanced down and knew why. Blood pooled in his lap. Soon he would bleed out. Rather than watch his life puddle beneath him, al-Jaburri looked to the side. Three feet away rested an object. He forced his mind to focus, then wished he hadn't.

A man's dying eyes should see something beautiful . . . glorious—not, as his did: the severed arm of a child.

CHAPTER 2

J. J. SAT NEXT to his team leader. The briefing was due to start thirty minutes before. Colonel Mac excused himself, stepped from the room, and failed to return. To pass the time, the team members took turns poking fun at J. J. At first he fought back with explanations and cutting quips of his own, but he was outnumbered and outgunned. He did what he knew he must: shut up and take it.

The ribbing was good natured, something he had participated in himself. It was much more fun, however, to poke fun than to be the target.

As the team's only practicing Christian, J. J. had taken his share of abuse, but none of it cruel. He had worked with these men for several years and trusted them with his life. In fact, he had done that on several occasions. That he was alive to be the butt of their jokes was testament to their skill. The feeling was mutual: he would lay down his life for any man on the team.

"Keep going, guys, I can take the best you have to offer."

"That a fact?" Rich said. "We haven't been using our best—"

The door to the briefing room opened and Colonel Mac poured in with someone on his six—a woman. At five-eight, she was just a few inches shorter than Colonel Mac. Auburn hair pulled into a ponytail hung to a spot between her shoulder blades. Her blue eyes danced around the room, fell on J. J., hesitated, then resumed their survey. She was thicker than a supermodel but not by much.

"What—?" J. J. started before his jaw dropped.

"They're called girls, J. J.," Moyer said. "Are you sure you're engaged?"

J. J. leaned close to the man the team called Boss. "I'm sure, all right. In fact, *she's* the one I'm engaged to."

Moyer snapped his head around so fast, J. J. expected to hear vertebrae snap. He said nothing.

Mac moved to the small wood podium at the front of the room. "Sorry for the delay, men, but someone had a question for me and since he had a star on his shoulder, I thought I should give him whatever time he wanted."

"Did she come from the general?" Pete Rasor asked.

"Can it, Junior," Moyer snapped.

"Um, okay Boss."

J. J. saw Moyer cut him a glance.

"Your immediate mission," Mac said, "is to act like gentlemen. Clear?"

"Clear," the men said in unison.

"This is Tess Rand, civilian advisor Special Operations. She's on loan to us from the War College where she teaches, among other things. She's going to brief you on background. I expect your absolute attention. Please act as if God has given you a brain—even you, Rich."

"What did I— Yes, sir."

"Ms. Rand is a specialist in suicide bombings, especially female suicide bombers." He turned to her and motioned to the podium.

"Ms. Rand." He stepped to the back of the room. J. J. imagined the colonel staring at him. He didn't dare turn around.

"Thank you, Colonel."

J. J. tried not to bite through his lip.

Tess picked up a small remote from the lectern and pushed a button. A projector screen hidden in the ceiling lowered and the lights automatically dimmed.

"The phrase 'suicide bomber' is now a familiar part of our vocabulary; not just for the military, but for all Americans. Few people in the West gave much attention to the topic until September 11, 2001, when nineteen hijackers commandeered two commercial airliners and flew them into the twin towers of the World Trade Center, leaving three thousand dead and sixty-three hundred injured. While technically no bombs were used, the hijackers used the aircraft as guided missiles.

"After the U.S. launched its War on Terrorism by invading Afghanistan and later Iraq, accounts of individuals using car bombs or strapping explosives to their bodies have become commonplace. For some, this seemed a new and despicable way to conduct war. It certainly is despicable, but it is not new. Some think the oldest example of killing the enemy by suicide goes back to Samson, who used his great strength to bring down a Philistine temple on his tormentors. The account is in the Old Testament book of Judges, chapter sixteen.

"Stories of injured soldiers blowing themselves up and the enemy around them rather than being captured span the globe and crosses centuries. German Luftwaffe suicide pilots flew their air-craft into bridges over the River Oder during the Battle for Berlin. Of course, *Kamikaze* attacks against Allied ships in the Pacific is a well-known suicide attack."

As she spoke, photos from World War II flashed on the screen behind her.

"Of concern to us today is the work of suicide terrorists—people willing to martyr themselves by driving a bomb-laden car or truck into a crowd, or strapping on an explosive vest, or carrying an explosive satchel into a crowd."

She pressed a button on the remote. Photos all too familiar to J. J. splashed on screen. He recognized the terrain of Afghanistan and Iraq.

"The number of suicide bombings has increased over the years. During the 1980s there were on average only five such efforts a year. From 2000 to 2005 the number rose to 180 per year. In 2005 there were more than 460 such attacks. These events took place not just in Afghanistan and Iraq, but also Sri Lanka, Israel, Beirut, Chechnya, and more. You might recall the 2002 attack on Russian civilians in the Dubrovka Theater in Moscow. Some of the Chechen attackers were women wearing bombs." She paused. "Some were pregnant."

Tess moved to the side of the lectern. "My studies have shown that most suicide bombers are Muslim males, but women are taking an increasing role. The first woman to make a suicide attack was Sana'a Mehaidli. On April 9, 1985, she detonated a car bomb that killed two Israeli soldiers and wounded two others. She was part of the Syrian Social Nationalist party. More than two hundred women in the Tamil Tigers have carried out such missions. Women in the Kurdistan Workers Party have conducted suicide missions. My point is this: The use of women in suicide bombing is not new."

Moyer motioned with his hand. "But something has changed; is that it?"

Tess nodded. "Taken as a whole, women comprise a very small number of suicide bombers. Most women are brought up to nurture, not destroy. It takes more effort to make a female suicide bomber than it does a male one."

"Why women?" Moyer asked.

"I suspect you already know at least part of the answer," Tess said. "First, women move more freely than men. I've read your files. I know you and members of your team have spent time in these countries. If you were manning a checkpoint and you became suspicious about a man approaching your area, you would detain him and search him. You'd tell him to remove his coat if he had one; to lift up his vest. You might even pat him down. Would you do that to a woman?"

Moyer shook his head. "There are protocols about the way we treat Muslim women."

"Exactly. In the more fundamentalist areas Muslim women follow a dress code." Tess closed her eyes for a moment as if searching file cabinets in her brain. "Clothing must cover the entire body; the material must be opaque and hang loose to disguise the shape of her body; garments must not resemble what men wear, or what unbelieving women wear; the garments should be free of bold designs meant to attract attention." She opened her eyes. "You can't very well ask an Islamic woman to lift her abaya."

"How do they get women to volunteer for this?" J. J. asked. His voice sounded half-an-octave higher than he meant. She smiled and for a moment he feared she would wink.

"Several ideas have been put forth. Early in 2009 Iraqi police arrested Samira Ahmed Jassim, a fifty-year-old woman who recruited eighty female suicide bombers and is suspected of arranging nearly thirty bombings. She calls herself the 'Mother of Believers.' She told horrific stories about recruiting vulnerable women: outcasts, the mentally impaired, and the disgraced. She said that men would be sent to rape the women. These women would be sent to her for motherly advice. The women felt disgraced and cast off from family and friends. Over time she would convince them they could redeem themselves by becoming a suicide bomber. Some of these women will do anything to remove shame from their families."

"So there's been a rise in suicide bombers?" Moyer asked.

"Not just suicide bombers—*female* bombers, and we're seeing it in other countries, not just those with fundamentalist Islamic leaders. In London, a woman walked into a mall and killed twenty-two people in a food court. In Barcelona, a woman detonated herself in a crowded movie theater. Another did the same in an elementary school. Twenty-two children died; another forty received life-changing injuries." She toyed with the remote for a moment. "We were late for this meeting because a woman in Baghdad bombed the lobby of one of the few remaining hospitals."

"Sick," Rich said. "But what can our team do about it? We can't hunt down every possible bomber."

"We think there's a single mastermind behind it all."

"You mean like that Jassim woman?" J. J. said.

"Jassim worked at the direction of others. We're thinking someone much higher up the food chain." She worked the remote and the image of a middle-aged man appeared. To J. J., he looked remarkably like Omar Sharif. "A concert of intelligence work including agencies from our country, the UK, and many other countries has led us to believe this man is more than he appears."

"How does he appear?" Moyer asked.

"His name is Ezzat El-Sayyed. At least that's what his Egyptian passport says. He leads several businesses, including a construction company and a mining company, and has vast holdings in a shipping firm. He has his fingers in several smaller operations as well. The guy is a walking-talking ATM machine."

Tess studied the screen for a moment. "He travels extensively but spends most of his time in Europe and Middle Eastern countries. He's built structures from casinos in Spain to high-end hotels in Bahrain. We have sketchy intel that places him in Iraq, Afghanistan, and Iran. He's never been to the United States and has said he will never put a foot on 'Satan's soil.'"

"Satan's soil, eh." Rich leaned back. "He likes to alliterate."

"He's no dummy. El-Sayyed took a degree in engineering from Oxford."

Rich angled his head. "Why are guys and gals of intel snooping through his underwear drawers when he's not home?"

"Because *we* intel people are weird." Tess let the words hang in the air. J. J. wrestled back a smirk. Just as Rich was about to sputter an apology, she went on. "As interesting as El-Sayyed's clothing might be, other things drew our attention, such as the number of suicide bombings following his arrival and departure from a country. Six of his last ten trips abroad were followed with one or more events, each carried out by a woman. We think he's funding and leading a group of extremists targeting the U.S. and our allies."

"That's where you come in, gentlemen." Colonel Mac moved to the front of the briefing room. "The spooks are 90 percent certain El-Sayyed is the man behind the rise in suicide bombers, especially those in Europe. The people who sign my check and yours want you on the ground ASAP. You'll get a full mission briefing tomorrow at 0800."

Moyer studied the man. "Exactly where are we going, Colonel?"

"Italy. I don't need to remind this group that you will not speak about this outside this room."

Rich laughed. "You can bet on that, sir. If I tell my wife I'm going to Italy without her, then the team will be short a man—if you catch my drift."

"In that case, maybe I'll tell her."

Rich flicked J. J.'s ear hard enough to make his toes hurt.

Colonel Mac watched the men for a moment, then said, "Dismissed."

CHAPTER 3

WILLIE BREE MOVED THROUGH the crowd with ease and grace, like a man who rubbed shoulders with the world's top fashion buyers every day. He smiled. He nodded. He raised a glass of wine and said, "Hello" and "You look gorgeous" in a French pummeled by a long suppressed Bronx accent. If someone raised an eyebrow, he smiled and said, "I had the misfortune of being born in America." It usually brought a laugh.

"I may just die here." Bree grinned at his assistant, a slightly heavy, short woman with straight black hair. She was twenty-four and an organizational genius, unlike her tall, thin, nervous boss. He comforted himself with constant reminders that details should be left to people like DiAnna. She never used her last name. For those living in the land of *Glamour,* a unique name goes a long way. Bree approved.

"You've made it through the first three of the Big Four; you'll live through this one."

The Big Four: New York then London then Milan and now Paris. He had attended these fashion shows every year for the last decade, but this was the first time he had been placed in charge and the first time a third of the designs came from his creative soul.

Bree had started in the business right out of high school, working two years to earn enough money for fashion school. The combined wages of a pair of elementary school teachers were not enough to pay for the best training. Grants, school loans, and his own hard-earned money got him through four years of the Fashion Institute of New York City.

He excelled there. Working in the supply room of one of New York's top design firms had given him a taste for the industry. Earning a bachelors degree in fashion design set him free. Over the next ten years he worked in every department, rising through the ranks by working harder and longer than anyone else—and by kissing more fannies. It was worth it. Now he was close to the top of his game. In two years he'd have enough money to start his own firm, and then he'd set the world on its ear. Just two years more.

"Please DiAnna, let a man have a few moments for a nervous breakdown. I've earned it."

"That's true enough. Your designs have also earned great praise. They'll like your stuff here."

"Stuff? You know, you're the only person on the planet I allow to call my designs *stuff.*"

"That's because I'm indispensable. If it weren't for me, you'd still be in Milan trying to find the airport . . ." She looked at her iPhone and punched a button on the screen. "Jesse just texted me. He wants you to talk to one of the models. She's refusing to wear her dress."

Bree rolled his eyes. "I bet I know which one. Let's go. How much time?"

"Ten minutes."

Bree moved through the milling crowd in the lobby and hallways of The Plaza Athénée Hotel. *"Excusez-moi. Merci.*

Excusez-moi, s'il vous plait." He drew several harsh stares and a few comments in French he didn't want translated.

A door to a service hall changed the world from one of glitz, tuxedoes, shoes that cost a week's salary, and a toxic cloud of perfume to one of stark business. In ten minutes the show would begin, and those seated in the large room sporting a catwalk spanning the sea of people like a bridge, would see a well-practiced procession of the world's most beautiful women strutting, one foot in front of the other, displaying on their narrow bodies this year's idea of style.

Another door opened into the dressing area, and for a moment Bree felt he had fallen into Dante's hell. Outside this room people drank wine and champagne, chatted, and laughed. Back here, models snipped at each other, snapped at their dressers, and forgot the amount of money they were paid for suffering such indignities.

The sight of half-naked women would have paralyzed any teenage boy. Bree had moved beyond the point of caring what state of dress a woman was in. Working his way through the pandemonium, he made his way to the area where his company's models dressed. A young Hispanic man wearing makeup threw his arms in the air.

"Finally, Mr. Bree. Finally. Miss Fussy Pants here won't put on the dress."

"I *have* a name." The woman was close to six feet tall and carried slightly more weight per vertical foot than the other models. Bree liked that. She looked like a real woman. Her olive skin was smooth and even colored. Moisture rimmed her dark eyes. Bree could see she was close to tears.

"Jasmine." Bree spoke just above a whisper and flashed a wide smile. "Every time I see you, I begin to think there is hope for this crazy business."

"Thank you, Bree, I . . . I . . ." She raised a finger to her eye and lightly touched the tear perched on her lower eyelash.

"Now, now, Jasmine. No tears. There's nothing we can't work out."

"I told her you wanted her to wear the abaya, but she got in a tizzy."

"Jesse?"

"Yes."

"Shut up. I know you're trying to do your job, but I don't need or want any attitude. Understood?"

"Yes, Mr. Bree." He stepped to the side.

Bree turned to face Jasmine. "So what's troubling my favorite model?"

"I can't wear the abaya. It would be wrong."

"Wrong? You know it's not a real abaya. It's nothing like what Islamic women wear."

"I know, but it's close enough. It will offend people."

"In Paris?" Bree laughed. "Two things I know for certain: a man cannot fly on his own; and one cannot offend a Parisian with clothing—or lack of it." He paused for a moment. "Is that it? You think it's too revealing?"

"Bree, I'm standing in front of you in my underwear. I don't embarrass easily."

"Then what?"

DiAnna spoke up. "Is it your grandmother?"

Jasmine nodded.

"Grandmother?" Bree raised an eyebrow.

Jasmine looked at DiAnna. She took the hint. "Jasmine's grandmother is a practicing Muslim. Wearing Muslim dress—especially the way you've reinterpreted it—might be offensive to her."

"It's supposed to be a political statement as well as fashion . . ." He pulled Jasmine close and kissed her on the forehead. "Okay, I understand. Jesse!"

"Yes, sir."

"Put Jasmine in something else—have her trade outfits with Ava. Ava won't mind."

A squeaking behind him drew Bree's attention. A woman in her twenties, with skin a shade darker than Jasmine's, pushed a large gray bin to the center of the room. Bree had seen such bins in every hotel he had ever stayed in. Maids collected dirty sheets and towels in them and wheeled them to the laundry. What Bree had never seen before was such a bin in the staging area of a fashion show.

The woman stopped and looked around. She wore a maid's uniform. From the apron pocket at the front of her outfit she removed a small electronic device and held it in front of her. "Western whores!"

Bree had just enough time to realize something was wrong when he felt the heat and the blast.

"YOU'RE KIDDING OL' RICH, aren't you?" Rich Harbison raised the beer to his lips.

J. J. shook his head. "Nope, that's her." J. J. couldn't bring himself to look the big man in the eyes. Instead, he focused on the plastic tumbler that held his Dr. Pepper.

"I don't buy it." Pete Rasor took another slice of pizza then spoke with his mouth full. "What are the odds? He's working us, guys. I can see it in his beady little eyes."

The team had gathered at a small pizzeria a mile from the base. It was a tradition. If a mission allowed them the time, they would meet, share a fast food meal for an hour, then go home to spend the remaining free time with family. Too many missions demanded they leave on a moment's notice. On a covert excursion into Venezuela a few months before, Moyer hadn't had time to go home and hug his wife and kids. It was the thing he most hated about his work. It was also the only thing he hated.

"Did you just get married, Pete? Why can't you believe I want the same thing?"

Pete's eyes widened. "How do I put this? I'm a far better catch than you. Besides Tess Run is, well, beautiful, and you are, well, you."

"Her name is Rand. Tess Rand."

"I sit corrected."

Jose, a thick-across-the-chest man with black hair, leaned J. J.'s direction. "Don't let these cretins get under your skin. They can't help themselves. After all, she is too good for you. Why, if I weren't married—"

"And didn't have a house full of kids . . ."

"I was getting to that, Boss."

Moyer smiled. The team medic was old-school Catholic. At the rate he and his wife were going, he would need to move his family into a warehouse.

"Okay, gentlemen, it's time to leave poor J. J. to his dreams."

"It's not a dream, Boss. We're gonna get married."

"Answer me this, pal," Rich said. "Did you know she was going to be briefing us today?"

J. J. shook his head. "Not a clue. I was surprised."

"Judging by the look on her face, she was surprised to see you too."

"You know how it is, Boss. We can't tell our family and friends what we do and where we go. I guess she can't tell me everything she does."

"But you knew she worked in some form of intelligence."

"Yeah. I knew she graduated from the War College and served as a civilian consultant to the DOD. She also told me she specialized in overseas conflicts. Since I have to keep secrets, it's only fair I let her have hers."

"No need to explain that to us." Rich pulled a slice from the flat pan. "Here, eat so you can grow up and be big and strong like me." He pushed the pizza pan J. J.'s way.

Moyer looked to the end of the table. Zinsser sat quietly, removed from the others. "You want another beer, Zinsser?"

"Nah, I'm good."

J. J. glanced at Moyer to check his response. J. J. was getting the feeling that Moyer had questions about the man.

"Tell us about yourself, Zinsser," Rich said. "I like to know who I'm entrusting my life to."

"Not much to tell. I'm an Army brat. Dad put in thirty years. Artillery. Did several tours in Nam, picked up a Purple Heart, but lost a leg in the process. He finished his career teaching recruits."

"Another hero, eh?" Rich said. "You got family?"

"Nope."

"A cat?"

"Hate cats."

Rich looked at Moyer, who shrugged. No words were spoken, but the team heard the same message.

"You up to talking about Kismayo?" Moyer asked.

"I think it's all in my service jacket."

Moyer nodded. "I read it before coming over here. It's impressive, but notes in a man's file are not the same thing as hearing from the man himself."

Zinsser lowered his head. J. J. had seen soldiers do this before. The work they did as soldiers extracted a high price. Ugly memories were branded on the brain and the wound never heals. While at church one Sunday, the pastor honored an elderly man in the congregation. He had served in the Navy during World War II and had three ships shot out from beneath him. The pastor joked that

that was the reason no one would go fishing with the man. The honoree and congregation laughed, but J. J. could see the pain on the man's face, just below the surface.

The pastor told of the man's efforts to save a dozen men in a burning engine room before the destroyer went beneath the waves twenty miles off the Philippines. He entered and reentered the burning space below decks to pull wounded men from the smoke-choked room. He saved twelve lives, throwing the men overboard before making the jump himself. In the water he found two of the most severely wounded and helped them stay afloat until rescue arrived.

The pastor held up a simple frame that held a typewritten accommodation from Admiral Nimitz. The congregation stood and applauded. The hero couldn't face the people. Later J. J. joined several other men who pressed for details to the story. The elderly man tried, but broke down two minutes in. Over sixty years later the sailor couldn't face what he had seen and done.

J. J. saw the same look on Zinsser's face. Apparently Moyer did too. "We'll have plenty of time to get to know each other later," Moyer said. He raised his glass of beer. "To the new guy."

The others raised their glasses in a toast.

Zinsser took a deep breath. "Thanks guys, I won't let you down."

"Our hour is up, men. Time for you to beat it. Go home. Enjoy the evening. I want everyone on base, on time, and ready to rock. Clear?"

"Hooah!"

CHAPTER 4

JERRY ZINSSER DIDN'T GO home. His bare apartment held no appeal. He had another destination in mind. He sat in his 2005 Chevrolet Silverado and starred at the lobby doors of Moncrief Army Community Hospital, Fort Jackson's medical facility. He closed his eyes, but the image of the doors and what lay behind them continued to play in his mind. He had never been a patient here. His wounds were first treated at a field hospital in Nariobi, Kenya, then in Landsthuhul, Germany.

Brian Taylor hadn't been so lucky. The doctors in Germany had been able to keep him alive, but they couldn't save his legs, his arm, or most of his colon. Despite his injuries, Brian "Echo" Taylor was more man than any person Zinsser had met.

Zinsser wiped his eyes, pulled a facial tissue from a box on the passenger seat, and blew his nose. Deep breath. Deep, cleansing, invigorating breath. He drew in air until his lungs hurt then released it in a slow jet from his lips. He looked at his hands. They shook. He flexed his fingers twenty-five times as he had done a thousand times in the last week. The tremors settled.

In a monumental battle of mind over body, Zinsser forced his jaw to unclench. His stomach still roiled with acid, but he could deal with that. He removed a small roll of Rolaids and ate half of them.

Five minutes later Zinsser convinced himself that he was still a brave man, exited the truck, and walked into the hospital.

Room 253 held only one occupant: Brian Taylor. The room was dark. Brian liked it that way. Zinsser took one step over the threshold then stopped. Brian's form lay on the bed, a clean white sheet covered him from his shoulders to just twenty-four inches below his hips. Where legs should have been there was just flat, white sheet. The portion of the sheet over his left shoulder covered the stump of his arm.

Zinsser's eyes began to burn. Careful not to wake his friend, Zinsser slipped across the floor and lowered himself into a yellow Naugahyde-covered chair. It squeaked lightly as he moved his frame across the chair's surface. Brian didn't move. Zinsser looked at the plastic bags hanging from the IV pole. He didn't have to rise and read the labels to know what they contained. Antibiotics and morphine. The latter kept Brian asleep most of the time.

The dim room provided Zinsser with a small sense of comfort. Like Brian, he'd come to appreciate the darkness. For Brian, it meant others would have trouble seeing him; for Zinsser darkness felt more familiar than light.

The IV pump kept track of each drop of fluid it moved through the plastic tubing, tabulating important information on a small, digital screen. Outside the door, nurses, doctors, and other visitors moved along the corridors. Although open, the door provided the demarcation between the normal world of healthy, active people, and the universe of the broken and busted. Those on the other side of the door pitied those on this side. Zinsser knew. He had spent two months in rehab and two months seeing a military psychologist before being returned to duty.

He was the lucky one.

Zinsser forced his eyes to trace the form of his friend, then corrected himself. Chief, Boss, and two others left their life's blood in Kismayo. They lost their lives and, despite the shame it brought him, Zinsser acknowledged the truth.

He envied them the most.

THE ACRID, BITING SMELL of spent gunpowder filled the still air of the room. From outside the window, the barrel of an AK-47 appeared. A moment later the head of its owner followed. Zinsser put a round in the man's forehead. What he wanted to do was yank the trigger back and never let go. At seven hundred rounds a minute, his clip would be empty in less than two seconds. Conservation was the ticket. Don't waste a shot; don't waste an opportunity.

"Can you watch the window?"

"Yeah." Brian pressed the words through clenched teeth. "But not for long."

Zinsser moved to Brian's right side. "I'm gonna make a tourniquet out of my belt. Don't let me get shot while I do it."

"It's no use, Data, I'm bleeding out. I can feel it. I'm bleeding inside. I'm busted up bad."

"Shut up." Zinsser removed his belt and slipped it around Brian's right thigh and positioned it between the man's wound and hip. "This might pinch just a little."

He yanked the belt hard. Brian screamed. Zinsser cinched the belt tight. A moment later he saw another bullet wound in Brian's left leg. It wasn't bleeding and Zinsser assumed it missed the artery. He also assumed the bullet had shattered the upper leg bone.

"Watch it!" Brian raised the 9mm and began firing. Hot casings spewed from the chamber, hitting Zinsser in the face. He recoiled and raised his M4. A Somali with a grenade launcher pointed through the window stood unmoving for a moment as if taking aim, but Brian's shot had put an end to that. No one could aim with half his head missing. The standing corpse dropped.

"How long before they rush us?" Brian asked.

Zinsser returned to his spot by the side wall. "I don't know why they haven't yet. They have enough bodies. I saw at least twenty-five men."

As if taking their cue from the discussion, the doorknob began to turn. Zinsser aimed his weapon at a head-high spot above the doorknob. He pressed the trigger and three rounds pierced the wood. "I hate people who don't knock."

Brian chuckled. "Only you would crack-wise at a time like this."

"Can't help it, buddy. I'm getting bored—"

The door exploded open, and several men poured into the room. Brian emptied his 9mm at them. Zinsser flipped the switch on his weapon back to automatic and released a burst of fire.

Men fell.

Several more followed. Movement to the side caught his attention. "Window!"

Something hot hit his shoulder. Fire raced into his chest. He had no time to cry out; no time to complain. Since his arm still moved he assumed the round had passed through his arm. He fingered the trigger again. Five shots spewed from the barrel.

He heard Brian drop the handgun and pick up the one Zinsser had given him before. The familiar sounds of handguns shredded the air.

The next time Zinsser pulled his trigger nothing happened. "Reloading."

The thirty-round clip fell from the belly of the weapon as Zinsser reached for another in his vest. Something punched him twice, driving his body armor into his chest. The air in his lungs fled. He stumbled back into the wall but didn't fall.

A thin man stepped his way, a large revolver in his hand. Zinsser could see down the barrel. The attacker grimaced as he stepped closer. Apparently he didn't want to hit body armor with his next shot.

Zinsser sprang forward, seized the gun and the man's hand, and twisted. The pain in his shoulder peaked. He could feel blood run from the wound, but it didn't matter—he and Brian were moments from death. Zinsser would not wait for it.

Snapping the man's arm behind him, Zinsser continued to twist his wrist until he felt the attacker's tendons give way. The man screamed, and Zinsser pulled the gun free. Using the man as a shield, Zinsser raised the revolver and fired at two other men coming through the door.

The men outside scattered for a moment. Zinsser pushed his captive forward. He ran for the door. Zinsser shot him in the spine.

The room seemed to tilt. His ears, pummeled by gunfire in a confined space, roared. A second later the roaring was joined with a distant pounding. He swayed. The room stopped tilting and began to spin. Seconds slowed to hours.

His weapon.

His M4.

He reached for it then rammed in his spare clip. "Come on! I'm ready for you! BRING IT." Vomit tried to rise in his throat.

Three Somali pirates appeared at the door.

Zinsser raised his weapon.

Brian pulled the trigger of his sidearm, but it only clicked.

The roaring in his ears lessened, but the pounding increased. Not pounding. Thumping.

The Somalis looked up and fled. A half-second later, bullets rained from the sky.

"Hey, pal, you all right?"

Zinsser turned to Brian, but he wasn't talking to anyone. Where had the voice come from?

"Open your eyes, Zinsser."

Zinsser looked up. A voice from heaven?

"WHAT?"

"Open your eyes, man. You're freaking me out."

Zinsser blinked several times. He was back in the hospital room. The voice wasn't from heaven; it was from the man on the hospital bed. Zinsser looked at his hands; they shook like leaves on a tree. He squeezed them into fists and took a ragged breath.

"Did I wake you?"

"Yeah. Screaming, 'Bring it' kinda got my attention." Brian smiled.

"Sorry. I must have been having a nightmare."

Brian chuckled. "Nightmares, is that what they call it? Night-terrors is a better description."

"It was just a dream."

Brian swore. "Sure, that's all they are: dreams. Just little dreams that make us wet ourselves and soak the sheets with sweat." He paused and studied Zinsser. "You told me you were over the dreams; that the doc made them go away."

"I am. It's just . . ."

"Don't sweat it, man. I knew you were lying."

"How?"

"Because I'm not over my dreams, and I'm a better man than you."

"That a fact, is it?"

"Watch what you say, Zinsser. You don't want me to get out of this bed and smack you around."

It took a moment for the words to come. "Yeah, yeah I do."

"We've been over this, Zinsser. My condition is not your fault. You saved my life."

"I know."

"You know it in your head but not in your heart." Brian pulled his one arm from beneath the covers and scratched his forehead.

Zinsser decided to change the subject. "When is your surgery?"

"Same as it was yesterday when you stopped by. Two days. One more time under the knife to get my plumbing realigned, then a couple of months of rest. After that they're going to torture me with prosthetic legs. They've been working on some new technology. Still, I won't be doing disco soon."

"Any word from Juliet?"

Brian frowned. "No. She's gone for good, Zinsser. I told her to leave. She married a whole man."

"That's just wrong on so many levels." A hot spear of emotion pierced Zinsser.

"It was hard on her. I've asked for divorce papers. She needs to be free to live her life."

"And she agreed to it?"

"No, but she will. It will take time for me to wear her down, but she'll leave because I tell her too."

"She loves you."

"Jerry, we've been through this. In this situation, love doesn't matter. She's only twenty-seven, just like me. This is as good as it's gonna get for me. I don't want to hold her back."

Zinsser tried to find words to change his friend's mind, but he came up empty.

"You don't have to come by every day, you know."

"What? You don't like my conversation skills?"

"What I don't like is you coming here to make yourself feel bad."

"I come here because you're my friend."

Brian sighed. "We made good teammates, but let's face it, we never hung out much."

"What we've been through creates a bond. You can't deny that."

Brian pursed his lips. "That's true, I guess."

"Well, you're going to get your wish. I won't be around for awhile. I've been reassigned."

"The docs really said you're fit for duty?"

"Since I am fit for duty, they had to." Zinsser's words carried an edge.

"Who did they assign you to? Another special ops team?"

"Yeah. I requested it. I'm on Eric Moyer's team now."

Brian thought for a moment. "I've heard of him. I hear he's a good man and a great soldier."

"I'll try not to hold him back too much."

"When do you deploy."

"Tomorrow. Early."

Brian looked thoughtful for a moment. Zinsser knew he wanted to ask about the mission but was too much of soldier to do so.

"Are you sure you're ready?"

"I'm ready, Brian. I'm more than ready."

CHAPTER 5

"I ALMOST FAINTED WHEN I walked in," Tess Rand said as she slipped into the corner booth of Tio Leo's Mexican restaurant, one of Columbia, South Carolina's upper-end eateries. She and J. J. had come here on their first date. He'd been trying to impress her, and she'd been willing to let him do it.

"It took me aback a little too." J. J. slipped into the booth beside her. "At first I thought the guys were pulling a joke and got you to go along." He paused. "They weren't, were they?"

"Sorry, I've been sworn to secrecy."

"So that's how it's going to be."

"Of course. It's part of the sneaky woman's code of conduct: Keep the men in your life guessing."

"Men? Plural?"

"Relax, soldier, you're the only guy for me."

A waiter approached and offered to take their drink order, but only after he suggested several types of margaritas. Tess and J. J. both ordered Dr. Pepper.

"Do you think we offended him by not ordering something with alcohol?"

"I'm sure he'll survive." He took her hand. It felt good.

"This is awkward."

J. J.'s eyebrows rose. "Holding hands is awkward? We're going to be married six months from now. I'm pretty sure we're going to be moving beyond the hand-holding stage."

"Not that, you goof. The work situation."

"Ah. You know, you're the only significant other that has an idea of our mission."

"Actually, I don't know that much. You know how compartmentalized this stuff is. I advised Colonel Mac and a few other of the brass, but they never discussed the mission with me. I'm still pretty much in the dark."

"That makes two of us. Moyer will give us the details tomorrow."

Tess stared at J. J. "He'll give *you* the details. I'm out of the loop until they call me in."

"It's better that way."

The comment irritated Tess. "How is it better?"

"What you don't know—"

She raised a hand. "Don't even go there. Not knowing means my imagination can take over, and I can imagine some pretty horrible things."

J. J. gave her hand a squeeze. "Do you remember when I proposed to you?"

She scratched her chin. "Can't say that I do. Was it recent?"

"Very funny."

"Of course I remember. I was there."

"I almost didn't propose."

Tess straightened. "Really? Well, I certainly feel loved now."

He moved closer and ran a finger through her hair. "You should. I wasn't going to back out because I don't love you. I do. More than I can say."

"Then why the cold feet?"

"Because of what is happening right now. We're lucky. We have the evening together. Most of the time, I get called up and have to race to the base. I've watched Moyer, Rich, and Jose when we get called up. There's a thrill about a new mission, but you can read the concern they have for their families. They wonder if they'll see them again. It's the thing these guys fear the most. I've seen them face impossible odds without blinking, but when it comes to family, well, it's very different."

"It must be hard."

"Hard isn't a strong enough word, but I don't have another to use in its place. It's like some living thing burrows into their gut and eats them from the inside out."

"Oh, gross. Can you be a little less poetic?"

"Sorry. Don't get me wrong. They would never step away from the mission, but this work takes its toll."

Tess narrowed her eyes. "And that made you reluctant to propose."

Before J. J. could answer, the waiter returned with a basket of chips, a bowl of salsa, and two sodas. They gave their order and the waiter disappeared again.

Tess waited for J. J. to continue. "I know you already know this. You can't do the work you do without some idea of what happens to couples at a call-up. I hesitated in proposing because I don't want to bring any pain to your life."

Tess picked up a chip, dipped it in the salsa, but never removed it. "I have an idea what it must be like, but I'll admit, I didn't truly understand until today. J. J., I'm scared for you."

"I'm not foolish enough to tell you not to be. It's the way of life. As long as I'm"—he looked around—"As long as I do what I do, these call-ups are going to be a part of our lives. It is what I do, and I'm good at it."

"I don't have to like it to live with it, do I?"

"No one likes it; we all live with it."

She forced a smile. "What I do is so different from what you do. We fight the same kind of battles, but all of mine is done on paper. I read, I research, I form opinions, then I go home to a warm bed."

"Don't sell yourself short, honey. You intel people make our job possible."

"I hope I don't come to regret that."

"We trust in God at all times."

"What's it like being the only Christian on your team?"

J. J. thought for a moment. "I've never thought about it. The team gives me a bad time about it, but they still show me a lot of respect. There's been a couple of times when they've turned to me for advice, but not many. Most of the time they just tolerate the fact."

"Do you witness to them; tell them about your faith?"

"Not directly. I don't know how to explain this. The men on my team—really, on any team like ours—are highly individualistic. They keep their cards close to their vest. We trust each other implicitly, and part of that trust means we don't invade one another's privacy. You have to be invited in. I try to show Christ by the way I live. I leave the sermons to my twin brother."

"Oh, have you asked him if he'll perform the wedding?"

"Yes."

"What did he say?"

"He asked how much money you have."

Tess moved away from J. J. "I see." She smiled.

"Get over here. He said he'd be honored to do the deed."

"He'd better."

J. J. motioned at the table. "You going to eat that chip?"

THE LIGHT FROM THE kitchen poured over the white tile counter and through the opening that separated it from the living room of the apartment. Jerry Zinsser sat as far from the light as possible. In his hand he held a tumbler half-filled with Chivas Regal. He sipped the scotch and enjoyed the burn it left in his throat, and savored the smooth, honey taste of the whisky.

This was his tradition. Soldiers had traditions—especially Special Ops. He knew men who went to certain restaurants the night before deployment. Others picked out lucky socks, worked out, went jogging, went to church, or ate specific foods. Zinsser's old team always gathered for a glass of Chivas, toasted the future, then went home to hug their families.

Zinsser had no family and those he counted as friends were dead, brought home in body bags. All except one, and Zinsser had left him in the hospital bed an hour before, no longer able to look at his damaged form. He raised the glass of booze and said to the darkness, "To Echo." He downed the remaining fluid in one gulp. It sent shivers through him. His head began to spin.

Taking the decorative bottle he poured another glass and raised it. "To Boss." It took two gulps to down the golden fluid.

His hand began to shake. Rising, Zinsser moved to his stereo and pressed play. The dulcet voice of Roy Orbison filled the dark room. Roy sang "Running Scared."

"You don't know the half of it, Roy. You don't know nuthin' from scared." The melody wrapped Zinsser's mind, and he began to sway, holding out the glass as if it were his dance partner. He two-stepped to the bottle of Scotch and refilled the glass.

"To Chief." He took his time with this drink. It was a breach of superstition, but he didn't want to vomit on the floor and lose all the good booze he'd been pouring down his throat.

By the time Roy Orbison had worked his way through "Oh, Pretty Woman," "Only the Lonely," "In Dreams," and "Crying," Zinsser could no longer walk a straight line. He had reached his goal: oblivion by drunkenness. His last conscious memory was stumbling into the bathroom, opening the felt-lined case holding his Distinguished Service Cross and pouring the last dregs of his drink on it. "Here's to courage under fire."

Zinsser began to weep.

THE AIR WAS FILLED with noise that pummeled Zinsser's already assaulted ears. The MH-60G Nighthawk helicopter unleashed a torrent of 7.62mm rounds from its Dillon minigun on the street in front of the building. The sound of weapons, the impact of bullets, the thunder of the helo's rotor blades, and the screams of the men burrowed through Zinsser's ears and into his brain. His mind raced. What he did in the next few seconds would determine if he lived or died.

He forced his ears to separate the sounds. He heard what he hoped: the syncopated pounding of another helo.

"Our ride is here. Time to get moving, Echo."

"You go, Zinsser. I can't last much longer. I can't stand."

Zinsser holstered his 9mm, ignoring the empty M4 on the concrete floor. Taking Brian by the front of his vest, he yanked the man up and over his shoulder. Brian's scream melted Zinsser's soul. He charged the door, peeked out the opening, then sprinted into the street. In a perfect world, the street would

be wide enough for one of the helos to land, or the roof strong enough to hold
the aircraft's weight. Of course, in a perfect world, he wouldn't be trotting
down the street with his dying friend over his shoulder and waiting for the
impact of a bullet striking the back of his head.

In the distance one of the helos was landing in a small field a hundred
yards away. Dust rose around the chopper. Zinsser forced himself forward.
His wounds screamed, and he could feel blood oozing down his arm. Still
he forced one step in front of the other. Adrenaline powered him like racing
fuel.

Two men rounded one of the buildings, stopped, and raised weapons.
Zinsser kept moving. A second later the men lowered their guns.

"Take him. He has several wounds."

The soldiers took Brian from Zinsser. "Can you follow us?"

"Yes."

"Let's move." The two special ops men headed toward the landed chopper.
Zinsser turned and ran back to the building.

He heard popping and saw bits of asphalt fly into the air. A thinking man
would have sought cover, but Zinsser gave up thinking. He was in reaction
mode. Years of training had taken over his conscious mind.

Moments later Zinsser dove through the door he and Brian had been
defending, stumbling and landing hard on the floor. He howled as the impact
jarred his damaged arm. He scampered to his feet and entered the windowless
room where the captives were chained.

Several of the men rifled through the pockets of the dead guards. Zinsser
joined them.

"Got it," a grizzled middle-aged man said.

"Give it to me." Zinsser reached for the key.

"Behind you!"

Zinsser spun and saw a tall Somali in a striped shirt and ripped jeans duck
in the door. He didn't bother to check the room. Instead he raised a Russian-
made rocket-propelled grenade launcher and pointed at something in the air.
Zinsser knew what that something was.

Sprinting from the room, he lowered a shoulder and executed a "crack-back" tackle on the man, sending them both tumbling into the street. Again electric bolts of pain ran through Zinsser's body.

The loud roar of the M-134 Gatling gun rolled over them. Bits of asphalt and of plaster shrapnel punctured their skin, but no bullets touched them. The Nighthawk gunner had released the trigger just in time.

Zinsser could feel his strength ebbing. He couldn't last much longer, and wrestling with a twenty-something-year-old Somali pirate would tax him too much.

Without thought.

Without regret.

Without hesitation, Zinsser drew his 9mm, forced the business end into the young man's side, and pulled the trigger. He rose and scampered back into the building, leaving the man dying in the street.

That was when Zinsser stopped feeling anything.

CHAPTER 6

TESS RAND LAY IN her hotel bed staring at the ceiling. The clock by her bed glowed 2:30 a.m. She had tried all the tricks to sleep: warm milk, thinking of quiet happy places, listening to a late-night radio program, but nothing worked.

After dinner J. J. had taken her to a movie, but she couldn't recall which one. When she was a girl, her mother advised her, "Love is the most wonderful torture you'll ever experience." It didn't make sense then. Now, alone in the darkness of worry, she understood. Tomorrow, J. J. would leave for Europe and might never come home. The mission—at least on paper—wasn't as dangerous as some, but she had been around enough, read enough reports, briefed enough teams to know that easy missions could go badly. Many names on the killed-in-action list got there while on "routine patrol."

She pushed herself up, crossed her legs, and sat on the bed. Tess wanted a cigarette. It was the first time she had felt the urge since giving up the habit her freshman year in college. That was the year everything changed for her; the year she began to live for someone other than herself; the year she found herself in an on-campus Bible study listening to someone teach from the Gospel of John.

She attended again the next week, and the week after that. By her junior year, she was leading the study. Sometime during that first year, her universe widened to include God. An international studies major, Tess graduated near the top of her class. International banking was her goal, but while working on her master's degree at George Washington University, she developed an interest in the way countries dealt with one another. By the time she finished her PhD she'd been recruited by a major think tank, the CIA, a private consulting firm, and two other organizations slow to reveal their names and natures. None of those groups interested her, but the invitation to do postdoc work at the Army War College in Carlisle, Pennsylvania, did. Soon she was an adjunct professor at the Strategic Studies Institute.

Tess hated war and violence, but she also recognized that, like weeds, evil grew wherever justice was allowed to languish. There were still many moments when her thoughts did battle, but at the end of each mental war, she remained convinced that she was saving lives by providing information to generals and senators.

It was during a briefing at Fort Jackson six months ago that she met J. J. The series of meetings required her to spend the weekend in Columbia, South Carolina. Sunday she attended services led by Army chaplain Paul Bartley. After the service Bartley stood by the door greeting worshippers as they left the chapel. Standing next to him was a good-looking man about the same age as the chaplain.

Bartley smiled as she shook his hand. "Is this your first time here?"

"Yes, I live in Carlisle, Pennsylvania. I'm down here for a few meetings."

Neither man asked what kind of meetings.

"Carlisle?" The other man studied her. "Carlisle as in Army War College?"

"Yes."

Chaplain Bartley said, "This is my nosey brother, J. J."

They exchanged pleasantries.

"Listen, some of us go out for lunch after service. Since you're from out of town, maybe you'd like to join us. It's nothing fancy, just five or six people sitting around a sandwich shop telling lies and jokes."

Tess grinned at the chaplain. "Lies? Are chaplains allowed to tell lies?"

"When a chaplain does it, it's called a sermon illustration." His smile was broad. "Come on and join us. It beats sitting alone in a hotel room watching television."

Tess agreed and J. J. offered to drive. Three hours and one tuna on rye later, Tess began to fall in love.

Prior to that moment, Tess had only her aging parents to worry about; now she had one more. J. J. captured her with his wit, his intelligence, his commitment, but most of all his faith. Tess spent her days surrounded by rugged, good-looking men, but she needed more. She needed someone with spiritual depth. J. J. had that by the truckload.

Over the months he spoke of his admiration for his teammates and team leader Eric Moyer. They were rough, crude, and often insensitive, but they were also brave, loyal, and committed to making their country safe and the world a little more evil free.

Two months into their courting, J. J. told her how the team lost a member on their last major mission. He left out many details such as the man's name, where he died, and why they were there. The details didn't matter; she saw the sorrow in his eyes and felt the pain in his soul.

Tess pushed back the covers, unfolded her legs, slipped on her robe, and walked to the sliding glass door that overlooked the hotel's courtyard three stories down. An alabaster moon hung in a cloudless sky. In the distance a siren wailed. The rumble and roar of eighteen-wheelers traveling nearby making early morning deliveries rode a gentle breeze.

Tess sat in a balcony chair and gazed at the moon. It looked peaceful in its orbit 240,000 miles away. It also looked lifeless.

A moment later Tess began to pray.

CHAPTER 7

THE ALARM NEXT TO Jerry Zinsser's head came to life, blaring a heavy-metal tune that threatened to liquefy his brain. The sudden noise activated his instinct and he pushed off the bed, fists clenched, and arms ready for a fight. It took five seconds for him to realize he was in his own bedroom. He quieted the alarm and stood in the dark. The numbers on the clock told him it was 0300, just as he had set it.

His head pounded; his stomach churned like a pan of acid over a blazing stove. He glanced at the bed. The covers had not been pulled back. He had no memory of how he got on the bed. He smacked his lips and grimaced at the taste of scotch residue.

Moving to the bathroom, he stepped to the toilet and vomited. It was a horrible feeling but better than the dreams he'd been having. After his stomach settled, he rinsed his mouth, then stared in the mirror. "You are one lousy piece of work, Zinsser. Someone should flush you."

His eyes drifted to the old double-edged razor he used to shave every morning. Electric razors were for sissies. He thought of the razor and how it had belonged to his father. He thought of the thin, sharp-edged blade inside—then he thought of his wrists.

It wouldn't take long. If he used hot water on his wrists first, it wouldn't even hurt. He thought of his legless, one-armed friend in the hospital.

Zinsser clamped his eyes shut.

He felt himself swaying. That or the room was spinning. He couldn't tell the difference.

He forced his eyes open. It was time to begin The Routine.

In the kitchen he started a pot of high-octane, African coffee. While the coffeemaker did its job, Zinsser drank a large glass of orange juice, then went to the treadmill he kept in his bedroom. He stripped to his underwear, then, barefooted, stepped on the device and started it. For ten minutes he walked at a slow pace, just two-and-a-half miles an hour. Once convinced he wouldn't topple over, he upped the speed to a fast walk. Five minutes after that he was jogging. Every step hurt; every stride was a struggle, but that was the point. The pain helped him dig his way out of the hangover.

Two miles later he stopped, consumed two cups of coffee, then slipped under the stream of cold water in his shower. The water felt icy on his skin. He shook. For the first ten minutes he thought his bones shivered as well.

The fog that draped his mind began to lift. By 0500 he felt functional and very nearly alive. By 0645 he could face himself in the mirror.

"Time to be a soldier."

He started for his front door, set a hand on the knob, then stopped. A foggy, thin thought stroked his subconscious. Turning from the door he moved to a China cabinet once owned by his mother. It looked like walnut but he knew it had been hastily made of poplar in some factory in the Midwest and stained to appear like the more expensive wood.

The high-backed cabinet had two shelves above a flat top, two pull doors at the bottom, and a single locked drawer. He removed his keys from his pocket and unlocked the drawer. Slowly he pulled it open. Inside rested the silverware his mother so prized. Time and inattention had left the silver tarnished and charcoal gray. Silverware didn't concern him. What lay just to the right did: a Colt 1911A1 pistol. The handgun had belonged to his grandfather who, as a twenty-year-old, carried it in several battles of World War II. It was dark and bore the scars of years of existence.

Papa Carl had given it to Zinsser as reward for graduating from basic training. The old man died six months later. Zinsser lifted the weapon and ejected the seven-round clip from the handle. The stubby bullets looked as fresh as when he placed them there five years before.

Papa Carl told fantastic stories of shooting Germans with the gun. As the man grew older and age began to eat at his mind, the stories changed from Germans to Japanese to Koreans. It didn't matter. Zinsser knew his grandfather had served his country for four years without complaint. So what if he couldn't remember when he was eighty.

The weapon felt heavier than it should; felt warmer.

Zinsser pulled back the slide and racked a round into the chamber.

The gun began to shake in his hand. He corrected himself. It was his hand that shook.

"Maybe this time . . . Now would be good; now would be perfect." If he didn't show, they would send someone to retrieve him. It would be a shock to find his body, but at least he wouldn't stink up the apartment with his rotting corpse. A lousy last image, but men like him didn't get to choose the last thing they saw in this life.

He lifted the .45, placed it to his temple, and fingered off the safety. His hand shook more. That wouldn't do. What if he missed?

What if the gun moved at the last second leaving him brain damaged but alive?

He lowered the weapon and rethought his actions. Then he lifted the collector's item again and placed the muzzle in his mouth. He tasted gun oil. He thought he tasted gunpowder.

Details mattered. The .45 had to be angled just right. Too shallow and he'd blow a hole in the back of his neck but might continue to live. Or die slowly. Too steep and he would only succeed in removing his face.

He pushed the muzzle to his palate. The front site scratched his gums.

His finger moved the trigger a millimeter then stopped. He relaxed, inhaled deeply through his nose, then again applied pressure to the trigger.

Seconds became minutes.

Do it. DO IT!

Tears streaked his face. He couldn't. God help him, he couldn't.

He removed the gun from his mouth, reset the safety, replaced the weapon in the drawer, and shut it.

Zinsser pulled his gear together, loaded his car, and started for Fort Jackson.

EZZAT EL-SAYYED WORE A black polo shirt, tan pants, and a pair of Salvatore Ferragamo Python Loafers. At $900 the shoes were not his most expensive pair, but he was dressing down for this occasion. Still, it only seemed right to wear Italian shoes in Italy.

The Mercedes E moved through the streets of Rome easily. It should. El-Sayyed's chauffer was one of his most trusted guards and had spent the week before his arrival driving these streets, familiarizing himself with the intricacies of every avenue, memorizing every turn and every possible place of ambush.

The Saint Bernadette Hotel stood ten stories and catered to traveling executives. It wasn't the most luxurious facility in the city, but it offered enough amenities to keep CEOs of mid-range businesses content, and the attention lavished on patrons by the staff made it a popular place to stay. For El-Sayyed its location, off the main street, and its reputation for employees who didn't ask questions and knew how to look the other way made it a suitable choice for a brief meeting.

Tony Nasser drove by the front entrance slowly, his eyes directed to a spot ten meters further along the walkway. A dark-skinned man leaned against the façade of the adjoining hotel. He was tall, thin, and seemed more interested in the cigarette he was smoking than the passing traffic. El-Sayyed knew better. As the Mercedes rolled along the man on the sidewalk raised his head, took a long draw on the cigarette, and blew the stream of blue smoke into the air. He then dropped the butt to the ground. It was the signal El-Sayyed hoped to see. He saw Nasser give a small nod. Before they had passed the man's location, he pivoted, walked to Saint Bernadette's front doors, and entered the lobby. Nasser drove on.

After driving side streets for ten minutes, the Mercedes arrived at the curb in front of the hotel. A young man in a red uniform stepped to the car and opened the back door. El-Sayyed exited. Nasser was by his side before the attendant could close the door. A second man in a yellow shirt and jeans appeared at El-Sayyed's side. He was of average height, and his build stretched the shoulder stitching of the sport coat he wore. The three men walked into the building.

The lobby sported a hand-painted ceiling showing ancient Romans doing whatever Romans did. El-Sayyed ignored the marble floor, the hand-crafted counter with a short line of people checking in, and made his way to the elevators. Brass doors parted, and three men in uniforms of pin-striped suits exited. El-Sayyed and his men filled the elevator. The cigarette-signal man joined them.

A bald man with a billiard-ball build started to enter the elevator cab but changed his mind when Nasser raised a hand. El-Sayyed smiled, shrugged, and stroked his mustache.

The elevator doors closed.

"You are satisfied with the room, Abasi?" El-Sayyed asked the signal man.

"Yes, sir. They arrived ten minutes ago. I searched the room before their arrival and swept for listening devices. The room was clean, but they've been alone in the room. I would assume you are being recorded and videotaped." He paused. "I do not trust these men."

"Do you trust anyone, Abasi?"

"My mother and you, El-Sayyed."

El-Sayyed placed a hand on Abasi's shoulder. "How is your mother? Is she still ill?"

"She died yesterday."

El-Sayyed turned to his employee. "May Allah give you peace."

"He has, sir. Allah is merciful."

El-Sayyed turned to Nasser. "After our meeting, Tony, I want you to arrange a plane for Abasi. Give him what he needs."

"Yes, sir."

"You are too kind, El-Sayyed, but I prefer to finish our mission. I can go home after our work is done."

"Take the month to be with your family. Celebrate the life of she who gave you life."

"I will, sir."

The elevators parted. Nasser and Abasi exited first, searching the corridor. Each had his hand under his jacket. Only after Nasser gave his approval did El-Sayyed exit.

They walked down the hall, Nasser and Abasi in front, the other guard behind El-Sayyed. Abasi stopped ten feet from the last door on the left. Only Nasser approached. Anyone could shoot through a hotel door.

Nasser knocked and stood with his arms to his side. Two seconds later, the door swung open.

"Is he here?"

Nasser didn't answer. He entered the room and exited sixty seconds later. He motioned for El-Sayyed to enter. Abasi stepped over the threshold first—one last effort to provide protection. The moment El-Sayyed entered, a brown-skinned man exited and stood next to the door. El-Sayyed's third guard did the same.

The room was small compared to those El-Sayyed knew existed on the top floor. Luxury wasn't required. He planned to be out of this room in five minutes.

A man with black hair, a round face, and a globe-like belly sat in a chair by the window smoking a cigar. El-Sayyed had no doubt the smoke had originated in Cuba. Standing to either side like bookends were two well-muscled men.

"You have kept me waiting, El-Sayyed. Again."

"Security has its price, Michael." He wondered, as he had many times before, if *Michael* was the man's real name.

"You disrespect me when you make me wait. You are a rude man."

Nasser took a step forward. Michael's guards took a similar step. El-Sayyed placed a hand in front of Nasser. "Insults from infidels mean nothing, my friend." He turned his attention back to Michael. "Shall we get down to business? I would like to do this quickly. I always leave these meetings feeling unwashed."

"Unwashed, is it?" Michael looked at his men. "The towel-head thinks we pollute him." They said nothing. Michael rolled the cigar between his fingers and squinted through the smoke. "My brother—for reasons I don't understand—likes you. He has asked me to tell you he is very happy with the test run."

"How has he shown his gratitude?"

Michael nodded at the guard to his right who reached behind the chair and removed a metal briefcase. He set it on the desk in the room and opened it. Stacks of euros filled the case. "Ten million as agreed, although that is little more than a child's allowance to a wealthy man like you."

"The money means nothing to me, but I accept it as proof of your brother's sincerity. You may thank him for me."

"I'll be sure to do that."

The guard closed the case and pushed it toward Nasser. Nasser didn't move.

"Does your brother have another message for me?"

Michael took his time answering. He stared at El-Sayyed and puffed on the cigar. El-Sayyed grew impatient.

"If you were man enough to grow a beard, my friend, you'd look like Fidel Castro."

"Thank you. He was very successful."

El-Sayyed laughed. "He became dictator of a small island nation and ruled over it until its people barely survive. There are greater successes to be had."

"This is why you do this? You risk so much for a dead ideology?"

"It is far from dead, and I take no risks. Now, does your brother have a message for me?"

Again, Michael refused to answer.

El-Sayyed motioned for Nasser to take the case. "We are done here. Tell your brother two things. First, our business is now concluded; second, he has a fool for a brother."

El-Sayyed turned to leave.

"Wait." Michael rose. "We move forward.'"

El-Sayyed gave a slight bow. "You may tell him, I will continue the next step. May Allah bring you to the light of Mohammed."

"Yeah? Well, *vaya con Dios* to you too."

CHAPTER 8

THE AIR FORCE C-37A went wheels-up from the Columbia Metro Airport at 1215 hours and skated into a black sky, passing through gossamer clouds on the way to its cruising altitude, which Moyer had been told would be 41,000 feet. Shortly after reaching altitude, the pilot would settle the craft at a brisk 600 miles per hour.

Moyer sat in one of the white leather seats near the entrance doors and enjoyed the sensation of flying upward at a forty-five-degree angle.

"I gotta ask, Boss, who'd ya have to kill to get this ride?" Shaq sat in the seat across the narrow aisle.

"You like this better than flying cargo on a transport plane?"

"Well, yeah. Don't you?"

"Sure beats commercial airlines." Moyer's seat was turned so he faced the back of the modified Gulfstream V. He saw seats for twelve passengers—plush leather seats, some with a simulated wood burl table between them. His team took six of the seats; three of the five flight crew took some of the other seats. Two of those were officers, one was an Airman Fifth Class, or First Class, or Third

Class—he never could keep the Air Force's rank system straight. At any rate, he was an enlisted man.

"I take it the Army has finally realized how valuable we are and has rewarded all our fine and sacrificial efforts."

Moyer looked at his second in command. "That or they're picking up some dignitary to bring back."

Rich tapped his teeth in thought. "Nah, it's because we're special."

The C-37A was one of nine such craft used by the Air Mobility Command in Illinois. Usually reserved for high-ranking government and DOD officials, the C-37A was an unexpected ride. They would be crossing the Atlantic in style. If he had to spend ten hours confined in a metal tube, this was the kind of tube he'd choose.

Ten minutes later the pilot's voice poured from overhead speakers. "All right, gentlemen, we have reached our cruising altitude nearly eight miles up. It looks clear ahead so feel free to move around the cabin. Please keep your lap belts fastened while seated in case we encounter clear-air turbulence . . . or I decide to do a few barrel rolls."

"Funny guy," Rich said.

"And for our Army passengers, please, no walking on the wings."

"Oh, this guy should go on the road." Rich chuckled despite his sarcasm.

The airman approached Moyer. "It's good to have you and your team aboard, Sergeant Major. I've been asked to offer you and your men lunch and something to drink."

Rich grinned. "Hey, we got a stewardess."

The airman, who looked barely older than Moyer's teenage son, studied Rich for a moment, then turned back to Moyer. "Did you choose him or did he choose you?"

"I'm being punished for my misspent youth. Thanks for the offer. We'll eat whatever you have."

"Very well, um . . . "

"What is it, Airman?"

"Six Army men in civilian clothes and a ton of equipment makes me think you're on a mission. May I ask what it is?"

"Sure. Go ahead."

"What kind of mission are you on?"

Moyer looked the kid in the eyes. "It's a training mission."

"I had a feeling you were going to say that. It seems like all you Army guys are on training missions."

"That's why we're so good, kid," Rich said. "I'll take a ginger ale."

The airman slipped to the back of the craft, stopping at each of Moyer's team and taking orders.

Before long, a microwaved plate of chicken breast, rice, green beans, and almonds was placed on the small table in front of him. "Man, if this is lunch, I can't wait to see dinner."

As he ate, Moyer gazed out the window at the passing world below. From this height he could see roadways and cities, but people were invisible. Six billion people on the planet, most of them good, honest, respectable. But there were the others. Moyer wasn't good enough at math to work out the percentages, but he knew that a few people could make life horrible for millions of others.

He had to find one such man.

MOYER WAS A YOUNG man at thirty-eight, but he was beginning to feel his age. Not so much physically, he could still bring it when he needed to, but his mind and worldview had aged faster than his body. In his twenties he never worried. The world was a toy. The Army trained him, equipped him, and empowered him to move beyond emotion. Even after he married Stacy, he never worried about dying on the field. She was young and could remarry easily. But when his children came along, Rob and Gina, that began to change. The idea of another man rearing his children ate at him. Still, he learned to live with it. Rob was now seventeen and until a few months ago had been a royal pain in the butt. Like many teen-agers, he withdrew, battled his parents about everything, and took an interest in anything that would irritate his father. Moyer had only made things worse. Being an Army brat was no easy thing; being an Army brat to the leader of a Spec Ops team was worse.

Gina, however, remained the jewel in his crown. Smart, sup-portive, she often saw things more clearly than adults. He hoped that she wouldn't change as she entered her teenage years. Moyer would be happy if his daughter remained perpetually thirteen.

Early on Moyer showed little concern for the families of his team. Then his own children arrived. Suddenly he saw things dif-ferently. He began to invite his team to his house for barbecue. He and his men would watch sports, preferably NASCAR racing, and the women would visit. Those times grew special.

Months ago, before beginning the mission to Venezuela, Moyer had thought he was seriously ill. Not wanting his superiors to know, he first went to a civilian doctor but received a call-up before the doc could run the needed test. The entire time he was in South America, Moyer believed he had colon cancer.

Moyer gazed down the aircraft and looked at his men. Rich Harbison was big, loud, funny, and seemingly impervious to pain or fear, but Moyer knew the man loved his wife more than most men are capable. He might joke about the hardships of marriage, but he would eat glass if Robyn asked him to do so. The highest compliment men like him could receive is, "He's a good soldier."

Rich was a *great* soldier and an excellent second in command. They didn't always agree, and Moyer had knocked heads with the big man more than once, but when bullets began to fly, he wanted to be next to Shaq.

Pete Rasor sat at a window over the wing, something he did every time he flew. He said it was a smoother ride. Pete was the youngest of the bunch, a fact that earned him the nickname, "Junior." He was smart, and like many young men his age, he loved anything tech. He was an early adopter. If anything tech came out that had a high "cool factor," Pete bought it. Even as Moyer watched him, Junior was playing a video game on his iPhone. When J. J. announced his engagement, Pete did the least of the teasing.

J. J. sat on the other side of the aisle from Pete, earbuds crammed into his ears. His eyes were closed as if asleep, but every few moments the Sergeant First Class bobbed his head. Moyer assumed the man was listening to music, but with J. J. it could be a sermon. He was an enigma Moyer had yet to fathom. Several of his team believed in God. It didn't mean they were churchgoers, Bible-thumpers, or goody-goody.

J. J. should fit those descriptions, but in many ways he didn't. He never preached to the others; never used guilt to make a point; never meddled. Still, he never kept his faith secret, would answer questions when asked, and provided a needed balance to the team. Although he was devout, no one could claim the young man wasn't a soldier. No one trained harder, and no one had shown more courage when the chips were down. Compared to the other team members, J. J. seemed the least likely to be the weapons and demolition guy. But he was and he excelled at it. His love of guns earned him the nickname, "Colt."

Sergeant First Class Jose Medina sat behind J. J. and across from Zinsser reading a newsmagazine. He looked Hispanic in every way: dark hair, rugged brown skin, and dark eyes that released glimpses of his intelligence. Considered one of the top medics in the Army, Medina had been approached by nearly every team leader in the country. Moyer had to threaten to break the thumbs of those trying to steal Medina away. He had four children at home. He used to boast that a man couldn't have enough children. That changed last year when his wife Lucy's pregnancy nearly cost her life.

Moyer let his eyes shift to Jerry Zinsser. New Guy sat in the back. Unlike the other team members, he passed the time staring straight ahead or out one of the small windows. Something about him gave Moyer pause. The man was a hero; he'd shown bravery in the worst of situations—the kind that usually left soldiers bleeding to death on the ground. Zinsser deserved every honor he received, but Moyer sensed there was something more. Looking at Zinsser, Moyer found one thought repeating in his head: *Some heroes came home whole and healthy; others came home broken. Fractured in ways that couldn't be seen.*

He could only hope Zinsser was in the former category. If not . . . Moyer didn't want to think about it

THE ROAR OF THE luxury jet's engine vibrated through the hull and bored into Zinsser's brain. He took a deep breath then let it out, releasing the air in a slow, steady stream. He repeated the action. His heart tumbled in his chest. His stomach twisted. The sound of automatic fire echoed in his skull. He pressed his eyes shut as if squeezing his lids hard enough would exorcise the images from his mind.

If only the jet would go down. That would end it.

It would end it all forever.

CHAPTER 9

DELARAM SAT AT THE outdoor coffee shop sipping espresso and gazing down the street. The late Rome night remained warm and the air carried a perfume of warm bread, rich sauces from the restaurant a half block down the narrow street—a street so narrow only foot traffic could travel its length. It was her favorite spot, the place she retired to when the day became too stressful—and every day was stressful.

Her attention flitted from a person at a nearby table to a man walking down the street. A young couple brushed past her. An elderly man with gray whiskers gazed at her from a second-floor window in a building across the lane. They were there; she knew it. Several people looked familiar, but she couldn't be certain they had watched her before.

They always watched her, and she had no doubt they had tapped her phone. Even now, as she sat under a darkening sky, she imagined men rummaging through her small apartment nestled in a complex of apartments a ten-minute walk away.

Let them look. Let them search all they wanted. She had done all they asked, provided no resistance, kept the police out of the matter. She had done it all. They would find nothing to fault her with. Not that it mattered.

Delaram looked into the small cup she held as if she could read the future in the black fluid; as if wisdom waited for her just below the surface. No amount of wisdom would save her. Her life ended two weeks ago with a hand-delivered letter containing photos.

She set the cup down. Holding it made her hand shake.

Locals spoke in soft Italian. Tourists strolled the uneven surface of the walkway, drawing in the ambiance of the quaint and quiet part of Rome. Delaram knew how they felt. Once she had been captivated by the charm of the neighborhood. She had traveled the world with her parents, and this had been one of her favorite spots to visit. Her mother loved Paris; her father London; both loved Mexico.

Water brimmed her eyes and she forced her mind away from those thoughts.

"He wishes to see you."

Delaram didn't bother looking up. She knew the voice. Knew it too well.

She rose and walked from the coffee shop, the dark-skinned man by her side.

DELARAM SAT IN THE backseat of an American-made SUV and watched the country scenery scroll by lit by a bone-colored moon. The skyline of Rome and its thick traffic receded in the distance. Delaram had been down this road countless times over the last two weeks. Each time she said it would be her last. She followed these men because she had to, and so tight was their grip on her mind and soul she had been unable to resist. Their cocky attitude allowed her to live on her own as long as they never had to go looking for her.

She should have run.

She should have sought help.

She should have done so many things, but she did nothing. How could she?

Her stomach began to roil as the first images invaded her mind again, just as they had a thousand times before. Just as they did every hour, sometimes every minute.

The pictures were horrible. The threats horrifying. The . . . She clamped her eyes shut willing the tears back. She refused to cry in front of these people.

Thirty minutes later the driver pulled from the road and motored down a graded dirt path. It would take five minutes before they reached their destination. She looked at the distant hills and wished she could be on the other side of them, far from this vehicle, far from the two men in the car.

The man next to her shifted in his seat. He had said nothing beyond the few words spoken at the coffee shop. He never did. Nor did he exchange words with the driver. Silence was the norm. Once, however, the driver had called the other man Abasi. All she knew about Abasi was that he was tall, thin, dark-skinned, spoke with an Egyptian accent, and smelled of strong cigarettes.

The road slowly rose to a crest. Once the vehicle crested the rise Delaram could see the ranging villa illuminated by the moon and decorative exterior lights that cast drapes of golden light on white stucco walls. Italian tile blanketed the roof. Delaram came from a very rich family. Her life was spent traveling or living in private schools around the world. She had lived in massive, rented mansions, each of equal or higher quality as the villa she was approaching.

From the outside the compound looked palatial. Inside was a different matter. While expensive art hung on walls, budget-breaking rugs covered teak floors, and the latest high-tech entertainment could be found in every room, there were things that made the building seem like the lobby to hell.

The car pulled to a massive iron gate and stopped. The driver turned on the overhead lights and flashed the vehicle's headlights three times.

An armed man stepped through an iron gate the size of a doorway and approached. The driver lowered the windows and sprung the latch to the back door that opened. The guard shone a light in the front seat, backseat, and searched the cargo area. Delaram thought it a waste of time. These men knew each other, worked together. Yet the procedure never changed.

A few moments later the large gate swung open and the driver pulled the car onto the long concrete drive that led to a tall, wide porte-cochere.

Delaram waited for the driver to open her door. Once she had let herself out, but a swift backhand had put an end to any future foolishness. Only after the driver arrived at the door did Abasi exit. Then they took positions to either side of Delaram like bookends and escorted her to the front door.

If she ran, she would die.

Maybe that wouldn't be so bad.

CHAPTER 10

A HAND ON MOYER'S shoulder woke him. "Sorry to wake you, Sergeant Major, but we're on final approach to Darby Air Force Base. I need you to swivel your seat back into place and raise the seat back. Also please make sure your seat belt is fastened."

"Thanks. Will do, Airman." Moyer glanced at his watch: 0400 local time.

The young man smiled, turned, woke Rich, and repeated the message. Soon he had awakened every member of the team and the off-duty crew.

As the steward came forward again, he engaged Moyer. "Ever been to Italy before?"

"Nope. I don't travel much."

The airman chuckled. "Yeah, I bet you don't. Once your . . . what did you call it? Training mission?"

"Yup."

"Once your training mission is over you should take a few days to visit the north country. Fabulous sites. Food is great."

"I'll remember that, son. I travel like a salesman."

The airman looked puzzled. "Excuse me?"

"I fly in, see the airport, see the base, see the airport again, and fly home."

"I'm familiar with the problem. My father is a business consultant. He's been in every major city in the U.S. and, according to him, seen none of them."

Moyer wanted to tell the man that he had seen parts of some cities no one should see, but let the conversation go. It was time to think of other things.

CAMP DARBY CONDUCTED ITS business near Pisa, Italy, and had done so since 1951. Named after General William O. Darby, who died in combat in northern Italy during World War II, the camp served as home to twenty-six Army, Air Force, and Department of Defense tenants. Among the military, the base's greatest claim to fame was its tourist appeal. Moyer's briefing revealed that 80,000 tourists visit the area annually. The base was one of the few in the world with access to the beach front. Not far away was the city of Pisa with its leaning tower. Any other time such sights would interest Moyer, but for the moment he had other things on his mind. The fact that many military personnel made the area their vacation spot created one more layer of secrecy for Moyer and the team.

The airman had been a little broad in his announcement that they'd land at Camp Darby. The aircraft touched down at Galileo Galilei International Airport, a facility that served the *Aeronautica Militare*, the Italian Air Force.

The men joked and chatted while they deplaned and climbed into the Fiat Ducato minibus that waited for them. As they headed toward the Via Aurella Sud, Rich Harbison gazed back at the C-37A. "I gotta get me one of those."

"On your salary?" Pete said. "You can't afford to have the thing washed."

"How do you know I'm not a man of means?"

"Because you're U.S. Army."

"Oh, yeah, that's right."

The banter died once the small bus pulled away from the airport. Moyer knew his men well enough to recognize their weariness. No one complained. They never complained. He also knew they were thinking about the mission. If they weren't sleeping, then they were thinking. It's how their mission worked. Moyer's own thoughts ricocheted from his family to his mission.

Female suicide bombers—the world has lost its mind. Battles should be fought by warriors willing to die for their cause; not cowards who hid behind civilians; who used noncombatants to do what they didn't have the guts to do themselves.

The early morning sun pushed the silvered moon back to the horizon. Traveling across the Atlantic played havoc with Moyer's sense of time. He looked at his watch and did the math: nearly ten hours in the air and local time was six hours ahead of the U.S. East Coast: that made it close to 2330 back home. That made it 0530 here. They had flown through the night. His body was yearning for bed while everyone in Pisa was having breakfast.

The van pulled to the main gate of Camp Darby and was waved in by a bored looking MP. Outside the single enlisted barracks, a boyish looking major met them.

"Welcome to Italy, the sweetest duty in the military."

Moyer snapped a salute as soon as his feet touched the macadam of the road. "Thank you, sir."

The major returned the salute. "Put your men at ease, Sergeant Major. It's breakfast time here, but I'm betting you guys could use a little time in the rack."

"We slept on the plane, sir."

The major smiled. "I've made that trip a few times. No one sleeps on a plane. At best, we nap. Let me show you the barracks. I have a room for each member of your team. Grab some shut-eye. You have a meeting in four hours and Colonel Tyson doesn't like to see any yawning, if you catch my drift."

"Understood, sir."

"You won't have any trouble finding your way around the barracks. I'll make sure you have some chow before the meeting. You want breakfast or lunch?"

"Lunch, sir. It's best if we eat at local time. Easier to adjust that way."

"I'll take both," Rich said. He grinned.

Major Barlow studied the big man for a moment. "I make it a point not to argue with men twice my size." He returned his attention to Moyer. "Get some rest. Fall out."

Moyer thought it the best order he had received in a long time.

CHAPTER 11

DELARAM DIDN'T SLEEP. AT least not that she remembered. The night crept by, minutes passing like hours, leaving her to stare at the ceiling. Pale light pressed past sheer drapes casting shadow monsters on the wall. The shadows didn't frighten her; the monsters on the other side of the door were the real ones.

When she stepped into the room she saw a figure curled beneath a white sheet in one of the two beds. The figure didn't move at the sound of the door opening and Delaram's entrance. The guard shut the door with a bang loud enough to wake a corpse, but still the woman on the bed refused to move. For a moment Delaram wondered if the thin woman was dead, expired from grief. Sitting on the second bed in the room, Delaram waited for her eyes to adjust to the dark. She saw the woman's chest rise and fall. Not dead; just too scared to move.

Delaram removed her slip-on sneakers and reclined on the bed. Her mind twisted and turned, unable to form a single line of thought. Emotion boiled just beneath the surface and she fought it, stuffing it into some narrow corner of her being.

A soft murmur bubbled from the other bed. Despite what must be heroic efforts, the other woman began to weep softly. Delaram wanted to comfort her, to utter words that would give the tortured soul a glimmer of hope, but she had no hope to give, no words of encouragement to offer. After an eon of moments, Delaram said, "Mother and father."

Ten seconds passed before the other woman said, "Husband and son."

The remaining hours of darkness passed in silence.

Moonlight surrendered to sunrise; pale ivory light yielded to salmon glow of the dawn. Delaram looked at her watch—6:45.

The door to the room swung open and a tall man with a ragged beard stepped in. He carried a small machine gun. "Get up." He spoke Arabic.

Delaram swung her feet over the bed and slipped her sneakers on. She hadn't bothered to undress. She stood.

The woman in the other bed didn't budge, the sheet covered her head.

"I said, get up."

When the woman refused to move, the man growled, stepped to the bed and pointed the weapon at the woman's head, gently laying the barrel over her temple. "Do not make me angry, woman."

Delaram crossed the room and laid a hand on the machine gun. She didn't have the courage to touch the man.

"She's frightened. Let me."

The man jerked the gun away, the front sight scrapping Delaram's hand. She let slip a cry of pain, then shook her hand. The man smiled at her. He had enjoyed inflicting the pain.

Using her other hand, Delaram slowly pulled back the sheet that covered her roommate. "You must get up. It does no good to anger—"

Delaram dropped the sheet and took a step back.

"Oh no."

The woman stared at the wall with unblinking, unmoving, unseeing eyes. An empty, light brown bottle with a white label lay near the captive's mouth.

"What did you do to her?" the man asked.

Delaram stared at him for a moment, uncertain she had heard right. "I did nothing to her."

"What is in the bottle?"

"How should I know?"

"Look at it."

The man didn't want to touch the body. He took a step back. Delaram moved closer, leaned over the dead woman, and picked up the small plastic bottle. "Sleeping pills. The bottle is empty." Looking closer, Delaram saw spittle and a small amount of vomit.

"And you know nothing about this?"

Delaram faced the man. "No, she was already in bed when I was brought here. She was alive then."

"How can you know?"

"She spoke to me. Just a few words. I also heard her crying."

"Why was she crying?"

Delaram tilted her to the side. *Idiot.* "Why do you think she was crying?"

He looked at her. "Fool. She could have died a martyr instead of a coward."

Delaram considered slapping the man. She was destined for death, what difference would it make. Then she thought of her parents.

"Shouldn't you tell someone?"

The man looked at the door. "Come with me."

THE MANSION'S RECREATION ROOM had been converted to a dining hall. Where once a billiard table stood, there were now folding tables set end-to-end. White sheets served as tablecloths. Thirteen women sat at the table, heads down, eyes fixed on the empty plates before them. Delaram made the fourteenth. An empty chair across from her seemed to mock her presence.

Delaram said nothing. She had spent the last week struggling to shut down every emotion. Tears would rise, but she would blink them away and, with sheer determination, squash every other emotion. Emotions did nothing to help her or solve the situation. She doubted anything could.

Slipping into her chair, she joined the others in staring at her empty plate. A moment later she cut her eyes to the end of the table. The guard who had retrieved her from the coffee shop the night before sat there. The man with the scruffy beard approached him and whispered in his ear. As he listened, he closed his eyes and tightened his jaw.

"That was your assignment?"

Scruffy beard nodded. "From midnight on."

"Take care of it."

"But—"

"Take care of it. Take two men with you."

The man with the machine gun spun and marched from the room. Delaram wondered what they would do with the body.

Two women emerged from the kitchen with bowls of fruit and breads, setting the items on the table. They exited and returned a moment later with more bowls of fruit, pitchers of juice, and carafes of coffee.

The tall man at the head of the table, the one she had overheard the driver call Abasi, rapped his knuckles on the table. "Allah has provided this feast. You will eat to honor him."

Abasi turned and left the room.

Delaram took a roll and an orange and began to eat. She could taste nothing.

EZZAT EL-SAYYED SAT AT a wide, golden oak table, eating while drinking strong coffee. He ate alone, just as he preferred. Over the years he had trained himself to appreciate each moment of life, especially if it involved something that stroked the senses. When El-Sayyed ate, he blocked all other business from his mind. When Abasi entered, El-Sayyed was thinking of a woman.

"I apologize for interrupting your meal," Abasi said.

It must be important. Abasi would never disturb him unless it was something that demanded his immediate attention.

"What is it, Abasi?"

"One of the women has died."

"Died?" El-Sayyed set his cup down. "How?"

"Sleeping pills. One of the men found her this morning while retrieving the women for breakfast."

"Suicide." El-Sayyed shook his head, then chuckled. "Allah loves irony."

"May his name be praised."

El-Sayyed pulled the linen napkin from his lap and dabbed at his mouth. "An inconvenience; nothing more. It is why we have more sacrifices than we need."

"Just one of the many brilliant jewels in your plan—still we must deal with the matter. I will take care of things so you will not have to be bothered. I felt you should know."

"Use your usual discretion, Abasi. I trust your choices." He set the napkin down. "Do the others know?"

"Just her roommate."

"How is she behaving after seeing such a shocking thing?"

Abasi said, "She seems in control and distant."

"Good. Is she eating and drinking?"

"I saw her take some food."

"Good, the medications will keep her calm." He rose. "Is the video conference ready?"

"We have tested the connections. Everything is functioning as it should."

"Good. Thank you, Abasi, you may go."

CHAPTER 12

FOUR HOURS OF SLEEP wasn't much, but since every second of it was spent in a bed instead of on the hard, bug-infested ground of some third-world country, it felt good. On several previous missions Moyer had to go days on just catnaps.

A peach-faced Private First Class knocked on Moyer's door and on the doors of the other team members then waited for them in the long plain hall of the barracks building. To Moyer the man looked no older than sixteen, but then all new recruits look like teenagers to him.

"If the Sergeant Major will follow me, Cookie has prepared lunch for you and your team."

"I hope he's a good cook," Rich said.

"They say the Navy has the best cooks in the service, but they haven't met Cookie. We have to run an extra three miles a week to undo the effects of Cookie's artistry."

"Artistry?" J. J. said. "You make the guy sound like Michelangelo."

The private smiled. "Up until now you only think you've had lasagna. And just for the record, I never said Cookie was a he."

The mess hall was a short march from the barracks. Moyer used the time to glance at his men to see if they appeared well rested. Each seemed relaxed and in good humor. Everyone except Zinsser. The new team member trailed the others as they walked to the mess hall. His eyes were red and his eyelids looked puffy as if he'd been awake for days.

Moyer looked him in the eye. "You feeling okay, Zinsser?"

"No worries, Boss. I'm good to go."

"You look like death warmed over."

Zinsser grinned. "Sorry, Boss. I'm used to sleeping 'til noon." The grin looked forced. "Seriously, Boss, I'm fine. Just a little jet-lagged."

"You'd tell me if there was a problem, wouldn't you?"

"Absolutely, Boss. I'm just not a morning person. Remember it's still the wee hours at home. You got to be a little drug out yourself."

Zinsser had him there. Moyer's eyes felt dry and twice their normal size.

"Okay, man. Just remember that we pride ourselves on honesty around here. Trust is a big deal with us."

"It is with me too, Boss. As I said, I'm good to go."

Moyer turned to the private. "You weren't pulling my leg about lasagna, were you?"

"I never kid about lasagna, Sergeant Master."

He returned his focus to Zinsser. "Maybe that will help wake you up."

"Heavy, cheese-laden food is sure to get the blood going."

Moyer caught the sarcasm.

DELARAM AND THE OTHERS were forced to sit at the table a half hour longer than necessary. No one dared complain, but being confined to the chairs made some of the others restless. Of the group, only she knew why they waited. Moving a corpse was no easy matter.

When she first caught sight of the young woman's corpse, she felt a moment of envy. The woman had lost all hope; Delaram still nurtured a flickering optimism. She had no idea if it would last the day.

Abasi stepped into the room. "Please follow me."

Please?

Delaram pushed back from the table, as did the other women. They kept their eyes down as if the floor were littered with shards of glass. She felt tempted to do the same, but just because she was in an uncontrollable situation she didn't have to sacrifice her self-assurance. Her captors may prefer downcast eyes in women, but she wasn't inclined to oblige.

From the rec-room-makeshift-dining room, they walked to a set of stairs that led, she guessed, to the basement. They walked single-file, like POWS. Delaram was the third to pass through a set of white double doors. The room was dim, lit by small overhead lights. Before she could take in her surroundings she was struck with a familiar odor. Not odor—aroma. Butter. Butter and popcorn. The unexpected smell confused her.

A moment later her eyes adjusted. Several rows of padded chairs stretched before her. On the far wall hung a silver screen. The side walls were draped in thick, pleated curtains.

A movie theater. A home movie theater.

She guessed the room held twenty thickly padded seats. A small alcove to the side was the only thing on the wall not covered with sound-absorbing fabric. A thin yellow light emitted from the front panel of a popcorn machine. A poster of Humphrey Bogart hung from one of the alcove's walls.

"Everyone forward, please," Abasi said. "Sit. Leave no open chairs between you."

The women complied without comment. Delaram sat in the first row, center seat. The movie screen was fifteen feet in front of her.

The room darkened as someone closed the doors to the room. Abasi stood in front of the screen, his hands clasped behind his back. He carried no weapon. For a moment Delaram wondered what would happen if they rushed him. Some of the women would certainly be hurt but there were enough of them to handle one man.

Of couse it wasn't just one man. Although she couldn't see them, Delaram knew other men were nearby. The women might incapacitate Abasi, but bullets would fly soon after. Besides, there was little chance the others would follow her lead in such an attack.

Once the last woman sat, the lights in the room went out. A second later a bright light reflected off the screen, stabbing Delaram's eyes. She blinked several times before the image on the screen became clear. She stared at the digital image of the dead woman in her room. The twelve-foot-tall screen made her look freakish, macabre. The others gasped.

Abasi didn't bother to turn to view the image. "I regret to tell you that one of your own has chosen to turn her back on the martyr's glory and end her life."

Several of the women began to weep. Delaram found the photo more disturbing than the real corpse she had seen ninety minutes before.

Abasi continued. "She not only betrayed the opportunity bestowed upon her, but she also turned her back on her husband and son." He nodded to the projection area. A live video feed replaced the static digital photo.

It took a moment for Delaram to believe her eyes. A man she judged to be in his late twenties and a boy of five or six years sat on wooden chairs, facing a camera. The area beneath the man's right eye was swollen and purple. The boy seemed unharmed. Last night the woman had uttered only three words in response to Delaram's prompt: "husband and son."

"Fila?"

The man gazed into the camera. Based on his actions, Delaram doubted he had a monitor on this side. "Fila, are you there?" Tears welled in his eyes.

Abasi turned and spoke to the screen as if the image of the dead woman's husband were really in the room. Delaram assumed Abasi wore a microphone.

"Fila is dead. She took her own life rather than saving yours. You have been freed of such a burdensome woman."

"Dead?" He lowered his head. "No." The man began to shake. His son began to cry.

"A wife who chooses death over her husband and son does not deserve to live."

"I kill you. I kill each one of you."

Abasi raised an eyebrow. "I doubt it."

Just as the screen went black two sounds poured from the large speakers in the room—two gunshots.

CHAPTER 13

THE CONFERENCE ROOM LOOKED similar to the one in the Concrete Palace back in the states. Chairs with fold-up half-desks that looked as if someone had stolen them from a local high school filled most of the room. Colonel Tyson and a tall, solid-looking man dressed in the uniform of the Italian Army stood at the front of the room.

"This is Major Ilario De Luca," Colonel Tyson said as Moyer and his team took their seats. Tyson was pure military, from his cropped gray hair to his sun-etched wrinkles and haunted eyes. Moyer knew better than to ask what the man had seen and done. Soldiers carried their ghosts and scars privately. Some soldiers' minds turned on them, tormenting brave men and leeching away their strength. No wonder the number of soldiers who committed suicide had grown through the conflicts in Afghanistan and Iraq.

Moyer understood it all too well. More than once it had taken double doses of sleeping aids to get him through long nights of vicious attacks by his memory. A man learned to live with it. It was part of being a warrior; part of facing enemies that threaten the innocent.

Live with it.

It was the only choice.

Moyer, like every experienced frontline soldier he knew, suffered the occasional flashback. They disturbed his sleep for a few days then disappeared. He was lucky.

"You with us, Moyer?"

"I am, Colonel."

Tyson ran his eyes over Moyer as if he could tune in his thoughts like a man tuned a radio. "I was saying this is Major Ilano De Luca. He is the liaison for the Italian military. He'll be accompanying you."

"Sir?"

"I know what you're thinking, Moyer. He's one of the most decorated spec ops men in the Italian military. Granted, you haven't trained together, but he knows his stuff. I don't want you or your men busting his chops. Is that clear?"

"Crystal, sir. No chop busting. It's just that—"

"Save it, soldier. We're on the soil of an ally and about to do covert work in their cities. This is the deal. No debate. No exceptions. Understood?"

The team response was immediate, if unenthusiastic: "Hooah."

"Go ahead, Major."

The Italian stepped to the front of the room and eyed each man. Moyer returned the look and would have bet a month's pay each of his men did the same.

"Welcome to my country, gentlemen." He hit the word *my* like a drummer strikes a base drum. His English came easily and with the kind of perfection that made Moyer guess the man spent a good deal of time in the U.S. or the UK. "As you know, there has been a substantial increase in human-carried bombings in Europe. We have had several in Italy. This is a matter of great concern, but not something we cannot handle ourselves."

"Then why are we here?"

Moyer heard the humor in Rich's jab. Apparently De Luca didn't. Neither did Colonel Tyson, who shot a look at Rich that Moyer was sure would set the big man's clothing on fire.

"I assure you, it is not my choice, but certain factors have influenced my superiors' decisions." De Luca seemed to force the words over a tense jaw. "You were briefed about El-Sayyed. Our president has indirect connections with the man's family."

Moyer crossed his arms. "And he needs an out?"

"If by 'an out' you mean a valid deniability factor, then yes. It is his desire to remain above any conflict and its results."

"What does that mean?" Jose sounded suspicious.

Moyer answered before the Major could. "It means if we kill El-Sayyed, the president can say it wasn't done by the Italian military."

"Ah. This way we get blamed. Works out nice."

Colonel Tyson cleared his throat, and the room fell silent.

De Luca closed his eyes for a moment, and Moyer half-expected him to click his heels together and chant, "There's no place like home. There's no place like home." Moyer pursed his lips to keep the corners of his mouth from rising. If the man was going to tag along, he might as well know what kind of men he was dealing with.

"Our intelligence organizations have been monitoring Internet traffic using sophisticated algorithms to filter e-mail, blog posting, audio and video transmissions, as well as other key factors. The process is similar to what is used to monitor suspected terrorist cells. We have recently intercepted a video conference between a place on the North American continent and an area not far from Rome. We have, over the last few weeks, intercepted similar communications as well as e-mail directed to El-Sayyed."

He placed his hands behind his back as if standing at ease. "The transmissions are heavily encrypted. We cannot say where in North America the connection was made, but intel analysts suspect Mexico. We had more luck on this end. We have an address."

De Luca began to pace. "The Italian source is tied to a mansion in the country east of Roma. El-Sayyed's plane is still parked at the airport and under twenty-four-hour surveillance. We'll know the minute it moves."

"So what do you think El-Sayyed is up to? Is he using Italy as a base of operations?"

"Sayyed has been in and out of Italy five times in the last two months. We have tracked the flights of his private jet in Europe. Naturally our ability to follow him in Middle East countries is problematic."

"But he's here now?"

De Luca gave Moyer a curt nod. "As of this morning. As to what he is up to, I fear he plans on bombing one of our historic monuments or churches. Working with the kind of extremist he does makes us think that he plans on detonating one or more bombs at a Christian shrine. Rome is the home to Christianity, as you know."

J. J. coughed.

"Is there a problem, Sergeant Bartley?" Tyson's question carried some heat.

"No, sir. No problem at all, I just thought Christianity began in Jerusalem. That's where the first church was founded and—"

"Save the history lesson, son. We have more important matters before us."

"Yes, sir."

De Luca tapped his lip, then continued. "Let me be more specific. Rome is home to the Holy Roman Church. The Holy Sea is here and is the center of faith for a billion Catholics. Rome is filled with historic churches and sites that would be a tempting target for Muslim extremists."

"Do you think they might try something at the Vatican?" Moyer asked.

"Perhaps, but the Vatican is one of the best guarded 110 acres in the world. It is a country unto itself and under the complete control of the Catholic Church. The Swiss guard, who protect the buildings and his Holiness himself, are some of the best trained soldiers in the world. The Vatican also has its own police force."

"Yet thousands of tourists visit the grounds daily," Moyer said. "We're dealing with suicide bombers here—human precision bombs. What's to keep one or more such bombers from strolling in with the other tourists?"

"It is possible, but access to the most valuable areas is limited. Since we confirmed El-Sayyed's presence, we have asked that the Holy Father be kept away from open areas, windows, and people who have not been cleared by their security. The Vatican has released a press report that his Holiness is spending time at Castel Gandolfo outside of Rome."

"That's where the Vatican observatory is," Rich said.

Moyer and the others looked at him.

"What? I read a lot."

"It is true. One of the two observatories run by the Church is in Castel Gandolfo."

"There are two?" J. J. asked.

"The other one is in Arizona," Rich said. "It operates in conjunction with the University of Arizona. . . . Okay I'm done."

"Bottom line is," Moyer said, "we have no idea where they will strike. All you have is speculation."

"Speculation and the mansion where El-Sayyed has been hiding."

Moyer looked to Tyson. "So what's our next step?"

"You go pay El-Sayyed a social call."

That made Moyer smile.

FOR THE FOURTEENTH TIME Delaram donned a tailored vest full of PE-4 explosive and ball bearings. The latter was a recent addition. Although she didn't need to be told, they told her anyway: the ball bearings would become fiery shrapnel, killing and maiming anyone within a hundred meters of her or the other women. Not that it would matter to her. Once the bomb went off she would know nothing but oblivion. No doubt some of the women believed in heaven, but not her. She was a John Lennon philosopher imagining no heaven and no hell.

The vest hung low on her, the rounded bulk of explosives resting just above her pelvis and pressing against her stomach. Once covered in a robe she would look like any pregnant woman in her third trimester. The irony ate at her. She would pretend to be a woman about to give life; then a button-push later she would become an angel of death.

Delaram looked around the large basement. Two long worktables ran the north and south walls. In the center of the room stood eight women of various ages. Two looked to be no older than high school students; five were in their early twenties; one looked to be her grandmother's age. Although their ages were different, their expressions were the same: bone-melting terror. Tears lined the faces of most. A few looked numb, their minds having shut down. Delaram understood. She had to fight to keep from giving in to emotional shock. It was a fight she was losing.

Running her hand along the smooth exterior of the vest, she thought about the death resting on her belly. She would never know pregnancy; never hold a child to whom she had given life.

Would there be children there? Would she kill them? Would she leave the "lucky" children crippled and bleeding in some street or building? Disguised as a pregnant woman, would she kill a woman truly with child—a woman with a mind filled with the great possibilities of the future?

"You have done well, Delaram."

She cut her eyes to see the thickly built man with dark skin and neatly trimmed goatee with streaks of gray. Under the dim light of overhead fluorescents, the man looked jaundiced. She didn't know his name, nor did she care to know.

He set his hands on her shoulders, let them linger, then pulled on the straps. "The fit is better. The payload hangs naturally. How does it feel?"

"How does it feel? It feels like a bomb strapped to my body. How is it supposed to feel?"

He frowned. "Fear is normal, but you must remain strong. You are doing a brave thing. You will be a martyr. You will spend eternity in glory and—"

"I'm not Muslim."

"Christians have martyrs too."

"I'm not a Christian either."

His mouth dipped toward his shoulders. "You are worse than an infidel."

Delaram chose not to respond. A stone would provide better conversation than this man.

He stepped to the rack of clothing situated to one side and removed a maternity dress. "Put this on. I want to make certain the detonator switch fits the inner pocket.

"Do you mean this thing?" Delaram lifted a push-button switch wired to the plastic explosive in her vest.

"Of course."

A half-thought passed through Delaram's mind.

She pressed the button.

CHAPTER 14

DELARAM EXPECTED TO FEEL nothing. Not this scorching pain racing from her face, down her neck, and to her knees—which buckled under the impact. She lay on the cold basement floor staring into the lights above—lights that blurred and dimmed.

"Nasser!"

Delaram thought she was seeing the world through translucent, fogged glass, the kind used in bathrooms to protect privacy. A man stood over her, bent at the waist with his arm in the air. It took a moment for her to realize he was about to send a jaw-breaking punch to her face. Just as the arm began to move, another figure appeared. The punch never arrived.

After several blinks Delaram's vision improved and she saw goatee-man with his fist in the air, stopped by Abasi.

"The fool thought the bombs were active. She tried to detonate it. She tried to kill us all." It was the man Abasi called Nasser.

"That's why we take precautions."

"She deserves punishment."

"Of course she does, but not her face. A bruised and swollen face draws unwanted attention. She must look normal."

Nasser threw an angry glance at Abasi as if he blamed him for the world's problems, then the mask of fury faded. "Not the face?"

"That's right. Leave her face alone. And remember: we need her."

A smile crossed Nasser's face. He nodded, then kicked Delaram in the thigh. He kicked her again.

Someone screamed. It took Delaram a moment to recognize her own voice.

IN SOME WAYS MOYER preferred urban missions. He and his team were fully trained in traditional warfare, hand-to-hand combat, and some had been schooled in technical and electronic attacks. Battle had morphed over the years. As a boy, he had watched the television shows *Combat* and *Rat Pack* with his father. Those black-and-white episodes were his first introduction to the Army. His father never served in the armed forces, prohibited by a congenital hip problem. Still, he instilled in young Moyer the need to have principles worth fighting for. An extremely patriotic man, Moyer's father imparted a love for country to his only son.

That parental teaching budded in those old television shows. Growing up, he often relived episodes of a small band of men who fought Germans as they worked through forests and bombed out streets. At the age of eight, Eric Moyer became an Army man.

Ten years later, and two months out of high school, he was sharing a barracks with other shaven-headed young men enduring boot camp at Fort Benning.

Ranger training almost killed him. Long days with little to

no sleep, living daily under a 90-pound rucksack forced more and more soldiers to drop out, but Moyer determined to persevere even if it meant he was the last man standing. The more difficult the training, the more he loved the Army. No masochist, he hated the pain but loved what the pain made of him.

Then came tours in Panama, Kuwait, Somalia, Afghanistan, and Iraq. Each mission gave him opportunity to grow as a soldier and a leader of men. Like most career soldiers, he came to hate war and love service. He didn't become a soldier to kill; he became a soldier to protect people and ideals precious to him.

Spec Ops gave him new training and a new way to wage war: small teams doing tactical, surgical work. Small actions often negated the need for major battles. Such was this mission.

The satellite map on the table, provided by a U.S. satellite, showed a mansion surrounded by acres of open ground. The house sat by itself. Surrounding the expansive property was farm land. The nearest house was two miles away.

"As you can see, we have very little cover." De Luca pointed to the image of the home. "The house has windows on all sides."

Moyer stared at the photo. "We have to go in at night. Any idea how much electronic security they have?"

De Luca pulled a thick roll of architectural drawings from a cardboard tube and spread it over the satellite photo. "These are the architectural drawings with inspector notes. Our building department is very demanding and thorough."

Moyer's eyes drew in the details. He said nothing as he studied the plans. Finally, he shook his head. "The house is enormous. There's gotta be, what, twenty thousand square feet spread over two floors and a basement?"

"Twenty-thousand-two hundred. The CEO of a major bank in Italy built it. The global recession of 2009 did him in. He declared bankruptcy and left the country. The house went up for sale, but very few people can afford such a villa. The property was seized by the bank and they rent it to businesses for corporate retreats. It sits empty most of the time."

Moyer nodded. "The house is wired for security, and we have to assume that El-Sayyed may have added more."

"It would be wise to do so."

The door to the room opened and Rich poked his head in. "Trucks are loaded, Boss."

"Good, round up the team. It's show-and-tell time."

"Will do."

EL-SAYYED STUDIED THE DIGITAL photo he had received over the Internet. He waited for the guilt to come, the remorse, the pity, but the emotions never arrived. No surprise. He handed the picture to Abasi. "Give it to the girl."

"Delaram."

El-Sayyed waved his hand. "Names are unimportant. She is still capable of carrying out our task?"

"Yes. Tony took care in administering her punishment. She might limp some."

"Give her something for her pain. We don't want her to think we are animals. The transportation?"

"All is ready, just as you ordered. We can leave at any time."

El-Sayyed stood. "We leave in fifteen minutes. Tony will drive me along the main road and into the city in case there are eyes on us. My leaving will provide a distraction. You take the women down the back roads. Drive until you are sure you are not being followed. Keep your eyes turned toward the heavens."

"To Allah."

"I was thinking of helicopters, Abasi."

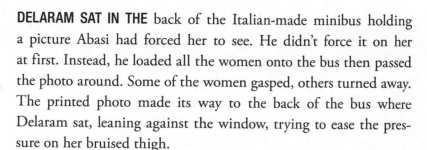

DELARAM SAT IN THE back of the Italian-made minibus holding a picture Abasi had forced her to see. He didn't force it on her at first. Instead, he loaded all the women onto the bus then passed the photo around. Some of the women gasped, others turned away. The printed photo made its way to the back of the bus where Delaram sat, leaning against the window, trying to ease the pressure on her bruised thigh.

She took the photo certain she could feel no more physical or emotional pain. In the photo she saw her mother sitting on the floor cradling her father's head in her lap. His left eye was swollen shut and dried blood clung to his nose and lips.

Delaram envied the girl who committed suicide.

ALDO GRONCHI CAUGHT A glimpse of his image in the tinted glass of the police boat. His eyes lingered on the dim reflection. He was a vain man and made no apology for it. Tall, smooth dark skin, serious eyes, and a mouth quick to smile, he knew he was what the Americans called a *babe magnet*. He resisted the urge to pose for himself, tempting as such an action was. He was on duty, and the only thing he loved more than himself was his role as a captain in the Naples police department. Ten years on the job, he had risen quickly through the ranks. Good looks, good humor, quick wit, and unflagging courage meant he would climb many more rungs of success's ladder. He wouldn't be satisfied until he was *Capo della Polizia*.

He would face no danger today. The task for this early evening was to analyze the ability of his men to patrol the Bay of Naples and the smaller bays that served as home to the hundreds of pleasure craft and yachts that plied the cerulean waters of the famous city.

Gronchi raised binoculars to his eyes and scanned the many hotels that lined the shores. Blocks of commercial buildings and homes covered the slope upon which the city of more than a million people had been built. He was proud of the city and its rich heritage. Less than seventy years ago, Allied pilots bombed the city repeatedly until they had broken the back of Fascism. He thought about how things changed. During that same time, Japan attacked the U.S., bombing Pearl Harbor to the brink of nonexistence. Now Americans competed for Japanese cars. They also traveled to Italy by the droves to take in its history and charm.

Such was the heritage that forced Gronchi to work fourteen-hour days for the last month.

"See anything?" A young officer stepped to Gronchi's side. He was shorter than Gronchi's six-foot-two yet weighed considerably more.

Gronchi gazed at the man. "Your green tint clashes with your uniform, Lorenzo."

The man shrugged. "I am not much of a sailor."

"Perhaps a little food would help you. I believe the captain brought sardines for lunch."

Lorenzo's tint darkened, but he didn't complain. Disappointed, Gronchi returned the binoculars to his eyes. "Did you make the contacts as I asked?"

"Yes, sir. We will have our final briefing with the navy this evening at nine o'clock."

"Good. The sniper posts?"

"All established per your orders."

Gronchi lowered the glasses. "Did you double-check the sight lines along all streets near the hotel?"

Lorenzo nodded. "Several times. We can observe the entrance from ten different positions; street access from a dozen additional points. The hotel staff has been checked, and only those with the cleanest records will be working tomorrow."

"I want undercover officers in the mix: kitchen, maid service, front desk, food services, everywhere."

"The hotel will be empty except for the G-20. There will be no other guests."

"I know that, Lorenzo, but we will err on the side of caution. No one walks into that building without having his identification checked."

"Understood, sir."

Gronchi shook his head. "Our careers rest on doing this right, Lorenzo. Allow no room for failure."

"The arrival of twenty of the world's leaders to our city is an honor and a great reason for concern."

"I hear it was the American president who wanted the meeting moved here from London. I suppose the suicide bombing in London forced his hand."

"It is a wise decision," Gronchi said. "The Brits are having trouble keeping their own backyard safe. Besides, Naples is small enough to make full security possible, but large enough to provide trained men and military."

"The fact that the American president is a student of history must have provided greater motivation. Is he still planning to visit Pompeii?"

"Yes, and Castel del Ovo, the Palazzo Reale and the National Library, the Cathedral of San Gennaro, and the Church of

San Domenico Maggiore, where Saint Thomas Aquinas lived and taught. Someone should tell him he is the president of the United States, not a tourist."

"Historians are passionate about history, Capitano."

"His passion is our pain. Even his Secret Service director is beside himself."

"He told you his concern?"

"No, I saw it in the man's eyes. He is uncomfortable with the extra stops."

"Who can blame him? President Huffington seems to get whatever he wants."

Gronchi gazed at Mount Vesuvius in the distance. "It's our job to make sure he doesn't get more than he wants."

CHAPTER 15

"WHATCHA GOT, DATA?" MOYER whispered the question into the small boom mike hung over his ear and taped to the side of his face.

No response.

Moyer looked to his right. Zinsser appeared green through Moyer's night vision goggles. Without the electronic goggles he wouldn't be able to see Zinsser or any other member of his team. Too little moonlight, especially when each man wore black from head to toe, including balaclava masks. With the goggles, Zinsser's image was distinct but otherworldly. Moyer could see the man looking through the handheld FLIR. The Forward Looking Infrared device was the latest in technology, able to "see" through most walls.

"Data, do you copy?" Moyer saw the man snap his head around.

"I gotcha, Boss."

"Report."

Zinsser's word came over in a whisper. "I'm getting nonspecific heat sigs from some of the rooms, but no targets."

Moyer gazed at the mansion. He and his team had parked a quarter mile off the access road, hiding the two vans they had traveled in from Camp Darby. The drive had been long, and most of his team took advantage of the time to sleep. After concealing the vehicles they had marched through the surrounding woods. They found no perimeter security. Moyer was grateful for that but guessed that the easy part was over. They divided into teams of two. Moyer ordered De Luca to stay with him, making Moyer's team a band of three. Zinsser earned a hero's medal, but he was untested with Moyer's team. De Luca seemed well trained, but Moyer had not seen him in action. That made them both rookies as far as he and his team were concerned.

"Colt, report." Colt was at least a quarter mile to the east.

"I got nuthin', Boss," J. J. answered. "No movement in the backyard . . . maybe I should say back acreage. I can see through a half dozen windows. No movement. Same lights are on per last report."

"Roger that, Colt. Shaq, you got anything for me?"

"Negative, Boss. A cemetery has more action."

"What cemetery do you hang out in, Shaq?"

"Can it, Colt." A mental image of the property and house formed in Moyer's mind. His team had set up a three-point surveillance perimeter, allowing them to eyeball every part of the property and building.

"Junior, you got anything on audio?" In his mind, Moyer could see Pete Rasor aim a directional mike at the villa.

"Nada, Boss. I've been straining my eardrums, and the most I hear is the house cooling and what sounds like a water heater firing up. No voices, no snoring, no television, or radio."

De Luca lay on the ground next to Moyer, binoculars pressed to his eyes. He lowered the high-powered glasses and, on one elbow, put his mouth closer to Moyer's ear. Whatever the man wanted to say, he didn't want it going out over the radio.

"You're doubting our intel, aren't you?"

"Something's not right. That's for sure."

"I assure you, our people are very good."

"Ease up, Polo. No one is blaming you or your intel team for anything. You do enough missions you learn nothing goes according to plan."

De Luca sighed. "Polo. You Americans like your code names."

"You don't like Polo? Marco Polo was a great man. He brought spaghetti from China to Italy."

Moyer heard another sigh. He checked his watch. The luminous hands showed him it was 0233. A solid hour of watching and waiting had yielded nothing. It was time to do something. "Data, give me one more sweep."

"Roger."

Through the goggles Moyer watched Zinsser remove a small electronic device from his vest. He had kept it in hand through the duration of their hike. Designed to pick up radio transmissions across a wide spectrum, it was invaluable in locating wireless sensors that might detect their presence and send a signal to an alarm in the house.

Thirty seconds later. "Nothing, Boss. We're clear for at least a mile around."

"Everyone get that?"

"Loud and clear."

"Roger."

"Okay," Moyer said, "on my mark, we move. No one enters until they hear from me." He took a deep breath. "Three, two, one, mark."

Moyer was on his feet moving forward in a crouch, his M4A1 held close to his chest. He glanced to his right. Zinsser was

matching him step for step. To his left he saw Le Duca with his
Beretta AR70 at the ready. He looked like a man who had done this
a dozen times. Moyer was glad to see it.

EATING DINNER AT THE Red Lobster in Mechanicsburg, Pennsylvania,
just outside Carlisle was a weekly treat for Tess. It was close enough
that she could drive to it without trouble, but far away enough to
make the destination seem special. Tess had no problems dining
alone. Usually she brought a novel to read. So much of her life was
spent reading reports and technical manuals that a novel brought
a mental break while still providing intellectually stimulating
material.

In front of her rested a plate of broiled sole, rice, and shrimp
scampi. To the side was a metal basket with one and a half garlic
biscuits, what remained of the three the waitress had brought.

Next to the plate, open to page 104, sat a Dean Koontz novel.
She had stopped reading when her meal arrived. Tess shifted her
gaze to the traffic motoring along the road in front of the restaurant. The food was good as always, but her appetite had fled a few
moments before, and she didn't know why.

Tess forced herself to face the plate and eat, but her mind
drifted to a distant land and to J. J. Every bite of food turned her
stomach. No, it wasn't the food; it was something else. What? Fear.
She recognized the emotion. Her stomach tightened into a fist.

"More Boston tea?"

Tess looked up at the waitress, a young brunette with three
earrings in her left ear.

"Um, no thanks."

"Is something wrong with the food?"

"No. I'm just a little off today. Everything is fine."

"Okay." The young woman slipped away, apparently happy over not having to return a plate to the kitchen.

Tess inhaled deeply. She had no reason to believe she was in danger, but she still glanced around the room. Elderly couples took up a third of the tables and booths; business men in dress shirts and ties talked and laughed. Several young families with children rounded out the clientele. No terrorists, no robbers, no gang members.

An Army major sat with a young blonde Tess took to be his wife. The man's uniform triggered a new wave of apprehension. Her fear had nothing to do with her but with J. J.

Something seemed wrong. She didn't believe in intuition or psychic powers, but she couldn't shake the acidic taste of fear.

Just after 0230 in Italy. Tess closed her eyes and began to pray.

ZINSSER SMELLED THE SEA. He heard the cry of gulls. He felt an ocean breeze. Despite the screaming of his subconscious, it all seemed right to him. He forced himself to focus. Before him waited the mansion the Somali pirates used to imprison their . . . captives.

Mansion? *That's right—a mansion. I think.*

Something didn't seem right.

Gulls? Sea breezes? He glanced to his left. Two men dressed in black and wearing masks ran alongside him. *Pirates?* No. They were running *with* him not *at* him. Zinsser felt grass and soft ground beneath his boots, not macadam or concrete.

The sound of sea birds faded, the salty scent of ocean departed, replaced by the aroma of manicured lawn and nearby forest. He wasn't in Somalia; he was in stealth mode and approaching a villa in the countryside of Italy. Why did he think he was half a world away?

Get with it, Zinsser. Bear down. Focus, before you make yourself and the others dead. He blinked hard, and the real world crashed on his mind like a wave on the shore.

The present plan rose to the forefront of his mind. He was not alone. He had two men with him on this side of the house—Moyer and the Italian De Luca. Two teams of two were approaching the building from the back and side. That was reality. That was what he had to focus on. Seven good guys; unknown bad guys. *If it comes to shooting, don't shoot the good guys.*

Hunched and silent, they moved to the north wall. Three windows broke the solid stucco surface. Zinsser stepped to the side of the easternmost window. Moyer took the middle window and De Luca the third. Zinsser strained his ears to hear any sounds of occupants or guard dogs. They had surveilled the house with the best electronics and saw no indication of inhabitants, but, despite his love of technology, he trusted his human senses more.

Moyer raised two fingers to his eyes then pointed at Zinsser's window. Zinsser glanced right then left then rose from his crouch, his back against the wall. He pulled a small electronic device from his vest and unwound a coil of fiber-optic cable. With one thumb he flicked the power switch, and a small monitor on the transistor radio-sized device began to glow. Pointing the end of the cable at the window pane, he scanned the room. A light had been left on, so he could see without trouble. The monitor showed a desk, a leather sofa, a long and overstuffed bookshelf. The den was empty.

Zinsser signaled "clear," then moved to Moyer's position. He used the camera to peer in. The room was dark, and Zinsser compensated by thumbing a switch for infrared. The monitor showed boxy structures and a long table. Laundry room, Zinsser assumed. Again, he signaled clear.

Zinsser didn't waste time going to De Luca's window. It was translucent textured glass, making the spy camera useless. When they first scanned the house from a distance, they determined that window served a bathroom.

Crouching again, Zinsser put his head close to Moyers. "Laundry and a den on this side."

"Roger." Moyer keyed his mike. "Clear on this side."

J. J.'s voice came over the headset. "South side clear."

Pete followed. "East side clear."

Moyer looked at Zinsser. "Time to go."

Zinsser's heart kicked into fifth gear. "Ready when you are, Boss."

"On my mark," Moyer said into his radio, then started for the front of the house. Zinsser followed with De Luca in his wake. Passive surveillance was about to turn into forced entry. They had planned the next step hours before they arrived, and Zinsser had rehearsed every detail in his mind more times than he could count. The south side of the building had a large deck, outdoor kitchen, an entertainment area larger than Zinsser's apartment, and—more importantly—a large array of French doors. Shaq would lead the assault from that end of the house. With him would be J. J., Pete, and Jose. Zinsser, Moyer, and De Luca would come through the front entrance.

The front door looked to be handcrafted mahogany. On either side of the door were tall, three-foot-wide panes of stained glass. *Someone paid a lot of money for those.* Zinsser forced the thought from his mind. Focus. Focus. Focus.

Zinsser watched Moyer step in front of one of the stained-glass panels, look at his watch, then pull a small explosive charge from his vest. Before Moyer could place it, Zinsser raised a hand stopping him, stepped forward, and slowly turned the doorknob.

It was unlocked.

CHAPTER 16

MOYER COULDN'T BELIEVE HIS eyes. He activated the radio and said one word: "Go."

Zinsser pushed the door open and Moyer stepped into the dark foyer. The house smelled of many things: leather, new carpet, lingering food orders, and a few things Moyer didn't recognize. A rail light attached to Moyer's M4 split the darkness. Zinsser's and De Luca's light did the same.

Moyer led his team through the entrance and room by room, the muzzle of his weapon pointed ahead of him, his finger just to the side of the trigger.

The foyer was clear. The living room was clear, as was a sitting room, a powder room, and a large dining room. The room held a long table littered with dirty dishes.

A sound came from the kitchen. Moyer raised his weapon so did Zinsser and De Luca. The door between the kitchen and dining room opened slowly. A second later Moyer was looking down the barrel of an automatic weapon.

Countless hours of training and experience prevented Moyer from shooting Rich Harbison in the forehead.

"Kitchen and rec room are clear," Rich whispered. "Colt noticed the coffee pot was still plugged in and warm."

"Understood, Shaq. We'll take upstairs. You take the basement."

"We're on it."

Rich motioned for his team to follow. Moyer started for a wide set of stairs. The best he could tell in the limited light, the treads of the stairs were made of the same mahogany as the door. He was no woodworker, but he knew high grade mahogany was expensive—well beyond a soldier's pay.

A thick carpet ran up the middle of the stairs, protecting the treads from damaging shoes and those who use the stairs from slipping on polished wood. Moyer appreciated the carpet for a different reason: it muffled the sound of his steps.

Upstairs was a wide hall of white plaster. Paintings hung along the wall. Moyer and his team took turns leading the group into bedrooms. Moyer counted eight in all. Each room had several beds, most of which didn't fit the décor. Clearly extra beds had been brought in. All of the bed sheets were mussed, twisted, or lying on the floor.

"Look at this." De Luca shone his light at the base of one of the windows. "The slider portion of the window has been screwed shut, and the screw head stripped. The only way out would be to break the glass and jump."

"Hard to do quietly," Zinsser said.

"It appears we have the right place, but where is everyone?"

"No idea," Zinsser said.

After they checked the last room, Moyer radioed. "Second floor clear."

Rich's response wasn't what Moyer expected. "No rush, Boss, but you may want to see this."

MOYER FOUND HIS TEAM gathered at the landing of the stairs that led from the main floor. The way they held their weapons revealed a relaxed state, but Moyer could sense tension. He expected it since he felt the same sense of inner conflict. Warriors were like other men. They felt fear and excitement. Their training equipped them to manage both. Seven men had just forced their way into a structure they had been told might be heavily guarded and found it empty. In the hours leading up to the mission they sharpened their minds and emotions like a butcher sharpens knives. They came in ready to kill or be killed. Instead of armed and well-trained enemies, they got nothing. It took time to get rid of energy like that and near superhuman strength to contain it.

Moyer removed his balaclava and tucked it into his back pocket. The others did the same. "Whatcha got, Shaq?"

"Three rooms, Boss." He pointed to the back of the basement. "Believe it or not, there's a small movie theater behind those double doors. We checked it and it's clear."

"That explains the popcorn smell," Moyer said.

"What we have behind these doors"—Rich motioned to another large pair of open double doors—"is a type of workshop. Not nearly as entertaining as a movie theater, but it has a few interesting points." Rich turned and walked into the room. Moyer and the others followed. "Okay to flip the lights, Boss?"

"Sure. Apparently we're the only ones here to see it."

Rich flipped a light switch and stepped to the side. Moyer glanced around the room. Long work tables, roughly built from two-by-fours and solid-core doors for the work surface, dominated the space. An aluminum rack to one side stood nearly empty, supporting only two long, dark robes.

Moyer moved deeper into the room and saw a metal drum that bore a label: PE-4. It looked to be about fifty gallons.

"Colt?"

"PE-4." J. J. stepped to Moyer's side. "Very much like our C-4. PE stands for plastic explosive. Think FORMEX. The designation tells us it's British. The Italians call theirs T-4."

"I know what it is, Colt. I'm asking if you've checked it out?"

"Oh, sorry. I have. The barrel is only a third full."

"Judging by the container, it's commercial grade."

J. J. nodded. "Used on structures, road building, and the like. It's still in powder form."

Moyer watched the barrel as if he expected it to move. When mixed with water, the material became pliable and easy to stretch, perfect for creating bombs that fit around a body.

"Any idea how many bombs they could make with two-thirds of a barrel?"

"A lot." J. J.'s jaw tensed. "More than I care to think about."

It was more than Moyer wanted to consider, too. "Polo, get whatever numbers you can off the label and get your people on it. See if we can't trace it back to the supplier."

"What good will that do?"

"It will make me happy."

Moyer's tone chilled the room. "We missed them. We got here too late." He took a moment to rein in his anger. "All right, let's get busy. Shaq, take Junior and Doc and search the upstairs, and I mean *search* it. I want to know if there's so much as a cockroach with a limp. J. J., you're the demo guy, I want you to see if you can't find something of use in this work room. Data and I will take the first floor. Polo, as soon as you get your people running down the info on the PE-4 supplier, you join us. Are we clear?"

Each man answered in the affirmative, but before Moyer dismissed them, Zinsser spoke up. "Boss, when I was using the spy cam to check the rooms before we entered, I saw a den with a computer. I'd like to check that out."

"Do it." Moyer glanced at the others. "All right, ladies, let's get busy."

"LOOKS LIKE YOU'VE WORKED a computer before?" Moyer stood two feet back of the seated Zinsser, watching him enter keystrokes so fast his fingers seemed to blur.

"Who hasn't? It's all part of the new Army, Boss. They don't call me Data for nothing."

"What are you doing?"

"I'm trying to milk info from this thing, but the hard drive has been wiped. Apparently our friends want to keep a few things secret."

"An untrusting bunch. If the hard drive has been scrubbed, then why are you messing with it? Let Polo take it back to his people."

"Time, Boss. I have an uneasy feeling that there is more going on than we know about."

"How so?"

"I'm just guessing, right now, but there seems to be a pattern in the chaos. Think about the bombings we assume are related to El-Sayyed: a Baghdad hospital; a London shopping mall; a movie theater in Barcelona; an elementary school in the same town; and Paris."

"Go on."

"If you pardon the pun, Boss, they're all over the map. Baghdad makes sense. Suicide bombings will continue there for decades."

"I hope you're wrong."

"So do I, but I doubt it. London also makes sense. England has a huge and growing Islamic population. A small percentage of those are extremists. Maybe we can make the same argument for Barcelona and Paris, but it seems a stretch. Why so many suicide bombings? Why all female bombers? There has to be a motive."

"Everyone agrees with that. That's why we're here."

"Agreed, Boss, but we missed them. If we know their motive, then we might be able to stop them before they finish their task."

"And you're going to get that off the hard drive?"

"Doubtful, but I think it's worth a try. The only way to completely clean a hard drive is to give it an acid bath or pound it to powder. I want to try something first, Boss . . . with your permission of course."

"What do you have in mind?"

"It will take a few minutes, but I think I can get this baby to go online. If so, I'll download a recovery program and see if I can't rebuild something useful. FBI does it all the time."

"Boss?"

Moyer watched Shaq enter the room. "I found this in one of the bedrooms. It was under the mattress."

"You found toilet paper under the mattress?"

"You said to search the place. You say *search* and I search. It's why I'm your favorite."

"Careful, you'll make the others jealous." Moyer took the folded tissue.

"Go easy with it, Boss. There's something inside. Several somethings."

Moyer unfolded the thin, white paper. He could feel small, hard objects inside. "This isn't going to make me gag, is it? Why did you fold it all up again?"

"I wanted you to experience the full effect.

Moyer peeled back the last layer and stared at the contents. He couldn't think of anything to say.

"Yeah," Shaq said, "I had the same response."

"Fingernails? Why would anyone hide fingernails under a mattress?"

"Look closer, Boss."

Moyer pushed the fingernail ends to the side and saw a word written in pink: Mexico. There was also a number: 110877. Moyer keyed his radio. "Polo. I need you in the den." He released the key, then activated it again, "Sir." Moyer was team leader and in complete charge of the mission, but he forced himself to remember that De Luca held officer status and they were in his country.

Thirty seconds later De Luca plowed into the room like a freighter. The man exuded industrial strength confidence. "Found something?"

"Shaq and his team found this." He held out the opened package. "What do you make of it?"

"Fingernails? A woman's fingernails."

"We got that much," Shaq said. "If El-Sayyed held women here, we might expect to find female fingernails."

De Luca glanced at the big man. "They have nail polish on them."

"Yeah, so . . . Oh."

"Since when do Islamic women wear fingernail polish?" De Luca studied the fragments and toilet paper. "Mexico and a license plate number."

"Of course," Moyer said.

"It's a commercial number; the kind used for trucks and buses." He bent over Moyer's outstretched hand. "Are you married, Boss?"

"I am."

"Then you know what lip liner is," De Luca said. "The person who did this had access to makeup."

Shaq frowned. "Why would the black hats let the women keep makeup?"

"Why wouldn't they?" Moyer thought for a moment. "Shaq, the room you found this in, does it overlook the driveway?"

"It sure does, Boss."

"So she could have seen any vehicles parked there?"

"Affirmative."

Moyer nodded. "Polo, can you get a chopper in the air to search for a bus."

"Yes. It's still dark, but we have military craft that can see in the dark."

"Make the call, then help Shaq check outside for any tracks that fit a large vehicle."

"Will do," Shaq said.

"Fingernails," Moyer said to himself. "This has to be a first." Then to Zinsser he said, "Hand me the satellite phone. It's time to report in."

"Don't sound so down, Boss. You had no way of knowing this was a dry hole."

"I'll let you tell Colonel Mac that."

"No thanks."

CHAPTER 17

TESS, HER DINNER RUINED by imagined fears and believing sleep would be impossible, returned to her office. It was nearly 10:00, but she didn't care. She didn't want to be home alone with her thoughts. She had just finished the last swallow of vanilla latte when the phone in her small office rang. The sound of the phone seemed out of place at this hour. "Tess Rand."

"Dr. Rand"—the caller spoke in a heavy French accent—"this is Inspector Adnot D'Aubigne with ICPO. I expected an answering service."

Tess did a mental search to unravel the initialisms. "ICPO—International Criminal Police Organization?" Tess had often thought how the designation made it sound like the organization was populated by criminal police.

"*Oui*, Dr. Rand—Interpol. I am sorry to bother you at this late hour."

"No problem. It may be late here but it must be the wee hours there. You are in Europe aren't you?"

"Oui. Paris. My work requires some odd hours. We understand that you are doing research on female suicide bombers."

Tess had sent out a formal request to military and police organizations for information. "I am. I take it you have something for me."

"Oui." He paused. "Are you able to understand me, Dr. Rand? I am told by my American friends that my accent is a little . . . what is the word?"

"Thick?"

"Oui, thick."

"I understand you just fine. Your English is much better than my French."

"Thank you." D'Aubigne paused then launched into the matter. "We have been working on the bombing that recently took place in Paris."

"The one at the fashion show."

"Precisely. As I'm certain you know, it is important that details of such investigations be kept secret, but we have something that may interest you, but I must ask that you keep this in the strictest confidence. Of course you can tell your superiors."

"I understand the need for discretion."

"Of course. We have been examining the body of the bomber. As you might guess, such an examination takes time and is quite difficult since very little identifiable biological material remains. We recovered several large bones and a good portion of the skull as well as a fair amount of skin tissue."

The image turned Tess's stomach. No matter how difficult her job seemed, it could never be as bad as the crime scene investigators who had to gather body parts and sort them.

"Are you still with me, Dr. Rand?"

"I am, Inspector. Just making a few notes." *And trying to keep my dinner down.*

"Of course, we sent DNA samples out for examination and possible identification. The bomber was a woman named Michele Tulle, Middle Eastern descent, twenty-four years old, and a well-known entity to French police."

"Well-known entity?"

"She had a criminal record and was known to be a prostitute."

"You're kidding."

"I am being serious, Dr. Rand."

"I know you are, Inspector. Please go on."

"Prostitution is not illegal here. Brothels and procuring is, but not the individual's right to sell sexual favors."

"Procuring?"

D'Aubigne hesitated. "Helping someone sell sexual acts . . . um, I believe you call it *pimping*."

"I see."

"Most of Michele Tulle's skin was burned, but we did find some whole segments. They were heavily tattooed."

"Let me get this right. The suicide bomber was a tattooed prostitute?"

"Yes, she also had been arrested several times, the last time just two weeks before she blew herself up."

"This is unexpected."

"You assumed she was radical Islamic?"

"Perhaps, or, at very least a practicing Islamic woman." Tess leaned over the desk, resting her elbows on the surface as if the news had deprived her of breath.

"We made the same assumption. This does not fit the pattern we've come to expect."

"Why would such a woman turn herself into a walking bomb?"

"My experience tells me anyone will do anything if properly coerced."

"What would coerce a young woman to slip on an explosive vest and kill herself and everyone around her?"

"I only know of one thing with that kind of power, Dr. Rand."

"What is that?"

"Love."

"THAT FITS." COLONEL MAC sounded sleepy. Tess had sent him an encrypted e-mail, then called a half hour after she finished her call with Inspector D'Aubigne. Since they were talking over an unsecure line, most of the conversation was done in innuendo.

"Fits? How does it fit?"

"Someone recently suggested the same thing."

Someone? "Anyone I know?"

"I believe you met, recently. He's a neat freak. Fingernail clippings drive him nuts."

Fingernail clippings.

"You don't wear pink fingernail polish, do you?"

"Pink? You probably mean coral, and no, I wear a dark red. Coral is so yesterday."

Colonel Mac laughed. "Women and their war paint."

"Is he enjoying being on the road?" Tess bit her lip to keep from asking about J. J. and the others.

"So far. I think he's a little bored."

Tess took that to mean that the team was safe and had not been in an armed conflict.

"Boredom can be a good thing."

"You're probably right."

"Boredom is temporary." *Death is permanent.*

"I know exactly what you mean. Keep me in the loop." Colonel Mac hung up.

"And you keep me in the loop too," Tess said to the dial tone.

DE LUCA STEPPED INTO the den where Moyer paced like a hungry cat. Waiting was not his strong suit. "What ya got, Major?"

The Italian straightened. "The license number comes back to a 2008 eighteen-seat Irisbus mini. It's a rental out of Rome."

"I don't suppose it came equipped with a tracking device."

De Luca shook his head.

Zinsser looked up from the computer. "Eighteen seats tells us something."

"True. A man doesn't rent an eighteen-seat bus for four or five people." He turned his attention to De Luca. "What about the helo?"

"It should be airborne in the next few minutes."

"In that case, we need to be ready to rock." He walked to a spot behind Zinsser. "How you doing, Data?"

"It's going to take more time than we've got to recover more than a handful of files. I did find one thing interesting. The computer is on a network. It recently accessed a teleconference site. I bet the Major could make a call and find out where the other end of the teleconference is located."

"Make it happen. I want us on the move in fifteen. Got it?"

"Got it, Boss."

THE PAIN IN DELARAM'S thigh grew. She ran a hand along the back of her leg and the inside of her thigh. The gentle touch felt like another beating. Her right leg had swollen over the last hour, and the rough road only made things worse. It was clear they had left the private road for a dirt path better suited for a four-wheel drive than a boxy minibus. Every few moments one corner or another of the vehicle would drop into a pothole and bounce out, jarring her and the other passengers. Each bump sent nails of pain through her hip and up her spine. At times she had to cover her mouth to keep from crying out. She might be helpless, but that didn't mean she had to give them cause for satisfaction.

She shifted in the seat, seeking a less painful position. She gave up trying to be comfortable. If she could just move from excruciating pain to mere horrible discomfort, she'd consider herself lucky.

Lucky. She had always considered herself fortunate. Born to a well-to-do family, free to attend the best schools, encouraged to travel the world without a care, she had a life most of the world would envy. No one would envy her now. Parents held halfway around the world, subject to beating and most likely awaiting their execution. Their only hope rested on her willingness to kill herself and a few dozen innocent bystanders.

Delaram had been in the Italian countryside several times before and believed it to be some of the most beautiful scenery she had seen. Now, outside her window scrolled a twilight land of nearly black gloom; a stygian panorama.

Dark as it was outside, the mood in the bus was darker. The women sat in silence. Occasionally, someone would sniff, and she knew they were fighting tears. Like her, they had not only their lives to lose, but those of their loved ones also.

More than ever, she wished the bomb vest she had been wearing had been set to go off when she pressed the button. She would have killed herself, her captors, and, yes, the other girls, but maybe she might have saved many more lives. At least she wouldn't be sitting in this bus.

Despair darkened the night and thickened her depression. Like a ping-pong ball in a tornado, her thoughts flew in tight circles of ever-increasing speed. She tried to force her mind onto a single track, to hold one image, one question, one hope, one anything, but she failed at every attempt. For a few seconds she thought of her battered parents; for the next few seconds she thought of her impending death; the next few moments made her focus on the hatred she felt for the men who were doing this; every once in awhile, she thought of the other women.

The bus shuddered to a stop, and Delaram felt the tires skid in the dirt. The men in the bus rose. One turned to them. "Everyone—out."

"MEXICO?" MOYER FROWNED. "AGAIN with Mexico. I don't get it. What does Mexico have to do with our mission?"

"I can't say, Boss." Zinsser stood next to Moyer, who had joined the others in the basement workshop. "Data made a few calls and I searched the computer. We confirmed that a teleconference occurred with someone in Mexico."

"Do we know who?"

"No," De Luca answered. "It was routed through several countries. Whoever did it has someone who knows how to manipulate the Internet."

"I found something else," Zinsser said. "I was able to reconstruct some pictures."

"Pictures of whom?"

"Not who, Boss; pictures of what. The pictures were screen captures of satellite services. You know, like Google Maps. There were pics from several servers including a private company. All satellite shots of the same place."

"And that place is . . ."

"Naples, Boss."

Moyer felt the blood drain from his face.

"Yeah." Zinsser's expression was grim. "I had the same thought."

"What?" J. J. looked from one to the other. "I'm not making the connection."

"G-20. Didn't I hear that it had been moved to Naples?"

"G-20?" J. J. frowned at Moyer.

"Group of Twenty. It's a gathering of government leaders. They meet from time to time to discuss economics."

"I thought it was the G-8," Rich said.

"It used to be the leaders from the top economic powers: Canada, France, Germany, Italy, Japan, Russia, the United Kingdom, and the United States. It started back in the mid-seventies. The number changes from time to time."

Zinsser ticked off the countries on his fingers. "Brazil, China, India, and Mexico have been included. This meeting includes several countries from South America and a few others."

Everyone stared at him.

"What? You think Shaq is the only one who reads?"

"You think these guys are thinking of doing something at the G-20 meeting?" Shaq asked.

Moyer thought for a moment. The puzzle pieces in his mind began to assemble. "It could be. Think about it: women bombers struck a hospital, a school, a fashion show, and the like. Bombers usually try to do their work in crowds, but each of these involved entering a building. It's one thing to set yourself off in a religious procession or an open air market, but to do so in a building presents challenges."

"Those were practice runs?" J. J. asked.

"Maybe. Data, get me command. Polo, get on the horn with your people."

"Then what?" Rich said.

"Then we hightail it out of here."

CHAPTER 18

PRESIDENT TED HUFFINGTON SCOOTED to the edge of the limo's back-seat and peered through the bulletproof glass. The driver stopped the presidential limo right on target. In a moment one of the Secret Service Protection Detail would open his door, and he and his wife, Marni, would move from the limo to the covered walkway. The cover, a bright red canopy, had been added to the side entrance to block the view of a sniper—not that a sniper could find purchase on any building within sight of the *Miramare Hotel Grande*.

The door swung open; Huffington exited the vehicle and slipped into predawn air, Marni just a step behind. Secret Service agents bracketed them and led them up a red carpet to the side entrance door. On either side of the carpet stood a row of Naples police officers dressed in dark blue uniforms with white gun belts and a matching diagonal support strap. Every man faced out, watching for movement that might indicate danger.

A tall man with ebony skin, prematurely gray hair, and a Secret Service pin stuck in his suit coat stepped to the president's side. "I need a moment with you, sir."

"Why does that statement always fill me with dread, Mitchell?"

"I don't know, sir. My mother always speaks kindly of me."

"What's that set you back . . . a month?" Huffington walked down the first-floor hall. He moved quickly to keep pace with the agents in front. Passing a mirror he saw the image of a sixty-year-old man with gray hair, laugh lines etched into his face, and growing bags under his eyes.

When had he started to look so much like his father?

"Not as much as you might think, sir."

"Okay. Give us ten minutes to freshen up then come up to the room."

"Thank you, Mr. President."

Moments later Huffington let out a relaxed breath. He'd ditched the dark blue suit and yellow power tie for a dark green Polo shirt and tan slacks. Much better. When Marni came from the dressing room, she also looked more relaxed in her loose-fitting jeans and bone-colored shell top.

She was still the most beautiful woman he'd ever seen.

The plan was to stay in for the morning and try to catch up on their sleep. Huffington knew it was futile.

Someone knocked on the door and he sighed. "Come in."

"Oh Huff, open the door." Marni eased into an overstuffed chair. "It's the polite thing to do."

"It's just Mitchell. It's how guys communicate. We shout through doors."

"I'm sure that'll go over big when you meet the Chinese prime minister next month."

The door opened, and Mitchell Baker entered. At his side was Helen "Brownie" Brown. A stern-looking woman with chestnut hair that hung to just below her jaw line, her brown eyes had a hardness about them. But then, as the first female chief of staff, she had to be tough. She had an unrivaled intellect, an acid tongue to everyone but the president and his wife, laser-beam focus, and a take-no-captive attitude. It was rumored that she had once made the speaker of the house weep. A fact that made Huffington grin every time he thought about it.

"Hey, Brownie. Early morning suits you." She didn't grimace at the nickname. Of course, only he was allowed to use the name.

"If you say so, sir." Helen closed the door behind them.

"If I didn't know better, I'd say you were being sarcastic."

"I would never be sarcastic with you, sir." And yet . . . her smile seemed forced.

"That a fact?"

"A solid fact, Mr. President."

Huffington motioned to the sitting area of the luxury suite. Helen and Mitchell took seats on one sofa; Huffington lowered himself into the love seat four feet opposite the sofa.

"Excuse me." Marni rose from the chair and started for the bedroom area.

"Hang on, sweets." Huffington turned to Helen. "Any reason Marni can't sit in on this? Poor thing has to leave every time someone wants to talk to me."

"I know of no reason." Mitchell glanced at the woman next to him. "Helen?"

She hesitated and Huffington could tell she was weighing the question. "Of course Mrs. Huffington can stay." The words seemed uncomfortable to speak.

"Great." Huffington patted the cushion next to him. Marni approached, then sat. "Okay, I believe you called this meeting, Mitchell. What's up?"

Mitchell Baker had been the head of the presidential security detail for the last six months and Huffington was glad for it. He possessed a stellar record: ten years in the Navy, eight as a decorated Navy SEAL; five years with the Treasury Department before transferring to the Secret Service division and protection detail. A serious man, he spoke seldom, made his words count, and tried to stay out of the president's way. Although professional distinction kept him from saying so, Huffington considered the man a friend.

"There may be trouble at the G-20 forum."

"That's to be expected. We've already discussed this. There's always trouble. A few years ago 225,000 marched on the G-8 meeting in Gleneagles, Scotland. There will always be protesters."

"Yes, sir. You may recall that suicide bombers killed over fifty people on the London Underground and on a bus." Mitchell hesitated. "You are aware of recent suicide bombings in London, Paris, and other cities."

"Of course."

"What you may not be aware of, Mr. President, is that there is a covert operation going in Italy."

"A covert operation? By our people?"

Helen nodded. "Yes, sir. Army Spec Ops. They're tracking a man named El-Sayyed—"

Huffington swore.

"Ted!" Marni snapped.

He felt his cheeks redden and offered a small grin. "Sorry, hon." He turned to his advisors. "She hates it when I swear. It's that Presbyterian upbringing." He'd told that story uncountable times, but it was still funny to him.

"Who is El-Sayyed?"

There was a hint of concern in Marni's question. Maybe he shouldn't have asked for her to stay. There was no need to worry her. Still, she deserved an answer. "A suspected terrorist. No one has been able to lay indisputable proof on the table, but we know he's funded and perhaps been involved in several events. He's slimy and that makes him slippery."

"As I was saying, Mr. President." Helen once again took control, something she was remarkably good at. "Mitchell has received word that an Army team is tracking El-Sayyed in Italy. It seems El-Sayyed is involved in the recent spat of suicide bombings."

"Who contacted you, Mitchell?"

"The commanding officer of Army Spec Ops—"

"Colonel MacGregor?"

"Yes, sir."

"Good man, built like a tank."

"I've never met him, sir. Anyway, he contacted the head of the Secret Service detail. Word then came to me."

"They think El-Sayyed will try something at tomorrow's G-20?" Huffington leaned forward.

"The in-country team leader thinks so. They tracked El-Sayyed to a villa outside Rome. The Italians think that he's massing female suicide bombers to attack Christian sites in Rome."

"The Italians know about the operation?"

"Not officially, of course," Helen said. "We assume their president has kept it at arm's length. Probably wants deniability."

"Same reason you kept me out of the loop."

"Exactly, sir."

Huffington wasn't angry. It was impossible for a president to be kept up to speed about every military operation. Many things went on without his knowledge or consent. It was why he needed people he could trust making those decisions.

He turned his attention back to Mitchell. "We can't cancel the G-20. Most of the heads-of-state are already here, and we've let these clowns move us out of our original cities. I'm tired of getting pushed around."

"We now think that the previous bombings were meant to force a move."

"What do they hope to achieve by that? The streets are going to be cleared around the meeting area. The Naples police have set up barricades. A dog won't be able to approach a fire hydrant without security clearance."

"Yes, sir, I know. We've been working closely with local police," Mitchell said. "We just want you to know that things may move a little more slowly as we take extra precautions."

Huffington saw his wife's face blanch, and she placed a hand on his arm.

"Maybe you and the others should postpone the forum."

"It doesn't matter when or where we have it, hon." He spoke softly. "This is a global problem. We have terrorists on our own soil. Mitch will keep me safe. Security details for the other countries will keep their leaders safe. Naples may be the most secure place on the planet."

Huffington stood and thanked Mitchell and Helen. "I want to be kept apprised of everything. For now, we continue as planned."

"Yes, Mr. President," Mitchell said.

"Sir, I have several domestic affairs briefings to go over with you this evening."

"After supper, Brownie. I need some sleep."

"Yes, sir."

Mitchell led the way to the door and exited. Just as Helen was about to cross the threshold, Huffington stopped her. "Brownie."

"Sir?"

"It's been awhile since I've told you how much I respect you and the work you do. You're the best."

"Thank you, sir."

"Now that I'm aware of the ops, I want to be kept up to speed. Clear?"

"Very clear, Mr. President."

"IF YOU DON'T MIND me saying so, Capitano, you look like a corpse."

Aldo Gronchi looked at his aide Lorenzo, who stood in the doorway of Aldo's office. The sound of early morning traffic pressed into the room from outside the La Stazione di Polizia. "I can see why you are so loved by the women. Who could resist such a tongue of gold?"

Lorenzo looked sad. "I did not mean to offend. I only meant you look very tired. Did you not sleep well last night?"

"Of course I did—for two hours, which is an hour more than I got the night before."

"Three hours in two nights? That is not good for the health. Try a glass of wine."

"I'd need the whole bottle." Aldo set his reading glasses on the desk and rubbed his eyes. He looked up and saw the same weary expression on Lorenzo's face he saw in his own mirror. "Everyone has an agenda and better idea how to do things. Unfortunately the French security team wants precedence over the British, who feel more entitled than everyone else."

"And the Americans?"

"Civil, courteous, insistent. Everyone thinks their president or prime minister is more important than the others. It's impossible to make everyone play nice. Now this." He tapped a file on the desk. "Suicide bombers."

"The file is uncertain about their target," Lorenzo said.

"It doesn't matter what their target is, people die, sometimes by the dozen. Our job is to make certain none of those people are members of the G-20."

"Fortunately we already have everything in place." Lorenzo made a questioning motion toward the chair in front of Aldo's desk.

Aldo nodded. "Of course. Sit."

Lorenzo did. "I've just returned from inspecting the barricade equipment. Everything is in order. We have experienced men on every street. Every manhole in the area has been welded shut, a task that is easier to do than undo."

"An old procedure and a wise one. I don't want to know how much this is costing our government. Euros must be flowing like water."

"No doubt, sir. I am glad that it is not coming out of my pocket." Lorenzo straightened. "The teams you sent to the other hotels and office buildings in the area have spoken to everyone who might open a window facing the *Grande Hotel di Napoli*."

Aldo picked up a pencil and tapped the eraser end on his desk. "Protestors?"

"Several have applied for permission to assemble, but we know of a half dozen other groups who will show up and make noise."

"Anyone out of the ordinary?"

"No, sir. The usual antiglobalization groups as well as the people on both sides of the free trade issue."

"Any change in the estimated numbers?"

"The largest group may reach six thousand. All the rest are smaller. If they congregate in one area, then we may see numbers as high as twelve thousand. The downturn in the global economy has increased frustration."

"While you were looking at manhole covers, I was meeting with department heads and military leaders. The biggest fear is what one group may do to the other. It will be a miracle if no one gets killed."

"I like to think Italians are more civilized than that."

"You remain the optimist, Lorenzo. People are people, and when they get together bad things happen. You have been a police officer long enough to know that."

"I know it, Capitano. I just find it easier to believe otherwise."

"I find it beneficial to assume the worst, so let me ask you. How would *you* attack the G-20 forum?"

Lorenzo shrugged. "We made it impossible for snipers. No one can get close to the building while the meeting is going on. All vehicles will be kept a quarter mile away—except for police, military, and government cars. The hotel's employees have been screened. Security forces from a dozen nations have reviewed our measures and added their own. I don't think anyone can make a valid threat. Our efforts are perfect."

Aldo stared at Lorenzo for a moment but didn't see the man. Instead, his mind was filled with images of disaster. "I want the perimeter pushed back another two blocks."

Lorenzo sighed then rose. "I'll get started."

CHAPTER 19

THE CELL PHONE IN De Luca's vest sounded. Moyer watched him retrieve it and place it to his ear. Moyer kept his hands on the steering wheel and snapped his eyes back to the dark road in front of them. Driving a dirt road at night was risky enough, but doing so without lights was insane.

Moyer raised a hand and wiped away a bead of sweat from above his eyebrow. The jog back through the woods to the vehicles they had sequestered was not especially taxing, but it did force a sweat.

The van Moyer drove rocked on the rough road and bounced hard in potholes.

"I think you missed one, Boss," J. J. said from the backseat. "You going to turn around and try again?"

"How about we tie you to the front of the vehicle and you can warn us when a pothole is coming up?"

"No need, Boss. You're doing great."

Moyer glanced in his side mirror and saw the second van following a mere twenty feet behind. If Moyer had to hit the brakes, Shaq would run his vehicle up Moyer's tailpipe.

De Luca switched off the phone. "Helicopter has something. Probably a vehicle. It's hidden under a canopy of trees, but the FLIR picked up a heat signature in keeping with a vehicle engine."

"Where?" Moyer asked.

De Luca punched numbers into a handheld GPS unit. "About five miles ahead and a mile north."

Moyer thought for a moment. "What about people? Did the FLIR pick up human heat signatures?"

"No," De Luca said.

"So they changed vehicles," Pete Rasor said. He sat next to J. J.

"It's what I'd do," Moyer said. "I'm not surprised."

Moyer was about to ask another question when De Luca anticipated him. "The chopper continues to search for any vehicles."

Moyer was starting to like the man. "They can outrun us, but they can't outrun the helo." With eyes still fixed on the dark road, Moyer said, "Colt, bring Shaq up to speed."

J. J. acknowledged the order and made the call.

Moyer pressed the accelerator another half inch to the floor.

THE TEAM ROLLED TO a stop about a click from the site where the helo discovered the bus. Although the infrared camera showed no human activity, Moyer wasn't in the mood to take chances. Dying while on mission was acceptable; dying stupid wasn't.

He split the team as he had while surveilling the villa and making entry.

"We go in slow and sure," he said. "Stay focused and don't shoot unless you're sure of your target. Clear?" The comments were unnecessary, but they served to focus each man's attention and give them a second to adjust the flow of adrenaline.

"Move out," Moyer ordered. He gave Rich a moment to lead J. J., Jose, and Pete to a northerly approach. His would be the longer journey.

"You want me to take point, Boss?" Zinsser asked.

Moyer started to say no, then changed his mind. He had a tendency to be overprotective of any new member of his team. Zinsser was with him instead of Rich, but Zinsser wasn't a raw recruit.

"Take it, Data. Just don't fall down any rabbit holes."

"You know what you get when you pour melted butter down a rabbit hole, Boss?"

"Do I want to hear the rest of this?"

"You get hot cross bunnies."

Moyer lowered his head. "Please tell me you got better jokes than that."

"Sorry, Boss. That's my A material."

De Luca looked at Moyer. "We're doomed."

"Ready to rock, Boss." He pulled his balaclava over his face.

"Do it." Moyer donned his black mask.

Zinsser started forward in a slow, careful jog. Moyer followed two meters behind, his eyes straining against the dark.

ZINSSER SOON FELL INTO a well practiced breathing pattern, forcing himself to inhale deeply and exhale fully. His boots landed in even footfalls. Tempted as he was to fix his eyes on the ground before him, he forced himself to scan everything in front of him. Tripping might be bad; getting a bullet in the head would be worse.

He had little fear of the latter. Zinsser trusted technology. It had helped him get through the endless hours he spent in the hospital. If the FLIR said no humans were in the area, then there were no humans in the area. Still, being "Army strong" meant being Army smart. He had no problem playing it by the book.

His heart increased its pounding but brought no strain. The pace was easy. Soon all he could hear was the sound of his boots impacting the grass-covered ground.

His ears picked out a distant sound.

A pop.

A whiz.

His head began to tingle as if ants were crawling through his hair.

A shot.

An AK-47.

Zinsser dropped to the ground, head down. A second later he raised his head to scan the terrain. Where had the shot come from?

Voices. Distant voices. Somali voices.

"Data."

To his right?

Another shot.

No, to his left.

"Data?"

That voice was clear and close. Someone needed him. "Brian . . . Echo."

"Zinsser!"

Zinsser activated his radio. "Echo, this is Zinsser, where are you?"

"I'm down." The voice wasn't in his radio. It came from inside his head. Something was wrong.

"Say again, Data?"

That voice came over his earpiece, but the timbre was wrong. It was deeper, thicker.

"Data, this is Shaq. Say again."

Someone touched his shoulder. He rolled on his side and reached for his sidearm. The 9mm slipped from the holster easily, and Zinsser started to bring it to bear when a heavy weight landed on him, driving the air from his lungs. His arm was pinned.

"Get off me, you dirty—"

A hand clamped his mouth shut.

"Zinsser!" The voice was familiar and just above a whisper— and the urgency was unmistakable.

Zinsser blinked. The sounds were gone. The terrain was no longer a Somali street but an open field.

"Boss, you guys okay?"

"Standby, Shaq. Hold your position."

"Roger that."

Zinsser's brain tried to settle the confused images in his mind. Lying two feet from him was an angry Moyer. De Luca sat on Zinsser, pinning his arm and sidearm to his body, his hand pressed over Zinsser's mouth.

It couldn't be. It couldn't have happened. Not here. Not now. Not with these people. Zinsser closed his eyes and wished his heart would stop beating.

"Look at me, Data." Moyer spoke through clenched teeth. "I said *look at me.*"

Zinsser gazed at Moyer and pictured, behind the black knit mask Moyer wore, a stone face chiseled with anger. Moyer's eyes, however, which should have flashed with fury, were tempered with concern. "Are you with me?"

"Yeah, Boss. I'm with you."

"You have ten seconds to tell me what just happened."

Zinsser thought quickly. "I thought I heard something."

"Who is Echo?"

"Echo? Echo was on my last team. Did I say Echo? I meant Shaq."

Moyer's eyes narrowed and Zinsser could imagine the gears of his team leader's brain turning. "You were going to shoot me, weren't you?"

"Shoot you? Why would I shoot you?"

"Then why did you draw your handgun?"

"I wouldn't shoot you, Boss. It would be a bad career move on my part. Why would I do that?"

"Because you thought you were somewhere else. Where were you?"

"I'm right here—in Italy—chasing bad guys with you."

"Listen to me, Data, and listen good. We got a situation here. I need to know you're with me mentally."

"I'm with you, Boss, body and mind. You got all of me." Zinsser could see some of the tension leave Moyer's face. "I'm fine, Boss. Good to go. I know where we are and what we're doing."

"That a fact?"

Zinsser took a breath. "We're in Italy, in the countryside outside of Rome. We are a seven-member team. You're leading me and Polo here on a direct approach to what we believe is an abandoned bus used to carry female suicide bombers. Shaq is leading the rest of the team—Colt, Doc, and Junior—on an approach from the north."

Moyer said nothing.

"Any chance you can get the Italian off of me? He's making it hard to breathe."

Moyer spoke into his radio. "Shaq, report."

"We're in position, Boss. The area appears clear. No movement in or around the bus. You guys okay?"

"Yeah. Hold your position. We'll be there in three."

"Holding position. See you in three."

Moyer pushed to his knees then put his face close to Zinsser's. Zinsser could smell coffee on Moyer's breath. "I don't know what just happened, but I have suspicions. We're going to carry on with our approach and you're going to stay focused on this mission. Is that clear?"

"Clear as glass, Boss."

Moyer paused, then added, "I've never had to shoot a team member before, but if I think you're about to draw down on me or any other member of the team, I'll drop you. Got it?"

"Yes, Boss."

"You continue on point. I want you in front of me."

"Will do, Boss."

"Let him up, Polo."

De Luca crawled off Zinsser but kept a grip on the hand that held the sidearm. Slowly Zinsser slipped the weapon back into its holster. "Waiting on your word, Boss."

"Move out."

Zinsser was on his feet, moving forward as he had been a few moments before. The night vision goggles narrowed his peripheral vision, and he was glad. He didn't want to see how often Moyer and De Luca were checking him out.

AS EXPECTED, THE BUS was empty. Moyer, Zinsser, and De Luca arrived at the coppice of trees three minutes after they resumed their stealth approach. Rich and the others had waited as told. During that time they saw no one. The area was clear of potential enemies. Still, Moyer sent them as if black hats were waiting inside the bus for anyone stupid enough to approach.

"Clear," Rich declared once he and J. J. made entry into the minibus.

"Still a step ahead," J. J. said. "By the way, what happened to you guys? We heard Data's transmission, but it didn't make sense."

Time to nip this in the bud. He couldn't afford to have the team speculating. "Nothing happened. Now—"

"But we heard—"

Moyer skewered J. J. with a glare. "I said nothing happened."

J. J. lowered his head. "Gotcha, Boss."

Moyer turned to De Luca, who was placing his cell phone to his vest. "Well?"

"Nothing. The pilot has been doing a circular search pattern but hasn't found anything but a few small vehicles on the roads— nothing the size of a minibus or a caravan that could hold enough people to fill even half this bus."

"They could have hidden several cars here and driven off in different directions," Jose said.

"Maybe, Doc, maybe." Moyer thought for a moment. "Okay, fan out. Let's see if we can find some kind of tracks or clues. Don't waste time; we're already behind."

The team began to move when Moyer said, "Zinsser, you're with me."

Moyer led the newest member of his team to the edge of the small grove, then stopped and gave him a narrow-eyed stare. "So, do I send you back or what?"

Zinsser looked away.

"I asked you a question."

"I want to stay."

Moyer ran a hand across his chin, glad to have the mask off. "How bad is it?"

"What?"

"Your PTSD."

"The docs checked me out for months and gave me the all-clear. I don't have a problem with post-traumatic stress disorder."

Irritation heated Moyer's chest—and his words. "Any soldier who's seen what you have is probably struggling with it. Don't lie to me. I have to be able to trust you. For all I know, if De Luca hadn't pounced on you, you might have put a hole in my head. I want the straight skinny."

Zinsser looked down for a moment and then raised his head to look Moyer in the eye. "Every once in awhile, I flash back."

Good. The truth. He could work with the truth. "Like you did at the villa?"

"Yeah, it usually lasts only a few moments. Most of the time I can control it."

Most of the time? Is that what I heard? *Most* of the time? I need you and your brain present 100 percent of the time. Ninety-nine percent isn't enough."

"Understood, Boss."

"Protocol requires I pull you from this mission and send you home. You are a danger to this mission and to the team."

"I . . . understood, Boss."

Moyer looked around. "If we were close to base . . . We can't afford to waste any more time. For the moment we're stuck with you. Shaq is assistant team leader so I'll have to let him in on this, and he isn't going to like it." Moyer raised a finger. "I'll get you home first chance I get. And if one of the team gets so much as a splinter because you fail to perform, I'll make sure you're drummed out of the service. If I lose a man because of you—"

"I know, Boss, you'll hunt me down and put a bullet in my brain."

"Oh no, I'll do much worse than that. I'll make sure you live a long, miserable life with your failure. Understood?"

"Understood."

"Dismissed."

As Zinsser jogged to join the others, Moyer wondered if his threats would help or hurt.

CHAPTER 20

THE AGUSTAWESTLAND AW109 SLOWED its descent and its retractable landing gear appeared. Moyer and the team stood twenty meters away from the landing site. J. J. had made the discovery and called Moyer to an area a short distance away from the stand of trees.

"Looks like prop wash to me, Boss." He pointed to an area of tall grass that had been pressed to the ground. J. J. squatted and touched the ground. He motioned with his flashlight beam. "The soil is soft and there are two long narrow depressions."

"Like helicopter skids." Moyer looked around them. "It would have to be one of the larger copters."

"A Bell 412 corporate chopper carries something like fifteen passengers."

"That'd probably do it," J. J. said.

"This just gets better and better." Moyer pinched the bridge of his nose and tried to force his thoughts into formation. "The helicopter would give a level of mobility they'd never have with a car, not to mention speed."

"They'd have to fly low to stay off radar," Shaq said.

"Another advantage."

Moyer had De Luca put in a call for transportation. The Italian Army sent the AW109. Less than sixty seconds after its gear touched down, the team was aboard and headed to Naples.

Over the horizon the sun rose, pushing its rays through a bank of clouds. The color reminded Moyer of blood.

LORENZO FILIPEPI GAZED AT the rising sun. He had waited all night for its arrival. There had been many occasions when events required he stay awake through the night. Those nights crept along, one minute slowly morphing into the next.

A gentle cough, softer than a kitten's mew, drew his attention from the window. He turned and gazed at the small form asleep on the hospital bed in the center of his tiny, dirty apartment. The form shifted, grimaced, and rolled to her side.

A moment later the eight-year-old girl with straight black hair was asleep again. He watched the thin blanket that concealed her form rise and fall with each breath—a ballet of life.

Seeing her made him ache, delivered a pain so hot and so deep he had to force back tears. Eight years old. Just eight. And for the last two years, Mia had seen almost nothing of the outside, just what passed by the car window whenever Lorenzo took her to the hospital.

He glanced around the apartment. It was small, with only one bedroom and one bathroom. It was all he could afford, and half of the time he was in arrears on the rent. The landlord, a blimp of a woman with a matching heart, often looked the other way.

A gentle knock came from the door. Lorenzo opened it, and the cool dawn air rolled into the room. Standing in the pale glow of the yellow porch light stood Ornella, Lorenzo's sister. Despite the early hour, she looked fresh, rested, and ready to greet the day.

"I'm sorry to ask you to come so early," Lorenzo said, stepping aside.

"Nonsense, it's only a couple of hours and I rise early anyway."

Lorenzo closed the door. "It's just that I have to be at work early."

"I understand. It is not every day that so many dignitaries come to our city." Ornella stepped to the tiny dining area, hung her long coat over the back of a chair, and set her purse on the table.

"How did she sleep last night?" Ornella spoke softly and let her eyes drift to the child.

"She slept through the night," Lorenzo said, matching her tone. "We had a little episode about two this morning. Choking. But it passed quickly."

"That's good. When did she last eat?"

"We had some ice cream about ten o'clock last night."

"I mean really eat."

"About six. I heated up a can of chicken noodle soup and made toast. That's her favorite."

Ornella walked to the hospital bed and straightened the snow-white sheets, careful not to wake her sleeping charge.

Lorenzo removed his blue uniform coat from the closet and slipped it on. "I may be late. I will get home as soon as I can."

"Don't worry yourself about it. Mia and I are best friends. I can stay all night if necessary."

Lorenzo bent over his daughter's form and kissed her on the forehead, then walked to the door. He turned to face his sister. "If the landlady comes by, please tell her that I will try to have the rent ready in a few days. She's been very understanding."

"But won't you let me handle that, Lorenzo? I've spoken with my husband—"

"No, it's my responsibility. You and Ricardo have financial needs of your own."

Ornella stared at him with kind eyes. "We can manage, brother. We are family and family sticks together."

"I can't allow it." Lorenzo pursed his lips.

"Well, since you won't be here, you can't stop me." She smiled. "Ricardo thinks you two should move in with us, and I agree. That way I wouldn't have to get up at dawn and come here. I could be of much more help if you and Mia lived with us."

"I appreciate the offer, Ornella, but it just isn't that easy."

"What is not easy for you is swallowing your pride, but we understand. The offer remains open. Mia needs a mother figure in her life. She's needed one ever since Isabella left you."

"I do not want to talk about Isabella."

He'd trusted her. Loved her. And she'd come to him one night saying she was leaving him for another man. A man who was not a police officer, who kept normal hours and would be home to take care of her. Just like that, she abandoned her husband and daughter. Lorenzo had not seen her for three years.

"I'm just saying that you would have more money for Mia if you lived with us. Perhaps better doctors could save . . ." She couldn't finish the sentence.

"It would not be enough. Ten times my salary would not be enough."

"Have your lawyers made any headway?"

"No. They're still trying to force the insurance company to live up to its promises, but they've made no progress. The insurance company has more lawyers."

Ornella stepped from Mia's bedside and joined her brother at the door. She kissed him on the cheek. "It is the lawyers and the doctors that keep you poor, brother. Don't let your pride make it worse." She removed a bit of lint from his lapel. "You look hand-some. You always look handsome." She wrapped her arms around him and squeezed. "I worry about you and Mia. I pray for you every night and during the day."

Lorenzo wrapped his arms around her shoulders and pulled her tight. He rested his cheek on her head. "Ornella, if something should happen to me—"

"Stop saying that." She pulled back. "It is as if you know something is going to happen. It frightens me."

"I just have to be sure you understand."

"I understand, brother. You have reminded me many times."

"I need to hear it for my own comfort."

"If something should happen to you," she said slowly, "I am to go to your desk and open the top drawer. There I will find a key that fits a safe deposit box in the Napoli Central Bank. Mia's important papers are there. I am to retrieve them."

"And you will do that for me? You'll do that for Mia?"

"Of course I will. You know I will. You shouldn't have to ask. But nothing is going to happen to you."

"Of course nothing is going to happen to me, I'm just being careful." He felt tears rise in his eyes. Before she could see, Lorenzo turned and left. He paused at his front window long enough to catch one more glance at his leukemia-ridden daughter.

BY THE TIME LORENZO pulled his tired Renault into the police parking lot, the sun had emerged full form from the horizon. He checked in with the desk officer and left the station in one of the department's newer patrol cars. It took fifteen minutes for him to work his way along the surface streets after the police barricades that he'd help set up. He parked a block away from the *Miramare Hotel Grande* and covered the remaining distance on foot.

This morning it was his job to check the status of the Naples police officers' stations. There had been a division of labor: Italian army provided snipers stationed on the roofs of many of the surrounding buildings. Secret Service agents and their equivalent from other countries provided in-hotel protection and transportation. The Naples police were to handle crowd control and traffic control. Lorenzo assumed there were other groups doing things he was not privy to. No doubt there were a dozen intelligence agencies hiding in the bushes.

His supervisor Aldo had called for several layers of blockades, each manned by uniformed officers. In every case but one, no one was allowed to pass. Deliveries passed through one blockade and only after each vehicle had been cleared. Should any one of the heads of government want to be driven from the premises, they had to obtain permission first.

Lorenzo made stops at three of the barricades, then made his way to the third of three checkpoints delivery trucks had to clear before being allowed to approach the building.

"There is a delivery van requesting permission to approach," a tall, dark-skinned officer said to Lorenzo.

"From what vendor? Do they have papers and badges?"

The officer said they did.

"Let them pass."

A few moments later a white Mercedes-Benz panel truck drove slowly to the checkpoint where Lorenzo stood. A logo and name on the side of the truck indicated it was owned by a large flower company near Rome.

"I'll take this." Lorenzo waved his hand, and three officers hurried to action. One used a small video camera on a pole to search the undercarriage for explosives; another walked around the vehicle looking for anything out of the ordinary. Lorenzo stepped to the driver's window. "Papers, please."

The man handed him a small stack of orders and a page that identified the driver and company. Lorenzo nodded. "Please pull the hood release."

The driver, a man in his thirties, did. One of the officers checked the engine compartment and pronounced it clear.

"Is the back unlocked?" Lorenzo asked.

"Yes."

"Please turn the engine off and hand me the keys." Lorenzo held out his hands.

The man laughed. "If I were going to run over you, I would have done so by now."

"Please, sir. The keys."

The driver handed them over, and Lorenzo went to the back of the vehicle and opened the double doors. Inside and mounted to the sides were several metal shelves. The floor was covered in buckets filled with flowers. From the back, Lorenzo could see the back of the driver's head and that of a female passenger.

He closed the doors and moved to the passenger side of the vehicle. The woman was young, with smooth, dark skin. She glanced at him then turned away. Around her neck hung a badge like the one the driver wore. Lorenzo recognized it. They were assigned to anyone who needed access to the building. Each badge had a bar code and a radio-frequency identification chip embedded in the plastic.

Lorenzo motioned for the chip reader and one of the officers brought a device that looked very much like a large television remote with a tiny LCD screen. Lorenzo passed it over the badge and nodded. He then returned to the other side of the vehicle and passed the scanner over the driver's badge.

"How long will you be in the building?"

"Until nearly noon," the driver said. "We have to cut and arrange the flowers to make the centerpieces for the lunch gathering."

"You must wear these badges at all times. Is that understood?"

"Si, officer."

Lorenzo looked to the woman. "Do you understand about the badges, signora?"

"Si."

"Let them pass." Lorenzo said and stepped away from the vehicle and watched it drive toward the building.

He felt ill.

DELARAM WAS A VICTIM, not a co-conspirator. At least she felt that way until the policeman looked her in the eye, read her badge, and she said nothing. The only image her mind could form was that of her parents being killed in the slowest, most painful manner.

"You behaved like a noble woman." Abasi glanced at her, his perfect white teeth shining between his lips. Delaram wondered if she were strong enough to knock any of them out.

Abasi drove the flower truck down a drive and into the basement of the hotel. Light from fluorescent fixtures encased in protective wire mesh replaced the first rays of sunshine.

Darkness seemed to follow Delaram. They had left the villa in the dead of night, traveled dark dirt roads, flown in a large helicopter over night-shrouded hills. She'd sat in the helicopter, half afraid they would crash, half afraid they wouldn't.

The helicopter landed at an abandoned private airport. Delaram had lost her sense of direction minutes after take off. She tried to use the pale glow on the horizon to determine which direction was east, but sunrise had been too far off. She couldn't tell if she was gazing at the sun's first rays or the glow of a city. To make matters worse, the pilot changed directions a dozen times. Filled with despair that mounted with every hour, Delaram gave up trying, gave up hoping, and gave up thinking.

By the time the helicopter landed and she and the other women were loaded into four SUVs of different makes, Delaram had fallen into such despair that she moved like a zombie. As far as she was concerned, her life had already ended. An hour, maybe two later, Abasi pulled the SUV onto the back alley of an industrial district. A string of warehouses bracketed the alley. The press of a button on a remote opened one of the wide loading doors. Abasi pulled the car in, stopped, exited, but left the motor running.

"You. Out." He pointed at Delaram. She slipped from her place in the backseat. The space was nearly empty. A white, flower delivery van was parked to one side. The space smelled of motor oil made slightly pleasant by an ocean breeze. She was close to the ocean.

"Get in the van. Passenger seat."

Delaram did. Perhaps it would all be over soon. Maybe her death could save her parents. The thought brought no comfort.

Waiting for them had been a round man in a jogging suit. He looked ridiculous and dangerous. He took Abasi's place behind the steering wheel and backed the SUV out of the work bay. The moment he was clear, the large, metal rolling door began to close.

Delaram caught Abasi staring at her. As the door closed, he raised an eyebrow.

CHAPTER 21

THE ITALIAN MILITARY PILOT landed the AW109 helicopter at the civilian airport. Two men stood a short distance away to avoid the rotor blast. Both wore suits.

Moyer waited for a moment for the pilot to power down the rotor, then slid the door open and led his team onto the tarmac. He wondered what an observer would have thought seeing seven men dressed in black from head to foot and carrying automatic weapons. It didn't seem to intimidate the two waiting men. Moyer marched to their position standing just a few feet away. No one spoke. The roar and whine of the helicopter's engine drowned out any possible conversation.

Moyer turned in time to see their ride lift off the pad and fly away.

"Sergeant Major Eric Moyer, I presume?" the shorter of the two men said. He was handsome and projected an air of unshakable confidence. He held out his hand. Moyer took it.

"I am. And you are?"

"Captain Aldo Gronchi of the Napoli police. My friend here is closer to your home. May I introduce Agent Mitchell Baker of the United States Secret Service."

Mitchell shook Moyer's hand. It was a strong grip, and Moyer could tell the man was very familiar with the gym. "Before we go any further, I need to ask a favor."

"A favor?"

"Please hold out your hand." Mitchell removed an electronic device from his inner suit pocket. It was about the size of a cell phone.

Moyer held out his right hand. Mitchell took hold of Moyer's index finger and placed it on the glass surface of the device. A second later it beeped.

"Sergeant Major Eric Moyer. Verified." Mitchell moved to Rich and repeated the procedure. "Rich Harbison, Master Sergeant." Mitchell continued through the team until each man had been verified.

"Does it say what I like on my hot dogs?" Rich asked.

"No, but it says you should call your mother more often."

The team laughed.

Mitchell turned to Moyer. "You understand my need to verify your identities. You are packing some heavy firepower."

"I understand. I'd have been worried if you hadn't."

"I assume you've been brought up to speed." Moyer spoke more to Mitchell than Aldo.

"We've been briefed by your commander. It is your opinion that El-Sayyed is headed here."

"He's probably already in the area. Scratch that. His history shows that he disappears shortly before any terrorist activity."

"And you think that activity is aimed at the G-20."

"It's our best guess so far. Captain thinks El-Sayyed might be targeting Christian sites in Rome."

"That seems to make sense," Aldo said.

"So does attacking the G-20."

Aldo smiled. "An impossible task, Sergeant Major. There are twenty security teams, one from each country. My men have gone to great lengths to coordinate and bolster the security that is already present. The Italian Army is involved."

"The place is locked up like a drum," Mitchell said. "Captain Gronchi is correct. The G-20 would be the worst possible target. Any attempt at assassination is doomed to failure. The Christian shrines in Rome make more sense. Although covered with security, they are more approachable targets."

Moyer's jaw tightened. "Are you suggesting we go home?"

"Of course not, just voicing my view," Mitchell said. "We have a van. Please follow me."

"Where are we going?" Rich asked.

"To prove our point."

THE LARGE FORD VAN moved through the streets of Naples, fighting airport traffic and the early morning rush hour. The sun had cleared the horizon and wasted no time climbing the morning sky. Moyer viewed it through tinted windows.

Aldo drove; Mitchell sat in the front seat, Moyer in the seat behind him. His men were spread out in the fifteen-passenger van. They sat in silence. Others would have missed it, but Moyer knew his team well enough to know that some serious teeth grinding was going on. They were not used to having their leader doubted.

"You have a military bearing, Agent Baker."

"Navy. Ten years."

Someone in the back snickered.

"Eight as a SEAL."

The snickering stopped. A Navy SEAL team had changed the tide in a firefight in Venezuela. Had they not shown at the right time, the team would be buried in a foreign cemetery.

"See any action?"

"Some here and there. You know the drill. Did a tour in the first Gulf War."

"What did you do there?" J. J. asked, breaking the team's silence.

"This and that."

The three words said it all. Agent Baker had been involved in Spec Ops. No details would be forthcoming.

"Why did you leave the Navy?"

"The Treasury Department recruited me. Being able to go home most days and tickle my kids made it an enticing offer."

"Understood," Moyer said, less angry with the man.

Twenty minutes later Aldo directed the van down a side street. Out the window Moyer could see men and women in police uniforms manning barricades. He also caught a glimpse of an Army sniper on the roof and a helicopter circling overhead.

"Tell me about the barricades," Zinsser asked.

Moyer shot him an icy glance.

"That's Captain Gronchi's area."

"There are three lines of barricades, and they stretch from the ocean around several blocks in which the G-20 hotel is located. The first barricade is manned by my officers. The streets and sidewalks are blocked by metal barriers. The next line of barricades has the same barriers with the addition of spike strips to stop any vehicle that runs the blockade. The third barricade line includes steel stanchions."

"What about foot traffic?" Moyer asked.

"Foot traffic is allowed only in certain areas. We have to allow for some movement since there are several office buildings and apartments in the inner ring."

"You're wondering if someone—like a suicide bomber—could walk into the hotel." Agent Mitchell turned to face Moyer. "We've taken that into account. No one can approach the hotel without clearing security and without the possession of a security card—a RFID badge. The system is foolproof."

"There's no such thing," Zinsser said. "There is always a chink in the armor somewhere."

"We know what we're doing, soldier," Mitchell said. "We've been at this for a long time."

Zinsser started to say something, but Moyer cut him off with an upraised hand. "No one doubts your professionalism, Agent. We're just curious."

Mitchell turned forward again and opened the glove compartment. When he turned again he was holding a handful of badges with neck strings. "These badges carry your necessary ID on a RFID chip. You must keep them on at all times in and around the G-20 hotel. We have monitors on every floor, in the elevators, and even the bathrooms. Lose your badge and pass one of the monitors and agents from my team will be on you like ugly on an ape."

"I assume the monitors keep a log of who passes by," Zinsser said.

"You must be the tech guy for the team," Mitchell said.

"Me and Pete."

"That's the big change in the military. Everything is digital."

"Except bullets," J. J. said.

"And you must be the weapons guy."

"Guilty as charged."

"You guys scare me."

J. J. smiled. "That's the point."

Mitchell handed the badges to Moyer, who passed them around.

Aldo pulled the van to a stop at a barricade. A peach-faced officer approached the driver's side window. "Good morning, Capitano. How are you?"

"I am fine. Everything fine here?"

"Boring, sir."

Aldo nodded. "As it should be."

The officer scanned Aldo's card with a handheld device. "How are your roses, sir?"

"Yellow as usual."

The man nodded and stepped away.

"Roses?" J. J. said. "You grow roses?"

Aldo chuckled. "I can't grow mold. The question was code. If I said anything other than yellow, we all would be looking down the boreholes of several weapons."

"Ah."

At the second barricade, the procedure was repeated. The police officers not only had to move the barricade but the spike strip in front of it.

"There it is," Mitchell said, pointing at a multistory hotel.

"Glamorous digs," Jose said.

"I wouldn't mind living here," Mitchell said.

Aldo pulled to the final barricade, standing twenty meters in front of the opening to the basement parking. This time several men approached the van. One carried a device on a pole that Moyer identified as a video camera used to check the undercarriage of the vehicle. Two other men circled the vehicle.

"How was the drive, Capitano?"

"Usual traffic, Lorenzo."

"May I scan your badge, sir?"

Aldo held it out.

"How was your meal last night, sir?"

"Not enough garlic."

More code.

"Please turn off your engine, sir, and unlock your doors."

Aldo did and the man he called Lorenzo walked to the passenger side. He opened the passenger side door and scanned Mitchell's badge. Moyer noticed the other officers stood back, one on each side of the vehicle, with their hands on their sidearms. A bad guy might be able to take down Lorenzo, but a second later the van would look like Bonnie and Clyde's car.

Moyer decided to be helpful: he slid open the side doors. A half second later, Lorenzo and his men had their weapons drawn and pointed into the passenger compartment. Moyer noticed that each weapon was held in steady hands.

"Don't move!" Lorenzo commanded.

"Um, Captain?" Moyer said to Aldo.

"I don't interfere with my men's work. I suggest you do as he says."

Moyer thought he heard Mitchell snicker.

Lorenzo approached, handgun extended. "Hands on your head."

"His English is good," Rich said.

Moyer and the others put their hands on their heads. Lorenzo shouted something in Italian. Officers, one with a Beretta AR-70, rounded the van and brought the sights to bear on Moyer and the others. Lorenzo holstered his weapon and approached. Without a word he snatched Moyer's badge and scanned it. He faced Rich, who sat next to Moyer. "Slowly remove your badge and hand it to me." Rich did and Lorenzo held it to the scanner. He repeated the procedure with each member of the team, then stepped away.

"My apologies, gentlemen," he said. The other officers lowered their weapons.

"For a moment we thought you might be up to no good. Next time, please wait for instruction."

"No apology necessary. At least not from you." Moyer turned his attention to Mitchell, who was doing his best to hold back laughter.

Lorenzo walked back to the driver's side window. "You are free to pass, sir."

"Thank you, Lorenzo."

The barricades were removed. Aldo started the van and crept forward.

"Was all that necessary?" Rich asked. "It's not like he didn't know you."

"If he had not acted as he did, I would have fired him."

A moment of silence passed, then Mitchell guffawed. His laughter filled the van.

"Something funny?" Moyer asked.

"The whole thing." Mitchell continued to laugh. "Wait until the president hears about this."

"Swell," Moyer said. "Just swell."

TONY NASSER PULLED THE sixty-five-foot super-yacht from a private dock in Salerno thirty miles south of Naples and directed the multimillion dollar craft toward open ocean. The *Sea Witch* cruised easily through the water and gentle swells, its sleek form parting the water at its bow as easily as a jet aircraft knifed through high-altitude air. Off her stern flew a Danish flag.

The yacht had once belonged to an oil executive with Denmark's leading oil company. Several bad deals, the dropping of oil prices, and an affair with the CEO's wife led to a change in his income. To pay legal fees and to counter allegations of insider trading, the man decided to liquidate some of his property, including the *Sea Witch*. El-Sayyed was happy to buy it—not directly of course, but through one of his dummy corporations. He bought it sight unseen and had never set foot on the vessel.

Nasser, however, had sailed her many times, all in preparation for this day. He learned quickly. While he would never trust himself to sail it across the Atlantic, he knew he could manage the mission before him.

Once clear of the bay, Nasser activated the auto pilot and left the cabin. On the rear deck, twenty bikini-clad beauties—none over the age of thirty—danced to loud music and sipped beer from bottles even though the sun was barely up. Each had brought a boyfriend.

The party had been planned and promoted for months. Nasser had spent time in upper-end night clubs catering to the upcoming generation of Hedonists. He never went home with the women, but he did buy drinks for them and their friends.

Today they were on an ocean-going party to celebrate Nasser's new acquisition: a Hollywood studio. When asked the company's name, he demurred, saying the lawyers had warned him to be discreet. He spent money like he printed it himself. That was proof enough.

He walked through the crowd. Several of the women approached him, running their hands over his shoulders or along his face. He could only imagine how they would behave once they were deep into the liquor.

DELARAM CUT THE STEMS of roses, placed them in thin glass vases, and framed them with baby's breath.

"Make them look good." Abasi removed another stack of flowers from the large, white pails they had transported them in. "Show some pride in your work."

Delaram looked at him. "There is no pride in what we do."

"It must be done. You do it to save your parents."

"And why do you do it?"

"I do it to further Allah's kingdom and to punish the infidels. You will be honored."

"None of your kind will remember me. Just my parents, assuming you keep your promise. Are you religious men people of your word?"

"If it serves the greater good."

"In other words, no."

He raised a hand to strike her.

"Careful," she said. "Someone will certainly notice the bruise."

He lowered his hand. "Do as you are told. Women like you cannot understand why brave men like me do what we do."

"Insanity?"

Abasi struck her on the back of head so hard her knees buckled.

"Get up. I know other places where bruises won't show."

Delaram steadied herself, forcing back the hot gorge that rose in her throat. A minute later the large dining room stopped spinning.

"No more talk. We are falling behind schedule."

Standing erect, Delaram tried to clear her mind. She lifted a hand and touched the heavy vest under her maternity dress. The irony struck her again: Those who saw her assumed she was about to give life; instead, she was about to take it.

CHAPTER 22

AFTER ALDO PARKED THE van, Mitchell led the team through the underground parking lot to a set of elevators. Before they exited the vehicle, Aldo said his goodbyes and shook Moyer's hand.

"Thanks for the ride . . . and the excitement." Aldo offered a small, polite smile. "You're going to go back to your men and have a good laugh, aren't you?"

"Certainly not. That would be rude."

"You'll forgive me if I don't believe you."

Mitchell swiped a keycard through a slot on the button panel. "Direct ascent to the top floor," he said.

"So, can I talk you out of telling the president about our being held at gunpoint by Italian police or do I have to shoot you?"

"It might be worth being shot." Mitchell moved his gaze from the lit floor numbers over the elevator door. "Maybe I'll just let you tell him."

"Yeah, right. I forgot to RSVP for lunch."

"He wants to see you," Mitchell said. "In fact, he insisted on it."

"When?" Moyer had trouble processing what he heard.

Mitchell looked at his watch. "In about fifteen minutes. You'll have only a few minutes with him. He's meeting with the Prime Minister of Canada and the President of Mexico. Sort of a North American Summit. First, I want to show you something."

"When you say the president wants to meet with you, do you mean just me, or the whole team?"

"The whole team. As you know, he loves the military. He never served, and I think he feels guilty about it."

"Well," J. J. said, "as commander in chief, he is serving now."

"Roger that," Mitchell said. "Just so you know, he cheers for Navy in the Army-Navy game."

"Then I won't bring up their embarrassing loss last December."

"You'd be wise not to."

The elevator stopped at the top floor with a slight lurch. When they stepped from the cab, several men in suits stopped, stared, and then reached under their suit coats.

"Stand down," Mitchell said firmly. "They're with me."

Moyer watched the eyes of half a dozen Secret Service agents shift to the ID card he wore around his neck.

"I'm thinking we ought to stow our gear," Rich said. "I'm getting tired of getting the evil eye."

"You won't be seeing POTUS with weapons in hand," Mitchell said. "You can keep them in the weapons locker in Oz."

"What does POTUS mean?" De Luca asked.

Mitchell glanced at the Italian. "President of the United States."

They stopped at the end of the hall. Two agents stood by a pair of double doors. Mitchell said nothing to them as they stepped aside. Mitchell ran his ID card over a reader mounted to the wall and a solid click emerged from the lock. Mitchell swung the doors open.

Inside Moyer saw an array of monitors with male and female agents watching them. A large table dominated the center of the room. Rolls of blueprints cluttered the surface. To one side was a large metal cabinet, the kind used to store weapons.

"This way." Mitchell walked to the cabinet, passed his ID card over the reader, and the doors swung open. "Sergeant Major, please secure your weapons and store them here."

"Will my ID open this?"

"Nope. You'll need me or one of our shift supervisors to open the locker."

Moyer didn't move.

"Look, gentlemen, I know you Army guys love your weapons. So do federal agents, but this hotel has the top leaders of twenty countries here. Certain rules had to be set up. This is one of them."

"Do as the man says," Moyer ordered.

"I suppose that means sidearms too," J. J. said.

"I'm afraid so: sidearms, body armor, knives—anything and everything that looks like a weapon."

Moyer looked in the locker and saw enough weapons to wage a war on a small country including sniper rifles, M5-A4s, and several Close Quarter Battle Receivers, a version of the M4A1 his team carried. Moyer set his M4 assault rifle in an empty portion of the rack and set his M9 on one of the shelves. He slipped from his "kit" and set it inside the locker. The others did the same.

"I want a receipt," J. J. said.

"You got something better—my word that no one will mess with your gear."

Mitchell closed the doors to the gun cabinet, and Moyer heard the lock set.

Mitchell checked his watch again. "We have enough time for me to put to rest some of your doubts." He looked at Zinsser. "The monitors you see are tied to street cameras mounted around the area. We can see everything for five blocks out and the ocean to our west. The small marina is closed to traffic for the next few days." He pointed at a special bank of monitors. "These monitor hot spots."

"Hot spots?" Rich said.

"If you've followed the meetings—the G-8, the G-20—there are always protests. The numbers can get pretty large, upwards of twenty thousand. The Italians thought it best to create areas where people can congregate. There will be media there so the protesters should be happy. The Naples police with the backing of the Italian army have those areas as part of their responsibility. Their job is to handle crowd control. It wouldn't do to have Americans taking on Italian citizens."

Mitchell touched his ear and tilted his head slightly to the right. Moyer had taken notice of the ear monitor the moment he stepped up to the agent at the airport. "The president is ready for you. Follow me."

Over his career Moyer had met high-ranking military leaders, briefed generals, and once gave a verbal report to the secretary of defense, and he had done so without a sense of intimidation. Meeting the president, however, was different. He had given scores of briefings to bigwigs, but he always had time to prepare. Just one more source of tension.

Moyer wished he had voted for the man.

DELARAM'S HEART AND MIND were numb.

Helplessness had given way to despondency. Hope seemed a distant memory, a foggy recollection that lived in a distant time that Delaram could barely remember. She was shutting down. With each minute that passed what remained of optimism dripped away.

She reconciled herself to the one fact that rattled most in her brain: Today was the day she would die.

The dining room began to vibrate with activity. Several men in suits gave orders to workers dressed in white who moved between round tables covered with white lace tablecloths. Five tables dominated the center of the room; a dozen others formed a perimeter around them. Their tablecloths were red. The center tables had eight padded chairs: enough for forty diners. Delaram noticed the workers had paired the seats so they formed four sets of two. Husbands and wives, she decided. She also decided the tables with the red tablecloths were for assistants, or maybe the media. She couldn't be certain.

Male and female workers set the tables with linen napkins, ornate silverware, crystal goblets, tumblers for drinks, and cups for coffee. The employees worked at a steady but unrushed pace. Abasi had told her they were setting flowers for a lunch meeting. A walnut lectern stood near the window wall that overlooked the ocean. The window was tinted, and Delaram guessed that people could see out the window but not in.

"Slower," Abasi said to Delaram. "We will wait until the servants have left the room before we set the vases."

"They're employees, not servants."

"What do I care? They work for infidels."

Delaram glanced at her captor. "The way I see it, so do you."

She saw him start to raise his hand, then lower it. He would not strike her in front of the others. Delaram returned to clipping the bottom of rose stems and setting them in the vases. The vest she wore rubbed against the worktable at which she stood. Because of her attempt to activate the vest back at the villa, her bomb had been altered. Abasi had to arm it first. Only then could she trigger the explosion. If she failed to do so, then Abasi could do it himself at a distance.

Delaram clipped another rose stem.

CHAPTER 23

MITCHELL, TRAILED BY MOYER and his men, walked to a pair of double doors a few strides from the communication center. Two agents eyed them as they approached. Mitchell nodded at the men. "Raptor is expecting us."

One of the agents knocked on the door.

"Raptor?" J. J. said.

"Every member of the presidential team gets a code name. The president is 'Raptor,' the first lady is 'Turtledove.'"

"Good thing it's not the other way around," Rich said.

"She picked her own name; we assigned his. The secretary of state is 'Vagabond.' Seems apropos."

"We know a little about nicknames," Moyer said.

A tall, thin man in a dark suit and red tie answered the door.

"Good morning, Mitch." The man had a deep Southern accent. Moyer guessed Virginia.

"Morning, Jimmie."

Jimmie stepped aside, and the men entered the spacious suite. Once everyone had cleared the threshold, Jimmie closed the door and locked it.

The entrance led to a sitting room with expensive and antique looking furniture. A man in a yellow pullover sweater and a pair of khaki Dockers rose from the sofa. The woman sitting next to him turned and smiled. Both had gray hair, pleasant smiles, and tanned skin. The president seemed shorter than Moyer expected.

"Come in, gentlemen, come in." The president's voice was smooth, powerful, and rode on a wave of unshakable confidence.

"Mr. President," Agent Mitchell said. "May I present the Army Special Ops team we spoke of before? This is Sergeant Major Eric Moyer, team leader."

The president stepped forward and shook Moyer's hand. "Ted Huffington, Sergeant Major. I'm pleased to meet you."

"The pleasure is all mine," Moyer said. For a moment he felt he should bow then corrected himself. *The guys would never let me forget that.*

"This is my wife, Marni. She's the real brains of the operation."

"Not the brains, honey, just the heart."

Huffington chortled. "If you say so, dear." He looked back at Moyer and the others. "It pays to be diplomatic at home as well as on the world stage."

"Yes, sir," Moyer said.

The president turned to Jimmie. "We could use a few more chairs, Jimmie."

"I'll bring some from the dining area, sir."

"Pete," Moyer said.

"Yes." A second later. "Oh. Of course." He spoke to Jimmie. "Let me help."

A few minutes later four straight-back chairs were brought in. Moyer and Rich took seats on the second sofa directly opposite the president and his wife. De Luca sat in a leather reading chair. The rest of the team took spots on the dining room chairs. Mitchell stood by the door. It looked like something he did often.

Another knock came on the door. Mitchell answered before Jimmie could take two steps. A woman with dark hair entered. Moyer had seen her on television.

"Ah, glad you could make it, Brownie," the president said. "Gentlemen, this is Helen Brown, my chief of staff. She may be the smartest person you ever meet."

"Are you trying to make me blush, Mr. President?"

Moyer guessed the woman hadn't blushed in many years.

"Of course not. Facts are facts."

Marni Huffington rose. "Well, I'll let you talk. I'll watch Jimmie get your suit ready."

"Don't let her fool you. She's going to watch Italian soap operas."

"Don't make me hit you, dear," Marni said.

"She wouldn't dare. Mitchell would protect me. Isn't that right, Mitch?"

"Maybe."

The comment brought smiles. Moyer admired the president's ability to put people at ease.

Huffington patted the spot where his wife had sat a few moments before, and Helen sat.

"The sergeant major was about to introduce his team to me."

Moyer took his cue. He motioned to Rich. "This is Rich Harbison, assistant team leader; Jose Medina is the team medic; Pete Rasor specializes in surveillance and communications; J. J. Bartley, weapons and explosives; Jerry Zinsser, electronics and doubles on communications. Our Italian liaison is Captain Ilario De Luca, of the Italian Army. He's our in-country intel man."

The president's expression saddened. "When I was first made aware of your mission, I failed to make the connection." He paused for a moment. "You lost a man last year? In Venezuela?"

"Yes, sir. Martin Caraway. He was a good soldier."

"You did good work down there and got no credit for it."

"We were just doing our duty. We are proud to serve."

Huffington nodded. "It's men like you that make me proud to be commander in chief."

"Thank you, sir."

"Fill me in on your mission?"

"Sir?"

"I want to know how your mission is going."

"Excuse me, sir. I just assumed you were being briefed."

Huffington leaned forward. "Sometimes information is slower than I like, especially when I'm out of country."

Moyer noticed Helen Brown shift in her seat.

"Yes, sir." Moyer spent the next ten minutes briefing the president on everything they had experienced since being deployed.

"And you think that El-Sayyed has targeted the G-20?"

"It's our best guess, sir, and the most important one."

"The Italians think the target is in Rome. You don't think that's important?"

"It's very important, Mr. President, but not as important as the lives of twenty of the world's leaders, their spouses, and staff."

"Good answer."

"Captain De Luca has maintained contact with his people in Rome and a manhunt is underway."

Helen Brown spoke for the first time since entering the room. "Agent Baker tells me this facility is the safest place on the planet with the possible exception of Fort Knox. Is that right, Mitchell?"

"Yes, ma'am."

Helen turned back to Moyer. "So why the concern?"

Moyer didn't like her tone. "We've been given a mission, ma'am. My job is to successfully complete that mission as efficiently and secretly as possible. My gut tells me El-Sayyed has targeted this area."

"Your gut?" Helen smirked. "The president likes evidence a little more solid than a gut feeling."

"I can speak for myself, Brownie," Huffington said. "Mitchell?"

"Yes, Mr. President."

"You've done a few spec ops missions in your day. Given your experience, would you trust the work you and the others have done or the sergeant major's gut."

To Moyer's surprise, Mitchell Baker didn't respond immediately.

"Is there a problem, Mitch?" Huffington asked.

"No, Mr. President. No problem at all."

Helen furrowed her brow. "What? Are you saying that Mr. Moyer's gut takes precedence over months of planning and implantation? You've repeatedly told us this location is secure. So what is it? Your skill or his gut?"

Another several moments passed before Mitch said, "His gut."

"What?" Clearly the president's chief of staff was nonplussed. "You mean to tell me that the hotel isn't secure?"

"With all due respect, Helen, I said nothing of the kind. I would stake my life on our preparations. . . . Actually, I've staked your life on our preparations. . . ."

"But?"

"Let the man speak, Brownie."

"Mr. President, as you know I've seen my share of military missions. Sometimes all a sailor—soldier in this case—has to go on is his gut. I've seen the lives of men saved on gut-level responses. If the Sergeant Major says something is up, I say we take it seriously."

The president ran a hand over his chin. "I can't go changing the schedule at this late date, Mitch."

"Mr. President, I wouldn't change a thing that we have done. We have done everything possible. As far as I'm concerned, our security is perfect." He paused to glance at Zinsser. "I'm just saying that we shouldn't dismiss Moyer's intuition."

"So we continue on as planned."

"Yes, sir, unless something comes up."

"Why did you look at . . ." The president shifted his gaze to Zinsser.

"Jerry Zinsser, sir," Zinsser said.

"Why did you look at Zinsser a moment ago?"

Agent Baker hesitated again. Zinsser didn't. "I mentioned that no security plan is perfect."

"Really. You don't trust our Secret Service."

Moyer tensed and hoped Zinsser was thinking clearly.

"The skills of the Secret Service are legendary, sir. It's just that all complex systems have weak links."

"Weak links? Like what?"

Zinsser scooted to the edge of his chair. "The weak links are often overlooked. They tend to be mundane or obvious. For example, not long ago our country—the whole world really—was in a recession. Someone dubbed it Depression 2.0."

"I remember."

"Of course, sir. As you know, many businesses went belly-up . . . bankrupt. Hundreds of them. What do you suppose they did with all their paperwork?"

"Destroyed . . . no, they couldn't destroy it all. Many documents would have to be saved."

"Yes, sir. Many of them rented storage sheds and filled them to the rafters. Depending on the business . . . let's say a mortgage broker . . . those documents would contain sensitive material like social security numbers. If I wanted to steal a few thousand identities, I would pay off or threaten one of the workers at the storage company. Most of those people don't make much money, so a few thousand would go a long way in making someone look the other way."

"We've done background checks on everyone," Helen said.

"Really? How many employees are in the building right now?"

"Seventy-five," Mitchell said. "Not one has a police record."

"Do any of them have a sick child or parent? Do any of them owe bookie money? Are any of them financially stretched?"

"Not that we can tell," Mitchell said.

"That's my point," Zinsser said. "Any one of them could be bought off."

"I doubt that," Helen said.

"I don't. Our history is filled with people who committed traitorous acts. You can start with Benedict Arnold and move forward. Arnold was a war hero and trusted by everyone. Name an intelligence agency or branch of government and I can name someone who sold out."

"How does that affect what we're doing here?"

"El-Sayyed is a man of great wealth and influence." Zinsser pushed back in his seat. "We know that he's been able to influence women into turning themselves into walking bombs."

"Terrorists have used religious zealotry to recruit martyrs for centuries," the president said.

Zinsser looked at Moyer like a child who is afraid they have gone too far. "Finish it," Moyer said.

"Sir, the female bombers are not religious zealots. They could be anybody."

Huffington blinked a few times, then looked to Mitchell. "So now what?"

"We're ready, sir, but I'll alert the other security teams and the local police to be on the alert for anyone, especially women, who seem out of place."

The president stood and everyone in the room joined him. "I hope your gut is wrong, Moyer."

"Me too, Mr. President."

"Mitch, get these gentlemen some rooms and chow. They look tired and hungry."

"Yes, sir."

"Forgive me for being rude, gentlemen, but I'm expecting company in five minutes."

Mitchell opened the door, and Moyer led his men from the room.

CHAPTER 24

ERMANNO GRECO BANKED HIS F2 Eurofighter Typhoon north and took in the scenery of the Bay of Naples: the cerulean water, the soft colors of the buildings lining the coast, the white pleasure craft moored at private docks. Activity at the marina was almost nonexistent. Ermanno could see several large military vehicles blocking access to the service roads and walkways. Two police boats patrolled close to shore; two Italian navy MK V-C Interceptor patrol boats cruised deeper water in lazy circles. Lookouts stood on deck, binoculars to their eyes. In the distance a cargo ship pressed slowly through the water. A cruise ship, which Ermanno guessed was headed to Crete, plowed through the ocean leaving a long, white prop wash in its wake.

Ermanno had only been in the air fifteen minutes after relieving another pilot in another F2 Typhoon. He had several hours of slow patrol around Naples. At least he was flying and even a boring day flying was better than most days doing anything else. What he most wanted to do was push the thrusters to the stops, pull back on the control, and race skyward, but his mission didn't include flights of daring. He was to patrol and be ready for a problem.

The first part was ironic. Although he flew at just a few thousand feet above sea level, he knew radar would see any approaching aircraft before he did. He was in the air to stop any madman from flying a plane into the building. It had been done before. Several other military attack planes were armed and ready to take to the air on a moment's notice.

Leveling the aircraft, he began the inbound leg of his circuit. As he did, he took note of one other ocean craft: a large, sleek, white yacht making its way south. It was too distant for him to see with accuracy, but he was certain he saw a group of people on deck. Some looked like women. Ermanno decided he'd take a closer look on the next pass.

J. J. WAS TOO wired to sleep. He had only slept a few hours over the last two days, but instead of feeling exhaustion he was amped. He had just met the president. Wait until Tess heard about that. "The hand you now hold, sweetheart, once shook the hand of the most powerful man on the planet."

"It's sweaty."

The response took place only in J. J.'s mind, but he was certain it was the kind of quip Tess would make. It was one of the things he loved about her: she could give as well as she could take. He was used to exchanging barbs with the guys. It was one of the ways they dealt with the work they had to do.

Agent Mitchell Baker had taken the men to the first-floor restaurant for a hearty breakfast. Rich ate two meals, for which he endured a fusillade of kidding.

After breakfast Moyer dismissed the men to the rooms Mitchell had arranged. Only Pete and Jose took up the offer. De Luca excused himself and had his cell phone to his ear before he had exited the restaurant, no doubt reporting in with his superiors.

J. J. had tried to snag a few winks, but his mind would not shut down. He decided the strong Italian coffee he had consumed with breakfast had been unwise. Television was no good since he didn't speak Italian, and the only English channel he could find was the BBC showing reruns of *Dr. Who.*

Leaving his second-floor room, J. J. returned to the restaurant. The sight of most of his team in one of the booths didn't surprise him.

"Hey, look who came back," Rich said. "Sandman refused to visit?"

"He left a note saying he wore himself out trying to put you under."

Rich waved a dismissive hand. "The guy's a wimp. Besides, sleep is a crutch."

Moyer nodded. "You got that right."

J. J. took a seat and ordered a latte, then addressed Zinsser who sat at the end of the booth. "That was quite a lecture you gave the president."

"It wasn't a lecture, kid. I was just trying to correct a misconception. You know as well as I do that overconfidence kills."

"Absolutely," Rich said. "Still, you did lay it on a little thick."

"My social filter was damaged in Somalia."

"Yeah," Rich said, "I guess we leave a little of ourselves behind with each mission."

"So what now, Boss?" J. J. asked.

"Nothing. We're out of our element here. This operation is in the hands of others. I've reported in and have been told to stay put. Since the meetings officially began this morning, the Secret Service has cut off all inbound and outbound traffic. No one walks in; no one walks out without an escort, and Agent Baker said he can't spare the men."

"He's a cautious one, that Baker," Rich said.

"He's paid to be paranoid." Moyer spoke with admiration.

"Okay, if I'm out of line here, just say so," J. J. said. "But what happened back at the minibus? I never could figure out what you were saying, Zinsser."

Moyer didn't hesitate. "You're out of line."

"Understood, Boss." J. J. noticed Zinsser direct his gaze into his coffee cup.

"I'm not used to staying out of the way," Moyer said, pushing his coffee away. "Part of me hopes I'm wrong about El-Sayyed's plan; part of me wants to be right."

"This is a huge target," Rich said. "We all agreed that this must be what he has in mind—well, all but our Italian friend."

"He makes a good argument, but I think he's wrong. Sure, blowing up historic Christian sites in Rome would get the world's attention, but it doesn't fit with the other bombings. Several of those sites were considered for the G-20 meeting. It's as if El-Sayyed was herding the world leaders here."

"Makes sense to me." Rich yawned. "Well, I'm heading to my room to take care of all this coffee I've been drinking and to catch a little shut-eye. Someone will let me know before we bug out?"

"Maybe," J. J. said.

"Cute. Don't you have a Bible study to lead or something?"

"My brother is the chaplain, Shaq, not me. I'm just the plain, ordinary kind of Christian." J. J. moved so Rich could slip from the booth.

"Plain is right. I don't know what that beautiful fiancée sees in you."

"She loves my wit and high intelligence."

"Hang on, Rich. I'll walk with you."

J. J. watched the team leaders cross the restaurant and disappear into the lobby, then glanced at Zinsser, who was still gazing into his cup. "I'm sorry, man. I crossed the line with that question."

"Yeah, you did."

"Like I said, I'm sorry."

Zinsser looked up. To J. J., he looked like a man who hadn't slept in a month. "Don't sweat it. I'm sure Moyer will spill the beans after the mission."

"Sounds like you're going somewhere."

"Maybe. Who knows?"

J. J. studied the man. He had seen stressed out soldiers before and, at the moment, Zinsser could be their poster boy. "Okay, fair warning. I'm going to cross the line again so get prepared to tell me to shut up and mind my own business."

Zinsser gave a mirthless chuckle. "I'm always ready to do that."

"You look like a man who's carrying more than his fair share of guilt."

"Is this where you whip out a Bible and give me an unwanted sermon?"

"Bible? Oh, you're talking about Rich's dig about me being a Christian. Well, I'm guilty as charged."

"And proud of it."

J. J. shook his head. "I'm not ashamed, but *proud* is the wrong word. As far as a Bible goes, I have one—in my vest. I'll talk with you all day about my faith and the Bible, but you can relax. I don't do sermons and I don't force things down anyone's throat. I'll leave you alone if you want."

"Nah, I'm just . . . I'm just being me. Sorry." He paused. "What's a Christian like you doing in an Army like this? I've known other Christian soldiers but I never understood them. I mean, aren't they like polar opposites?"

"It sure seems like it at times."

"Not only are you Army, but you're spec ops—and the chief weapons and demo guy."

"I've asked that question of myself a million times, but it's clear I'm right where God wants me to be."

"Killing people?"

"The only people I kill are trying to kill me or the innocent . . ." J. J. broke eye contact and his heart seemed to labor.

"What? I know that look. I see it in the mirror every day. You regret something."

J. J. nodded. "Yeah, in a way."

"It's none of my business."

"Sure it is, Zinsser. You need to know who's fighting by your side."

"If you insist. I've got the time."

J. J. sipped his coffee. "We were doing a surveillance op in Afghanistan—I guess it was about a year and a half ago. We did a HALO drop and speed marched up one of the mountains and tried to get a bead on an insurgent camp. We were dug in when one of those stupid things happened. We had a team member. His name was Caraway."

"The guy I replaced."

"Yeah, he died on an op in Venezuela."

"A good soldier?"

"Yeah, but a lousy person. He hated me. Mostly because of my faith."

"And you seem so lovable." Apparently Zinsser was relaxing some.

"Somehow, Caraway's rucksack developed a tear. Probably from the rough landing on the parachute jump. Anyway, he liked to pack trail mix on missions. It was his superstition. A few half-starved goats got wind of the trail mix and gave away our position.

We tried to lay low but two men appeared a short distance away. Both carried AK-47s, but you know how it is in Afghanistan: every adult male carries an automatic weapon. They pointed our way. We assumed they might be a Taliban patrol."

"So you popped them."

"Yeah. Several of us fired, but I'm sure I got my rounds off first."

"Let me guess, you killed a couple of shepherds."

J. J. answered with a nod. "I doubt they had anything to do with the Taliban camp."

"Did they give you away?"

J. J. shrugged. "In a way. The shock of being shot made one of the men yank the trigger of his weapon. The noise brought bad guys running up the hill by the dozens."

"How did you get out?"

"We called for close-air support. It was a danger-close mission—"

Zinsser straightened. "You let a bunch of jet jockeys drop bombs on your position?"

"It seemed like a good idea at the time. We were dug in and the Taliban had a hundred or so men coming our way."

"You know I gotta ask—"

"Two times ICM, five meters."

"They dropped bombs over your position set to explode at fifteen feet above ground level. Man, that must have hurt."

"It was hard to overlook."

"And that did the job?"

"We're here, aren't we?"

Zinsser laughed. It was the first time J. J. had seen the man do so. J. J. joined him for a moment. He had relived those moments a thousand times, and this was the first time he felt he released some of the pent-up tension with laughter.

"Another guess: Those shepherds haunt you, don't they?"

J. J. saw a moment of concern in Zinsser's eyes. "Yeah, some. Every once in awhile it bothers me a lot."

"How do you deal with it?"

"Prayer mostly."

"You did what you had to do. No one is going to blame you for that."

J. J. pursed his lips. "It isn't what other people think that bothers me. It's that I killed, or at the very least helped kill, two men whose only crime was trying to find wayward goats."

"And if you hadn't, they might have ratted you out to Taliban fighters."

"I know that."

Zinsser looked to a distant horizon only he could see. "Does the prayer help?"

"A lot. I won't say I don't have my moments, but when I do, I have someone to talk it over with."

"God?"

"Yes. Does that sound strange to you?"

Zinsser looked back at his now empty coffee cup. "I don't believe in God. I stopped believing in Him when I lost my whole team."

J. J. lowered his voice. "Didn't someone else make it? I thought two of you made it out alive."

"Brian . . . Brian Taylor. I guess it depends how you define *alive*."

J. J. leaned over the table. "You guys were close?"

"You know how it is. I don't get close to people, but Brian was always good to me. I visit him when I can. He's a good man— a better man."

Thoughts tumbled in J. J.'s mind. Soldiers were a different breed of men, especially career warriors. They were complex beings that hid more than they revealed. There existed an unwritten code: never pry, never invade, and never go further than a man allowed.

"This is a crazy business we got ourselves into. Still, I can't see myself selling insurance." J. J. grinned.

"Just keep an M4 on your desk. People will buy whatever you're selling." Zinsser paused. "The prayer really works?"

"It always has. I grew up in the church, but that's not why I'm a believer. I'm a believer because I've seen the difference Jesus makes in a man's life."

"Here comes the sermon."

"No worries, man. I preached one sermon in my life and the congregation was very kind—then asked me not to do it again."

"That bad."

"It was pretty bad. I think it's best if I live my sermon and share with those who want to listen."

"Is it true God forgives?"

Zinsser's words were so soft J. J. had to process them twice to make sense of them. "Yeah, He does. That's the thing about faith; it's a place for busted up people. Jesus' whole ministry was about bringing forgiveness to whoever asks."

"People like me are too far gone for forgiveness."

"You bigger than God now?"

Zinsser's jaw clenched. "What?"

"I asked if you're bigger than God."

"What's that supposed to mean?"

"No one is too far gone for forgiveness. God is the same distance from every individual. You just have to decide if you're willing to talk to Him."

"I wouldn't know how."

"It's not calculus. You talk to God the way you talk to anyone. Just remember who He is and who you are."

"And light falls from heaven?"

"Cool as that would be, it doesn't happen that way. One of my favorite verses goes like this: 'But now in Christ Jesus you who once were far away have been brought near through the blood of Christ.'"

"And that means what?"

"That Jesus gave His all so we can be close to Him and Him to us."

Zinsser didn't respond, and J. J. couldn't read his expression.

"Do you know who the apostle Paul was?"

"I've heard the name."

"He was one of the first persecutors of the church. He hunted down believers and had them jailed. By his own admission he persecuted the church to the death—until he had an encounter with Christ. Half of the books in the New Testament came through him. He often referred to Christians as soldiers . . ." J. J. saw Zinsser's attention switch to someone approaching the booth. He turned and saw Moyer.

"Uh oh," Zinsser said. "This doesn't look good."

Moyer stopped a foot from the booth and fixed his gaze on Zinsser. "There's no good way to do this, Zinsser."

"What's happened?"

"I was just on the horn with Command. Brian Taylor died an hour ago. Complications from a surgery."

Zinsser closed his eyes.

"I'm sorry."

J. J. searched for words to say, but none of them made sense. He looked at Moyer. "We were just talking about him." He hesitated. "Hey look, Zinsser, if there's—"

Zinsser raised a hand. "Keep it, J. J." He scooted out from the booth then looked at Moyer. "Thanks for giving it to me straight, Boss."

"I wish I didn't have to."

Zinsser made eye contact with J. J. "That's some sense of humor your God has."

He walked away.

CHAPTER 25

HELEN BROWN WALKED WITH President Huffington as he left his suite. Agent Mitchell Baker led a small procession of agents—two in front of the president and two behind. They paused at the elevator. Helen and the president waited at the edge of the elevator lobby until agents cleared the cab.

"I see you're wearing your 'I'm invincible' tie." Huffington had hundreds of ties, many of them gifts from supporters and well-wishers. The solid silk tie was a little out of date, but its maroon color and diagonal pinstripe looked sharp. It was the tie he had worn when he accepted the Republican nomination for president five years earlier. He wore it again at his first and second inaugurations.

"I thought the meeting went well." Pride suffused Helen's tone. "You and the Canadian prime minister made headway with the Mexican president."

"President Gomez is a proud man. Our insistence on a border fence between the U.S. and Mexico while not insisting on the same thing with Canada smacks of racial prejudice."

"Which is nonsense. Our biggest immigration and drug problem is with Mexico, not the Canadians."

"He knows that, but he's a politician and concerned with
appearances. To his people it looks like we're hanging out the
unwelcome sign."

"Well—"

"Don't go there, Brownie. The Mexicans have a rich history
and are an honorable people. It's their weak economy that drives
the immigration problem. It wasn't that long ago when I thought
Americans might start crossing the border into Mexico. Our economy is on the upswing now, but the world was betting against us
just a year ago."

"Economic stress is one thing, Mr. President. Being a channel
for drugs is another."

"Let's not forget that the only reason drugs cross the border
from Mexico is because the drug lords have buyers over here.
Cutting off the supply is only one of the steps we need to take. We
need comprehensive medical treatment for anyone willing to kick
the habit."

"We have to convince six more senators before we have a prayer
of that happening, and you know what they're contending with."

"Yes. If we help Americans addicted to illegal drugs, we should
also help Americans addicted to cigarettes . . ."

"And alcohol and every other substance considered addictive."

"Just so long as we don't include caffeine on that list. I like my
coffee."

"Addict."

The president chuckled. "Don't get too cocky. I know about
that sweet tooth you have."

"Mr. President." Mitchell motioned to the elevator cab.

Huffington and Helen entered and faced the doors.

"Any questions about the schedule for this afternoon?" Helen asked.

"Enter the dining area on the second floor at 11:30; chat it up for a few minutes with a few of the other leaders . . ."

"Don't get drawn into any debates."

"Have I ever allowed that to happen?"

"Let's see, at the G-8 in Tokyo, you and the Chinese president delayed dinner by fifteen minutes by refusing to take your seats. Global warming, I believe it was."

"That's why we have these meetings. It's how things get done."

"I agree . . . just don't do it again."

"Yes, Mother."

"That's better."

"Hey, Mitch. I want you to meet the new leader of the United States of America: Helen Brown."

"President Brownie. I like it."

Helen cut him a glance. "You wouldn't be so snide if you weren't packing heat."

"Yes, ma'am."

She turned back to her boss. "And next?"

"The mayor of Naples will say a few things, welcome everyone. At noon, lunch will be served . . . what am I having? Not chicken I hope."

"Fish."

"Swell. Fish." He frowned.

"It's black bass. You like black bass."

"I pretend to like black bass; I'd rather have a steak."

"Maybe for dinner. What happens after lunch?"

"We hear from Japan, then the UK. Afterwards there will be a short press conference. I'll tell the world how well things are going."

"Sounds like you're ready. I'll be there to root you on."

The elevator opened and Huffington checked his watch, then followed Mitchell from the cab.

THE CAPACITY OF WESTERNERS to consume alcohol at any hour of the day never ceased to amaze Tony Nasser. True, they had begun drinking at an earlier party and just continued through the morning hours. The massive yacht bobbed in increasing swells of the open ocean. He glanced at his watch—11:30. Forty-five minutes ago he had turned the yacht on and crept along an easterly course. The Naples skyline was visible two miles in front of the bow.

For several hours the luxury craft moved through the water, loud music playing from the sound system. Nearly naked women and shirtless men danced to tunes that made Nasser's ears hurt.

He glanced to the north and saw what he had been waiting for: a twenty-foot sailboat. It flew a solid blue flag.

It was time.

Nasser stepped into the interior bridge and inserted a key into a recently installed lock. Before turning it, he removed a small transmitter and entered a five-digit code into the keypad. His mind played the image of a timer below decks coming to life—a timer attached to a dozen metal barrels of ammonium nitrate and fuel oil—an explosive mix used by Timothy McVeigh and Terry Nichols to bring down the Alfred P. Murray Federal Building in Oklahoma City. They managed to kill one-hundred-sixty-eight people in 1995. A few improvements had made Nasser's explosive mix even more effective.

Glancing out the window, Nasser saw a man on the sailboat pull in the skiff it towed behind and enter it. Timing was

everything. He waited until he saw the skiff start for his location. A
roar overhead drew his attention. The military jet that had been cir-
culating the city passed through the cloudless sky on another pass.

Nasser waited another two minutes then slipped into a bright
orange life jacket. He returned to the control panel and turned the
key. The yacht's engine roared to life and the large craft began to
gain speed. It had taken workers a week to set up a system that
would lock out all the controls. Nasser pulled the engine throttles
from the pilot's panel, something that would have taken a great deal
of time had the controls not been previously compromised.

The yacht could be controlled from a station topside, but
Nasser had already rendered those controls useless. Thanks to days
of planning and preparation, the multimillion-dollar vessel was
now an ocean-sailing smart bomb.

Nasser walked onto the back deck.

"Hey Tony, what's with the life vest?"

"Forget the vest, what are you doing to the engines?"

"There is nothing to worry about my friends. Allah controls
everything."

At the port-side safety rail, Nasser tossed the lockout key into
the water. The yacht pressed forward, gaining speed every second.
Off the stern the water turned to white froth as the propellers
churned the water.

"Good-bye my friends."

Tony Nasser climbed over the safety rail and dropped into the
water.

JUST EIGHTEEN YEARS OLD and standing only four-foot-eleven,
Anju Sharma had no trouble disappearing into the gathering crowd

six blocks from the *Miramare Hotel Grande*. She pushed toward the center of the mob. She made no attempt to guess the size of the crowd. It didn't matter. It was in the thousands—thousands of mostly young people carrying signs denouncing the West and the financial tyranny it forces on the world. One month ago she was barely aware of such protests. Anju had even less concern about mob politics now. She had only one task left in her life.

She thought of her home in India.

She thought of her sister and nephew.

She thought of the backpack slung over her shoulders.

FIVE BLOCKS AWAY, TWENTY-THREE-YEAR-OLD Zoya pulled into a Naples fueling station and parked the Renault Megane station wagon next to the pumps.

She slipped from behind the driver's seat carrying a long, nylon package tie. Inserting a debit card in the reader, she selected the mid-grade gas and inserted the nozzle into the vehicle's fuel port. She activated the nozzle then passed the nine-inch tie into the handle and cinched it tight. A moment later fuel began to flow into the tank.

Tears flowed down her face as she pulled the nozzle from the gas port and set it on the ground, then watched the gasoline flow into a rapidly growing pool.

A young woman pulled behind her. Zoya could see two children in the vehicle. The mother stopped when she saw Zoya standing in the pool of gasoline.

Zoya made eye contact. "Run."

J. J., BY HIS count, completed his twenty-third transit across the hotel lobby and down the corridor leading to the first-floor rooms. At the end of the hall, he turned and started back to the lobby and corridor on the other side. What now? Zinsser's response to the news of his friend's death was understandable. The man had been through a great deal and now lost the only other survivor of a mission gone terribly wrong. He had a right to be angry, a right to be emotional.

When J. J. reached the lobby, he found a deep, leather chair and lowered himself into it. The lobby was nearly empty. Two men stood behind the front desk chatting. Since the hotel had been closed to others, they had nothing to do but manage whatever requests that came from the entourages accompanying the planet's top leaders. Occasionally a Secret Service agent walked by, identified by the specialized lapel pins they wore. Out the glass entryway, J. J. saw cars used as barricades lining the street.

The problem with men was that they were emotional cripples. J. J. smiled. The idea was not original with him. Tess had made the observation not long after they met. *"Soldiers are worse. You are taught to suppress your emotions. Do that long enough and you don't know how to deal with them when they arise."*

She was right—at least partly. Soldiers in battle had to rein in emotion. Thinking was good; feeling could get in the way.

Still, Tess was mostly right. Zinsser was angry, hurt, and alone, and J. J. didn't know what to do about it. If the roles were reversed, he didn't know what he'd want Zinsser to do for him.

"This is crazy," J. J. whispered and rose. Zinsser would come out of it. All J. J. could do was pray for the man and give him his space.

He moved to the elevator. Bored, yet too weary to sleep, he punched the button. The cab stopped at the second floor and the doors parted. Mitchell Baker stepped on.

"J. J., isn't it? Or do you prefer to be called by rank?"

"J. J. is fine, sir."

"Shouldn't you be sleeping or something?"

"Can't unwind."

Mitchell grinned. "Yeah, I know. I always had trouble sleeping on mission."

"Shouldn't you be watching the president?"

"He's well covered. I have to check the protesters. We have a couple of agents in the crowd. The group is growing larger than expected. They're also getting noisy. Wanna come along?"

"You bet. It'll beat pacing the lobby."

The smell of scores of running computers and monitors and other electronics hung in the air. Some of the faces of the agents were different, no doubt the result of a shift change. J. J. was surprised to see Moyer standing over the shoulder of a woman seated at one of the monitors. "Hey Boss, what are you doing here?"

"I gotta be somewhere."

Mitchell nodded to a thickly built African-American. "What's going on with the crowd?"

"The group continues to grow. We estimate about eight thousand. They're getting pushy, too. The police have moved their riot squad into position."

Mitchell leaned close to the monitor. "Have you identified the leaders?"

"No. There are a few possibilities, but it looks more like an anarchy group."

J. J. glanced at another monitor, a closed-circuit video link to a dining room filled with dignitaries. He immediately noticed the president seated near the center of the room, his wife to his left. Someone he didn't recognize stood behind a podium. Another monitor scanned the room moving from one end to another.

J. J. started to shift his attention to the monitor trained on the protesters when something caught his eye. "Hey Mitch, can you zoom in with these cameras?"

"Sure. Why?"

"I don't know. I thought I saw something."

Mitchell and Moyer walked to J. J. "What?"

"Pan the camera back to the entry." The technician did. "There. That woman."

"The pregnant woman?" Mitchell frowned. "She was with the florist. I saw her in the room earlier, setting up the centerpieces."

"Can you zoom in closer?" J. J. said.

"Do it," Mitchell ordered.

"She looks nervous. Her hands. Focus on her hands."

The camera tightened its view.

"Pink. Pink fingernail polish."

Moyer stepped closer. "Short nails. Chewed nails."

"Someone had better clue me in—" Mitchell began, but a tech cut him off.

"I've got smoke!"

"About a mile away—"

The floor vibrated. J. J. turned to the monitor watching the protesters. Thousands were running from something. Some hobbled.

J. J. looked back at the young woman with the pink fingernails. "Oh . . . no . . ."

CHAPTER 26

"BOSS, THAT'S GOTTA BE her." Despite the activity on the other monitors, J. J. couldn't tear his attention away from the young woman in the maternity outfit. An RFID badge hung from her neck, but J. J. wasn't convinced.

Moyer didn't question him. It was one of the things J. J. admired about Moyer's leadership style: he trusted his men. "Agent Baker. We've got serious trouble."

J. J. started for the door. Moyer and Mitchell followed on his heels. Before J. J. could cross the threshold he heard Mitchell shouting. "Lockdown! I want a complete lockdown—"

J. J. didn't bother listening to the rest. He had other things on his mind.

The corridor filled with men and women in suits. Most looked confused, several looked angry without knowing why.

"Stairs," Moyer ordered.

J. J. had already turned that direction. The elevators would be too slow and possibly jammed with people. Most likely the Secret Service had seized control of the elevators.

Slamming the palm of his hand into the panic bar on the door of the stairway, J. J. sprinted into the narrow enclosure, descending the steps three at a time. He could hear the pounding of boot-clad shoes behind him. He heard other steps as well. A glance over his shoulder showed Moyer bearing down on him, Mitchell two steps behind, and a female agent fast-stepping to catch up.

A plastic sign hung by each door listing the floor. J. J. was thankful they weren't running up the stairs. Seconds passed like glaciers. At the fourth floor a searing realization hammered J. J.'s brain. His weapons were still locked away in the control room. It didn't matter, he decided. The Secret Service, local police, and other security forces protecting their heads of state would be armed. Not that it would matter.

He thought of the basement workshop in the villa he and the team had searched. The PE-4 plastic explosives had been disturbing enough, but the image of nails and ball bearings took what little breath he had left away. His Commander in Chief was moments from being rattled with bits of metal propelled by the explosive vest worn by the woman standing near the corner of the room.

When he reached the second floor, J. J. yanked the door open and plunged into the hallway. Secret Service agents stood near the entry doors to the meeting room. A line of metal carts holding food, glasses, pitchers, and other items necessary to serve an up-class meal to world leaders and their spouses lined one wall.

He started for the doors when a smallish Hispanic Secret Service agent stepped in his way and raised his service weapon until he had drawn a bead on J. J.'s head. J. J. put on the brakes, stopping just a few feet from the agent.

"I'm on your side."

"Stand back—"

Mitchell's voice came from near J. J.'s ear. "Ease up, Danny. He's with me."

The agent lowered his weapon.

"What have we got?"

"We've got the lockout in place," Agent Danny said. "Everyone inside knows something has happened but has remained calm. I'm assuming something happened outside."

"Something is going to happen inside if you don't let me in there," J. J. snapped.

Danny looked at Mitchell.

"Give me a rundown, J. J.," Mitchell said. "Make it the *Reader's Digest* version."

"The woman I pointed out to you. She's a suicide bomber."

"How can you know that?"

Moyer stepped between J. J. and Mitchell. "Maybe we could have this chat later. We may be out of time as it is."

J. J. watched Mitchell weigh the situation. "I'm the demo guy. I'm the guy you need to disarm the bomb."

"If she's a suicide bomber, then—"

"Make a decision, Agent." Moyer barked out the command. "This isn't practice. Two bombs have already gone off. We don't have time for a conversation."

Mitchell straightened. "Let's go."

J. J. inhaled so deeply his lungs hurt, then let out the air. Two seconds later he walked into a room that could be ablaze any moment.

DELARAM FINGERED THE BUTTON on the trigger inside the pocket of her maternity dress.

Push it.

Her eyes darted around the room. People, nervous about the lockdown, whispered insistently. Security personnel stood by the doors.

Push it.

The push-button activator felt heavy. She ran her thumb over the button. A simple movement would end it all. Just push the little green button down and it would be over. She'd never know what happened. The explosion would tear through her body, burning every inch of her inside and out. Bits of her bone would become shrapnel, but she would feel nothing.

Just press it. Do it now.

Delaram tried to muster the strength to complete the act. Fire and metal would spread through the whole room. The ocean-side windows would be shattered by the force of the concussion. Those standing near the windows might be carried along with the glass.

Push it, Delaram. Push it. Push it for your mother. Push it for your father. Just press the button and be done with the nightmare.

The image of her battered parents—her brutalized father resting his head in her mother's lap—played on her mind in vivid colors. She stopped seeing the others in the room. Tears began to flow.

"Hello."

Delaram raised her eyes. Before her stood a man about her age, dressed in black. He had a friendly smile and kind eyes.

"Do you speak English?"

Delaram applied a slight pressure to the button.

"My name is J. J." He touched his chest, then motioned to her.

"You don't want to be here."

"I'm guessing you don't either."

"I have to do this." Her voice sounded robotic, even to her own ears.

"I can help."

"No one can help. I have to do this. I have to do this now. Then it will all be over."

"I know what you're here to do."

"They left me here to do this alone. He left. He made me do this, then left."

"That's the way those animals are. Let me help you."

"It's too late."

"It's never too late. You left your fingernails for us."

Delaram wasn't sure she heard correctly. "You . . ."

"We found them at the villa outside of Rome. You were there, weren't you? You left them because you thought someone like me would find them."

She shook her head. "It's too late. If I don't do this, he will."

THE WOMAN'S BLEAK WORDS chilled J. J. to the marrow. "Who?"

"I don't know who he is. They call him Abasi. That's all I know . . . I have to do this."

"No you don't." J. J. lowered his tone. "I told you my name is J. J. What's yours?"

He heard rustling behind him.

"No one move!" Delaram's voice echoed off the walls.

J. J. looked over his shoulder. Mitchell and two other agents stood there, guns pointed at the woman's head. "Boss, I need working room here."

"Back off, Agent Baker," Moyer said.

Mitchell glared at him. "You don't call the shots here."

"I know that, but you're not helping. Take a step back."

J. J. watched as Mitchell and his crew withdrew one step. He looked into the woman's eyes and saw fear and surrender. "If I'm going to die, I'd at least like to know who I'm dying with."

"Delaram."

"Delaram. It's time we put an end to this. I can help. Will you let me? I know—"

"You know nothing!"

J. J. raised a hand. "I'm sorry. I'm just scared . . . scared like you."

"They have my parents. If I don't do this, they will kill them."

J. J.'s heart stuttered. A person would do almost anything to save a loved one. "I figured it was something like that. I can tell you're not a zealot."

"I don't believe in anything."

"I think you do. You've hesitated. You've hesitated because you believe there is a difference between right and wrong."

"I'm going to die anyway."

"I'm not going to leave you, Delaram, even if that means I die with you."

She lowered her head. "Nothing matters."

J. J. spoke softly. "You matter, Delaram. These people matter. I know you're in a horrible situation. Let me help."

"You can't. There is nothing you can do. Even if you shoot me, the bomb goes off."

J. J. didn't like the sound of that. "Delaram, look at me." She kept her eyes down. J. J. raised his voice. "Delaram, I said look at me." She did. "Look in my eyes. Do you think I'm lying to you?"

She shook her head.

"I'm going to help you, and you're going to let me. Understood?" She didn't respond. "The first thing we're going to do is empty the room."

"If I don't kill them, my parents will be killed. I don't care what happens to me—"

"But you do care what happens to these people. Let me help."

Tears cascaded down her face. J. J. turned to Moyer. "Clear the room, Boss."

Moyer studied Delaram. "I'm not sure that's a good idea, J. J."

"We can't wait any longer. I believe her when she says someone else could set off the bomb. We have very few choices." He turned back to Delaram. "I will stay with you. I will try to disarm the bomb."

"My parents . . ." She began to sob.

"I can't imagine how hard this is for you, but I know you will do what is right, even if it means the worst for your parents."

Delaram gave a slight nod.

"Do it, Boss. Take the team with you."

"What about you?"

"I'm going to disarm the thing."

"And if you can't?"

"Then I can't, but I'll be getting off easy. You're the one who'll have to tell Tess."

Moyer's gaze said volumes. "Agent Baker. Clear the room."

As the dignitaries filed from the room in silence, J. J. took a step closer to Delaram. "You've done the right thing." He placed a hand on her shoulder. "Tell me about the bomb."

MOYER BACKED INTO THE corridor to make room for the crowd to exit. He bumped into someone. At his shoulder stood Zinsser, behind him Rich, Pete, and Jose.

"We felt the rumble," Rich said before Moyer had a chance to ask. "Figured something might be up."

"How did you know to come here?"

Rich shrugged. "Simple. We followed the Secret Service agents."

Moyer was glad to have them there. "Here's the skinny. Two explosions outside, one about a mile distant, one in the middle of several thousand protesters . . ."

"Don't tell me—" Pete started.

"Yeah, one woman inside packing enough explosive to blow out a good size chunk of this floor."

"J. J.?"

Moyer looked at Zinsser. Did he sound worried? "He got the girl's confidence. He's going to try to disarm the bomb." Moyer explained about the remote detonator.

"Why not just pop her and beat feet out of here?" Rich asked.

"A dead woman can't give us answers. Besides, she said that even if we shoot her, the bomb goes off."

Zinsser took a step toward the door. "I need to get in there."

"No you don't." Moyer's tone stopped Zinsser cold. "I'm ordering you guys out."

Zinsser squared off. "Look, Boss, if there's a remote detonator, then a radio is involved. That makes it in my bailiwick—mine or Pete's. Look at him. Does he look in any condition to do this?"

Moyer stepped to the side to look at Pete. Before he could turn, Zinsser pushed past him and walked into the room.

CHAPTER 27

ALDO GRONCHI CROUCHED ON the hot asphalt as hundreds of pairs of feet landed near him. Screams choked the air. Several people tripped over him as they stampeded past. Beneath him, sheltered between his legs and arms, lay an eight-year-old, red-haired girl, who screamed in terror—the same scorching terror he felt.

Pain raced up his leg as a bulky man stepped on his right ankle, then crashed down next to him. A second later the man was on his feet, swearing in Italian, and running with the pack.

"Stay still, little one. Stay still." Could she even hear him? His ears rang from the sound of the explosion. He tried to force the images of flying body parts from his mind.

When he received word that more protesters than expected had shown up and they were moving closer to the barricades, Aldo had gone to take charge of the operation. Fifteen minutes after he arrived, he felt the ground rumble and heard a distant explosion. The second explosion was much louder and much closer.

The crowd reacted by running from the sound, the heat, and the bloody carnage, overrunning the barricades and the men who manned them. To Aldo it seemed as if he had been swept up in a wave, not of water, but of human flesh. Before he could issue an order, he went down. The little girl tumbled near him. He'd been a cop too long to wonder why anyone would be so stupid as to bring a child to a place like this. Someone tripped over her and landed hard on the macadam. Aldo scrambled to the girl, intending to pick her up, but the crowd thickened and rising proved impossible. He did the only thing he could: cover her with his body. Sheltering her made him a target—a larger obstacle to the fleeing crowd.

For several long minutes Aldo was certain the crowd would trample him into the street, leaving a dead and flattened version of himself. Aldo's mind told him the human stampede lasted only a few minutes, but it felt like days had passed.

"Are you hurt, Capitano?"

A young officer helped him to his feet. Aldo picked up the girl, who continued to wail. Placing a hand on her head, he pulled her close. "I don't think so." He looked at the officer and could tell the man had taken a beating. His uniform was torn in several places and covered with dirt. "You?"

"I'm fine, sir."

Aldo guessed he was lying, being brave for his commander. "Take the girl." The man did.

Turning slowly, Aldo took in the scene. It looked like a battlefield. Wounded people lay on the grass, the sidewalks, and in the streets. As he walked past the wounded, he pulled the radio from his belt. He didn't want to walk this direction but knew he had too.

Broken bodies gave way to burned and dismembered ones.

Aldo paused long enough to vomit.

"WE SHOULD CLOSE THE gate."

Lorenzo stared at the Naples police officer. The man was right. They had just received a report that a large crowd was headed their way. He glanced at the open maw that led to the hotel's underground parking, then hesitated.

"Sir?"

The flower van emerged, driving slowly, and pulled up the ramp.

"Of course. Close the security gate."

The officer raced to the opening while Lorenzo opened the barricade to let the van pass. He refused to look inside.

In the distance the ululations of fire trucks, ambulances, and police cars rose skyward along with a tall column of black smoke.

Lorenzo looked up at the tall hotel. "Any moment . . ." He drew his handgun and placed the muzzle next to his right temple.

He thought of his daughter—then pulled the trigger.

"ARE CHRISTIANS SUPPOSED TO do that?"

J. J. looked up and saw Zinsser approaching, then returned his attention to the zipper that ran down the front of Delaram's maternity dress.

"You shouldn't be here. It's unhealthy in this room."

"So I hear." Zinsser stepped closer. "I figured you could use some help."

J. J. gently pulled the zipper down until it reached its stop. "You figured wrong. I'm the demolition guy."

"Getting a little territorial, aren't you? I'm the electronics guru."

"If this goes south, pal, you're going to be more goo than guru. I can handle this."

Zinsser stepped behind Delaram and pulled the dress free of her shoulders. He let it drop to the floor. "By the way, who am I undressing?"

"My name is Delaram." Her voice shook.

"Nice to meet you, Delaram." Zinsser didn't offer his name. He stepped around to face her. J. J. had taken a step back. "Is that what I think it is?"

"It's a good thing Agent Baker didn't get his way."

"I take it he wanted to . . ."

"Shoot me in the head?" Delaram said. "I wish he had."

"If he had," J. J. said, "we'd all be dead." It took all the courage he could muster to step forward. Delaram stood straight and unmoving, dressed only in her underwear, the dress she had been wearing puddled at her feet. "I'll disable the radio receiver first."

"Sounds good," Zinsser said. "What do you want me to do?"

"Leave. I have a bad feeling about this."

"Forget it." Zinsser pointed at the round vest strapped to Delaram. "What do you see?"

"We don't have time for questions. Abasi could be about to push the button."

"Who?"

"Someone Delaram mentioned." J. J. reached for the radio.

"Hang on a sec. See the wires that run up the shoulder strap?"

J. J. looked up. "I missed that. Tamper mechanism?"

"I don't think so. They're attached to the motion detector."

"Is that true, Delaram?"

"I don't know. They made me practice putting on the vest, but this time they did things I couldn't see. They put a bag over my head."

"I can't wait any longer. Take off, Zinsser, I may not get this right."

Zinsser ignored him.

Delaram began to shake, then sway.

Zinsser slipped behind her and wrapped his arms around her. "Get busy, Colt. She's going to pass out."

J. J. laid a hand on the receiver. Duct tape held it in place. J. J. removed the tape and gently pulled the receiver away. Two insulated copper wires ran from the back and into the bulging vest. "The great thing about plastic explosive is how pliable it is." J. J. bit his lower lip, grabbed the wires, and yanked.

"We still alive, J. J.?" Zinsser asked.

"So far . . ."

Delaram's knees gave way and her head rolled to the side. Zinsser grunted. "Put some speed on, J. J."

J. J. didn't waste time with words; he turned his attention to the gray box he had determined was the motion detector. Zinsser bent under the dead weight of the woman.

"It looks simple. All I have to do is keep it level as I—" J. J. removed the tape that held the device in place. He saw a small glass tube filled with a yellow bubble, like a carpenter's level. The bubble was for the user's information during installation. The real sensors would be electronic—probably a mercury switch.

"You praying, J. J.?"

"Haven't stopped."

"Good. God's more likely to listen to you than me."

J. J. gently pulled the device away with one hand. Unlike the radio receiver, this device had two long, pointed metal pins protruding from the back. The pins had been pressed into the explosives.

"So far so good."

"Maybe for you. Can I set her down?"

"No. I don't trust the designer." He unbuckled the straps that held the vest to Delaram's form. "Okay. Let me hold her and you unbuckle the back of the vest."

J. J. placed a hand on each of Delaram's arms and squeezed. It was an awkward position and Delaram's dead weight made her as heavy as a large sack of rocks. It was his turn to grunt.

Zinsser had the vest unbuckled in seconds and slipped it forward, then let it drop. Together they lowered the unconscious woman to the floor. J. J. returned to the vest and checked for any source of ignition he might have missed.

"Can I start breathing again?"

"Sure," J. J. said. "I think we're safe now." J. J. sat on the floor and lowered his head onto his knees. Just a few minutes ago twenty of the world's leaders were within seconds of death.

"You okay, pal?"

"Peachy," J. J. said. "Just peachy."

ERMANNO GRECO RECEIVED THE radio call as he banked his F2 Typhoon to the west. To his left, from an area just a mile or so from the coast and the *Miramare Hotel Grande,* rose a thick coil of black smoke. Ermanno could see orange-red flame scratching at a nearby business. A half dozen fires blocked the streets. A few blocks further south, flashing red lights told the pilot something else was going on—something bad.

He resisted the urge to fly over the area. He had been given a mission, and nothing else mattered. Ermanno throttled up.

"Feet wet," he said as his craft crossed over the shore and streaked over the ocean. He spoke with a casualness that belied the pounding of his heart.

He had been given a detailed description and had no trouble finding the long, white yacht racing on a collision course with the marina on the ocean side of the hotel. Gunboats from the Italian navy bore down on the vessel from the south and the north. Each had twin 50-caliber rapid fire cannons on the bow. In moments they would be in range to open fire.

Ermanno eased the stick forward, lowering the nose, and set his sights on the yacht. He strained his eyes to see who, if anyone, stood at the wheel. He was too high and moving too fast to make a determination. He had no trouble, however, seeing the twenty or so people on the deck frantically waving at him. Their behavior made clear their terror.

Ermanno radioed base. "The yacht carries about twenty people. I think they're trapped onboard."

He was told to make another pass. As he did, several of the men and women pressed their hands together as if praying. They were pleading for help.

Nausea began to burn his stomach. He feared the order that might come his way.

On the next pass the northernmost gunboat reached the yacht and fired a round of tracers over the bow. The yacht continued on course and gave no sign of slowing.

"Flight Command, Eagle Two, the gunboats have fired warning shots. No change." He imagined someone on the gunboats was giving the same report to their superiors.

"Standby Eagle Two."

Seconds dripped by. Ermanno flew a mile out to sea, then began a sharp turn. The g-forces pressed him to the side and back in his seat.

"Eagle Two, you are directed to make a low flyby for observation."

"Roger. Beginning flyby."

Ermanno skimmed a hundred feet above the swells of the Bay of Naples. He slowed to just fifty kilometers above his stall speed. This time he could see the fear on the faces of the passengers. Not one looked older than twenty-five. He saw no one at the upper helm. Perhaps the captain was in the control area in the cabin, but if he was, why didn't the people on deck do anything to stop him?

Pulling back on the stick, Ermanno directed his F2 skyward and reported what he had seen. He was told to circle as support for the gunboats.

His commander didn't say it, but Ermanno knew what they were thinking. If the gunboats couldn't stop the craft, then someone would have to blow it out of the water. He guessed that someone would be him.

From his airborne vantage point, Ermanno watched as one of the gunships pulled alongside the yacht. He imagined them trying to make contact, giving orders to pull to and prepare to be boarded. The yacht stayed its course. It could only mean one thing. In less than a mile, the yacht—certainly laden with explosives—would crash into the marina. A boat that size could carry hundreds of pounds of explosives.

"Command, Eagle Two. Advise the gunboats to tell the passengers to jump." At the speed the yacht traveled, many of them would be injured, and if Ermanno had to do what he knew he would be ordered to do, several might be killed in the water. But it was the only hope they had.

Ermanno had to again direct the jet around in a lazy circle. As much as he could, he kept an eye on the yacht. Another voice came over his head set. "Eagle Two, this is Raven One. I will be at your position in two minutes."

"Understood, Raven One." *Backup. Just in case I can't follow his orders.*

As he passed the yacht again, he saw people jumping over the side of the yacht. Some seemed reluctant. Two muscular men were lifting anyone that couldn't muster the courage to leap and tossing them over the side. "Good men," he whispered. He also caught a glimpse of a woman throwing life vests over the stern. A moment later she launched herself into the water. The two men followed a second behind.

"Command, Eagle Two, craft appears evacuated."

"Roger that, Eagle Two. We believe the yacht is carrying high explosives. You are cleared to stop the boat. Repeat, stop the boat."

"I understand I am clear to sink the yacht."

"Roger that, Eagle Two. Raven One, you are to follow Eagle Two in. Verify."

"Follow Eagle Two in. Will do."

Ermanno crossed himself, began a wide turn until he was three miles from his target. He hoped the maneuver would give those in the water a slightly better chance at survival. He dropped his altitude to two hundred feet, powered the throttle, flipped the safety cover off the "pickle"—the flight and weapons stick—and took aim.

He pressed the launch button.

The F2 shivered as the first of two Raytheon Paveway IV 500-pound guided bombs let go of the undercarriage. Ermanno pressed the throttle to the stops and climbed, the acceleration pushing him back in his seat.

He jerked the control stick to the left and turned the aircraft in time to see a rolling, roiling ball of flame expand at unimaginable speeds and scorch the air.

"Command, Raven One, target eliminated. Repeat target is eliminated. Good job, Eagle Two."

Ermanno crossed himself again. "God help those in the water."

ABASI SAT IN A room two miles from the hotel that should be pouring smoke from the second floor. He had a clear view of the structure. He pressed the button on the transmitter again, just as he had done fifty times before. Twice he had switched the batteries. His system was foolproof, yet the bomb had not gone off. He was responsible for four suicide bombings. Two had worked as they should, but the one strapped to Delaram's belly failed. Of the three, it was the only one with a double backup—and yet it failed.

Abasi stepped from the balcony and moved into the bathroom. Bit by bit he dismantled the device and dropped its pieces into the toilet. Several flushes later the defective device was gone.

What would he tell El-Sayyed?

His cell phone sounded.

NASSER SAT ON THE stern of the twenty-foot Catalina sailboat flying a British flag. He wore an Aloha shirt, white shorts, flip-flops, and sunglasses. A beer he hadn't and wouldn't sip rested in a drink holder. He looked like any of a thousand pleasure sailors who plied the waters off Naples. Next to him rested a pair of high-powered binoculars, the same binoculars that allowed him to see an Italian jet put an end to his portion of the plan.

"We have failed," he said into the cell phone.

Abasi answered, "Yes. I will contact the home office."

"You do that."

"What are you going to do?"

Nasser switched off his cell phone.

CHAPTER 28

MOYER WATCHED THE PRESIDENT enter the sitting area of his suite from the bedroom. The man looked drawn, pale, and weary beyond his years. Moyer, his team, and the others stood.

"Remain seated." President Huffington made his way to an upholstered chair. The room was filled with people, many on cell phones.

Moyer studied the president. "How is Mrs. Huffington?"

"Physically she's fine, but she's understandably upset. She's lying down." Huffington rubbed his forehead. Clearly the man was shaken to the core. Who could blame him? "You know, I took this job knowing that sooner or later some nutcase was going to try and take me out, but my wife . . ." He gazed at the floor. "Family should be off-limits." He looked up. "Okay people, I need a little breathing room. Mitchell, you and Brownie stay. Moyer, I would like you and your men to remain as well."

As though anyone could make them leave the man's side right now. Moyer'd like to see someone try. "Police Captain Aldo Gronchi has some information for us. So does Captain De Luca."

"Very well. Everyone else out. I'll get to the rest of you as soon as I can."

Even after the others—including the press secretary, valet, and the president's personal physician—left, the room felt crowded.

"Give me the rundown, Mitchell."

Mitchell nodded. "A female suicide bomber pulled into a gas station about 1150 local time. Witnesses are still being interviewed, but the short of it is she poured gasoline on the ground and then set off her bomb."

"Unbelievable. Casualties?"

"Only two others, Mr. President. One witness said she told people to run." Mitchell looked at his notepad. "At approximately 1155 hours, a bomber entered the crowd of protesters. Forty-five dead; fifty more with life-threatening injuries; 235 wounded and maimed." He paused. "Those are the early numbers. I suspect they are underestimated."

Huffington leaned back in the chair and closed his eyes. "Go on."

"A third attempt at bombing was attempted using a yacht. The bomber had arranged a morning party on the deck. Twenty-five to thirty civilians were on board when the man rigged the yacht to run at top speed. The steering had been compromised. An Italian F2 blew it out of the water before it could reach shore and damage the hotel."

"Were the people still onboard?"

"No, they jumped before the jet fired. Apparently the Italian navy encouraged them to do so." Mitchell consulted his notebook again. "Five were killed from the explosion, ten were severely injured. The rest escaped with moderate injuries—mostly burns. We think the yacht was loaded with homemade explosives like ammonium nitrate and fuel oil. Experts are analyzing video taken from another jet in the area and the gunboats. We may not know the specifics, but it is certain that the explosion was greater than the plastic explosives would have generated on their own."

The president drew a deep breath. "This is almost too much to believe. Current status?"

"The facility is secure, the Italian police and military are searching the surrounding buildings. It is doubtful there will be another attack."

Helen Brown looked at the president. "Nonetheless, I think we need to get you back to the White House, sir."

Moyer couldn't say he disagreed.

"That would look like I'm running to the safety of home."

"No, sir, it won't." Helen leaned forward. "I've received word from several of my counterparts. Most of the heads of state are returning home. The American people need to know their president is safe."

Huffington sighed. "I had such high hopes for the meeting. How could that woman get into the building, let alone the meeting room?"

Aldo Gronchi stepped forward. "Mr. President, if I may. The fault is mine."

"Yours? How so?"

"I believe one of my men may have let her through. We found his body. He killed himself."

"Why would he do such a thing?"

Moyer studied the police captain. He looked hollow, fragile.

"I am having his home searched, his phone records examined, and interrogating his friends. He has always been a good officer."

"Maybe they got to him like they got to Delaram," Zinsser said.

The president looked at him. "That would make your weak link hypothesis right."

Zinsser shrugged. "I take no joy in it."

Huffington faced Moyer. "I owe you and your team my life. If that woman had succeeded, there's no telling what would have happened on the global stage."

Moyer looked at his men. "The credit goes to J. J. and Zinsser, sir."

"I will make sure your superiors know of the bravery you've shown. There's a medal in this; I can assure you of that."

Moyer smiled. "Thank you, Mr. President, but our mission isn't over. The people behind this won't stop because they failed today. They'll continue to slaughter innocent people."

"But who are they? Islamic fundamentalists? You made it clear the recent bombings were not carried out by religious zealots."

"That's right, sir," J. J. said. "Delaram said she didn't believe in anything. She was doing this to save her parents."

"Where is she now?"

Mitchell answered the president. "She's being held at a local military base. Italian intelligence is interrogating her."

De Luca spoke for the first time since the president's entrance into the room. "She is cooperating fully. Of course, she is depressed and worried. Still, she is answering every question."

"Of course, she's depressed!" J. J. looked thoroughly disgusted. "She thinks her parents are dead, or as good as dead."

"Mr. President," Moyer said. "I have a favor to ask."

"Name it."

BOOK II

CHAPTER 29

MOYER HAD NEVER BEEN on Air Force One before, but he decided he could get used to it: comfortable seats and every imaginable amenity. He'd assumed he and his men would sit in the press section of the plane, but the president insisted that they ride in the staff area. The greater part of Moyer wanted to put his feet up and nap the way back to the states—but there wasn't time.

And he wasn't going to the states.

He'd spent the last half hour making a mental checklist. The president's gratitude had given Moyer far greater latitude than he would normally have. First, he requested phone privileges for his men. Air Force One had the best communication equipment in the world. Once airborne, there was no place they couldn't call. On Moyer's orders, the men called home in reverse order of their rank, allowing each ten minutes. Spec Ops families had an unhealthy addiction to the news, knowing that any world event might involve their husbands and fathers.

Jose had called his wife and four children, learned that two had the flu and the youngest was teething. "Makes me kinda glad to be on mission."

Moyer smiled at Jose's lie.

Pete called his bride of less than a year. J. J. spoke with Tess. Of all the family and loved ones, only Tess would know what was happening. But she was on an unsecured line, so she and J. J. could only speak in euphemisms about his "business trip."

Rich, the biggest and toughest man Moyer knew, always grew teary when he called home from overseas. No one razzed him. No one dared.

Finally Moyer spent his ten minutes talking to his wife, daughter, and son. Over the last year his daughter had turned thirteen and was showing disturbing signs of womanhood. Boys were calling and, more than once, he'd reminded her how adversely his career would be impacted if he had to start killing her boyfriends. Gina always laughed; Moyer always kept a straight face.

Moyer wanted the boys to understand what he did for a living, but he couldn't tell them. None of his neighbors knew he was Army. To them, he was just another businessman who lived on their street. Still, he took special joy in speaking to his son. Seventeen-year-old Rob had, with the help of J. J.'s chaplain brother, found his way through the rebellious teenage years. Last year Moyer was sure the divide between him and his son could never be bridged.

After his call, Moyer accepted an offer the president made earlier. Huffington and his wife had retired to the bedroom, leaving the in-flight office open. Helen Brown informed Moyer the room was available.

Stepping into the staff seating area, Moyer nodded to Rich and Zinsser. "You two, you're with me."

The men rose from their seats and followed him into the president's private study. Simulated wood covered the bulkheads.

The thick carpet bore the presidential seal. A desk of matching wood was situated near the starboard side of the plane and seemed to merge seamlessly into the fuselage. A sofa ran along one of the walls. All the furnishings had been bolted to the deck.

"Have a seat, gentlemen." Moyer motioned to the sofa. Zinsser and Rich sat.

Rich glanced at the president's chair. "You gonna?"

"Not in this life, pal. I know my place." Moyer took one of the guest chairs that faced the desk and turned it so he could face the two. He fixed his eyes on Zinsser. "First, that was a brave thing you did in the hotel, Zinsser. You probably saved a lot of lives—at very least you saved J. J.'s."

"Thank you, Boss."

"Don't thank me, soldier. You did it against my orders."

"Yes, Boss, I did, but it wasn't personal."

Moyer felt his jaw tighten. "Not personal? This team runs on orders—*my* orders, and in my absence, on Rich's orders. Is that clear?"

"It is, Boss. Crystal."

"I could have you up on charges for that bit of rebellion. I could have you bounced out of the service."

"With all due respect, Boss, you're going to do that anyway." He looked at Rich. "I assume—"

"I brought him up to speed about the incident in the field. He's second in command and as such needs to be appraised of anything that affects this team."

"Good. Then we can talk freely."

"You getting smart?" Rich's tone was menacing.

"No way. I don't mean to sound flippant, but let's face it, guys. What I did in that field eclipses my skirting an order to evacuate the scene in the hotel. My career ended a couple of days ago." He thought for a moment. "Actually, it ended in Kismayo."

Moyer leaned back, torn between backhanding the man and putting a comforting arm around him. "How bad has it been? The flashbacks, I mean."

Zinsser shrugged. "They were worse at home. They come and go."

"What does that mean?" Rich asked.

"Sometimes I lose a grip on where I am. I flashback to Somalia."

Moyer watched the man's eyes glaze.

"Other times I just feel irritable and depressed. I can't control it."

"Have you seen the Army shrinks?" Rich asked.

"Yeah, but not specifically for this. Before I could return to service, I had to go through a battery of psych tests."

"And you passed?" Moyer glanced at Rich.

Zinsser shrugged. "I'm a pretty good liar."

"You're pretty good at understatement too."

Moyer eyed his second-in-command. "Ease off, Rich."

But the comment didn't seem to faze Zinsser. He raised his head and took a moment to look each man in the eye. "Okay, here's the deal, Boss. I'm smart. Real smart. I cruised through school, and if I had any discipline as a teenager, I could have made MIT, but I was sick of school. So I joined up and have never regretted it. Not even now that my brain has been branded with images that don't fade. Fooling the head-docs was easy. I even had you guys fooled for awhile." He looked at the opposite wall as if he could see the open air and clouds on the other side. "You know how I sleep at night? Want to know how I drive the demons away? I drown them in booze. Sometimes that doesn't work. Most of the time I'm the Zinsser I remember; other times I don't know who I am."

Moyer digested this new information. "Have you been drinking while on this mission?"

"No, Boss, and I would never do that—not that it's not tempting. The Army is what keeps me going, keeps me grounded. It's why I worked so hard to heal and get back on a team. The Army is the only medicine that works."

"It doesn't seem to be working."

"But it is, Shaq. Sure, I lost my senses in the field, but I've been able to keep it together otherwise. I've had bouts of confusion and depression, but those are less frequent."

"The field incident was less than two days ago," Moyer said.

"That's true." He sighed. "Look, I know what this is about, and I can't blame you."

Moyer's leaned forward. "If you know so much, then tell me what this is about."

"We're going to stop to refuel in England. Then you and the team are going on with the mission. You'll bounce me, and I'll be relieved of duty when I return to the states."

Moyer narrowed his gaze. "Are you suicidal? Is that why you went in to help J. J.?"

"No . . . yes . . . partly. I knew I could help, but if I failed, then the bomb would end it all for me."

Moyer sprang to his feet and began to pace, his mind racing like an Indy car. No one spoke for several minutes. As a leader he knew exactly what he should do: send Zinsser home, where he could get the help he needed. As a soldier on mission, he knew how valuable Zinsser had been. As a warrior he knew sudden dismissal would wound the man even more. Zinsser had shown himself to be a hero multiple times.

He shook his head. If only he could foist the decision off to a superior, but this was his call to make. "Rich."

"Yes, Boss."

"Tell me I'm wrong." He turned to face his friend and saw confusion.

"Excuse me?"

"Tell me I'm wrong."

"About what?"

"Rich, just do it."

"Okay, Boss, um, you're wrong."

"Tell me to change my mind."

"Boss, I have no idea what you're getting at."

"Rich!"

"Okay, okay. Boss, I'm telling you you're wrong, and I advise against this course of action . . . whatever it is."

"You strongly advise me against it."

"Um, sure, if you say so. I strongly advise you against . . . Are you trying to keep me off the hook?"

Moyer ignored Rich and stepped to Zinsser. "On your feet, soldier."

Zinsser shot up and came to attention. "I'm keeping you on the team. You will have no more breaks with reality—"

"Boss, I can't promise—"

He ground his teeth. "I did not give you permission to speak! You will have no more breaks with reality, and to make certain you don't, you will be accompanied by either Rich or myself. Is that clear?"

"Boss—"

"I asked you a question. Do you have a problem with my question?"

"No, Boss. I understand."

"Dismissed."

Shaq stood. "Boss, I strongly advise against this, and this time I mean it."

"Dismissed, Rich."

Rich's face hardened. On several occasions he had challenged Moyer's decisions, but he never failed to obey them.

"Yes, Boss." He pressed the words between clenched teeth.

"I CANNOT KNOW," EL-SAYYED said into the cell phone. He was in a luxury boat sailing up the Nile. "I was not there."

"You failed in your mission." Even over the distance from Mexico to Egypt, El-Sayyed could hear the man's anger. "My employer is unhappy."

"As am I."

"You have our money, but we do not have the results we paid for."

El-Sayyed spoke in an even tone. "You knew there was a risk of failure. This was not a simple operation, and complexity always increases the danger of a misstep."

"My employer wants to know what went wrong."

"Tell him what I have told you: I don't know. I wasn't there. You follow the news as I do. You know we created great destruction and death, proving that no security is foolproof."

"But the primary goal was not achieved, you stinkin' Arab."

"Careful, my friend," El-Sayyed said. "I have a limited capacity for insults. Think about that next time you or your boss start your cars."

"Are you threatening us?"

"I'm just warning a friend about the unwanted consequences that can come from hasty words."

The line went silent for a moment, and El-Sayyed let his gaze trace the farmland that bordered the Nile. Peasants worked the fields; sun-weathered men and children drew water from the ancient river and poured it into irrigation channels. Despite its great achievements, his country was still backwards in so many ways.

"My employer wants his money returned."

"I'm sorry, my friend, but a deal is a deal. We all took risks and knew that things might go wrong. It is the way in modern business. And please don't threaten me again. It will do you no good."

El-Sayyed rose from the lounge chair and paced the deck of the thirty-five-foot pleasure craft. In his free hand he held a small cup of strong coffee. *Dahabeeyahs* plied the Nile, the small boats crammed with tourists as they traveled up and down the famous river. Several other pleasure craft and commercial boats worked the waters. The roar of engines skipped along the surface. El-Sayyed saw a power boat racing faster than was wise. It approached quickly. "Stupid rich tourists."

"Did you say something, El-Sayyed?"

"Nothing to concern you, Michael."

The powerboat slowed as it approached El-Sayyed's craft. The man who stood behind the wheel held a phone to his ear. He waved. A second man sat at the stern.

"El-Sayyed?"

"Yes."

"Two can play your game."

"What does that mean?"

The second man stood and shouldered a rocket-propelled grenade launcher. Before El-Sayyed could shout a warning, the grenade struck.

Burning, sharp debris pierced the side of El-Sayyed's head and torso. He stumbled to the side and started to fall.

A second RPG hit the boat.

The last thing El-Sayyed's brain registered was the sound of the speedboat's engine piercing the air.

CHAPTER 30

TESS RAND HAD BARELY hung up from her brief *courtesy* call with J. J. when a man in uniform appeared at her door.

"I take it you're not selling cookies."

"No, ma'am. Colonel MacGregor has requested a few moments of your time."

"A few moments? Is he here? In Pennsylvania?"

"No, ma'am. He's at his office." The man looked to be thirty, had brown hair, and looked as if he hadn't smiled anytime in the last two years.

"Since his office is in South Carolina, this is going to take more than a few minutes."

"Arrangements have been made, Dr. Rand. If you'll follow me."

"Not until I get a few things I need."

"The Army will provide anything you need."

She glanced at the rank insignia on his khaki uniform. There was a pin affixed to a spot directly over his sternum. "Lieutenant, do you really want to go shopping for things a woman needs?"

He paused but showed no emotion. "I suppose five minutes wouldn't hurt, ma'am."

Four minutes later Tess was out the door. Ten minutes later she was the lone passenger on a Beechcraft C-12 Huron. The twin-engine prop plane wasted no time climbing to its cruising altitude. Early morning clouds gave way to a bright blue sky. The Pratt & Whitney turboprops made the aircraft vibrate as it climbed.

The army lieutenant who retrieved her from her apartment offered no information. Tess had tested the waters with a few probing questions, but if the man knew anything—which she doubted—he wasn't talking. All she could do was wait.

The craft touched down fewer than two hours later, and Tess exited to find another army lieutenant waiting by a car. He smiled, opened the door for her, waited until she was seated in the back, then closed the door. A few minutes later she passed through the gates to Fort Jackson and was driven straight to the Concrete Palace, where she'd briefed J. J.'s team.

Colonel Mac waited at the entry door and escorted her through the stages of security as he had done before. This time she was not led to the conference room but to a different space, one that required passing through two levels of biometric security. She stopped two steps into the room. Monitors hung on the walls, and a large table dominated the floor. Smaller desks lined one room. Tess had never been in the Situation Room in the White House, but she imagined it looked much like this.

"Is it unprofessional to say, 'Wow'?"

Colonel Mac chuckled. "I hope not. I said the same thing—basically."

"But with more, um, flair?"

"Flair. I like that."

"Is . . ."

"J. J. and the others are fine. That's not why you're here."

She felt the tension melt away. Someone to her right moved. He had been standing in the back corner of the room. He had a billiard build, and a head to match. He wore wire-rimmed glasses that made her think of John Denver.

"Dr. Tess Rand, meet Dr. Smith."

"Dr. Smith?" She held out her hand.

"It will do for now."

"Let me guess: The badge you wear at work has a different name."

He had a pleasant smile. "It might."

"Billions of dollars of taxpayers' money are spent each year on foreign intelligence, and the best pseudonym we can come up with is Smith."

"My wife's maiden name was Smith," Mac said.

Tess's cheeks warmed. "Sorry—not about your wife's name being Smith, but about . . . I'm going to quit while I'm ahead." She looked back at Smith. "Which branch of . . . Never mind. Why am I here?"

"First, we want to bring you into the loop," Smith said. His voice seemed a half-octave too high.

"Have a seat." Mac motioned to a chair at the table. Tess did as he suggested. Both men continued to stand, which made her nervous.

"We received this a few hours ago." Smith nodded at a man seated behind one of the monitors. Sound poured from overhead speakers.

"My employer wants his money returned."

"I'm sorry, my friend, but a deal is a deal. We all took risks and knew that things might go wrong. It is the way in modern business. And please don't threaten me again. It will do you no good."

A pause.

"Stupid rich tourists."

"Did you say something, El-Sayyed?"

"Nothing to concern you, Michael."

"El-Sayyed?"

"Yes."

"Two can play your game."

"What does that mean?"

Tess heard an ear-pounding noise and nothing more.

"You're kidding." As soon as she uttered the words, Tess felt stupid. "I mean . . . Where did this come from? Where's the rest of the conversation? What about—"

Smith raised a hand. "The conversation ended abruptly. You heard the thud?"

"Yes."

"It was the sound of a rocket propelled grenade hitting El-Sayyed's boat."

"Someone attacked him?"

Smith nodded.

"They did more than attack him, Dr. Rand. They put an end to his sorry, worthless existence."

"Killed? Someone killed El-Sayyed?"

"The Egyptian authorities have his body—well, most of it— enough of it." Smith put his hands behind his back. "There were eyewitnesses."

"Who is responsible for the assassination? And how did you record the phone call? It was a phone call, right?"

Smith smiled politely but said nothing.

Tess thought for a moment. She would never get a straight answer out of the portly spook, but she could make some guesses.

The attack on world leaders may have opened a door of international cooperation—at least for one purpose.

"Where was El-Sayyed when this little mishap occurred?"

"On the Nile," Mac said.

"They killed him in his own backyard?" Tess couldn't believe her ears.

"Apparently, he crossed the wrong man," Smith said.

"Who?"

"We're still working on that. We do know the other end of the call came from Mexico."

"You've been receiving briefings from my office," Mac said. "You see the connection?"

"The woman . . . the hesitant bomber. She said her parents were being held in Mexico."

"And?"

"And the team found evidence of video sent from somewhere in Mexico to a villa outside of Rome."

"True. What you don't know is the Internet routing from Mexico to Rome was nearly impossible to trace. The Italian intelligence agencies are working on narrowing it down, but there's a good chance they'll fail."

"Mexico is a huge country, Colonel."

"Yup, 760,000 square miles, more than 105 million people, and has the fifteenth largest economy in the world. I've done my homework."

"I'm not getting the connection," Tess admitted. "Mexico has been a supporter of the war on terrorism. Why would someone in Mexico want to kill or maim twenty . . . of . . . the world's . . . Oh." She pinched the bridge of her nose. "I've should have known. Narco-terroism."

Saying the word made Tess feel ill.

Mac stared at her. "What do you know about narco-terrorism?"

"It's not my primary field, but I know some things. I know they are far worse than most people in this country know. If memory serves, they smuggle forty billion dollars worth of drugs across the border and smuggle U.S. weapons back across the border. Close to fifteen thousand people have been killed in Mexico during the drug war over the last few years."

Unable to sit any longer, Tess stood and began to pace. "The attack on the world leaders in Naples had nothing to do with ideology. It had to do with money made on drugs. If that woman had been successful, she might have killed our president, the president of Mexico, maybe the Canadian leader as well."

"It's no secret that President Huffington is giving serious consideration to increasing our efforts along the border: fences, National Guard, and a few billion dollars into Mexico."

"I recently read about a thirteen-year-old who was forced to kill a man. Later he told a reporter he enjoyed it and that he knew he could get away with it." The details of the article burned in her brain. "But which drug lord could be responsible?"

"We may know that," Smith said. "We've analyzed the voice of the man El-Sayyed called Michael. He's a bad one. Rotten to the core. Killed his own parents when he was fifteen to prove he could be trusted by one drug lord."

"Who?"

"We don't have a name. For years there have been rumors about a man named Lobito—Little Wolf."

"There's nothing little about him," Mac said. "I've been talking to the DEA and others. They tell me Lobito is well armed and doesn't mind leaving bodies in his wake."

Tess thought for a moment. "Why am I here? I know a little about this problem, but my field is—"

"There is someone I want you to talk to."

The colonel's words drew her up short. "Who?"

"The woman who tried to kill the world's most important leaders."

HERNANDO SOTO SAT BENEATH the shade of a large umbrella and sipped beer from a bottle. Spread across a concrete outdoor table decorated with hand-painted Mexican tiles lay several newspapers, three from the United States and two from Mexico. Ancient, handcrafted Mayan figurines held the papers in place against the gentle breeze that pushed through shade trees and over the lush lawn. Overhead, a blue sky created a backdrop for the one thousand species of birds who called Mexico home. Hernando could only name a handful of birds and had no desire to learn more. His had been a study of human nature—especially the human need for addiction.

He set down the *New York Times* and gazed over the panorama before him. He owned everything his eye could see, including the two towns, each fifteen miles from his compound. He provided each town with protection and employment the citizens could find nowhere else. Less than two thousand people occupied the villages, but each person was dedicated to him. They had to be. Most worked in growing and processing the heroin, cocaine, and marijuana that had made him the wealthiest man, not only in Mexico, but Central America as well.

He was not the only drug cartel leader, but he was the most powerful. Over twenty years Hernando had unified several cartels under his leadership and eradicated those who refused to cooperate. His real genius lay in his ability to transport drugs across the U.S.

border. His heroin was distributed to the western U.S., Colombian heroin to the eastern part of the country. Not only had he made riches in creating the drugs others would sell, but he took a cut from other cartel leaders by transporting the drugs along his well-developed channels.

He had three rules: one, complete every promise; two, remain anonymous; three, eradicate anyone who wronged him.

Motion caught in Hernando's periphery vision drew his attention. A large man with a larger belly swaggered to the table. He held a cigar in his teeth.

"Is it done, Michael?" Hernando returned his attention to the *Times*.

"It is, brother. The television news is starting to carry the news about a terrorist attack on a wealthy Egyptian."

The irony made Hernando smile. "A terrorist attack on a terrorist. You did give him an opportunity to do right by me?"

Michael sat at the table, removed the cigar from his mouth, and stubbed it out on the ground. "Yes. I told him you wanted your money back. He refused."

Hernando shrugged. "Pity. I liked the man. He did some good work for us."

"Apparently, when it comes to money, he has no honor."

"When it comes to money, brother, no one has honor."

"Perhaps you are right. What now?"

"That depends on what the authorities do next. Our anonymity should still be in place. I doubt El-Sayyed ever revealed who he was working for."

"He can't now. They fished out some of his body, but it won't be talking." Michael laughed at his macabre joke.

"Was he alone?"

"No, our men saw several other people on the boat."

Hernando thought for a moment. "Could they identify anyone?"

Michael shook his head. "They took video footage. They will send it to us for analysis as soon as they are out of country and can arrange a secure Internet connection. They're a little busy fleeing for their lives."

"I imagine." Hernando put the paper down. "We lost a precious opportunity to send an unforgettable message. Now the U.S. and Mexican presidents live and continue to hinder our work."

"At least the world thinks it was Islamic terrorists who committed the acts."

"Maybe," Michael said.

"Never underestimate your enemy, Michael. They are usually smarter than we think."

"I'm not so sure, brother. No one has ever connected any of our . . . *work* with you, and even if they do, finding you is nearly impossible."

"Nothing is impossible these days."

Michael pulled another cigar from his shirt pocket but didn't light it, and Hernando knew he wouldn't. "I wish you would try one of these. They are fresh from Cuba."

"Smoke pollutes the body. You know my feelings about consuming unhealthy substances."

"Beer isn't unhealthy?" Michael pointed at the beer bottle with his cigar.

"Moderation in all things, brother. Beer has many healthy qualities; cigars have none."

"If you say so, brother." Michael changed the subject. "What shall we do with our guests?"

Hernando looked up at the sky again. "Keep them safe a little while longer. We may need them."

"Need them? For what?"

"Do we know why the primary suicide bomber's vest did not explode?"

Michael shrugged. "I assumed that El-Sayyed's men failed to set it up right."

"Perhaps, but what if she found a way to keep it from exploding? We have to assume she is still alive."

"So what? She knows nothing about us. She might know a few things about El-Sayyed's team, but your plan kept us at arm's distance. She knows nothing."

Hernando frowned. Even as a child Michael worked hard at not working. He worked equally hard at not thinking.

"Do as I say, Michael. We keep the others alive until we have a better handle on all that has happened. What did El-Sayyed do with the other girls? He only used three for the mission."

Michael shrugged again. "El-Sayyed did nothing with them. As usual, he left long before the plan went into action. He was already on his way to Egypt before the first move was made."

"That was part of the plan. We knew he'd do that. How else would I know where he was so I could have him killed?"

"You are right, of course, brother."

"Have you learned anything about his lieutenants?" Hernando took another sip of beer.

"Our spies in Naples kept track of them. We know the one named Nasser took the boat out—the one meant to ram the hotel marina. You already know what happened to the boat. The Naples media was able to talk to several of the people who had been on the boat. They said Nasser jumped overboard after he set the yacht on its collision course. If there is any justice in the world, then the propellers chopped the man into fish chum."

"But the world has no justice, so we must assume he escaped. Not that it matters. He was just a flunky." Hernando folded the newspaper. "What about the man that was with the girl in the hotel? Did he escape?"

Michael hesitated. "Our men lost him."

"Lost him?"

"There was great chaos after the explosions. Police and military were everywhere. He presents no problem. He will learn his master is dead and disappear into the sunset. I know these kinds of people."

"Do you? I'm not sure you do. In any case, keep the hostages alive for another day or two just in case we need them, but we need to move them.

"I know just the place."

"To be safe, make preparations to dispose of the bodies."

"It will be my pleasure."

"I'm sure it will, Michael. I'm sure it will."

CHAPTER 31

TESS SAT AT THE large table and gazed at the video wall. Colonel Mac had brought Tess up to speed. "The woman is being held in a secure hospital somewhere in Naples. She is under guard at all times. She has no debilitating physical injuries, but she is showing signs of stress and fatigue. She's been quite emotional."

"No wonder. I'd be a basket case if I went through what she's gone through. Will she be able to see me?"

"Yes, the Italian military has set up a camera and monitor on their end. Remember not to mention where you are, what building you're in, or anything else that might sacrifice security. Use only your first name."

"It's not like she can do anything more. . . . Oh, you're thinking someone might be listening in."

"We've taken every precaution, but technology changes overnight. We think we have every base covered. Still, it pays to be paranoid."

Five minutes later the video link was established, and Tess got her first look at the woman who almost brought chaos to the world.

Delaram looked fragile, like a broken ceramic pot hastily put back together. Tess immediately felt sorry for her, an emotion her logical mind checked by recalling the woman had been ready to kill a room full of world leaders. The suicide bomber wore a pink hospital gown and lay on a hospital bed with the covers pulled to her waist. Both arms were strapped to the bed.

Tess leaned toward the screen. "Can you hear me?"

The woman looked to the side and, for a moment, Tess was certain she was averting her eyes. Then she realized Delaram was looking at the monitor, not the camera. It was a human thing to do: to look at the person speaking even if the person was on a flat-screen monitor.

"I can hear you."

Delaram's voice bore a slight accent, one Tess couldn't recognize. "They tell me your name is Delaram."

She gave a slight nod. "Yes. I imagine they told you many things about me."

Tess smiled. "True. My name is Tess. How are you feeling?"

"I wish I were dead."

Tess didn't know what to say. "Why?"

"You are not serious with that question, are you?"

"Perhaps I shouldn't be, but I am."

"My life is over, not that that matters, but I failed my parents." She looked away. "Who are you?"

"As I said, my name is Tess."

Delaram frowned. "I didn't ask your name, I asked who you are."

"I'm a professor, Delaram. I study things, like suicide bombers."

"You're a spy?"

Tess tried to form a disarming smile. It didn't sit comfortably on her face. "No. I do research and I consult and teach."

"So am I your next subject?"

"Not today. I need your help."

"My help? I couldn't help my parents. I couldn't help myself. How can I help you?"

Tess kept her voice soft, gentle. The woman on the monitor had the strength of tissue paper. The wrong word could rip a hole in her. "I'm not going to pretend I know what you're going through. I can't comprehend it, and I doubt anyone else can. However, I don't believe your life is over."

"It might as well be. The best that waits for me is prison. Execution, if I'm lucky."

"Why?"

She laughed, but it came out hollow. "Maybe they didn't tell you everything. Not long ago I tried to kill many people. Judging by your accent, I tried to kill your president."

"Did you?"

"I was the only one in the room with a bomb strapped beneath her dress."

"Did you press the button?"

Delaram closed her eyes.

"Delaram, I asked you a question. Did you set off the bomb?"

"No." The word came so quietly that Tess barely heard it. From the corner of her eye, Tess noticed Colonel Mac talking to Dr. Smith. "Why not?"

"I don't know."

"I think you do, Delaram. I think it was impossible for you to detonate that bomb."

"I didn't want to die then, but I do now."

"That's not what stopped you. It wasn't that you couldn't push the button; you *refused* to press it. Isn't that right?"

"I don't know."

"Delaram, I've heard all the details. I even spoke to someone who was very close to you—" Colonel Mac cleared his throat. Tess continued as if she hadn't heard it. "You left a clue at the villa in Rome. You left your fingernails. Why?"

"I don't know."

"Yes, you do. You guessed that someone might come looking for your kidnappers. You wanted them to know that you weren't a Muslim extremist. You wanted to leave behind a little bit of DNA. Am I right?"

Delaram nodded. Tess could see tears forming in the young woman's eyes.

"I guess."

Tess leaned back. "Listen, girl, some people consider you a hero."

"I'm not a hero. A hero would not have been there at all. A hero would have saved her parents."

"I won't lie to you, Delaram. I have no idea what will happen to you. I am a person with very little authority, but I will do my best to tell your story the way it should be told: You are a victim who so loved her family, you were willing to die to save them."

"And kill others to save them."

"That's how it looks, but it isn't the truth. Your refusal to detonate that bomb shows me you valued the lives of the others in the room."

Tears flowed like rivers. "Someone else could have set off the bomb. I'm sure they told you that."

"They did, but that doesn't matter. The point is, you chose not to."

"I went in the room knowing that if I didn't set the thing off, *he* would . . ." She dissolved into sobs. Tears dripped from her cheeks, mucus puddled beneath her nose.

"Someone get the woman a tissue!" Tess had no authority to give orders, but she guessed those on the other side didn't know that. "And release one of her hands so she can use it."

"Easy, Tess."

She cut Colonel Mac a harsh glance, then whispered, "You want to cut the link, or do you want me to do what you asked me to do?"

He didn't respond. Tess watched as a uniformed soldier removed the restraint on Delaram's right wrist and handed her a tissue. There was nothing more she could do but wait for Delaram to regain her composure. The woman's façade had fallen.

It took five minutes for Delaram to compose herself. Such an achievement, made in so little time, was remarkable. "Delaram, may I ask you a few questions?"

"I am not going anywhere."

"We want to find your parents."

Delaram looked stunned. "They are dead."

"How do you know?"

She dabbed at her eyes. "Because I failed and the whole world knows about the bombings."

"All the world knows is that two bombs went off near the G-20 hotel. The media knows nothing about you."

Delaram shook her head. "That does not matter. Abasi would know, and if he knows, then his owner knows. They said if I failed, my parents would die."

"Abasi was the man with you?" Tess already knew the answer but wanted to keep Delaram talking.

"I only know two names. I've told the people here this. Abasi and Nasser. I overheard their names. I don't know any more."

"That doesn't matter, Delaram. We know about them." She paused, uncertain which way to go. "We know that digital information, most likely a video, or a large photo—maybe a series of photos—came to the villa where you were held. Our experts have done some tracing, and it seems like it came from Mexico. Does that mean anything to you?"

"Yes." She offered nothing more.

"Can you tell me about it?" Tess wanted to press her softly. Even over the monitors, she could tell Delaram was recalling something.

"One of the girls committed suicide. Her name was Fila. They made us watch the execution of her husband and son."

Tess's stomach turned. "They made you watch the execution?"

"The screen went blank, but we heard two shots. I'm sure they have done the same to my parents."

"Maybe not. We're going on the assumption they're still alive. Were your parents in Mexico?"

She nodded. "They are perpetual tourists. My family has money and they love to travel. They've taken me all over the world. My father enjoys architecture, especially cathedrals. Mexico has many interesting buildings."

"Did your father want to see any particular building?"

"Yes, the Sinking Palace in Mexico City."

Tess furrowed her brow. "Sinking Palace?"

"It is an art museum. My father told me it had sunk more than four meters since it was completed in the late thirties."

"Four meters . . . twelve feet?"

"I think a little more than that."

"Did they call you when they traveled?"

"Yes. Often."

"Where were they when you last heard from them?"

"Monterrey. There is a cathedral there that has been standing since the late 1700s."

"That was the last word you had from them?"

"Yes."

"Delaram, when your parents traveled, did they rent a car?"

"Usually. My mother has a bad back and needs a luxury car to travel in comfort."

Tess let that sink in. "I need you to give me your parents' cell phone number."

"Which one? My mother's or my father's."

"Both."

Delaram recited the numbers. "My father also carried a business phone. He didn't like business calls coming in on his personal phone."

"You'd better give me that number too."

Delaram did. "Do you really think they are still alive?"

"We hope so, Delaram. No one can be sure."

"But you said you'd look for them."

"We will." *If we find them, then we might find who did this.*

"May I ask a question?"

"Sure," Tess said. "You let me ask a bunch."

"Do you know a man named J. J.?"

Tess's stomach flipped. She knew J. J. had been in the building with Delaram, but nothing more. "I've heard of him. Why do you ask?"

Delaram looked away. "Can you get a message to him?"

"I can try."

"He saved my life. He saved everyone's lives. He stayed with me and disarmed the bomb so I could live. I want you to tell him— thank you."

The image of J. J. inches from an improvised plastic explosive bomb made Tess ill. She began to tremble and folded her hands to keep it from showing. "He's the one who disarmed the bomb?"

"Yes. Another man helped, but he was the one who freed me from the bomb. He could have died with me. If the bomb had gone off while he was so close, his face by the explosive—"

"I will do my best to make sure he knows how grateful you are."

"Thank you."

The video link went blank.

"Are you okay?"

Tess ignored the colonel's question. Instead she rose, stepped to an empty trash can by the door, lifted the can, and vomited.

CHAPTER 32

TP-01, A BOEING 757-225 belonging to the Mexican Air Force, lifted off from Heathrow Airport with Moyer and his team. President Huffington had made calls and pulled in favors to make the trip possible. Most of Moyer would have preferred to finish the flight to the U.S. in Air Force One, but his mission wasn't over, which made the other part of Moyer happy.

Not as large or as sophisticated as Air Force One, TP-01 was no slacker in the presidential transportation department. Most of Moyer's team sat in reclined seats, napping. He couldn't blame them. A nice, firm bed sounded tempting. Instead of sleeping, though, Moyer reviewed the information he received before deplaning in Heathrow. Using onboard communications, he had conferred with Colonel Mac about the next few steps.

"The president has cleared the way for operations in Mexico," Colonel Mac said. "You have been given an unprecedented opportunity. The Mexican military doesn't like us playing on their field anymore than the Italians. Their military has worked with ours in the past, but just as recently as last year they ruled out joint raids against drug lords."

"If I remember right, Colonel, they wanted our help with logistics and equipment, but not boots on the ground."

"Exactly. That's changed with the rise of violence along the border and drug lord invasion of U.S. cities—that and the fact your team kept Mexico's president from being shredded by a bomb."

"Small favors go a long way, Colonel."

"Yes, they do." Mac paused for a moment. Over the headphones he wore in the communication room Moyer heard the sound of rustling paper. "You'll land in Mexico City. It will be after dark. After the president and his entourage deplane, you and your team will remain aboard for two additional hours."

"That's a long time, sir," Moyer said. "Considering our mission, I mean."

"I'm aware of that. You will remain for two additional hours to give time for the press to leave and for the Mexican army to make ready for you. From TP-01, you will be taken aboard a military helo to the airport in Monterrey. By that time we may have a better address for you."

"I'd hate to show up at the wrong door."

"That would be bad, Moyer. Real bad. That's why we have to do this right. You will have full military operational latitude. Just don't shoot any of the good guys."

"We'll be careful, sir. May I ask a question?"

"Ask it."

"What are the odds the hostages are still alive?"

"It's not impossible, but it's not likely. I'll have more info for you later. Operations are beginning."

"Understood, sir."

"Oh, one last thing. Tess wants you to give J. J. a kiss for her."

"Colonel, that ain't gonna happen."

"I told her so."

Moyer removed the headset and handed it to the communication's officer seated to his right. He rose from his chair and wondered what the next few hours held.

ZINSSER FELT A BEAD of sweat trickle along his temple. He wiped it off with the back of his hand, then reached up to the fresh air port above his head and gave it another twist, increasing the flow. His vision blurred, then narrowed, then returned to normal. He took a ragged breath and looked around. The Mexican president's plane had grown quiet. Some passengers slept; most of his unit slept. The recent events, the near disaster, had left every reporter, every aide, and every team member exhausted.

Zinsser wanted to sleep, but he was afraid to close his eyes—afraid of what waited for him in the darkness.

A resounding *pop* made him jump. He looked around. It sounded like a gunshot. No, it couldn't be a gunshot. Something must have happened to the hull's integrity. He glanced up waiting for orange oxygen masks to drop. None did.

Something pounded his chest, beating from the inside like a man trying to kick open a locked door. His lungs stopped, then restarted a few moments later. Despite his fear, he closed his eyes.

Gunfire. Hot salty air. Crowd noises. The crackling of a radio in his ear. "Data, it's Echo. I'm hit. I'M HIT." He heard AK-47 fire and felt a bullet sail by his ear. His temple pounded. His scalp felt on fire. *"Data, it's Echo. I need you, man. I need you. Don't let me die here. Where are you?"*

"No," Zinsser whispered. "It's not real. It didn't happen that way."

The sound of distant helicopters.

He forced his eyes open. The 757 was gone. The passengers were gone. In their place were the buildings and streets of Kismayo. He could smell the acrid odor of spent gunpowder. He knew it was wrong, understood that it was impossible. He was strapped to a seat of a plane flying 35,000 feet over the Atlantic.

"Move over."

"Data, I'm hit. Where are you? They're coming for—"

A sharp pain raced down Zinsser's left arm. "I *said*, move over." He looked up and saw the massive head and black face of Rich Harbison. Rich was always quick with a smile and a joke, but he wasn't smiling. Or joking.

"What? Um, sure." Zinsser popped his seat belt and moved one seat over, then decided it might be wiser to move to the window seat.

Rich dropped his large frame into the aisle seat and moved the armrest to his right up and out of the way. Zinsser watched the man study him like he could vacuum him up through his eyes. "You okay?" His words were soft.

Zinsser grinned. "Sure. Great. Why?"

"Because you were about to push your fingers through the arm rests, and I'm pretty sure our government would have to pay for new ones."

"Really? I hadn't noticed."

Rich leaned toward Zinsser, and Zinsser leaned back against the plastic hull covering. "I don't scare, Zinsser. You know that, right? Not much scares me."

"I'd never doubt your bravery."

"Yeah, well, you scare me, pal. You give me the shivers."

Zinsser didn't like Rich's tone. If it came down to a fistfight, Zinsser figured he could get in maybe three good punches before the big man folded him like a blanket and stuffed him under one of the seats.

"That was never my intent." The rapid fire of an AK-47 set on auto echoed in his head. He ignored it.

"Data, I need you."

"I've told Boss this and now I'm going to tell you. I think he was wrong and continues to be wrong. I would have sent you home."

"If it's any comfort, Rich. I would have sent me home, too."

"Yet here you are." The words were hot but soft.

That did it. Zinsser leaned closer, their noses just inches apart. "May I speak freely?"

"Do it."

Zinsser could smell the man's breath. "I didn't ask for this thing in my head. If I thought it would go as far as it has, I would have disqualified myself."

"But you didn't."

"No, Shaq, I didn't. Maybe someday I'll be as perfect as you think you are."

Rich raised a finger. "I will not let you screw up this mission. Understood? You will do as you're told. I'll be there to make sure you do."

"I've got it under control."

"That's not what I just saw." Rich stood. "Heaven help you if you get one of the unit killed."

Zinsser's anger rose. "You got a bullet with my name on it? A target that fits my back?"

Rich stepped back to the seat.

"Stow it, gentlemen."

Zinsser looked over the seat back to see Moyer moving his direction. "What's the problem here?"

"No problem, Boss. We were just discussing strategy."

"Strategy, eh? That true, Rich?"

"Just opening the lines of communication a little more."

Moyer's eyes narrowed. "Come with me, Rich."

"Boss—" Zinsser began.

"I don't want to hear it."

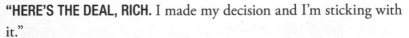

"HERE'S THE DEAL, RICH. I made my decision and I'm sticking with it."

"Boss, the man is a menace. We can't depend on him. He shouldn't be on the team."

Moyer closed his eyes, then opened them slowly. "Rich, I'm only going to say this once. You're my friend, and you're the best soldier on the team, but I'm the one in charge. I make the decisions. I call the shots. You may not like them, but you will obey them. I don't expect you to agree, and I went out of my way to make sure none of this can be laid at your feet. Is any of that unclear?"

"No, Boss. It's just—"

"There are no 'it's justs,' Rich. My gut tells me we need him. He made connections we overlooked or couldn't find."

"He pulled a gun on you."

"Yeah, I was there, remember? I'm a good soldier, and I know a good soldier when I see one. If you want, you can write me up when we get home. Better yet, I've been given full access to onboard communications. I can call Colonel Mac right now, and you can tell him the unit leader isn't doing things the way you want. You want to do that, Rich?"

"No, of course not."

"Good. Let's put this issue to bed. Can we do that?"

"Yes, Boss."

"Good, because we've got a mission to plan."

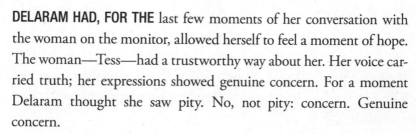

DELARAM HAD, FOR THE last few moments of her conversation with the woman on the monitor, allowed herself to feel a moment of hope. The woman—Tess—had a trustworthy way about her. Her voice carried truth; her expressions showed genuine concern. For a moment Delaram thought she saw pity. No, not pity: concern. Genuine concern.

Turning her head Delaram looked out the window. She was on the fourth floor, and the only view she had was the cluttered rooftop of another shorter wing of the hospital. She shifted her focus to the glass in the window. She estimated the window to be three feet wide and its sill three or three-and-a-half feet above the floor.

She had not been allowed to look out the window, and she wondered if it offered an unobstructed fall to the ground below.

She wondered if she could throw her body against the glass hard enough to shatter it and propel her body through. If she tried, there would only be one opportunity.

She was still strapped to the bed.

There was always someone in the room with her.

Still, if the opportunity presented itself . . .

An odd thought floated into her mind. *What would Tess think?*

ABASI STRAIGHTENED HIS YELLOW tie and slipped into his blue suit. He checked his wallet and his passport. The name on the passport and on his Egyptian driver's license read "Baya Bakari." He examined himself in the mirror. He looked like any of ten thousand international businessmen traveling today. His eyes concerned him: they were red and puffy from hours of weeping.

He first learned of El-Sayyed's death from a BBC broadcast. The revelation came like a hot dagger to the stomach. Of course, the news spent most of its time on the events in Naples, but they managed to squeeze in a short story about a wealthy Egyptian killed on the Nile by terrorists. He didn't have to ask who had committed the crime.

Vacillating between rage and abject sorrow, Abasi had stayed in his room and away from the hotel staff. Repeatedly he asked Allah how such a great and kind man as El-Sayyed could be allowed to die this way. Perhaps Allah would consider the great man's death a martyr's demise.

Abasi decided it was time to carry on. Plans had been made for his departure; he saw no reason to change them. He would drive the one hundred fifty-three miles to Rome and board EgyptAir flight 792. Four hours later he would be in Cairo, where he'd buy another ticket.

To Mexico.

CHAPTER 33

J. J. KNEW MANY soldiers shut down their emotions. A few had become more robot than human, especially on missions. He'd been taught to keep emotions in check. It was difficult to shoot straight while screaming like a Girl Scout. His training had also taught him that directed emotion could sharpen the senses and make a man more efficient. Some emotions, however, were never useful.

Impatience being one of them.

TP-01 had landed smoothly in Mexico City, and all but the team had deplaned. Every person on board had been sworn to secrecy by the president of Mexico himself, and everyone seemed to take his words as promise and threat.

Two hours passed in near silence. Sleeping seemed the wise thing to do, and J. J. gave it a shot. No dice. Pete and Jose found a deck of cards and played some game J. J. didn't recognize. J. J. tried to read a newspaper someone left behind, but his Spanish was too lacking to make out more than a few sentences. He tried pacing, but the others gave him the stink eye, so he settled in one of the seats.

He wanted to look out the window, but the plastic shades had been closed. Workmen had set the craft to receive power from the airport. That meant air flowed and the lights worked. It also meant the communications station was operational. Not that anyone was using it.

Moyer and Rich sat at the back of the plane, talking softly, asking "What if" questions. J. J. guessed they lacked any hard intel to do more than guess at a worthwhile mission approach. The first thing J. J. learned after enlisting was how to wait without complaining. In the early days of his Army career, he'd felt like he spent a third of every day waiting to be told what to do. It was one reason many soldiers took up cigarettes. J. J. avoided that, but he understood the desire to have something to do.

He leaned his head back and closed his eyes. Images of Tess pressed to the forefront of his mind. He could see her; he could smell the shampoo she used and the spritz of perfume she preferred. Lord willing, he would soon be introducing her as his wife instead of fiancée.

"What are you grinning about?"

J. J. looked up to see Jose standing next to him. "That's my secret."

"Trust me, it's no secret. Does she know you drool when you sleep?"

J. J. sat up. "No, I don't."

"I've seen it, buddy. Time and time again. Two words: rubber pillows."

"Very funny, Medina. You been sampling the morphine in your med kit?"

"Never. Now if the med kit came with beer . . ."

J. J. grinned. "I bet you could find some in the galley."

"I thought of that. The boss man nixed the idea."

"So you thought you'd interrupt my reverie. Bored with Pete?"

Jose shook his head. "We're trying to stir up a poker game to kill time. You wanna play."

"Nah, but thanks."

"You sure? It's your paycheck we're betting on."

"Funny man."

"Hey, I got a bunch of kids to support—"

A pounding sound came from the front of the aircraft. Moyer and Rich appeared from the back. "Pete," Moyer said.

J. J. saw Moyer motion to the front door. Leaning into the aisle, J. J. watched Pete step to the passenger entrance door just behind the cockpit area. He peered out the porthole. The pounding returned, and Pete turned. The noise came from the front starboard emergency exit. He looked through that door's window, then stepped back.

Moyer pushed past Jose and moved forward like an ice cutter in the Arctic. From the small steward's storage closet Moyer pulled a 9mm handgun and handed it to Pete. He took one for himself. They had stored their weapons before takeoff in Italy.

The rest of the team went forward and received handguns from Moyer then spread out through the seating.

"Open it, Pete."

Pete Rasor turned the long, silver release handle. The door swung in. As it did, Moyer and Pete raised their weapons. J. J., like the other team members, kept the muzzle of his weapon down.

"Avon calling." The voice came from a man J. J. couldn't see. The accent was decidedly American. A moment later, "I presume one of you is Sergeant Major Eric Moyer."

"Identify yourself," Pete demanded.

"Smith. Dr. Larry Smith. Colonel Mac sends his regards. So does Tess Rand."

J. J. heard her name and his heart quickened. "She said to tell J. J. . . . wait, I want to make sure I get this right . . . that he needs to be careful because life isn't worth living without him."

Several snickers echoed down the 757.

Moyer lowered his weapon.

MOYER LOWERED HIS WEAPON and took in the scene. A man with a barrel-shaped body and bald head stood in what looked like a small shipping container. It took a moment for Moyer to make sense of it. He had seen workers at airports drive a vehicle to the side of an airliner, and then, using a scissors lift, raise a boxy container to the side door of the aircraft. It was how airline caterers off-loaded the drinks and goodies to be distributed on the flight.

"I didn't expect this kind of entrance."

"It's important to keep up appearances. Permission to come aboard?" The man held a large brown envelope.

"I don't know," Pete said. "That sounds like Navy talk."

"Just my attempt at humor. I'm still trying to grow a funny bone."

"I think we have room for one more." Moyer stepped back and Smith moved in. "I hope you're here to spring us. We were told to wait two hours—"

"And it's been closer to four. Sorry. I couldn't get here faster, and it wouldn't have mattered if I did. Intel wasn't ready."

"Is it ready now?"

"We have a few things to discuss, yes."

Moyer introduced Smith to the team. When he introduced J. J., Smith smiled. "So you're the lucky man."

J. J. blushed, something Moyer hadn't seen before.

"Okay, let's talk," Smith said. "Do you want me to brief you alone or with everyone present?"

"Everyone. It'll save me from repeating the info."

"Got it. Take a seat, gentlemen." He opened the large envelope. "We've been busy. Colonel Mac played a wild card and got a good result. He had Tess Rand speak to the bomber chick—"

"Delaram," J. J. said.

"Yes, Delaram. He felt she could get more out of her than an intel officer or a man in uniform. As an expert in female suicide bombers, she might make more headway than any of us. Besides, she already knows the mission, and that kept us from pulling in another person. She proved very effective."

"How so?" Moyer asked.

"As you know, the bombers were not typical. None appear to be martyrs scattering their body parts for the cause. You already know about the abductees of which Delaram was one. We also know that El-Sayyed—who is dead, if you haven't heard—was not the only man behind the scheme to blow up twenty of the world's leaders."

Zinsser's forehead creased. "Dead?"

"Yup. Someone sent a couple of RPGs into the man's luxury boat. He and the boat are no more."

"I'm assuming his partner did that," Moyer said.

"Yeah," Smith said, "a little over the top way of ending a partnership."

"So who is his partner?"

"Forgive me if I repeat anything you already know, but here it is in a nutshell. We were monitoring El-Sayyed in Egypt. He received a cell call that we traced to Mexico—which is why you're here. Turns out the call originated on a landline. We've been working with Mexican authorities to trace it. The call was made from a small village called Frontera."

"Border."

Moyer glanced at Jose. "What?"

"The word is the feminine for *border.*"

Smith nodded. "Makes sense. It's not far from the U.S. border. Far enough away to keep it from observing eyes in the U.S. but close enough to be a problem. There is another town near by: Colina Verde. Neither is much to look at."

"And our man is in one of these towns?" Moyer asked.

"No, but we think he might be nearby. The villages are small but the inhabitants seem to be doing well. They have no industry so that makes me think they work in drug processing."

Rich arched a brow. "Does this man have a name?"

Smith frowned. "No, but the DEA and their Mexican counterparts hear stories of Lobito—Little Wolf. We do know that there is a mastermind who had managed to create a confederation of drug lords. The impact on U.S. cities has been stunning. Violence that used to be confined to border areas now extends as far north as Seattle. We think the mastermind of that coalition is the same guy that brought El-Sayyed into the picture."

"And he tried to kill the world leaders because our president and the Mexican president are discussing a border fence."

"Among other things. Those two were most likely his targets, but, by killing the other leaders, he would be making quite a statement." He handed Moyer a photo. "We have satellite surveillance. We also have been allowed to fly an MQ-1 UAV Predator over the area for real-time recon."

Moyer had seen the unmanned aerial vehicle several times. It had been used in Iraq, Afghanistan, Serbia, and Yemen. The remotely piloted vehicle could do anything from reconnaissance to hunter-killer missions. The MQ-9, a larger version of the MQ-1, was capable of firing Hellfire II missiles into ground targets.

"Here are some night shots taken earlier this evening." Smith handed out the pictures. "The U.S. Border Patrol ran the mission. They were in place and ready to go. They also have experience flying the border area. As you can see, there are the two villages I mentioned. What else do you see?"

Both the daytime satellite photo and the Predator image revealed a sprawling mansion. "I see a house built by someone who likes his privacy."

"Exactly. We think our man lives there."

Moyer studied the images for a moment then handed them to Rich. "What about the hostages. Are they in this guy's house?"

"Doubtful. Delaram gave us two bits of info that proved especially useful. One, her parents rented a car. She said they were prone to luxury vehicles because of her mother's back."

"You have to have a bad back to like a nice car?" Rich said.

"Their motive doesn't matter. We checked with rental companies, and, sure enough, a Cadillac Escalade out of Mexico City has gone missing." Smith removed another photo and handed it to Moyer. "This is from a flyover of Frontera."

Moyer saw several boxy buildings lining a dark street. Had it not been for the low-light camera aboard the Predator, Moyer wouldn't be able to see anything. A dark vehicle was parked next to a small warehouse. "That could be a Caddy. Doesn't fit with the other cars, none of which looks newer than the mid-eighties. Still, how do you know this is their rental?"

"Recon over Colina Verde doesn't show any vehicle that could be mistaken for a late model SUV, but the real kicker is this: Delaram gave us the cell phone numbers for her parents. We've been able to get their call records. The personal phone for her dad and the one for her mother haven't been used since the abduction. In fact, there's been no signal from them at all. We assume the phones were taken and destroyed."

"Makes sense," Rich said.

"But we caught a break. Delaram's dad also carried a high-end smart phone for his business. She said that he would only check it a few times a day when he was traveling. He liked to keep it in the glove box of the car he was using."

Zinsser nodded. "You triangulated the signal."

"Yup. Believe it or not, there's good cell coverage in the area. Many outlying regions get cell phone coverage before anything else. These two towns look like they should be in a third-world country, but they have Internet, satellite television, and cell phones. Most likely Lobito arranged for such things."

"The phone in the car is still working?" Zinsser pressed.

"Yes. I doubt it will last much longer without a charge."

Moyer looked from Smith to his team. "So we have two missions. A rescue mission in Frontera, and a late-night visit to the mansion."

"You may want to forget Frontera," Smith said. "We have grave doubts about any hostage being alive. These are not nice people we're dealing with." Once again, he removed a photo but held onto it. "This isn't pleasant."

Moyer held out his hand and took the photo. He glanced at it, closed his eyes, and tried to keep his stomach down. He handed the picture to Rich, whose hand began to shake. The photo made the rounds. When it reached J. J., Moyer heard, "Blessed Jesus." Had the words come from anyone else, Moyer would have heard it as a meaningless gut reaction. Coming from J. J., the words were a sincere prayer.

He swallowed. "I take it those are the missing women. There were only three bombers that we know of. We found evidence of there being ten or so women."

Smith cleared his throat. "Yes. A man named De Luca found this van. The bodies were inside. Preliminary coroner's report says each had been shot in the head and the van set afire. At least they were dead when the fire got to them."

Every muscle in Moyer's body tensed as one desire, one dream, burned inside him: strangling the people behind this. He forced the thoughts to the back of his mind. "We go after the hostages first. Then we pay a surprise visit to the man in the mansion."

"Colonel Mac said you'd go for the hostages no matter what. He appears to know you very well."

"At times, too well." Moyer stood. "Anyone here feel like setting things right?"

"HOOAH!"

CHAPTER 34

IT SEEMED LIKE DAYS ago when Smith appeared on TP-01 and briefed the team, but Zinsser knew it had only been a matter of hours. Since then, they had gathered what gear they had brought with them, entered the catering truck that hid their exit from prying eyes, and rode in the trailer as it lowered on the scissor lifts and was delivered to a spot beneath one of the airport's terminals. From there they were driven to a private jet that flew them to Base Aérea Militar No. 14 near Monterrey.

An Army captain waited for them in one of the hangers. Two long folding tables held gear, which Zinsser immediately recognized. The items didn't surprise him, nor did the C-130 warming up on the tarmac.

The captain returned salutes. "I'm Matthew Boyle, Fort Bliss. I hear you need a ride." He was lanky but solid. He seemed a tad older than most captains, and Zinsser assumed he began his career as an enlisted man.

"We appreciate that, Captain. We'd be on foot otherwise."

Zinsser watched the officer eye Moyer and detected approval.

"Your men have fifteen minutes to check their equipment, hit the latrine, and get on board the C-130."

"Understood. We'll be on time."

"Good. I want to get the thing back before the base commander knows it's missing."

Moyer looked surprise. "You're kidding me, right, sir?"

"Yeah, I am. Just trying to lighten the moment."

"A little levity is always appreciated, sir."

"Unfortunately we have to get down to business." Captain Boyle turned to the unit. "Gather up, men. I've only got time to say this once." Zinsser and the others formed a semicircle around the man. "I will be your static jumpmaster for this mission. That means I'll be going up with you, but you'll be leaving alone. You already know some of this, but let me give you the details. We will be wheels up in fifteen and head north to the target area. We will come in at 30 feet and 30 miles out you will make a HAHO jump. The moment the last man is out, we will stay in area until we hear a report of safe landing. An extraction team will be in the air shortly and in area an hour after you bail. They will take on fresh fuel before crossing the border. You will bear in mind that these guys will need time to come in. If they get too close, anyone on the ground can hear them—so try and stay out of any kind of trouble that requires immediate aid. Clear?"

As usual, Moyer spoke for them all. "Clear, sir."

Boyle eyed the men. "I'm told that each of you has done High Altitude, High Open jumps. Is that fact?"

"Fact, sir," Moyer said.

"Good, then I'll leave out the trivial stuff, but to make sure we're all on the same page, I'll hit the highlights. You're opening high so the aircraft noise and the noise of your chutes won't alert the enemy. We are assuming the area to be hostile with heavily armed bad guys. At angels thirty you'll exit the aerial platform and deploy fifteen seconds out. Who will be first man out?"

Moyer nodded. "That'd be me, sir."

"Very good. Your gear and that of your men have a compass and GPS. You will be landing in the dark, two hours before sunup. I hear you had to leave equipment behind in the previous theater of operation. Do I have that right?"

"Yes, sir," Moyer said.

"I've taken the liberty of bringing night vision gear and a few other items you may need, including the items you requested. Questions?"

No one spoke.

Boyle looked each man in the eyes, then smiled. "I've done a lot of missions, and part of me wishes I was going with you, but now that I think of it, I'm glad I'm not."

Several of the men chuckled. Zinsser was new to the team but he couldn't imagine anyone of the unit offering his spot to the captain.

The captain clasped his hands behind his back. "I don't know you personally, but I know your kind. I'm one of you. I'm going to ask a question and I want the straight skinny: Does anyone have a reason not to make the jump?"

No reply.

"I don't have the time to ask you individually, so it's up to you to tell me."

Zinsser caught Rich glancing at him. He refused to return the gaze. Instead he kept his eyes on Boyle.

Boyle turned to Moyer. "It's your team, Sergeant Major. You wanna ground anyone?"

Zinsser knew why Boyle belabored the question. They were about to board an aircraft, fly to an altitude where temperatures were well below zero and the atmosphere too thin to hold sufficient oxygen for a man to breathe, leap out the back, try to sail thirty or so miles to the landing zone, and not one of the men had more than a few hours of often interrupted sleep over the last thirty-six hours.

"No," Moyer said. "We're good to go."

Boyle looked at the others. "That true, men? You're ready to kick some bad guy butt?"

"Hooah!"

"You have fifteen minutes to check your gear and dress. Fall out."

WEARINESS BURNED J. J. eyes, but his mind raced with the work before him. He donned the polypropylene knit undergarment to help fight the cold he was about to face, checked his chute, examined the oxygen bottle he would be carrying, and checked the altitude gauge and GPS unit. He went over what seemed like a hundred details. He did one thing none of the others in his team did. He slipped his small field Bible into the leg pocket of his ACU and sealed the Velcro flap.

Thirteen minutes later, he sat in one of the fold-out chairs along the side of the C-130. On his head rested an MICH helmet with modified mask connectors that allowed him to wear night vision goggles. An oxygen mask hung to one side. J. J. buckled himself in and attached his oxygen mask to a feed that would deliver 100-percent oxygen to his lungs, helping him purge nitrogen from his bloodstream. High-altitude jumps, especially those where the soldier opened his canopy early, forcing him to stay at high altitudes longer than a low open jump, could lead to Cassion's Disease—decompression sickness—because of the rapid rise of the jump aircraft. At altitude, the lack of oxygen could lead to hypoxia.

The C-130 rumbled down the runway and slowly lifted into the air. The sound of the landing gear rising rumbled through the hull. Unlike a commercial aircraft, this plane was designed to carry cargo more than people, but its ability to lower a tail ramp while flying made it ideal for jumping.

The first time J. J. jumped out of a plane, he prayed all the way up and all the way down. He saw no need to change the habit now, except he felt no compulsion to pray for himself. He made eye contact with each member of his team. They had been together long enough to know what he was doing. Not one of them followed his faith; not one of them was critical of it. He looked at Moyer and prayed not only for his leader's safety, but wisdom. Moyer returned the gaze and nodded an unspoken *thank you*. Rich did the same, as did the others. When he set his eyes on Zinsser, the man blinked.

J. J. prayed for something else too. He prayed for the captives, should they be alive.

He breathed the oxygen in steady inhalations. Strapped to his body was a small oxygen bottle he would use when he left the aircraft.

He took another look at the men who made up his unit—men he called friends. Jose held a photo of his family; Rich bobbed his head to music only he could hear—probably something from a musical; Pete drummed his fingers on his leg; Moyer stared straight ahead, no doubt working and reworking the plan in his mind; Zinsser stared at the door.

MOYER WAS SECOND-GUESSING HIMSELF, something he seldom did. Maybe he should have pulled Zinsser. What if Rich was right, that the man was a liability?

He studied Zinsser, noted how the man stared at the back of the C-130. Where they'd jump. Was Zinsser thinking of suicide?

You couldn't find a much better way to end a life than to walk out of an airplane.

IT WOULD BE EASY.

Zinsser tried to push the thought from his mind, but he had to admit it was perfect. If this were a static line jump, then he would have to hook a release to a line running along the ceiling of the aircraft. The line would deploy the chute. But that wasn't the case. Every man of the team would waddle to the open end, turn, and jump. Once he did that, he'd be in complete control of his destiny. He could lower his head and raise his feet like a diver, and take the plunge into solid ground.

Someplace in the darkness of his mind he heard gunfire . . . felt the heat of Somalia . . . and saw his now-dead friend.

Yup. No better way to end it all than stepping out of an airplane.

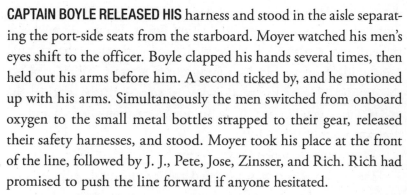

CAPTAIN BOYLE RELEASED HIS harness and stood in the aisle separating the port-side seats from the starboard. Moyer watched his men's eyes shift to the officer. Boyle clapped his hands several times, then held out his arms before him. A second ticked by, and he motioned up with his arms. Simultaneously the men switched from onboard oxygen to the small metal bottles strapped to their gear, released their safety harnesses, and stood. Moyer took his place at the front of the line, followed by J. J., Pete, Jose, Zinsser, and Rich. Rich had promised to push the line forward if anyone hesitated.

Moyer doubted the act would be needed.

"Check your airflow," Boyle ordered. Moyer checked his gauge. The tank was full, and cool air flowed into his mask.

"NVGs on," Boyle snapped. Each man activated his night vision goggles. The inside of the aircraft went black.

Boyle said something into his headset. He stood for a moment, then the rear ramp of the massive plane began to lower. Freezing air poured in. Moyer pulled at his gloves. It wouldn't take long to get frostbite at this altitude.

"Go on my mark." Every eye turned to the light panel. It went from red to yellow. Moyer could hear himself sucking air and willed himself to slow his breathing.

Over the com system he heard Pete. "Hey Colt, you really gonna jump with that chute? It doesn't look right to me." Pete chuckled.

"Yeah, whatever, Junior. If things go bad, I'll just take a seat on Boss's rig. He won't mind."

"Can the chatter," Moyer ordered.

The yellow light went out and the green came alive.

"Go!"

Moyer waddled forward, his leg movement hindered by the large chute on his back and the air pack full of equipment that hung down and between his legs. Every protective instinct in his mind sounded—a chorus of sirens and ships' horns. No matter how well trained and experienced, there were moments when the rational mind said, "Sane people don't jump out of aircraft five miles above the ground." He took several awkward steps until he reached the end of the ramp and, in a single motion, turned on one foot and fell backward out of the C-130.

The night enveloped him.

The air, thin as it was, whipped around his mask, goggles, and helmet. It shrieked in his ears.

"One . . . two . . . three . . . four . . ." Six more counts until he activated his chute.

His stomach climbed into his throat. Below he could see nothing but darkness. In the sky, a fingernail moon watched him plummet. In the distance, faint lights glowed on the ground.

". . . eight . . . nine . . . ten." He opened his chute and felt his velocity change. It was as if a rubber band attached to his back had jerked him skyward. It was an illusion. He was still descending, but at a much slower rate.

He looked up to check his parachute. It was nearly impossible to see, but he could make out the rectangle of the steerable parachute. The purpose of a high altitude open was to give insertion teams time to find their landing zone and come in as quietly as possible. If things went well, they would land a mile south of Frontera.

The icy air bit what little facial skin Moyer had exposed. It felt like needles being shot into his skin.

Boyle's voice pressed into Moyer's ears. "All are away."

"Understood, all away." Moyer waited a second. "Report. Shaq?"

"A lovely evening."

"Colt?"

"Here, Boss. I have you in sight."

"Junior?"

"On Colt's tail."

"Doc?"

"Doin' bueno, Boss."

"Data?"

No answer.

"Data, report."

Silence.

"Shaq. You got a visual on Data?"

"He went out head first, Boss. I can't tell whose chute is whose from my position."

Moyer's mind raced. "Data, report."

"Gotcha, Boss." Zinsser's voice. "Radio wasn't working. Seems to be working now."

"You okay?"

"Peachy, Boss. Just a little miffed at my radio, I don't know why it wouldn't transmit."

Moyer closed his eyes. He had been certain Zinsser had chosen to do a header from the airplane. "Okay team, find the guy in front of you and follow him. We'll be in warmer air in a few minutes."

Moyer's heart had pounded before he jumped. When Zinsser didn't respond, it doubled its pace and tripled its force. For a moment Moyer thought it would break from his rib cage.

Zinsser was making him an old man.

From overhead came the decreasing sound of the C-130 heading for the border. It was a lonely sound. Moyer checked his GPS, then his compass. He pulled on his rig, and his stomach confirmed the digital information from the compass. He had successfully changed direction.

At 20,000 feet he made another adjustment. Every few minutes he called for a report, and each team member reported. When he dropped below 5,000 feet, he knew he was coming down a full mile away from the town, but that didn't mean he couldn't land on someone's barn. He found a clearing surrounded by trees and steered his parachute toward it.

A few minutes later Moyer landed in a field—in someone's crop. Two-foot high plants surrounded him, but he paid them little attention. His first job was to rein in his chute before it could catch a breeze and drag him along the ground. He landed as close to the trees as possible without hitting them, making it possible for him and his men to stay out of the open and get out of their chutes in seconds.

He bundled his chute and removed his jump harness, cramming as much of the chute into its holder as possible. He stayed in position until he heard that each man was down. Through his night vision goggles he watched each man land within fifty yards of his spot. "Not bad ladies, not bad."

"Graceful as a gazelle, I am." Shaq grinned.

Doc grimaced. "Sure you are."

The conversation stopped before Moyer could quiet them. He removed his helmet and slipped on his black balaclava mask. He heard footsteps behind him.

"Coming up on your six, Boss." It was J. J. Moments later the team had rid themselves of the gear they didn't need. They were no longer parachutists, but foot soldiers.

"Um, Boss," Doc said. "Do you know what we're standing in?"

"As long as it's not poison ivy, I don't care."

"You might, Boss. Take a good look."

Moyer pulled his small, red-lensed, tactical flashlight and shone it on the ground around him. He plucked a leaf off one of the plants. It had six or seven long leaves. "Is this what I think it is?"

"If you think it's marijuana, Boss, then you'd be right."

"I brought us down in a field of weed?"

"And don't think we're going to let you forget." Shaq sounded way too happy.

Moyer shook his head. "I trust I don't have to check anyone's pockets."

"Not with this group," Pete said. "J. J. might start preaching."

"I guess this shouldn't surprise us." Moyer glanced around. "We *are* in drug-lord country. Let's move out." He dropped the leaf, switched off his light, reported to Boyle the team was down, then led his men north.

CHAPTER 35

THIS WAS TAKING TOO long.

Moyer moved through the field with care. He'd never made an assault on a drug lord's location before, but it didn't take a genius to know booby traps could be waiting anywhere: in a footpath, under rubble, or at the base of walls. Moyer reminded his men of the danger then started forward in a slow trot. He wanted to move faster, but he'd make no progress if he blew his foot off.

The team lined up behind him. They'd try to stay on the same course as Moyer; if he didn't trigger a land mine, they likely wouldn't either.

Darkness made things worse. Night vision goggles helped, but detail could often be lost. Several times Moyer raised a clenched fist, commanding the team to freeze. He did so again and lowered himself to one knee. They'd been moving along a footpath through the plant material. In the middle of the path rested a cardboard box, its open side to the ground. Moyer's training won out, squashing the nearly overpowering urge to look under the box. The object might be a forgotten cardboard box, or it could be hiding an improvised explosive device. In the movies a team member might try to disarm it, but in real-world combat operations the protocol was simple: leave it alone or it could kill you.

Moyer stood and slowly worked his way from the footpath into the knee-high crop. He'd seen his share of traps in Afghanistan and Iraq and knew the enemy often paired devices to catch intruders as they bypassed the first trap. He took one deliberate step after another, never assuming he was safe. An explosion would do more than maim or kill him; it would also alert the enemy to their presence. Moyer decided this was going to be the longest and slowest mile he had ever traveled.

He led the team ten yards past the cardboard box then returned to the footpath. This time he set a slow walking pace. Adrenaline fueled his heart and tensed his muscles, but he had to move slowly. There could be other traps: trip wires that activated explosives; pits with spikes designed to pierce the soles of combat boots; rusty fishing hooks hung at eye-level, mines that bounced up from the ground and blew up in a man's face, crush-wire mines, and a hundred other demented designs to protect the illegal crop.

Each step heightened the tension.

Again, Moyer signaled *Freeze.* Three steps ahead of him was a small pile of disturbed dirt, as if someone had dug a hole and covered it over. Instinctively Moyer started to key his mike but stopped. His radio was off. All the radios were off. Before moving out, they discussed the kinds of traps they might encounter. Zinsser made a point: "We know Lobito has brought in cell technology and other things. There's a chance that he might have his fields set with radio activated devices. We could set something off just by using our radios. Recommend we kill radios until we're out of the field."

Moyer accepted the recommendation immediately. Everything would be hand signals until they were reasonably certain there were no IEDs about.

Every step counted, but so did time. They wanted to make their assault before dawn. Moyer focused on the area before him and around him. It amazed him that the drug war had become so much like real war. Drug lords were well armed and utilized well-trained men—many who served in the military of different countries. He had even read about policemen who switched sides.

They came to the end of the field. A wide, clear dirt path extended to their right and left. On the other side were a few trees and uneven ground. The path looked hard and compact—no recently dug holes to raise Moyer's fears. No rubble or boxes under which a bomb might be hidden. No tripwires.

Moyer turned to his team and saw five faces focused on him. He pointed at himself then indicated that he was going to cross the path. He signaled that each man was to follow one at a time. Moyer turned and stepped onto the dirt border. He stopped three steps later. Something wasn't right. He gazed at a spot just two feet in front of his boots. A straight line in the dirt, like something had been buried. How could anyone work in this field? Of course, they knew where all the traps were.

Putting one foot on the other side of whatever was just beneath the soil, Moyer pointed at J. J. and motioned for him to come. He stopped J. J. a few feet from where he straddled the assumed trigger and pointed at a spot between his feet. J. J. nodded, stepped over the line, and continued forward. Moyer held his position so each man would know where not to step. As each man reached the other side, they hit the ground, using several small mounds as cover. Moyer joined them face down on the ground. J. J. was looking at him. One breath later Moyer knew why. Stench worked its way into his nose—a stench he knew: rotting flesh.

J. J. leaned close to Moyer's ear. "This mound . . . I think it's a shallow grave, Boss."

Moyer studied the mound. It was the right size and shape for a mass grave. His heart sank.

"We can't know for sure, Boss," J. J. whispered.

Moyer nodded. "We stick to the plan."

From their position Moyer could see the end of the town's main street—its only street. Images from the satellite photo and the Predator flyover appeared in his mind. He had memorized every detail. All his men had. The main street was little more than a wide, packed dirt road. Several narrow alleys ran parallel to the street. The town was small. It had one recently built apartment complex they assumed harbored workers and guards. There was one cantina that still had its lights on—no 2:00 a.m. curfew here. There were a few other shops, a mechanic's garage, houses, a mission-style church . . .

And a large warehouse. Their target.

J. J. CRAWLED OVER the grave and tried to ignore what he was doing. His thoughts had to be focused—his life and the lives of his friends depended on it. Still, he couldn't stop the macabre images of what lay under the mound. He told himself it was a dead animal, a horse or a pig, or anything other than what he knew it to be.

On Moyer's signal, J. J. moved east until he was a block past the street, then ran up one of the alleys. A minute later he found the shed he had seen on the surveillance photos. The builder had made it from rough wood and covered it with tar paper. Slinging his weapon over his shoulder, J. J. upturned a trash can and used it as a step to the low roof. He moved quickly but quietly.

He unshouldered his weapon. Boyle had brought sweet gear. As the team's weapons and explosives expert, it fell to J. J. to take the sniper's role. The Army had better trained snipers, but there was no time to call in a shooter team. On many occasions J. J. had demonstrated he was the unit's best shot.

His weapon was an M110 SASS—Semi-Automatic Sniper System. Unlike earlier bolt-action sniper rifles, this one could be fired in semi-automatic mode, making it more useful for close-combat situations like this one. J. J. inched his way to the front end of the shed. Across the wide dirt street stood the warehouse, lit by a mercury vapor light that bathed the front of the building in bluish light.

Plenty of light.

Now, away from the field, the team had activated their radios. Still, most communication would occur by hand signals. However the team would not be able to see J. J. Radio was a must.

"In position, Boss."

J. J. heard Moyer respond with two clicks on the radio. He extended the small bipod attached to the front of the M110 and set the short legs on the front of the sloped room. He pulled the rubber covers off the scope and trained it at the building. The weapon was good up to a thousand meters. J. J. was less than thirty meters away.

Placing his eye to the scope, he did a quick sweep of the building. "Hand-applied stucco exterior," he whispered into the radio. "One entrance door at the south end, looks to be wood; one large metal roll-up door at the north end of the building; one window next to an entrance door; can't see the north end, but I see light—assume another window. No movement—standby."

A large, obese man in a plaid shirt and dirty jeans rounded the northeast corner. He looked the size of Rich. He wore a holster and carried what looked to be an Uzi in his right hand.

"Boss, one man, large, sidearm looks to be 9mm. He's carrying an Uzi." The last part concerned J. J. The tried-and-true Uzi could fire six hundred rounds a minute—ten rounds every second. No one wanted to be looking down the muzzle of that.

J. J. brought the scope up to the window. He saw two figures inside. "Two targets near the corner window."

Two more clicks from Moyer.

J. J. released the safety on his weapon and took slow deep breaths. Somewhere in his subconscious, he was praying.

ZINSSER CROSSED THE ROAD and just reached the back of the warehouse when he heard the sound of a car motor. He ducked behind a stack of empty wooden boxes. The sound of the engine lessened and Zinsser could hear tires on gravel and dirt. Light from the vehicle's headlamps spilled across the ground. The vehicle stopped at the south end of the building, just around the corner from Zinsser's spot. Zinsser didn't move.

"Boss?" he whispered.

"One man. Armed."

Zinsser caught a whiff of food.

"Drop 'em." Moyer's voice sounded relaxed through the ear piece. Zinsser had to admire the man. Slipping from his hiding spot behind the crates, Zinsser moved to the corner and peeked around it. The man was six-two, in his late twenties, and looked strong enough to lift the Jeep he had arrived in. A cigarette hung from his mouth. He pulled several bags of food from the Jeep, probably obtained from the cantina, and a flashlight. He turned on the light and did a quick scan of the area—no doubt part of his job. He showed no sign of interest in the work until he swung the light across the dirt perimeter that separated the village from the field. He paused. Zinsser saw what the man saw. One of the team lay face down in the dirt. From the size of him, it was Rich. He must have been crossing the open area when the man in the Jeep arrived.

The driver dropped the bags of food and withdrew a handgun from his holster.

Zinsser moved forward, reaching to his leg as he did so.

The driver opened his mouth to shout, but Zinsser closed it with his gloved hand. He twisted the man's head to one side, raised his combat knife, set his eyes on the spot where neck met shoulder, then brought the seven-inch blade down.

He held the man until he stopped moving.

His rushing blood made his face hot. He let the man drop.

"Must you always make a mess?"

Zinsser turned to see Rich by his side. Before Zinsser could answer, another sound drew his attention. A large man in a plaid shirt rounded the corner and pointed the barrel of an Uzi at his head.

CHAPTER 36

J. J. PAUSED HIS breathing.

He squeezed the trigger with slow, steady pressure.

The recoil of the M110 slammed his shoulder.

J. J. saw a wet spray emanate from the guard's head.

SOMETHING WET HIT ZINSSER in the face. He looked at the man on the ground at his feet. No question about his life status.

The sound of booted footsteps to Zinsser's right drew his attention from the gory sight on the ground. Zinsser froze. The inside of his skull itched. He looked up. Did he hear helicopters?

"Data, I need you."

Zinsser slammed his eyes shut.

Moyer's voice hissed at him. "Data, you with us?"

"Yeah, Boss. Of course."

"Check out the window."

Zinsser said nothing more as he returned his Benchmade knife to its sheath and poked his head around the corner. Seeing no other guards, he moved to the one window in the building and squatted below the sill. Pulling a small video device from his vest, he attached a gooseneck spy camera and raised the small lens just over the sill. He studied it for a moment, then returned the device to his vest. He raised a hand to his eyes then raised three fingers: three men inside.

A moment later Moyer crept past and took a position by the door. Rich did the same. Jose followed on his heels. Pete stopped by Zinsser's side. The next action had been planned and discussed at length on the flight here. Zinsser kept his eyes trained on Moyer.

Moyer raised three fingers, then retracted them one at a time, counting down. When the last finger disappeared, Zinsser stood.

MOYER TENSED.

This was the weakest link of the plan. In a perfect mission there were no unknowns. Too bad there were no perfect missions. J. J. had reported two men inside, but his vision was restricted to the window. Zinsser had had a better look through a digital periscope, and he reported three armed men. No one knew how many more might be in the storage area of the warehouse. For all Moyer knew, there could be twenty men ready to do battle. He doubted it, but the doubt didn't make him feel any better.

He raised his hand, three fingers ticking off the seconds to action. He studied Zinsser; the man's mind better still be with them. Zinsser's skill and willingness to engage the enemy without hesitation had kept the guard from sounding the alarm. If the man had opened up with his weapon, then one or more of Moyer's men might be dead.

He pulled in his last finger and saw Zinsser and Pete pop up. Zinsser put the butt of his M-4 through the glass, then spun away from the window. Pete tossed a small cylinder through the opening, then stepped back and turned his face away. The M84 "nine-banger" stun grenade exploded, releasing nine mini-explosions of blinding light and ear-shredding noise.

A moment after Pete tossed the grenade, Moyer nodded to Rich, who kicked the door just to the right of the knob. It exploded inward. Moyer was first in, his silenced service sidearm drawn. The effects of the nine-banger grenade would only last a few seconds.

The door opened into a shabby office area with a battered dinner table for a desk. On the table was a deck of playing cards. Three men stood near the table, their chairs knocked over backward. Two steadied themselves against the table, and one plugged his ears with his fingers. Tears, the result of the grenade's intense light, ran down their faces. Each man wore a sidearm. Two AK-47s were propped next to the wall. Two men reached for the automatic weapons, the third pulled his hand from his ear and dropped it to the holster hanging on his right hip.

Moyer squeezed the trigger twice and saw the escaping gas from Rich's weapon. The three men crumpled to the floor.

Jose brushed past Moyer and stepped to the door that stood between the storage area of the warehouse and the office. Three whispered shots told Moyer that Pete had found more men. He turned and followed his medic into the room. The sound of footfalls behind him told him the rest of the team had arrived. A movement to the left snagged Moyer's attention. He spun, weapon at the ready. He saw a man raising some kind of automatic pistol. Moyer was faster. The man's head snapped back, but not before he unleashed a stream of bullets, rounds fired without benefit of a noise suppressor. The sound of it stabbed Moyers ears, but worse, he was sure the sound traveled outside. The flash-bang grenade had been a concession Moyer had to make, but the closed environment most likely muffled the sound. Now he hoped the warehouse would contain the sound of weapons fire.

Most of the space was filled with large bundles of plant material wrapped in plastic. Boxes of smaller bags filled with white powder were stacked in the corner. Moyer didn't waste time focusing on such things.

He had to make sure the area was secure.

J. J. REMAINED UNMOVING on the shed roof, his sniper rifle at the ready. His breathing was regular, his limbs steady, his heart calm. His brain, however, raced like an Indy car out of control. "Come on, Boss. Come on. Talk to me."

He knew better than to tie up the radio. His unit mates might need to contact him. The noise of the flash-bang he expected. But the unsuppressed gunfire—exactly the sound he'd prayed he wouldn't hear. "Someone talk to me."

He was just about to key the radio when two things caught his attention. First, just moments after the team made entrance, a dirty, ancient-looking SUV pulled onto the street and started north. It didn't slow. J. J. couldn't make out the driver, but he appeared to be lost. When the sound of gunfire pierced the air, the car slowed, then sped off.

The second thing J. J. noticed made his heart tumble. Lights in some of the buildings came on. Seconds later several men emerged from the cantina. "Not good," he said to himself. "So . . . not . . . good."

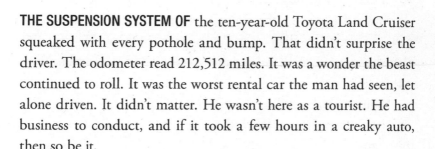

THE SUSPENSION SYSTEM OF the ten-year-old Toyota Land Cruiser squeaked with every pothole and bump. That didn't surprise the driver. The odometer read 212,512 miles. It was a wonder the beast continued to roll. It was the worst rental car the man had seen, let alone driven. It didn't matter. He wasn't here as a tourist. He had business to conduct, and if it took a few hours in a creaky auto, then so be it.

A few moments before the driver had turned the vehicle from a horrible dirt road onto an almost passable one. Frontera was everything he expected it to be: small, dirty, poor, and asleep. It should have been asleep. Just as he turned on the main road, he heard gunfire and ducked, lowering himself to the seat. When no bullets struck his car, he pressed the accelerator and pulled away. He had not been alone in noticing the noise. Five or six men poured from what looked like a bar.

The driver didn't wait to see what happened.

He just didn't care.

"WE'VE BEEN COMPROMISED."

J. J.'s voice poured into Moyer's ear. "Understood. Time?"

"Two minutes tops, Boss. Make that ninety seconds."

"Number?"

"I count five men. All are armed with handguns."

"Roger that, Colt. Hold your position. Sounds like we're going to need you again." Moyer looked at the others. They'd heard the broadcast. "Doc, Junior, take positions at the window and door. You too, Data." The three men sprinted to the office area.

"I don't get it, Boss. We were sure the hostages were here."

Moyer stepped to the only empty corner in the area. Dark stains covered the floor and the lower portion of the wall. He turned and saw a small video camera standing in the corner. "This is the place."

"You think they killed them."

"I think we were hunkered down behind their graves a short time ago—"

One of the guards groaned. Moyer stepped to a dark-skinned man with a beard. He looked to be fifty. Blood oozed from his chest. The man looked like a fish stranded on the dock, moving his mouth to suck in air. *Pneumothorax.* The bullet had punctured the lung and the pleura. He couldn't inflate his lungs.

Moyer squatted by him. "Do you speak English?"

The man's eyes went wide, and he nodded.

Moyer watched the rise and fall of the man's chest, then at the right moment, he placed a gloved hand over the wound closing off the hole. The man took several good breaths. Moyer saw the fear of death in his eyes. "Listen, amigo, you are going to die, and I can't do anything about it. I'm going to give you a chance to do one good thing with your miserable life; something you can take with you when you go. I don't know if it will help or not. It's just a chance you're going to have to take. Do you understand?"

The man nodded.

"I only have time to ask this once. Are any of the hostages still alive?"

He nodded. "Two."

"Where are they?"

He hesitated, but when it looked as if Moyer were going to remove his hand, he said, "The church."

Moyer nodded. "Give me your left hand." The man did. Moyer pressed the man's hand over the sucking chest wound. "Keep the hole closed." He stood.

"Doc teach you that?" Rich asked.

"I saw something similar during my first tour in Iraq."

"We have company, Boss," Pete said, his voice rock solid. "They've drawn their weapons."

"Doc, tell them to ditch the hardware. This will be their only warning." Moyer started for the office. He heard Jose give the order in Spanish.

"Nuthin' doing, Boss," Jose said.

"Listen up," Moyer said into the radio. "Colt, take your shot. The rest of you open up when the first man drops. Conserve your ammo. We have another stop to make."

J. J. SET THE crosshairs on the last man. He heard Jose shout something, but it had no effect on the approaching men. He put pressure on the trigger. The recoil surprised him—just as it should.

Before J. J. could bring his weapon to bear on another target, the remaining men staggered and collapsed.

"Colt?"

"Clear at the moment, Boss, but some lights have gone on in the apartment building. If we're going to bug out, now might be a good time."

"Bug out!" Moyer commanded. "Colt, we'll meet you in the alley at your location."

"Roger that, Boss."

J. J. snapped the bipod back to the barrel and slid down the roof, lowered himself to the inverted trash can and stepped into the alley just as the rest of the team arrived.

"What now, Boss?"

"We go to church, Colt."

"Really? It's about time."

"On the double." As Moyer started forward, the back door of a small home opened. A young woman looked out.

"*Volver en la casa!*"

At Doc's shout, the woman slipped back inside without question.

Rich grinned. "Doc, you have a way with women."

"Well, Spanish is a romantic language."

"Let's move." Moyer set off in a jog, his men lined up behind him. His mind raced faster than his feet.

J. J.'S STOMACH TURNED. He would never hesitate to do his job just as he had done it, but he never wanted to become so calloused as to not care that he had just killed several men. He had no doubt they would have killed him or any one of this team. Still, dead men littered the streets. Before the night ended, there could be more. He prayed none of those bodies would be his friends.

CHAPTER 37

PADRE GRADOS NOVENOS STOOD in the dark basement, lit only by a forty-watt bulb hanging from the ceiling. Anytime one of the men above walked across the floor, the bulb would sway, sending shadows dancing like demons around an open fire. Those demons did not frighten him; the ones above with guns did.

His eyes traced the forms on the old cots. Both slept fitfully, the man more from illness; the woman more from emotional exhaustion. Thinking about what Lobito's men might have done to these two made him ill, an illness made worse by his knowledge of what was to become of them. He knew what had happened to the other captives. There was no way he couldn't know. In a village this small, Padre Grados knew everything. Still he stayed. By choice.

He moved to the woman's side, removed a simple white rag from a bucket of water, wrung it out, and dabbed it on the woman's forehead. She was feverish, the result of infection that had set in around the raw and broken skin beneath the shackle around her wrists. At his touch, she awoke.

"Thank you, Father." She offered the smallest of smiles.

"Shush, child, you must rest."

"I was dreaming of my daughter." She closed her eyes, and a tear raced to the dirty, feather pillow. "She was happy and safe."

"The dream is a gift from God. To help you sleep. Perhaps you will have more good dreams."

"Are you praying for her, Father? You said you would pray for Delaram."

"Yes, child, I have been praying for her and for you and your husband. All night I have been praying."

She raised a manacled hand and touched his wrist. "Why are you here, Father? Of all places in the world, why here?"

He had asked himself the same question. Many times. "I have to be somewhere. I serve the Light and light shines best in darkness. This place needs light." He didn't tell her Frontera was his home. He had been born here sixty-two years before and had been baptized in this very church. Frontera was his home. It had always been a poor town, but often people do not know they are poor if they don't know what others have. That was how it had been for him. Poverty was just a word. His home had no indoor plumbing, but he still had a home.

As a boy he served the priest, helping with daily chores and as an altar boy. When he felt the call of God on his life, the village saved funds to send him to a catholic seminary. He had promised to return—a promise he happily kept.

That was before Lobito came. Lobito. The name made him laugh. Hernando Soto had been a troublesome child who grew into a troublesome adult. For decades Frontera had been as peaceful as it had been poor. Most families lived on sustenance farming, but they still knew how to laugh. Padre Grados couldn't remember the last time he heard genuine laughter.

Hernando Soto and his brother Michael had changed things. The people only grew drug crops now, with just enough land dedicated to feed their families. Soto stocked the store and paid the workers more than they could get anywhere else. He brought technology to the village, but he took its heart in exchange.

The people had modern medicine, entertainment, and more, but they no longer had their freedom, or happiness. Frontera had become a village of zombies, people who did their work because they had no other choice.

A tiny bit of music worked its way down the basement stairs, the sound of a cell phone ringing in the predawn hours. One of the men answered.

Padre Grados heard the sound of running feet.

"HERNANDO. HERNANDO, GET UP."

Hernando felt a strong hand on his shoulder. He opened his eyes to see his brother standing over him. "What is it, Michael?" He sat up.

"Trouble in the village. Armed men. Maybe military."

"Our guards?"

"I've just received a report that seven or eight are dead, maybe more. No one wants to go into the warehouse to count."

"The warehouse?" Hernando swung his legs over the side of the bed.

"You were right to move the man and woman, brother. If you hadn't, they might be gone now."

"What is our status here?" He stood up and reached for a red silk robe.

"There has been no trouble here."

Hernando thought for a moment. "Send our men down there to help. We'll be safe here. You stay with me."

Michael sprinted from the room.

WITH THE LAND CRUISER hidden twenty yards off the long driveway that snaked up a low grade, the driver worked his way through knee-high grass. He avoided the road, staying behind low-lying bushes. Every step brought him closer to his destination. He could see lights glowing on the second floor and from several rooms on the lower floor. He still had a problem. An eight-foot-high chain-link fence ran around the property. To his knowledge, only one gate allowed entry, and it was certain to be guarded. Still he hiked up the grade.

He neared the fence and raised a pair of light-amplifying binoculars to his eyes. First he searched for security cameras and saw several. Next he searched the area near the mansion. Movement caught his eye—rapid movement. A pair of vans were pulling away and driving toward the front gate. He had a decision to make. If he approached the gate, the security cameras would detect him; but if the vans were leaving the premises, then the gates would be open.

Tossing the binoculars to the side, the driver ran toward the gate. As he closed the distance, he pulled a gun from the holster behind his back. He no longer cared if he were seen.

ZINSSER WAS THE CABOOSE in the line, Rich just a few steps before him. Six men moving through hostile territory after a firefight, their only means of transportation was their own boot-laden feet. Their survival depended on the ready status and alertness of each man. Six pairs of eyes could scan a lot of space, peer into a lot of dark corners. Six pairs of ears could hear better than one. Zinsser wasn't listening, wasn't watching—but he was seeing and hearing.

The sound of a gun battle fought on a different continent rolled in his brain; ghostly images of wounded soldiers and angry Somalis flooded his eyes. His heart began to pound beyond his present exertion.

Zinsser fought the images, focusing on Rich's back. He couldn't fall behind, couldn't give in to the demons. He began to count his steps. He took notice of his breathing, taking slightly deeper breaths and longer exhalations. His boots pounded the hard dirt.

For the moment he could tell the difference between the gunfire in his head and reality. For the moment. He heard distant, tardy helicopters. He heard Brian Taylor calling his name.

Zinsser smashed into Rich's back, the abrupt stop jerking him back to reality.

Rich turned. "Ease up, pal."

"Sorry, big guy. Didn't see your brake lights." The words were barely audible.

"You still with us, Data?"

"All the way, Shaq."

Rich eyed him as if sucking the truth from his mind.

"Data, I'm down."

Zinsser ignored it. He leaned to the side to see Moyer circle his hand, signaling the men to rally. Zinsser stepped to Moyer's position.

"We have to assume we've been compromised and that more men are on their way to make our lives miserable. We have two hostages in the church and unknown opposition. We need to do this fast and surgical."

Moyer's voice filled Zinsser's head, pushing out every other image and voice. Zinsser was grateful. "All we have is the exterior layout. No idea what's on the inside?"

Jose leaned in to keep his voice low. "I've toured many missions. My wife loves them. Lots of them have basements."

"Makes sense," Moyer said. "Okay, we assume that to be true in this case. Here's what we do: two teams. I'll lead Alpha team; Shaq you'll lead Bravo. Colt, Data, you're with me. Doc, Junior, you're with Shaq." Moyer laid out the next steps. The meeting lasted less than ninety seconds.

CHAPTER 38

PADRE GRADOS HAD BEEN ordered to stay in the basement. He hated giving the men upstairs free rein of the church. Who knew what manner of defilement they had brought within the mission walls. If the condition of the man and woman were any indication, then Grados could only fear the worst.

The stomping above had ceased, and for a few moments Grados hoped something had forced them to flee. He didn't know what could force heartless, callous, armed men to flee, but he'd welcome it.

Hearing nothing for several minutes, the priest walked up the wooden stairs slowly, pausing when he could see the upper floor. The stairs led to a narrow hall that prevented him from seeing very far. He strained his ears to hear the sound of the men and heard nothing. He took a few more steps and paused again. Fear made him sick to his stomach, but he continued up the risers, moving as quietly as possible. "In God have I put my trust: I will not be afraid of what man can do to me." He quoted the psalm over and over, his voice so low only he could hear it.

The floorboards beneath his feet creaked, and he stopped, as if
the sound had turned him to stone. He took another step. The hall
ended in the church kitchen. The room was old and the painted
plaster chipped, but the appliances were new—gifts from a man
who thought he could buy acceptance and forgiveness. Grados
wanted to reject the stainless steel, commercial grade refrigerator
and freezer, the matching stove and double oven, but Hernando
Soto was not a man one said no to.

In slow steps he crossed the large kitchen and entered the
fellowship hall, a wide space filled with folding tables and folding
chairs. The light in the kitchen had been on, meaning the men had
been helping themselves to the food. He wondered when the couple
on the cots in the basement had last eaten.

The fellowship hall was dark. As Padre Grados stood in the
doorway, light from the kitchen cast his shadow into the room,
filling the rectangle of illuminated floor. His heart pounded so
hard, he was surprised the windows didn't reverberate in rhythm
with it.

A wide opening in the wall opposite him led to the narthex
and the nave. He moved to the door that opened to the large space
where the congregants sat each Sunday. The space was much larger
than needed. A century ago the church believed the small villages
it served would grow and so they built for future crowds, that never
arrived. Prayer candles were the only light in the room, but it was
enough for Grados to see two men with automatic rifles peering
through the shutters that sealed the opening facing the courtyard.
The only glass in the sanctuary was century-old stained glass. All
other openings in the walls—where glass windows might be in a
contemporary church—bore hinged shutters that could be opened
and closed from the inside.

It took a moment for Grados to realize what he was seeing.

The two men were set up for an ambush. An ambush of whom? Realization settled on him: *Federales*. The government was making an assault on Hernando's drug empire—and these men were lying in wait for them. Blood was about to be spilled on church grounds.

Grados stepped back, praying the floor would not squeak under his weight. Over the years he had grown used to hearing the noises and no longer paid them attention. Now, it was his greatest concern. Knowing the floorboards were more secure near the walls, the priest moved along the partition that separated the narthex from the nave until he reached the large, oak double doors. Each door had a small square opening covered with decorative wrought iron. Placing his face near one of the openings, Grados stared across the courtyard with its central fountain and at the four-foot high stucco wall that enclosed the space. Centered in the wall was an opening with an arch above. Congregants walked through that opening and into the courtyard every Sunday, often gathering in the courtyard after services to share gossip.

Something moved near the courtyard entrance. Something dark; almost impossible to see. Something human shaped. Grados's eyes traced the wall. He saw another form. They were here. They were approaching. They were about to walk into the crossfire of evil men.

"Blessed Jesus!" Grados crossed himself. He was about to witness murder.

A man dressed in black slipped under the arch and moved toward the fountain, crouched like a cat ready to spring. In his mind he could see the two men in the sanctuary tightening their fingers on their respective triggers.

Grados's hands shook so that he had trouble working the iron-door latch. He hesitated. His lungs ceased drawing air. His heart refused to beat.

Again, Grados crossed himself, then flung open the door. He forced his feet to move, to run. Pointing at the shuttered windows, he shouted at the top of his lungs: *"¡Cuidado! ¡Peligro!"*

Padre Grados heard something.

Something loud.

ZINSSER HAD BEEN THE first on direct approach. Moyer gave him the signal, and he rounded the wall, stepped through the gateless opening, and sprinted to the fountain in the middle of the courtyard. He had only taken a few steps when a crazy old man bolted from the front doors of the church yelling something in Spanish. Instinctively Zinsser turned his weapon on the man but stopped short of pulling the trigger. The man wore a long robe with long sleeves and what appeared to be a white rope around his waist. The priest?

Zinsser had no idea what the man was saying, but he understood. He dove for cover behind the fountain just before something chipped off a large piece of decorative tile. No one had to tell Zinsser what that something was. He lowered his head and pulled his helmet tight.

Another shot.

The man stopped his screaming.

Zinsser glanced to his side in time to see the man fall to the ground. His head bounced off the adobe skirt that circled the bottom of the fountain. Zinsser reached an arm to the man, seized the hood at the back of his robe, and pulled him behind the fountain. The priest's open, lifeless eyes told him it had been a useless gesture.

"Data?"

"I'm fine for the moment, Boss. The priest is dead. He was pointing to the two windows facing the courtyard."

"We got a clear angle on them." Rich's voice came through the monitor in Zinsser's ear.

"Take it, Shaq." Moyer didn't hesitate and Zinsser was glad.

Before Zinsser could raise his head, a fusillade of noise-suppressed gunfire erupted. The wooded shutters in the window exploded into countless splinters. Zinsser pushed to his feet and charged the front doors. When he was two strides from the entrance, a large man with an AK-47 appeared. Zinsser pressed the trigger and sent a burst of bullets into the man's chest. He fell across the threshold. Zinsser planted a foot on his back as he propelled himself through the door.

From his left came the *ratta-tatta* of automatic gunfire, followed by the whistle of bullets and thudding as rounds impacted the thick plaster walls. Through the opening between what Zinsser thought of as the lobby and meeting hall, he saw a skinny man with an automatic weapon.

Zinsser put three rounds into him.

"Boss, Data, two EKIA." Two enemy killed in action.

"Other hostiles?"

"Unknown."

Zinsser stepped into the church. Long wooden pews formed an aisle leading to the front. A handcrafted pulpit sat upon a dais. He brought his weapon to his shoulder and moved quickly down the side aisle, looking for bad guys who might be hiding.

"Boss, Data, church clear."

"Hold your position."

Zinsser stepped from the church and back into the foyer, stopping short of the threshold into the next room. He dropped to a knee and kept the barrel pointed into the unsearched room.

"Coming in."

Zinsser didn't look up at the sound of boots at the door. Moyer and J. J. appeared; each took a position on either side of the doorway. Moyer motioned to J. J., held up three fingers, and did the countdown. J. J. was through the door before the last finger retracted. Moyer followed, and Zinsser after him. What appeared to be a dining room was empty.

The three men poured into the kitchen. Moyer must have seen the hallway. He pivoted and pointed his weapon down the narrow corridor. A closed door was on the opposite wall. Moyer pointed to Zinsser and gestured at the door. J. J. stepped to the door and set his hand on the doorknob. Zinsser raised his weapon, stopping just a foot away from the door. He nodded, and J. J. turned the knob, throwing the door open. Zinsser plunged in, J. J. a half step behind.

The room was small and spare. A bed with a worn mattress was situated to the side. A small desk was on the other wall. A large crucifix hung on the wall. *The priest's bedroom.* Zinsser thought of the man lying dead by the fountain.

Zinsser and J. J. retreated from the bedroom and gave the signal for all clear. Zinsser stepped behind Moyer, and J. J. stepped behind him. Zinsser squeezed his team leader's shoulder. Moyer started forward. Two steps in, a voice came over the radio.

"Boss, Shaq. Perimeter."

"Understood."

"Boss, I think we may have company. I'm hearing engine noises."

"Take cover."

Moyer pushed through the narrow corridor to the stairs. Zinsser tensed. Stairs could be a problem. Once a soldier was on a staircase, his movement was limited to forward and back, and back in this case was uphill. The railing and wall limited lateral movement. There was nothing they could do but take the chance.

Zinsser's primary concern at that moment was not to accidentally shoot Moyer should something go south.

Thirteen steps later they were in a barely lit basement. Two people lay on rickety cots: one male, one female. Only the female was conscious. She pushed back, trying to put distance between her and the men in the black masks carrying guns.

Zinsser and the others swept the room and found no hostiles.

Moyer moved to the woman. "We're not here to hurt you. How many men brought you here?"

She didn't answer. Zinsser could see fear in her eyes. "Is Delaram your daughter?"

"Yes, yes! Is she safe?"

"She's alive and being taken care of," J. J. said. "I got to meet her. Now please answer his question. We don't have much time."

"Two. Two men brought us here. My husband won't wake up."

Another voice in the ear. "Boss, Shaq, we got company. Two vans, approaching."

"Take positions in the church. We're in the basement. Building is clear."

Zinsser stepped to the woman and looked at the shackles that bound the couple to the wall. A metal plate that held one end of the shackle had been bolted to the wall and a chain welded to it. At the woman's wrist was a hinged cuff with a padlock securing the two parts together. "Did one of the men use a key to lock your cuff?"

"Yes. He put it in his pocket."

Moyer turned to J. J. "Colt, get upstairs, get that key and get Doc down here. We have to find a way to wake the man."

J. J. was gone before Moyer could put a period on the end of the sentence.

CHAPTER 39

THE GATE CLOSED BEHIND him. He had waited until the last possible moment to sprint through the automatic gate. He had almost waited too long, and he wondered what would have happened had his wide body become trapped in the device. Would it have crushed him?

He didn't harbor the questions for long. He had other things on his mind, and those *things* were waiting just a few yards ahead of him. He had toyed with several ideas about how to approach the mansion. Seeing heavily armed men race from the grounds in two vans gave him a little more confidence. Something else was going on, something that demanded the attention of the guards. Perhaps they had left the place unguarded.

He took his time walking up the drive, trying to look as if he belonged there. A backpack hung from his shoulder. He knew there were cameras watching the large property. Lawn and low-lying shrubs populated the grounds, leaving no place for an unwanted visitor to hide. If someone was manning the security camera area,

316 BLAZE OF GLORY

then he had been seen. He should have been seen several minutes ago, but no one approached him.

The man had a new fear. Maybe the house was empty. No matter, he could wait.

He took the porch steps one at a time, as if he had walked this path a hundred times before. In a way he had. He had rehearsed this in his mind more times than he could count.

At the door he took hold of the knob and, to his surprise, turned it. He stepped into the lobby.

MOYER TURNED AT THE sound of Jose trotting down the steps. "What we got, Boss?"

"The woman is conscious, but the man is out. I've tried to revive him, but he seems too far under. See what you can do, Doc."

"He's not . . ." Jose trailed off as he looked at the woman.

"I got a pulse."

"Here," Jose handed a key to Moyer. "Found it on the guy in the doorway."

Moyer took the brass colored key and unlocked the cuff on the woman's wrist. She rubbed the raw skin beneath. He did the same for the man as Jose examined him. Jose asked the woman, "When was the last time you had water?"

"Two, maybe three days."

Jose nodded. "He's dehydrated. His pulse is weak and thready. I need to give him an IV."

"We don't have time for that, Doc. Any other ideas?"

Jose shook his head. "My field bag doesn't carry stimulants. I've got stuff to dull pain; not sharpen senses."

"So we carry him or leave him behind."

"You can't leave him!" the woman said.

Jose said, "I'll be right back." Moyer watched him race up the steps. A few moment's later he reappeared with a deep, white plastic tray.

"What's that?" Moyer asked.

"Ice. I need your help, Boss." Jose handed plastic bags to Moyer. "Fill these with ice."

Moyer did and handed the first bag to Jose, who had just finished unbuckling the man's belt. "Give me two more." He took the first bag and shoved it down the front of the man's pants.

"That doesn't look very medical, Doc."

"My dad was a paramedic. He told me they used to do this to drug overdoses. Kept them from slipping into comas."

"And your dad said it worked?"

"He said it did. Give me the other bag." Jose pulled open the man's shirt and placed the ice bag under his right arm. When Moyer handed him the third bag, he placed it under the left arm.

"That's gotta be uncomfortable," Moyer said.

"That's the idea." He reached into his med bag and removed two chemical ice packs and activated both, placing one under the man's neck and one on his belly. A moment later he moaned and tried to push the pack off his stomach. "Bingo."

Rich's voice slipped from Moyer's earpiece. "Party crashers, Boss. I count ten."

"Understood. On my way." He paused. "Um, Doc."

"Just a sec, Boss." Jose turned to the woman. "What's your name, ma'am?"

"Everyone calls me Char. It's easier to pronounce."

"Come here, Char."

She wobbled to him.

"I have to go help my pals. I want you to stay down here and try to revive your husband. Don't be afraid to get a little rough.

Once he comes to, you can remove the ice packs; just don't let him go under again."

"I may not be able to stop it."

"You have to try. Clear?"

"Yes. You won't leave us, will you?"

Jose looked at Moyer, who shook his head. "No, ma'am. We came a long way to get you and the others. When we go, you go."

"The others are dead," she whispered.

Moyer nodded. "We know." He took a deep breath. "Let's go, Doc."

ZINSSER BIT HIS TONGUE—ON purpose. He tasted blood. Still it was better than listening to voices in his head. He stood at the window where the skinny man had fired on his team a short time ago. Rich stood at the other window.

J. J. walked into the worship center. "We sealed the front doors again. It's not much of a lock. A couple of swift kicks and they're in."

"There is no way they're getting close to the door—"

A roar of gunfire erupted, and plaster from the walls flew like shrapnel. Zinsser and the others hit the floor.

"What the—" Shaq began.

"That sounded like my old M249 SAW." J. J. grimaced. "If it is, we're in big trouble."

The Squad Automatic Weapon could fire a thousand rounds a minute and, since it was fed by an ammo belt, could fire a long time without reloading.

Another barrage of bullets chewed through the wall.

"I was wrong," J. J. said. "It sounds like *two* M249s."

"Ever our ray of sunshine, aren't you, Colt?"

"Just trying to be helpful, Shaq."

Zinsser lifted his head to see Moyer crawling along the floor. "I can't leave you guys alone for a minute. Junior, get a message off and report our situation."

Pete pulled a satellite phone from the pocket on his vest.

"Where's Doc?" Rich asked.

"He's taken a position in the dining room. It has windows facing the courtyard, too."

Again a volley of bullets ground away at the wall and wooden shutters. "I don't think the mission was built for a full-on attack," Zinsser said. "Rounds are cutting through the stucco and plaster like they're paper."

"Ya think?"

Zinsser ignored Shaq's sarcasm and rolled on his back, removed the digital periscope from his vest, turned it on, and extended the gooseneck camera over the sill.

"See anything?"

"Not much. Too dark. I see the vans and some movement along the wall around the courtyard. I can't make out details."

"Okay, we're about equal in number, but they have superior fire power," Moyer said.

"Let's hope they don't have RPGs or worse," Shaq said.

"Now who's a ray of sunshine?" J. J. gave a grim smile.

The sound of muffled M-4 fire rolled through the lobby and into the sanctuary. Zinsser could hear the *clink-clink-clink* of spent shells landing on the wooden floor. Another round of machine gun fire hit the church. This time the gunners fired on Doc's location.

Zinsser was on his feet, his weapon pointed out the window. If they were shooting at the other side of the church, then they must not be aiming at this side. Zinsser released burst after burst. Rich must have had the same idea. He lay down a stream of bullets. Both ducked a second. They heard a man—maybe two—screaming in the distance.

"Loading," Zinsser said as he ejected his spent clip and inserted another.

"Junior," Moyer ordered, "go help Doc. Keep your head down."

Pete crawled along the floor.

"Think we took out the SAW?" As Rich spoke, scores of high-impact bullets hit the wall again. "Never mind."

"We can't get the extraction team in with those guys out there," Moyer said.

"Who has the flash-bangs?" Zinsser glanced at the others.

Moyer shook his head. "Doesn't matter. They're too far away and the sound won't work that well outside."

"I'm not thinking of the bang, Boss; I'm thinking of the flash."

"They're still too far."

"I can hit them from the roof, and if I can't, at least I'll have a better angle of attack."

Zinsser watched Moyer mull it over. "How are you going to get on the roof?"

"I'll need a boost."

Shaq looked at Moyer. "I'll do it. I can probably just toss him onto the roof."

Moyer nodded. "All right. When you're ready, we'll lay down cover fire."

Shaq turned to Zinsser. "Where?"

"The priest's bedroom had a window on the back wall."

"Lead on, Data."

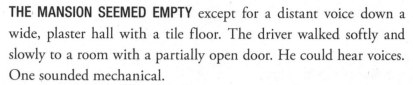

THE MANSION SEEMED EMPTY except for a distant voice down a wide, plaster hall with a tile floor. The driver walked softly and slowly to a room with a partially open door. He could hear voices. One sounded mechanical.

"Two dead, but we have them pinned down. We have men watching the back."

"Stay on them. I want to hear that every one of them is dead." The voice was familiar.

Things were working out.

"NOT MUCH OF A window," Shaq said.

Zinsser looked at the window, at Rich, then back at the window. "Think you can make it, big guy?"

"I have to. Someone has to keep an eye on you."

Zinsser moved close to the double-hung window and peeked outside. He saw no movement, just the darkness resisting the dawn. "We still have plenty of darkness, but we'll have to do this quickly. I'll go first so I can lay down cover if necessary."

"I'm sorry, I seem to have forgotten. Who's the assistant team leader? You or me?"

"That'd be you, Shaq. I meant it as a suggestion. How do you want to do this?"

Rich looked at the window. "Here's what we're gonna do. You're going through first and set up to lay down cover for me since it will take me a few moments longer."

"Genius."

The sound of bullets striking the front of the mission drove both men to the floor. The walls, plaster, and lathe prevented rounds from the small gunfire from coming into the room. The large machine gun was another matter.

Zinsser stepped to the window, took another look around, then removed his battle knife.

"What ya doin'?"

"Making your life easier." Zinsser drove the blade of the knife into the wooden sash that held the lower sliding portion of the window and pried it away and returned his knife. He lifted the lower pane a couple of inches, slipped his fingers through the opening, clamped his hands on the frame, placed a foot on the wall, and yanked. The whole unit came loose. Zinsser tossed it to the side. "Do you think I'll burn in hell for damaging a church?"

"Probably, but you'll have to ask J. J."

Zinsser reached for his knife again.

"Step back, Data. I have a different approach." Rich raised his weapon, waited for the next round of gunfire, then smashed the butt of the M-4 into the upper glass pane. He cleared out the glass, seized the wooden frame, and pulled it from the wall as if it were held in place with tacks.

"Man, remind me never to make you angry."

"Too late, pal. If we live through this, I'll have a few things to say to you."

"Can't wait." Zinsser scanned the area again, fearful that they had made too much noise, but he was pretty sure the constant give and take of gunfire made that impossible. He slipped his weapon through the window, put his hands on the sill. "Give me a boost—"

Zinsser landed outside before he could finish the sentence. He vaguely recalled something grabbing his vest and belt. The next thing he knew, he had a mouthful of dirt. *Cute.* He sprang to his feet and retrieved his weapon.

The area was clear. Something dropped at his feet: Shaq's vest.

"Go," Zinsser whispered. He turned to see Rich trying to work his way through the window. The hot popping of automatic weapons filled the air. Zinsser seized the back of Rich's uniform and pulled for all he was worth. The big man landed hard, and Zinsser knew if they weren't moving as covertly as possible, Shaq would have filled the air with enough curses to make birds drop dead from the sky.

The men exchanged glances. Shaq's could have melted a glacier. Zinsser set his weapon down, put his back to the wall, and linked his fingers to form a stirrup. Rich shook his head. "You first." Rich slipped his vest back on.

"I can't pull you up on the roof. You need to go up first."

It must have made sense, because Rich slipped the strap of his weapon over his shoulder, put his foot in Zinsser's hand, and used it as a step. Zinsser lifted, trying to give Shaq an extra six inches of height to reach the roof. It was like lifting a car.

The weight disappeared, and Zinsser could hear Rich scrabbling up the wall. Then he heard something else. Someone was approaching. Before he could turn, he felt the muzzle of a gun behind his ear. He didn't hesitate, didn't bother weighing his options. Zinsser spun, swatting the weapon aside and drove the heel of his hand into the man's sternum. The attacker staggered back. Fearful the man could call for help or discharge his weapon, alerting the others to their presence at the side of the building, Zinsser sent his fist into the man's throat. His eyes widened but then closed a moment later. Zinsser twisted his wrist then removed his knife from the man's gut.

He dropped.

Zinsser retrieved his weapon and tossed it to Shaq. He took two steps back, then charged the wall, planting his right boot on the wall, and reached for the roof. A vise-like hand seized his wrist and Zinsser felt himself rising skyward.

CHAPTER 40

MOYER'S FEAR MORPHED INTO annoyance. There was no shame in fear. No soldier denied being afraid. Instead they took pride in conquering fear.

"Tell me you got through, Junior."

"I got through, Boss, but I haven't heard back. I'm feeling jilted." Pete had taken Rich's place at the bullet-riddled window.

Moyer's mind raced. This had turned into a royal mess. There was nothing they could have done better. They had come up with the best plan possible; they had executed it without fault; but no team, no matter how well trained, could predict the unpredictable.

For the last few minutes they had, in an effort to preserve their limited ammo, been rotating their return fire. If any of the men shooting at them had military backgrounds—and there was a very good chance they did—then they would know the team's ammo was limited and begin to advance.

"Boss," Pete said, the satellite phone to his ear, "no joy here. Our extraction helo is out of commission. Something about a fractured rotor."

"Swell. Just swell."

"Command has something else working. They will advise."

"That's good. Any chance they might get to that soon?"

"They didn't say, but they're aware of the problem."

The crash of breaking glass rolled through the room. Moyer turned in time to see the barrel of an AK-47 come through one of the stained glass windows. He rolled on his back and turned the muzzle of his weapon toward the window. He saw the attacker's barrel turn his way—then disappear in a spray of red. Standing in the doorway between the sanctuary and the foyer was J. J., his M100 aimed at the broken window.

"I owe you a steak," Moyer said.

"Two."

"We've lost our advantage, Boss. They're going to advance on our position soon."

"Let's give Shaq and Data a chance."

"You think Data can do it, Boss?"

"Once a hero, Junior, always a hero . . . I hope."

A voice pressed through Moyer's earpiece. "Boss, Data. We've taken our positions. That's the good news."

"There's bad news?"

"Roger that, Boss: Three more vans and two trucks are headed up the street. I think they called for reinforcements from the other town."

"Colina Verde," Moyer muttered. "Junior, advise Command."

"Will do."

As soon as Pete made the call, Moyer said, "Listen up, team: This is about to go Alamo. We have to hold on until we get some support. When Shaq and Data give us the word, we open up. J. J., you got Willie Petes?"

"Yes, Boss."

"I hate to ask this . . ."

"No sweat, Boss. If it helps, I volunteer."

Moyer never felt more proud of the young man. "Okay, here's what we're going to do . . ."

ZINSSER PEERED OVER THE roof parapet. The image in night vision goggles came through sharp and clear. The rising sun threatened to crawl up the sky and push the dark back like a window shade. Although not yet visible, the red slit along the eastern horizon told of the sun's imminent return. What Zinsser couldn't decide was if that was good or bad news. With more light, they would be able to see the enemy better—and the enemy would see them clearer.

Zinsser glanced at Rich and saw him nod. "On my count. Three, two, one—go."

A burst of gunfire came from the church.

Shaq popped his head over the parapet and let loose a long stream of fire. Zinsser pushed to his feet, pulled the safety, and threw one, then another M84 flash-bang grenade. Most soldiers could toss a grenade thirty-five meters. Zinsser had the advantage of adrenaline and height above ground.

He dropped facedown on the roof and closed his eyes. Two bangs told him the grenades had gone out. The screams told him the bright light had temporarily blinded the shooters.

Rich was on his feet, tapping the trigger of his weapon and firing short bursts at the enemy behind the courtyard wall. Zinsser joined him. He could hear the others below doing the same. Zinsser heard something else: the front doors of the church flying open and slamming the walls hard enough to shake the building. In the dim light, Zinsser saw two objects fly through the air. Again Zinsser dropped facedown to the roof and shielded his eyes.

He heard two explosions.

He heard screams that threatened to melt the marrow in his bones.

Looking over the parapet, Zinsser saw fire burning the vehicles. He also saw burning bodies.

A WILLIE PETE—A WHITE phosphorous grenade—is effective, devastating, and horrible. It had been used by Army personnel for decades to signal, to create smoke, and occasionally to clear an enemy location. What J. J. had done was necessary to save the lives of his team. Still, his stomach burned almost as hot as the phosphorus on the other side of the courtyard wall.

"Shaq, report!"

"Targets hit, Boss. Approaching vehicles have stopped in the middle of the street."

"We bought time." Moyer's tone was still grim. "Question is, how much?"

J. J. had dove back into the church as soon as he threw the WP. He did so to put himself out of the line of fire. He also didn't want to see what was about to happen.

"Good job, Colt."

J. J. heard the voice, but the words made no sense.

"You with us, Colt?"

J. J. blinked. "With you? Yes, Boss. I'm with you." He rose and raised his M110. He had killed men before. He had killed men that day. Somehow the sun-bright phosphorus and fire unnerved him. He took three deep breaths, and the images faded. He could question himself later. Right now his team needed him; two hostages needed him.

MOYER STUDIED J. J. For a few moments he'd expected the young man to crumble, then he saw the fire return to Colt's eyes. J. J. never complained. In many ways he was the perfect soldier, but he was also a man of sensitivity. Moyer had known soldiers who longed to kill, but most were like J. J.—they did what had to be done. While they loved the adventure, appreciated the danger, and found fulfillment in completing missions that made a difference, few relished taking life. Moyer could always tell J. J. regretted taking a life, even the life of the enemy. Even so, he never hesitated.

Moyer knew he'd be all right.

"Boss—"

Moyer turned to Pete.

"We have incoming friendlies."

"DATA, IT'S ECHO. I'M down. Repeat . . . I'm hit."

Zinsser squeezed his eyelids shut so tight spots floated in his eyes.

"We need support. Data, where is our support?" A scream of pain. "Oh dear God. Don't let me die in this dump."

Stop it. Stop it, Brian . . . Zinsser pressed his head against the roof, pushing his helmet into the tar that sealed the surface. His lungs burned. It took a moment for him to realize he had stopped breathing.

"Chief is gone! Data, get us that support!"

Zinsser's heart bounced more than beat.

"Data, do you read me?"

"Data, do you hear me?" A different voice.

Zinsser's blood thickened and burned his arteries. Every breath was like inhaling gasoline.

Something touched his shoulder. He swatted it away. It touched him again, and again Zinsser knocked it away. This time the touch was not gentle. He was pulled two feet to the left, his body scraping the roof. Zinsser snapped his eyes open and saw another pair of eyes—those of a black man wearing a black mask. Zinsser felt fear. He reached for his knife.

The punch sent pain shooting through his nose, up his eyes, and around his head.

"You will not go loopy on me now. Understand?"

A familiar voice. An angry voice. Zinsser's nose pulsed with pain. The man was holding Zinsser's nose and twisting.

"I'm talking to you, Data. You hear me? You pull it together or so help me I will throw you off this roof."

Roof? Sweat ran down his face. Roof. Church. Mexico.

"I'm here, Shaq."

"You sure?"

Zinsser shot a hand forward and seized Rich's nose. "We can play this all night. Really, Shaq, I'm here . . . I'm back."

"You had better be. Clear?"

"Clear."

Zinsser released Shaq's nose. Shaq gave another twist before letting go.

"Ow! What was that for?"

"Because you are really starting to irritate me."

Zinsser heard a roar and looked to the street below. The vans and trucks were starting forward at full speed.

CHAPTER 41

ZINSSER LET LOOSE A burst of bullets into the windshield of the lead van. It jerked right, then left. To his left, Rich was reporting to Moyer: "We see three vans and two pickups. There are men in the beds of the trucks. Best guess: forty men."

Forty men. Zinsser knew what that meant. *We're toast.*

He had no doubts about the ability of his fellow soldiers, but they carried limited ammunition. A protracted firefight against forty new guns was bound to end badly. Pinned down with no easy way out made for a bleak future. He didn't care if he died. He'd longed for death for months. But the others deserved to live. They had family. He had nothing.

The passenger van collided with a short stone wall. Men poured from the back. Zinsser counted seven—he must have killed one or two when he fired through the windshield. He looked at Rich then back at the approaching men.

The two fired as they dashed for cover.

"Shaq, I got me an idea."

"I hope it's a good one."

Zinsser triggered his mike. "Boss, Data. I've been thinking . . ." He gave the high points of his scheme in twenty seconds.

Over his earpiece he heard Moyer address Rich with a single but loaded word: "Shaq?"

Zinsser didn't need an explanation. Moyer wanted to know if Rich thought he was in his right mind. Rich eyed him. "Yeah, but I want to go with him."

"Better if I go alone. Shaq can provide cover from up here—and I'm going to need serious cover. Recommend sending Colt up."

The radio link stayed quiet. Zinsser could almost feel Moyer thinking. Then came the word. "Shaq, Colt will be at the window in sixty. Get him to the roof. Data . . ." The pause seemed to last a year. "Data, you're cleared to go."

Rich clamped a crushing hand on Zinsser's arm. "So help me, Data . . . so help me, if this is a suicide run because you don't have the guts to face your problems, I will . . . I'll . . ."

"Relax big guy, it's just war." Zinsser smiled, then looked in Rich's eyes. "This isn't about me, man; it's about you and the others. I'm for real."

Rich let go. "You had better be." He rose to a hunkered position and moved to the edge of the roof where he and Zinsser had climbed out the window. Zinsser swept the battle area to provide cover, then sprinted to the same spot.

J. J. came flying over the parapet, pulled by the adrenaline-strengthened arm of Shaq.

"Nice digs," J. J. said.

"Ya think?" Shaq turned to Zinsser. "I'll help you over—"

"No need." Zinsser stepped over the edge.

THE MAN SHIFTED HIS backpack, pushed the partially closed door open, and took several silent steps into the room. Hernando and Michael were listening to radio reports from their men.

Michael paced. "I should be down there."

"I can stand to lose many things, Michael, but not my only brother."

A perfect opening. He stepped forward. "There's nothing like family."

Michael and Hernando turned from the radio.

Michael's eyes widened. "You!"

"You remember me? Of course, it's only been a few days since we last spoke."

"What are you doing here?"

The man raised his gun. "Business."

"Who is this?" Hernando asked.

"His name is Abasi. He was one of El-Sayyed's dogs. He seems to be off his leash."

"What kind of business?" Hernando stepped away from Michael. Abasi smiled, lifted his gun, and shot Michael in the knee and Hernando in the hip. The men screamed in pain.

Casually Abasi pulled a chair to the center of the room and sat, setting the backpack between his feet. "My business is revenge. El-Sayyed sent me."

Michael spoke through clenched teeth. "El-Sayyed is dead."

"Dead or alive, he is my leader. I know what he would want me to do, so I plan to do it."

"I'm bleeding," Hernando said. "I'm going to bleed to death."

Abasi smiled. "I can assure you that you won't." He removed a bomb made of plastic explosives from the backpack and set it two feet in front of him.

Michael turned defiant. "Do it. If you want to blow us up, then do it. Stop playing games."

Abasi wagged a finger. "I'm sorry, but you haven't suffered enough. You haven't experienced enough pain—the same pain."

"El-Sayyed felt no pain."

"I did. I do. I will avenge his death and ease my grief by making you suffer for as long as possible." He rose from the chair, stepped to Michael, and shot him in the right hip. Michael bellowed. Abasi moved to Hernando and shot him in the knee. More wailing. Again, Abasi smiled. "Look, matching wounds. I love symmetry, don't you?"

"You're crazy!" Michael ground the words out.

"Yes. I do believe you are right." Abasi shrugged. "Somehow that doesn't seem to matter right now."

Abasi watched as blood began to pool beneath the men and thought it a lovely sight.

TESS RAND WOKE EARLY. Dawn was just scratching at the night sky. Something else scratched at her insides—something she couldn't identify. Her night had been filled with nightmares she could no longer remember, but although the images were gone, the terror remained. For an hour she fought a losing battle with the bed, then gave up. She moved into the kitchen of her apartment and started a pot of coffee, paced the floor, then decided to shower.

The hot water ran over her head, slipped over her shoulders, and ran down her body. In every other area of her life she conserved water, but not showers. The shower was her idea chamber, her retreat, her cocoon . . .

But this morning the cocoon was fractured. Five minutes later she began to weep.

She had no belief in psychic phenomenon and couldn't explain why she felt such dread. Her search for answers came up empty. Tess lowered herself to the floor of the shower and let the water pound her body. Waves of grief erupted from her.

In the shower, under the constant flow of hot water, in the darkness of fear and dread, Tess began to pray for J. J.

MOYER HAD TAKEN AN ammo survey of his men and didn't like the answers he received. If they weren't careful, they'd be down to one bullet per bad guy. The Willie Petes J. J. had thrown had killed or wounded many of the remaining first wave. The others retreated, but Moyer knew they wouldn't be gone for long, not with a large number of reinforcements arriving. They could wait them out, wait for daylight. What bothered Moyer most was their ability to completely surround the church.

Time was the problem. It was possible the inbound help might arrive too late.

"Excuse me." A woman's voice—a voice full of tears.

Moyer turned and saw the woman from the basement. Her dirty face was marred by streaks of tears. "Get down!"

"I think he's dead. I think my husband is dead."

Moyer started to rise, but Jose was faster. He sprang to his feet, grabbed her, and pushed her to the floor.

She began to weep in earnest. "He's dead. I know he's dead."

"Doc."

"I'm on it, Boss." Jose grabbed her arm, helped her to her feet, and pushed her toward the stairs that led to the basement, keeping his body between her and the bullet-riddled wall. Moyer and Pete fired into the darkness just to keep enemy heads down while Jose and the woman moved across the floor.

Five minutes later Jose appeared. "She's right, Boss. Her husband is dead. Nothing I can do for him."

Moyer closed his eyes and sighed. No one would be bragging about this mission.

DUTY AND HONOR HAD been powerful words in Zinsser's life. Now they were annoyances. All he had longed for was death and the courage to do himself in. The courage never came, and he was still alive. He had the perfect opportunity when he helped disarm the bomb on Delaram and another opportunity during the HAHO jump. Each time he chickened out. Even a few minutes ago he could have simply stood up and taken bullets provided by the bad guys. That would have done the job. But no, he spent time doing to others what he hoped they'd do to him.

Now as he worked his way over the church's side yard wall, he was in the perfect position to put an end to his miserable life, to the haunting visions and the never-ceasing voices. All he had to do was let the enemy see him. That was it. Just step out, say hello, and take a dozen rounds in the head and body—the last member of his previous team to die.

That, however, would leave his current team down one member, one weapon. They already faced impossible odds, and his absence would make things worse. He cursed honor and duty.

He moved from the wall to a drainage ditch that ran along-side the road. Moving quickly he silently slipped into the ditch. It reeked with a familiar and unpleasant odor. He was trekking through a sewage ditch.

He had to move more slowly than he'd like to prevent splashing water and alerting others to his presence.

He heard voices and dropped to the side of the ditch. Several men jogged past, no doubt looking for a way to approach the church without getting cut down in the process. Zinsser's first temptation was to drop the men as they jogged by, but that would alert their partners and put an end to his plan.

"Data, Boss. Report."

The last thing Zinsser could do was speak. He keyed his mike twice but said nothing, knowing Moyer would hear two clicks on his side. Nothing further came over the radio.

The men moved on, and Zinsser resumed along the ditch, thankful the human sense that tired easiest was the sense of smell. By his estimation, he had traveled eighty or ninety meters, putting him just past the last vehicle in the recently arrived caravan.

Slowly he crawled from the ditch and surveilled the area. From his vantage point he could see men moving along the courtyard wall. Others were slowly circling around the church. They had left the vans unattended.

Zinsser eased his way to the van at the front, the one with the windshield he had shattered. With his 9mm in his hand, Zinsser approached the driver's side of the vehicle. The driver leaned against the door, bleeding from his throat and head. The front seat passenger was crumpled in the seat. The van's airbags had deployed when it hit the low wall that paralleled the ditch.

The engine of the van continued to run, something Zinsser considered an advantage. Starting an engine would draw unwanted attention. He opened the driver's door, seized the dead man's bloody shirt and pulled him to the ground, then took his place. Pulling his bloody knife from its holder, Zinsser cut away the expended airbag and tossed it behind him. The wide side door was locked open. *Perfect.*

He whispered into his mike. "Boss, your limo awaits."

"Understood, Data, be advised: friendlies overhead in two minutes."

"They know not to shoot this van?"

"Maybe I should have mentioned that."

Cute. "Ready to rock on your command."

"Wait sixty then go."

"Roger. Wait sixty."

Zinsser squeezed the steering wheel and waited.

It was the longest minute of his life.

MOYER RAN THOUGH THE next few minutes in his mind. At last he had a reason to hope. Less than three minutes out were three aircraft: two A-10 Thunderbolt II aircraft and a V-22 Osprey. The latter craft used tiltrotor technology, allowing it to fly at very slow speeds and to land or take off vertically. It operated like a helicopter with wings. It was the last item that concerned Moyer. The only place the Osprey had room to land was the marijuana field where they started their mission.

The A-10s were designed for air-to-ground combat and close air support. Unlike most fighter aircraft, the A-10s could come in slower and stay in the general area longer than a high-speed fighter jet.

"Incoming, Boss."

"Understood."

The situation was delicate. All the A-10s had to do was disperse the insurgents without cutting off Moyer's path of egress. They also had to keep from filling Zinsser full of holes.

"Doc, get the woman."

Jose disappeared, then returned seconds later. "She doesn't want to leave her husband's body, Boss."

Moyer trained his eyes out the window. "Doc, you're going to have to—" He turned and saw the woman slung over his shoulder.

A roar in the distance grew.

"Pin 'em down, boys." Moyer raised his weapon and squeezed the trigger. Pete did the same. Overhead he could hear the fire from J. J.'s M110 and Shaq's M-4.

The church shook.

A hundred explosions sounded from the air overhead, and Moyer saw dirt flying from the 30mm Avenger Gatling gun. At well over 4,000 rounds per minute, the gun could cut down a building like a lumberjack fells a tree. It could place 80 percent of its rounds on target. For a moment Moyer felt bad for the men on the other side of the wall.

The moment passed.

The aircraft roared off only to be replaced by the second escort craft, unleashing another ground-shredding burst. The attack aircraft were capable of firing AGM-65 Maverick missiles, but Moyer had concerns about shrapnel injuring his men on the roof and Zinsser in the van.

"Hit it, Data." Moyer started for the church doors. To the rest of the men he ordered, "Bug out. Repeat, bug out."

CHAPTER 42

THE VAN'S ENGINE ROARED as Zinsser threw it in reverse and backed away from the garden wall. He dropped the gear into drive and slammed the accelerator to the floor. The heavy vehicle lurched forward then gained speed. Before him were the burning hulks of vehicles and bodies from the first wave of attackers. Zinsser caught a glimpse of a large form flying overhead and heard the thudding of powerful propellers clawing the air. He had watched the A-10s come in and unload. If he had been one of the attackers who survived the attack, he would be on his way to anyplace but here. Zinsser had seen what A-10s could do, but seeing them up close and this deadly made his insides melt.

The early morning air, laden with the acrid smell of spent gunpowder, burning phosphorus, and flaming autos, poured through the large side passenger door. He glanced at the dead man in the front passenger seat.

"Sorry, pal. I didn't have time to drop you off."

He heard popping and banging. Something hit the side of the van. It took a moment for him to realize that something was a bullet—a bunch of bullets. How crazy did someone have to be to stay behind after an air attack like that? "Taking fire, Boss."

"Understood."

Zinsser pressed on, the van bouncing over debris and other things he didn't care to think about. He directed the van through the gate to the courtyard. The sides of the arch peeled paint off the sides of the vehicle and struck the sliding door. He couldn't worry about that. He continued forward, jerking the wheel to the right to avoid the fountain and the priest's body, then screeched to a halt in front of the church. He popped open his door with his left hand and leveled his M-4 in the direction of the shots that struck the van. He pulled the trigger and sprayed the area.

A loud thud came from behind and above him. Another followed. A glance told him J. J. and Rich had leapt from the roof, using the roof of the van to decrease the distance of their fall. Familiar fire came from behind the van. Rich was following Zinsser's lead in laying down cover fire.

The A-10s finished their tight turn over the area and strafed the ground on the other side of the wall. It was the most terrible and exhilarating thing Zinsser had seen.

The van wobbled behind him as the rest of the team poured into the back of the vehicle. Zinsser pulled his trigger again but nothing happened. He heard nothing but dry fire. He jumped back in the driver's seat, tossing his empty weapon onto the floorboard in front of the passenger seat. The door opened and Zinsser saw Moyer freeze for a moment.

"Geez, Data."

"Sorry, didn't have time to clean the van before I picked you up."

Moyer pulled the corpse from the seat and crawled in. "That's your problem, Data, no pride of ownership."

Zinsser looked over his shoulder. "Where's our other guest?"

"Dead," Doc said. "Let's go."

Zinsser slammed the accelerator again and turned the wheel to direct the van around the fountain and toward the gate.

More popping.

A scream. Zinsser let go of the wheel for a second but took hold again.

"I'm hit, Boss!"

Zinsser didn't have to look to know it was J. J. who screamed.

MOYER TURNED. "DOC!"

Jose had already crawled forward from the backseat. "I need room, Shaq."

With a grace Moyer couldn't image, Rich found a way to crawl over the middle seat to give Jose access to J. J.

"Where?" Jose asked.

More popping. Windows shattered. Moyer was sick of being shot at. "Pete, tell the A-10s they missed a few."

"Will do."

"Talk to me, J. J. Where are you hit?"

The fact that Jose didn't use J. J.'s mission name told Moyer how concerned he was.

"Leg. Thigh. Man, this hurts. Nobody told me being shot hurt."

Moyer turned in the seat, removed his flashlight, and shone the beam on J. J.'s leg. His beam fell on a growing wet spot halfway up the man's left thigh. Jose pulled his knife from its sheath and cut open J. J.'s pant leg. A stream of blood hit him in the face.

"Arterial bleed." Jose stuck his finger in the hole. J. J.'s scream almost liquefied Moyer's brain.

"Shaq!" Jose kept his tone even. "Open my kit. I need a tourniquet."

Shaq didn't waste a moment. Moments passed like hours and Moyer could do nothing but watch. The only sounds were J. J.'s groans and the weeping of Delaram's mother. Jose cinched the tourniquet and J. J. writhed.

"In and out." Jose placed one hand just above the knee and one just below J. J.'s hip. "Sorry, pal, but this is gonna hurt real bad." He pressed the top of the leg down while lifting the lower an inch. The whole leg moved. This time J. J. didn't make a sound. "Missed the bone. That's good."

"I'm one lucky fella."

J. J.'s grim humor almost made Moyer smile. Almost. "You just hang in there, son. If you check out on us, your girl is gonna kick our butts."

"You got . . . that . . . right . . ."

Moyer met Jose's eyes. Doc understood the question. "He's loss a fair amount of blood. I can't be sure how much."

"Should you give him something for the pain, Doc?" Pete asked.

"No. I'll give him morphine once we're airborne. Until then, we need to keep him conscious."

"Uh oh."

Moyer turned at Zinsser's soft warning. He followed Zinsser's nod.

Ahead of them a farm tractor towed a trailer in front of the street, blocking their path. A man leapt from the rig and took a position behind the engine. He had a weapon of some sort.

"Can you get around him, Data?" Moyer asked.

"I doubt it, but I can try. If he doesn't shoot us first."

"Junior, get on the horn with the A-10—"

A narrow object trailing fire streaked from the sky. The tractor, the trailer, and the man flew into the air, spinning to the side. One of the A-10s had sent a Maverick missile into the roadblock.

"Never mind," Moyer said.

"Ya gotta admit, that's pretty impressive," Rich said.

Zinsser slowed as they reached the end of the road, steering around tractor debris and the crater the Maverick left behind. It was like driving through a Hollywood's vision of hell. Fuel and oil from the tractor burned in the streets. Moyer could only guess what people who lived in the village thought. He doubted they would sleep again any time soon.

Zinsser coughed. It sounded wet.

"You okay, Data?"

"Peachy. Our ride is here."

Moyer looked and spotted a large, dark object slowly settling in the field. The van's headlights skimmed the tops of the plants. Moyer held his breath, hoping the craft wouldn't settle on a booby-trap. It settled safely.

Zinsser directed the vehicle forward and into the field. A few meters in, it bogged down in the soft dirt. "I think . . . that's . . . it."

"Data."

"Go. Get Colt on board." Zinsser opened his door and stepped out.

Moyer slipped from his seat and took up a defensive position at the back of the van. "Go, go, go."

He heard the team and woman leave the van and caught a glimpse of Doc and Junior helping J. J. to the aircraft and up the ramp at the craft's rear. Moyer took two steps back, turned and started for the Osprey, its tiltrotors aimed skyward, beating down the surrounding plants. He began to sprint toward the craft when something caught his eye. Zinsser lay facedown in the dirt. A movement to his right made Moyer turn.

"I got him." Rich lifted Zinsser as if he weighed no more that a bag of dog food then started for the Osprey, racing up the ramp and into the guts of the craft.

A moment later the roar of the engines increased and the V-22 began to rise.

ABASI STUDIED THE TWO men bleeding to death before him. He waited patiently and it finally arrived. Michael begged for help.

"I'm sorry. It wasn't personal. It was business. We've got money. We can pay you more than you . . . can dream of."

"I have no need of your money."

"Then what do you want?" Hernando screamed.

"I told you. Revenge."

Abasi picked up the plunger switch and fingered the button.

"DOC, WE NEED YOU," Moyer said as Rich set Zinsser on the deck.

Jose moved from J. J. to Zinsser. As Rich pulled away, Moyer saw blood on his arms.

"I need more light, Boss."

Again, Moyer pulled his flashlight. Rich did the same. Their beams traced Zinsser's body and settled on his abdomen.

"Gut shot."

The grim words needed no clarification. Everyone knows how bad such an injury can be.

Jose pulled his med kit close and opened it, retrieving a large gauze pad. He also pulled out a pair of surgical scissors and cut open Zinsser's shirt. Zinsser didn't move. There was a small hole an inch above and two inches to the right of his navel. "Help me roll him."

Before Moyer could act, Rich was kneeling by Zinsser's side. He rolled the man to his side. Moyer saw a gaping, ragged hole in the back. The exit wound was far worse than the entry.

Jose placed the sterile pad on the back wound and another on the entry wound. "He needs a hospital and needs one fast. I'm not seeing extreme bleeding so I think the bullet missed major vessels, but I'm sure it's done a job on his internal organs. I'm pretty sure it missed his liver and stomach. His intestines—that's another matter."

"You think he's gonna make it, Doc?"

Moyer heard an unexpected concern in Rich's voice.

"If we can get him to a hospital. He's going to need surgery." Jose looked at Moyer. "It's going to be close."

Moyer nodded and moved forward to the cockpit. "I've got two injured men. We need to move it, Lieutenant."

"Understood. We'll move at best possible speed—"

A bright light in the hills lit the sky.

"What was that?" the pilot asked.

The only thing Moyer could remember being in that area was a mansion.

"Maybe someone did our job for us."

"Boss?" Pete stood behind Moyer. "J. J. wants to see you."

Moyer moved to the back again. "How you doing, son?"

"Good to go, Boss. Always good to go."

"You're not going to ask me to deliver some kind of final message are you? Cause it's not your time."

"I have a favor to ask . . ."

THE V-22 OSPREY LOWERED its rear ramp and made a slow pass over the marijuana field. J. J. stood near the opening, Rich to one side, Moyer to the other. The three wore safety straps. J. J. held a Willie Pete grenade retrieved from Zinsser's vest.

He pulled the safety pin.

He took a deep breath and balanced on his one good leg.

The green indicator light lit, indicating they were over the target area.

J. J. tossed the phosphorus grenade out the back. A few moments later a blinding light lit the sky. As the Osprey flew toward the U.S./Mexico border, J. J. saw the fire begin to spread across the field.

CHAPTER 43

HOT. HE WAS HOT.

And dry. His eyeballs felt cracked and shrunken. Pain ran up his side and filled his body, but it had lost its edge.

He heard noise: the humming and drumming of powerful engines. Vibrations rose from the hard surface beneath his back. Opening his eyes, he saw dim lights overhead. Darkness framed the periphery of his vision. He couldn't focus.

"Water."

A large black face appeared in his vision. "Sorry, pal. Can't do it. Gut wound."

"Shaq?"

"Thought you died and were seeing angels, didn't you? Understandable. I hate to be the one to tell you, but you're still alive."

"Team?"

Rich smiled. "We're all here and headed home."

"J. J. . . ."

"Doing fine. Don't worry about him. You focus on staying alive."

Zinsser nodded, then tried to rise. Scorching pain pushed him back.

"Stay put, man. Doc is working on you. We have a gift . . ."

Darkness filled Zinsser's eyes. The sound of engines faded. A moment later Zinsser was in Somalia.

"DOC?" MOYER SAID.

Jose put two fingers on Zinsser's throat. "He's still with us, but I'm not sure he'll last much longer if I don't get this done. He's lost a lot of blood."

"How can we he help?" Moyer studied Zinsser. He looked one step above a corpse.

"In this bag is a blood collection system—plastic bag with clear tubing. Pull it out."

Moyer took hold of the bag, thankful someone thought to bring a more complete med kit than Jose could carry in the field. He found the empty, plastic IV bag.

"Okay, Rich. On your back."

"Where?"

"Anywhere. I'm going to draw off about 450ccs of blood."

Moyer understood the dangers of what Jose was doing. "Walking Blood Bank" transfusions carried inherent risk. Jose wouldn't be attempting this if he didn't think Zinsser was close to death. Rich's blood type matched Zinsser's.

"They teach us not to trust dog tags or a soldier's opinion," Jose said before he tested Rich's and Zinsser's blood. It was a match. He inserted a large needle into Rich's arm.

"Ow. Did you have to get a running start with that thing, Doc?"

"Stop being a baby and be still."

"I'm just saying . . ."

"We'll put you in for a Purple Heart, big guy," Moyer said.

"Really? Cool."

Blood flowed through the catheter and along the tubing. It seemed to Moyer to be taking a long time.

"Hold this."

Moyer took the bag from Jose, who moved to Zinsser and cut away the man's sleeve. Pulling a container of povidone iodine from the kit, he cleaned Zinsser's arm. Once the bag was full of Rich's blood, Jose changed needles and inserted it in Zinsser's arm. Data didn't flinch.

Slowly the blood passed through the tubing and into Zinsser's arm.

"What are his chances, Doc?" Pete asked.

"This will help keep blood volume up and aid in carrying oxygen through his body. Assuming he doesn't react to the blood, then he stands a chance—a slim chance, but a chance. What he really needs is a surgeon. I think the bleeding has stopped." Jose shook his head. "The guy didn't make a sound when he was hit; he just kept driving our sorry heinies to the extraction area."

"Yeah, well, it wasn't like we had time to talk about it." Rich sat up, still holding a cotton ball over the small hole Jose had left in his arm. A second later he looked at Moyer. "You were right to keep him, Boss."

Moyer wondered.

THE OSPREY SET DOWN at Martindale Army Airfield, an inactive airport near Fort Sam Houston. Ambulances were waiting for them, as was a minibus. Jose and the waiting medics moved J. J., Zinsser, and the lone surviving hostage from the aircraft to the ambulances. Moyer knew they'd be in good hands at San Antonio Military Medical Center. He wanted to ride with his injured men but knew he would only be in the way. Stowing their gear on the Osprey, Moyer led what was left of his team into the bus and took the first seat he saw. Fatigue washed over him like a high tide and for several moments he thought he would drown in it.

Every muscle ached. Every joint protested. Technically his mission was over, but personally it wouldn't end until he knew J. J. and Zinsser would be all right.

The bus pulled away, and the team rode in silence, each lost in his thoughts. Moyer longed for the sweet release of sleep, but his mind would not allow it. Events played over and over in his head. He heard the unending gunfire, felt the sting of plaster as it struck his face. He replayed every communication, reran every scenario. What could he have done better? Two of his men were wounded. That came with the work they did. Each man knew the current mission could be their last, but they never believed it. Moyer had lost a man on a recent mission, and now there was a chance he'd lose another. The thought of it made him ill.

Voices rang in his head; J. J.'s scream echoed inside his skull; the sight of Zinsser lying facedown in the marijuana field played in his mind. Is this what Zinsser experienced? He didn't know, but if it was, he'd be more sympathetic with the man.

THE SAN ANTONIO MILITARY Medical Center was a multistory, modern affair, and Moyer was relieved at the pilot's choice. Thousands of medics had trained here, including Jose. They waited in the lobby of the ER, three men dressed in black, dirty from running through fields and enduring a firefight.

A tall, thin, bespectacled physician who looked too young to be a doctor approached Moyer. "Who's going to be first?"

"First?" Moyer said. "I'm sorry, Captain, what do you mean by 'first'?"

"I have orders to examine you and your men."

"We're fine." Moyer waved his hand. "Any news on my injured men?"

"They're in good hands. I don't want to belabor the point . . ."

Moyer saw the doctor's eyes looking for rank insignia. Neither Moyer nor any of his men wore one. "Sergeant Major Eric Moyer, sir." He introduced Rich and Pete.

"Captain Reynolds, Sergeant Major. Shall we start with you?"

"I said we're fine—"

"And I said I have orders to examine you and your men. My orders are your orders, Sergeant Major. If you cooperate, we can be done in no time."

Moyer frowned. "You go first, Rich."

"Why me?"

"Because you have that gaping wound Doc gave you."

"Gaping wound?" Captain Reynolds's eyes widened.

"Relax, Doc. I had some time on my hands so I gave a little blood."

Reynolds shook his head. "You special ops types are all the same."

CHAPTER 44

MOYER WAS THE LAST to be examined. When he exited the exam room he saw two familiar faces walking into the ER waiting area. Outside the sun bathed the Texas sky in light. Colonel Mac escorted Tess Rand through the doors, his hand on her elbow. He looked rock solid; she looked ready to collapse.

Moyer greeted them. Tess was in no mood for pleasantries. "Have you heard anything?"

"Last word I had was J. J. and Zinsser are in surgery. How did you get here?"

Colonel Mac answered. "I know a guy who knows a guy." He forced a smile. "I left as soon as I heard you were airborne. I picked Tess up on the way."

"Philadelphia is on the way?"

Colonel Mac shrugged. "It all depends on how you look at it."

Another familiar face entered the ER. Moyer shook hands with Chaplain Bartley, J. J.'s brother. "No news yet, sir."

"What can you tell us?" Bartley asked.

"Wait a sec." Mac walked to a nurse who had just come down the hall and then, a moment later, motioned for Moyer and the others to follow. Soon they were seated in a small conference room. "I wanted a little privacy. I've also arranged for coffee and food."

"We're fine, sir."

"I ordered it, Moyer. You will eat the food and drink the coffee, then tell me how wonderful it was. Clear?"

"Clear, sir."

"Okay, answer the chaplain's question."

Moyer took a breath. "We were under heavy fire and attempting escape to our extraction point. Jerry Zinsser worked his way around the hostiles, commandeered a van, and broke through another line of attackers as the A-10s were getting ready to make another pass." He told the story of being pinned down in the church and the heroics of his team. "As we were speeding down the main road we took fire. A round went through the side of the van and hit J. J. in the thigh. Doc, who is still in the ER, stopped the bleeding or J. J. would have bled out before we could get on the V-22. Sometime during the escape Zinsser took a round in the gut." He tried to soften the details. He knew Colonel Mac would want the information straight, but Moyer feared the impact on Tess.

As he was speaking, Doc walked into the room. Behind him followed cafeteria personnel with food and coffee.

"They told me I'd find you here," Jose said.

"You look like a hundred miles of bad road, Doc," Mac said.

"It's good to see you too, sir." Jose plopped into a chair and rubbed his eyes. "I'm going to sleep for a week."

"What's the word?" Moyer pressed.

Doc sighed and leaned back. "They're working on J. J. now. The docs agree that the bullet passed through cleanly, but it did nick his femoral artery. Fortunately we got the bleeding stopped. The surgeons won't know what needs to be done until they get in there, but I can tell you his leg looked good: pink and warm. I don't think he'll lose it."

Tess gasped. "It was that bad?"

"I'm sorry, Tess, I'm not at my best. I lose all tact when I'm tired." He paused. "Yes, the wound was bad, but I was more concerned about the effects of the tourniquet. Cutting off blood flow can severely damage a limb. During the flight Pete and I loosened the tourniquet to allow some blood flow. The human body is an amazing machine. Sometimes artery wounds will seal themselves. I've seen arteries in severed limbs retract and cut off blood flow on their own. Right now, my guess is J. J. will be chasing you around the sofa in no time."

"Zinsser?" Mac said.

Jose shook his head. "He's in rough shape. The bullet tore up his insides worse than I thought. He's going to be in surgery for some time."

"But you think he'll live," Mac said.

Jose shrugged.

Moyer studied the two people most impacted by the news: Tess and Chaplain Bartley. Bartley looked stoic. As a chaplain he had dealt with many tragedies. This, however, was personal. Moyer sensed he was being brave for Tess. She kept control of her emotions, but Moyer recognized fear when he saw it. Still, she showed more strength and grace than he thought possible.

Bartley straightened and took Tess's hand. "I don't know about the rest of you, but I need to pray. Would anyone object if I led us in prayer?"

Tess squeezed Bartley's hand.

No one objected.

MINUTES BECAME HOURS. COLONEL Mac tried to send the team to one of the base's barracks for sleep. Since he fell short of making it an order, no one budged. Moyer wouldn't leave and he wouldn't compel any of his team to do so. They survived the firefight. Now they fought a different kind of battle—one with nerves and the fear of losing teammates.

Lunch came and went. At two that afternoon, a man in uniform, a PFC, entered with a folder. He handed it to Colonel Mac, then stepped outside. Mac opened it. Inside were daylight photos of Frontera. "You guys made a real mess." He paused and glanced at Tess. "Do you mind stretching your legs for a few minutes? The chaplain will be happy to keep you company."

They got the hint, rose, and slipped from the room without a word.

"Confidential report?" Moyer said.

"Yeah, but I sent her out for another reason." He passed the photos around. Bodies littered the church, some burned beyond recognition. "She doesn't need to see this."

Moyer took a look at the photos. He wasn't thrilled at having to see them. Each man took a turn studying the images while Mac read a brief report. "The Mexican government has boots on the ground looking at your handiwork. We may have lost our place on their Christmas list. Twenty-two dead; eleven wounded. One marijuana field burned to the ground. Several dead in a local warehouse."

He read more. "They have found some shallow graves. This is just a preliminary report, but they think the hostages are buried there."

"Speaking of hostages . . ." Rich said.

Jose answered. "I checked on her earlier. Dehydrated, distraught, and confused, but she's going to be fine."

Mac nodded. "They found her husband's body in the church basement." Mac tilted his head. "You guys blew up Hernando Soto's mansion? When did you have time to do that?"

"We didn't," Moyer said. "I saw a flash of light as we were flying out."

"I guess that's going to be a mystery for the Mexicans to solve."

Someone knocked on the door. Bartley poked his head in. "J. J.'s doctor is here."

Mac gathered up the photos and returned them to the file and resealed it. "Bring him in. Send in the PFC too." Mac returned the folder with the words, "Keep me posted," then sent the messenger away.

The doctor was a brick of a man, as if he had been chiseled from stone rather than born. His sharp features looked tired. Dark bags hung beneath his eyes. He found a seat and lowered himself into it, rubbed the back of his neck, then raised his head. "Man, what a day." He sighed and looked around. He pointed at Tess. "I take it you're the fiancée?"

"Yes. How is he?"

"The rest of you are part of his team?"

"That's right," Mac said.

"That makes you family enough for me. Your man is going to be fine. He's a tough one, and I'll admit that we almost lost him on the table. While trying to repair the artery, he started to bleed out again. We hung several units of whole blood and kept at it. We repaired the artery, did some work on the leg muscle, and set up a drain for the wound. He's going to be off his feet for a while and most likely need a cane for a couple of months. I expect a full recovery if he'll follow through with physical therapy."

"He'll follow through." Tess and Moyer said it in unison, then laughed.

"You guys practice that?"

Tess offered her first real smile since she'd arrived. "No."

Moyer wanted to ask if J. J. would be able to return to the team but decided to wait until Tess couldn't answer for him.

"When can I see him?"

"He's still a little out of it. We'll keep him in the recovery room for another hour; then you can visit if you promise not to wear him out."

"Thank you, Doctor," Tess said.

"Who's the team medic?"

Jose stood. "I am."

The doctor studied him for a moment then held out his hand. "Fine work. You not only saved his life; you saved his leg." The doctor moved to the door, then paused. "Oh, I almost forgot. When we brought him out of the anesthesia, he started mumbling about moving the wedding up."

Tess smiled. "Sounds good to me. Real good."

Bartley put his arm around his future sister-in-law. His grin stretched ear to ear.

THREE HOURS LATER ANOTHER surgeon entered the conference room. Unlike J. J.'s surgeon this man looked to be in his sixties and was movie-star handsome. He glanced around the room. "Who's here for Jerry Zinsser?"

Only Moyer, Rich, and Mac remained in the room. The others were visiting J. J. "All of us."

The doctor shrugged. "He's out of surgery but in critical condition. I've got him in surgical ICU. We'll have to watch him for a few days. The bullet tore up his intestines. We had to do a lot of repair and clean up. My biggest fear is infection. He's on heavy antibiotics and pain meds. You can visit him in a couple of hours. The pain meds will make him a little dopey, so go easy on him."

"But he'll live?" Rich asked.

"As long as something else doesn't develop. We'll know more tomorrow. Right now he needs rest. Lots of rest." The doctor looked at Colonel Mac. "Are you his commanding officer?"

"I am."

"You should know that there is very little chance he'll return to field duty."

"Understood, Doctor."

JERRY ZINSSER GAZED AT the ceiling above him. It looked blurry and ill defined. It took several moments for him to realize he was in a hospital. *Hospital!* Fear flooded him, filling him with dread.

"Easy, pal."

The voice was familiar. He shifted his gaze to see Moyer, Rich, and Colonel Mac standing by his bedside. Moyer and Rich were still dressed in black.

"Where am I?"

"San Antonio," Moyer said. "Fort Sam Houston."

Zinsser's breathing quickened. His heart shifted to double time.

"Are you okay, son?" Mac asked.

Zinsser didn't answer. Instead he slowly raised his left arm and was relieved to see it there. He lifted his right arm and it responded. He tried to sit up.

"No you don't," Rich said. "No sit-ups until you're well. Don't make me sit on you."

"I need a . . . favor." His voice wavered.

"Name it," Moyer said.

"Someone touch my legs."

"What?"

"Just do it!"

Moyer squeezed Zinsser's left then right ankles. "Something wrong with your legs?"

The image of legless Brian Taylor rattled in Zinsser's mind. "Tell me they're there. Tell me I still have my legs."

"Of course you have your legs," Moyer said. "You were shot in the belly, not in the legs."

Relief washed over Zinsser. "Okay. Thanks. Sorry."

"You're thinking of your friend?"

Zinsser nodded.

"You still have all your parts, Jerry, and you are going to be fine."

He closed his eyes. He couldn't face them.

Mac's deep voice washed over him. "I hear you saved the team. I want to thank you for that. Moyer owes me money, and I wouldn't know how to collect if he were dead."

Zinsser smiled and took several deep breaths. "I think you'd find a way, sir." He paused. "I don't remember anything after we hit the field."

"Yeah," Moyer said. "You sorta checked out on us there. Rich had to carry you into the Osprey. He even gave you some of his blood."

Zinsser groaned. "Tell me you're kidding. I have his blood in me?"

"What?" Rich straightened. "You got a problem with a black man's blood in your white body?"

"Not at all. It just explains my sudden urge to sing show tunes."

Rich laughed. "See, you're a better man already."

CHAPTER 45

THE DOCTORS HAD CLEARED Delaram to leave the hospital. Italian intelligence, working with local police, moved her to a safe house in Rome. It was a small stone building at the southern end of the city, well away from tourists and locals. She had full run of one of the two bedrooms and the living room. The other bedroom remained reserved for one of the three guards who kept track of her.

Outside a warm evening breeze rustled through an olive tree in the front yard. Delaram was not wise in such things, but she was smart and guessed that hidden cameras covered every corner of the property and every room of the house. She wondered if there were hidden cameras in the bathroom.

She made no complaints. She had been treated far better than she deserved. Perhaps they understood that she was a victim trying to save the lives of the parents she loved. Still, she had participated—unwilling as she was—in an effort to kill not one, but twenty world leaders. Others would consider it a selfish act, and she would agree. Had she been older, wiser, able to think more clearly, she might have been able to make the hard decision to let the two people she loved most be tortured and killed. There was a reason, she realized, why these people selected young, more impressionable, more easily frightened women.

It was no excuse. She had no excuses. People with various badges and identifications quizzed her until she dissolved into convulsive sobs. She knew so very little, had so little to offer. If she could, she'd lead the authorities to the front door of the men who had manipulated her, but she couldn't.

Her emotions moved like a ball on a professional tennis court. One moment she feared what would happen to her; the next she didn't care. The only emotion that remained constant was the fear she felt for her parents. Not knowing their fate devoured her strength and hope.

The front door opened and the man she had spoken to many times entered. "Hello, Delaram." Captain De Luca had always been firm, probing, but polite.

"Hello."

"How are you feeling?"

"Does it matter?"

He didn't respond and she had no idea what she'd expected. He motioned to a padded chair in the living room. Next to it sat a small table with a phone that looked as if it had been manufactured fifty years before. She sat and De Luca pulled an ottoman close and lowered himself until he was seated.

"Delaram, there is someone who wishes to speak to you."

"Who?"

He raised a finger indicating she should wait. The phone rang a moment later and De Luca snatched up the handpiece. He greeted the caller, then listened for a moment. He handed the phone to her.

"Who is it?"

De Luca waved the phone at her. "Take it."

"Hello?"

"Delaram, this is Tess. We spoke over a video link the other day."

She recognized the voice. "I remember."

"There is someone who wants to speak to you. Please hold the line."

Now what? What was going—

"Delaram?"

Her heart stopped. *"Mother?"*

Sobbing came over the line.

"Mother, are you all right?"

"I'm fine, but your father . . . your father . . ." More sobs.

"Is he . . . dead?"

"Yes."

Delaram slid from the chair to her knees and wept into the phone.

COLONEL MAC LEANED OVER his well-used desk and glanced over the team report. He probed for every detail and knew every word in the document was true. Still, even he had trouble believing it. As far as the world was concerned, two suicide bombers tried to disrupt the G-20 meeting in Naples, resulting in the death of scores of people. What the world didn't know was what happened inside the *Miramare Hotel Grande.* News of the bomb-laden yacht could not be kept secret. Clearly an orchestrated attack had occurred, an attack designed to disrupt or kill some of the world leaders. What the newspapers and news shows did not carry was Delaram's nearly successful attempt to assassinate the presidents of the United States and Mexico, as well as other leaders who had declared a war on drugs.

Rumors leaked from a small village northeast of Monterrey, Mexico, but few paid attention. The idea that U.S. military would fly over a sovereign nation as well as wage a ground war seemed beyond the ability of even conspiracy theorists to believe.

But there were several who believed it.

They had lived it.

He was proud of each one.

EPILOGUE

ARLINGTON NATIONAL CEMETERY IN Arlington, Virginia, smelled of green grass. Row upon row of white headstones bore mute testimony to the cost of freedom, to the price paid by the few for the many. Too many remained forgotten except by family. The public acknowledged their sacrifice on a day or two each year. More than three hundred thousand individuals lay in the 624 acres—some dating back to the Civil War.

Here rested heroes. Here rested men and women who loved country over self. So many gravestones; so many white, rigid marble headstones. Rivalry among the service had no place here. Army heroes were the same as Navy heroes, Air Force the same as Marine.

Eight men stood around one grave. The headstone read SGT. 1ST CLASS BRIAN TAYLOR, UNITED STATES ARMY. Jerry Zinsser stood closest to the covered grave. Taylor had been buried two months before, but Zinsser wasn't able to leave the hospital until two weeks after and was unable to travel for several more weeks. It had been

J. J.'s idea to hold a second service, and his brother agreed to say a few words.

Standing with Zinsser and Chaplain Bartley were men he now counted as friends: Colonel MacGregor, Eric Moyer, J. J. Bartley—leaning on a cane—Pete Rasor, Jose Medina, and Rich Harbison—Boss, Colt, Junior, Doc, and Shaq.

Zinsser kept his eyes fixed on the grave as Bartley read from the Bible. Time seemed to stretch. Seconds and minutes had no value to Zinsser. Time had stopped until he heard the voice of Colonel Mac: "Group ten-*hut!*"

Zinsser straightened his spine and squared his shoulders.

"Present arms!"

With painstaking slowness, the soldiers, dressed in their dress blues, raised their arms in the traditional salute. Zinsser's hand began to shake. A few steps away a bugler played "Taps," the mournful tune crossing the cemetery as it did almost every day.

The men eased their salutes then went to "at ease."

Zinsser lowered his head and began to weep. He was suddenly aware of someone standing beside him. On his left was the massive form of Rich Harbison. On his right stood Moyer. The others gathered behind him.

Rich put a hand on Zinsser's shoulder.

JERRY SAT AT THE end of the table in the pizza parlor where he first spent time with the team. Moyer sat to his right; the others were gathered around the table. Several nearly empty pizza pans littered the table. It had only been a few weeks since he came to in the hospital. His days had been filled with bag after bag of antibiotics and later physical therapy. Almost every day one of the team members came by to visit. At first he assumed they were there to encourage J. J. who, in some hospital humor, had been assigned to share a room with him. Both had been transported from Texas to the hospital at Fort Jackson. J. J. was released four days later but had to return for physical therapy several times a week. Each time he did, he came by to share his brand of joy and lousy jokes. As time passed, Zinsser began to look forward to the days. He even began to appreciate hearing J. J. talk about his faith.

Much of his focus rested on what the Army would do to him. He had not been forthcoming about his problems; he had even lied on several occasions. The one thing that ate at him the most was how close he had come to harming Moyer and destroying the mission.

The others considered him a hero. Rumor had it that Moyer had put his name in for a commendation. Zinsser hoped it was nothing more than a rumor. Most of his heroics had been done in hope that a bad guy would do for him what he could not do for himself—bring death close and personal.

Yet he continued to survive, and he didn't know why. J. J. said God had plans for him, but Zinsser doubted it, no matter how much he wanted it to be true. Still he listened.

First time he sat around this table, he saw only a bunch of men, strangers linked only by uniform and training. Now he saw friends, co-patriots, fellow warriors, each willing to die for the others.

Their missions had been largely successful although each man regretted not being able to save the other hostages. They had done their best, saved the lives of their president and a score of other world leaders, but the innocent dead haunted them.

What they did would only be known by a few. Friends and family would be forever in the dark. Just as well. Few would believe it anyway.

"How long you gonna keep us in suspense, Zinsser?" Rich leaned his elbows on the table. "You called this get-together."

"Can't a man just want a pizza with friends?"

"Friends?" Rich said. "Now I'm blushing."

"Okay, Rich, you're right. I did have a reason for asking you guys to be here." He looked at Moyer. "Have you said anything?"

Moyer shook his head. "Nope. Not my place."

"Of course it's your place, Boss, but thanks." Zinsser took a deep breath and let it out. He felt less anxiety doing the HAHO jump. "I'm leaving the team."

No one spoke. No one moved.

"Come on, guys, you knew it would come to this. I've been seeing the doctors—head doctors, I mean—and we've been talking about my little problem."

"You have a problem?" Pete looked around. "I hadn't heard."

"Then you must be in a coma. Let me get this out. I suffer from post-traumatic stress disorder. Not that that is news to you, but the doctors think it helps when I say it out loud. Things have gotten better. I'm not as depressed and I don't think about offing myself any more. Still, I'm not cured and there's a good chance I never will be."

He leaned over the table and interlaced his fingers. "I very nearly blew everything. I was so lost in myself and in my . . . problems. You'll be happy to know the voices have stopped."

"At least you were never alone," Rich quipped.

"Alone isn't always bad—at least, that kind of alone."

J. J. spoke softly. "They're not drumming you out of the Army, are they?"

"No, but they gave me the opportunity to walk away."

J. J. looked away. "So you're going back to civilian life."

"Nah, I don't fit out there. The Army is my family. I'm just changing directions. I won't be going on any more ops—for obvious reasons. Flashbacks tend to be a little distracting."

"So what are you going to do?" Jose asked.

"I'm going to teach at the Advanced Individual Training Infantry School. Someone has to whip new recruits into usable soldiers."

"That's great," J. J. said. "New guys will love you."

Moyer pinned J. J. with a look. "Did *you* love your AIT instructors?"

"Well, not so much."

The others laughed.

"It was Boss's idea. He put in a good word and so did Colonel Mac."

Moyer grinned. "As I recall, the president threw his considerable weight behind the idea."

"Yeah, but he doesn't have the influence you do," Zinsser said.

"That's true." Moyer nodded. "It is wonderful to be me."

"You'll be a great instructor, Jerry," Rich said. He looked down. "I've been meaning to tell you—"

"Stop right there, big guy. If you're about to apologize then don't. I don't want your apology. I'd rather you paid for the pizza."

"Ain't gonna happen," Rich said with a smile.

Zinsser lowered his voice. "I only had the opportunity to do one mission with you—"

"On two continents," J. J. said.

"True. Now shut up and let me finish. As I was saying: One mission might not be much, but I consider it the highlight of my service. If you guys need anything, then come to me. I'll do whatever I can. Thanks for being there for me." He turned to Moyer. "Thanks for the second chance."

"I knew we'd need you. I'm more than a pretty face, you know."

"Maybe you should be seeing the doctors I've been seeing."

"When do you start?" Pete asked.

"I still have some physical therapy to do and more psych evals, but soon. I've also been talking to J. J.'s brother. He's helping me deal with some of the guilt issues I have. Among other things."

"The chaplain is a good man," Jose said. "He was there for my family when we needed him."

Moyer picked up his drink. "As far as we're concerned, Data, you will always be part of this team." He raised his plastic cup. The others followed suit. "To Data."

"To Data."

J. J. HADN'T BEEN this scared in all his life. Things had happened so quickly and so unexpectedly. It was one thing to get married, but to have the ceremony in the Rose Garden of the White House with the president and his wife in attendance was another. The offer was as kind as it was unexpected, but the president insisted that he be allowed to do something special for the man who disarmed a suicide bomber, not only saving the president's life but that of his wife.

Wearing his formal blues, J. J. tried to listen to his brother conduct the wedding, but the words made little sense. Thank heaven he'd already placed the wedding ring on the correct finger, something he would not have done correctly had not Tess raised her left hand so he wouldn't have to guess which was her right hand and which her left.

". . . you husband and wife."

J. J. looked up. His brother stared at him.

"You may kiss your bride."

J. J. did. Her lips were soft. The sweet fragrance of her hair surrounded him. He'd been told that battle made a man feel alive. But J. J. had never been more alive than at this moment. He lingered.

He kissed her again, then used all his strength and determination to pull back.

"Hooah!"

Rich. Who else?

Tess on his arm, the two turned and started down the aisle. Attendees stood and applauded. The scent of roses filled the air. J. J. tried to focus on his steps to ensure that his leg, which was still tricky at times, wouldn't give out, but his eyes kept tracking to his girl—his *wife*. Her hair glowed, her eyes sparkled, her smile stunned him. If he had not already fallen in love with her, he would have done so at this moment.

At the end of the aisle stood twelve men in dress blues matching his own, each with a military saber raised touching the saber of the man opposite him. The dress swords formed an arch. J. J. led his bride under the arch. As they passed beneath each pair of sabers, the men lowered their swords behind the couple. The last two swordsmen were Moyer and Rich. Before the new couple could pass, Moyer and Rich lowered their swords, blocking J. J. and Tess's path. J. J. smiled, turned to his bride, and kissed her.

"Welcome to the United States Army, ma'am," Shaq said; then he and Moyer raised their swords so the couple could pass.

Not one to ignore tradition, Rich swatted Tess on the fanny with his saber.

The crowd erupted with laughter.

THE RECEPTION WAS IN full swing.

Holding the wedding at the White House had brought out friends J. J. hadn't seen in years. He didn't mind. The more people, the happier Tess grew. He would have been happy with just a few people on some beach. He had never dreamed he would be celebrating his wedding on the lawn of the world's most famous building.

"Hey, J. J., you got a sec?"

J. J. turned as Zinsser approached. He held a wooden box with a hinged top. "Sure." He and Tess excused themselves from the conversation they had been in with Moyer and his family.

"I got you a little something." Zinsser held out the box. It had a weight to it. The box looked new and bore a shiny finish. "Is this rosewood?"

"Good eye. I had it made. The guy did a good job."

"It's beautiful," Tess said.

Zinsser chuckled. "You guys know the gift is inside, right?"

"You want us to open it now?"

Zinsser nodded. "Yeah, I want to see your face."

"Now I'm nervous. Is it filled with snakes or something?" Tess took a step back.

"I hope you like it. Go on, kid. Pop the top."

J. J. shrugged. "If you insist." He lifted the lid, which rode on a pair of brass hinges—then stared. He felt his mouth drop open. "You're kidding me."

"You're the weapons guy. I thought you might like this for your collection."

J. J. blinked several times. "I don't have a gun collection."

"You do now."

Tess peered in the box. "Is that what I think it is?"

Inside, resting on a royal blue, velvet pad was a Colt .45 1911A1 handgun. It was clean and recently polished. "Is this real . . . I mean it's not a replica?"

"My grandfather carried it in World War II. It's as real as can be. You can see why I didn't want to leave it on the gift table."

J. J. stared down at the gun, then shook his head. "I can't take this. Not if it belonged to your grandfather."

"Nonsense. You'll treat it better than I have. Besides, it fits you."

Tess gave Zinsser a puzzled look. "What do you mean?"

"A Colt handgun for a man whose friends call him Colt."

It was a good thing the guys weren't standing around. They'd never let J. J. forget he was standing there all soggy eyed.

THE MOON SHONE THROUGH a cloudless sky over Tehran. Several security men escorted Tony Nasser in to the Iranian president's office. The men hugged.

It had been a long journey here. The sailboat captain had sailed slowly south along the Italian coast, stopping in nearly every port to throw off suspicion. In each port Nasser had remained below decks to avoid eyes that might identify him. A week later they sailed past Sicily and on to Tunisia. From Tunis he flew to Alexandria, Egypt. He arrived after El-Sayyed. His followers had scattered. There was nothing left in Egypt for him.

It had taken days of working the back channels of communication, but Nasser had been able to arrange this meeting.

The Iranian president tented his fingers. "So, I hear you have had quite an adventure."

"My life has been spared so that my service may continue."

"I was grieved to hear of your leader's murder. Tragic. Immoral. The work of cowards."

"I agree, Mr. President. My heart is broken into a thousand pieces. I weep for him every night. Still I must face the future."

"You have something in mind, my friend Nasser."

"I do, Mr. President." He couldn't restrain the smile. "Indeed, I do."

ACKNOWLEDGMENTS

Special thanks to Jonathan Clements at Wheelhouse Literary Group, to Julie and Karen at B&H, and to the Wilhite and Waller families. And thanks most of all to my King, Jesus Christ, for giving me the gifts of faith, family, and friends.